THE
BLADEBONE

AUSMA ZEHANAT KHAN holds a Ph.D. in International human rights law with a specialization in military intervention and war crimes in the Balkans.

She is a former adjunct law professor and Editor-in-Chief of *Muslim Girl* magazine, the first magazine targeted to young Muslim women in North America. She is also the award-winning author of *The Unquiet Dead* and *The Bloodprint*, the first book in The Khorasan Archives.

A British-born Canadian, Khan now lives in Colorado with her husband.

Follow Ausma on:
Ausmazehanatkhan.com/
/ausmazehanatkhan
@AusmaZehanat

Also by Ausma Zehanat Khan

The Khorasan Archives

The Bloodprint

The Black Khan

The Blue Eye

The Esa Khattak/Rachel Getty Mystery Series:

The Unquiet Dead

The Language of Secrets

A Death in Sarajevo (a novella)

Among the Ruins

No Place of Refuge

A Deadly Divide

THE
BLADEBONE

Book Four of the Khorasan Archives

AUSMA ZEHANAT KHAN

HARPER
Voyager

Harper*Voyager*
An imprint of HarperCollins*Publishers* Ltd
1 London Bridge Street
London SE1 9GF

www.harpercollins.co.uk

HarperCollinsPublishers
1st Floor, Watermarque Building, Ringsend Road
Dublin 4, Ireland

First published by HarperCollins*Publishers* 2020

This paperback edition 2021
1

Maps created by Ashley P Halsey, inspired by Ayesha Shaikh
Map backgrounds by caesart/Shutterstock, Inc.

Ausma Zehanat Khan asserts the moral right to
be identified as the author of this work

A catalogue record for this book is available from the British Library

ISBN: 978-0-00-817175-9

This novel is entirely a work of fiction.
The names, characters and incidents portrayed in it are
the work of the author's imagination. Any resemblance to
actual persons, living or dead, events or localities is
entirely coincidental.

Printed and bound in Great Britain by CPI Group (UK) Ltd,
Croydon CR0 4YY

MIX
Paper from
responsible sources
FSC™ C007454

This book is produced from independently certified FSC™ paper
to ensure responsible forest management.

For more information visit: www.harpercollins.co.uk/green

For Malala, from one Yusufzai to another,
and for all the Pashtun girls

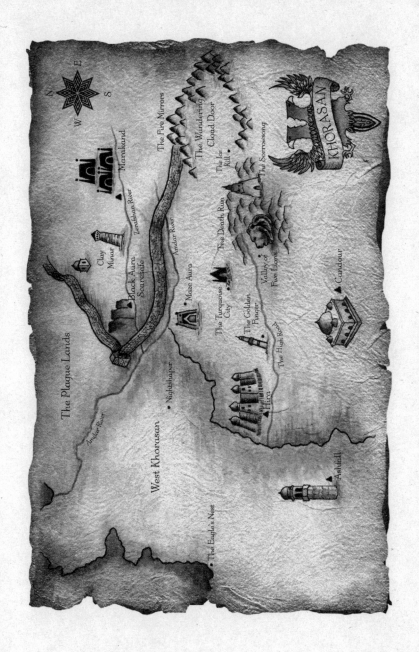

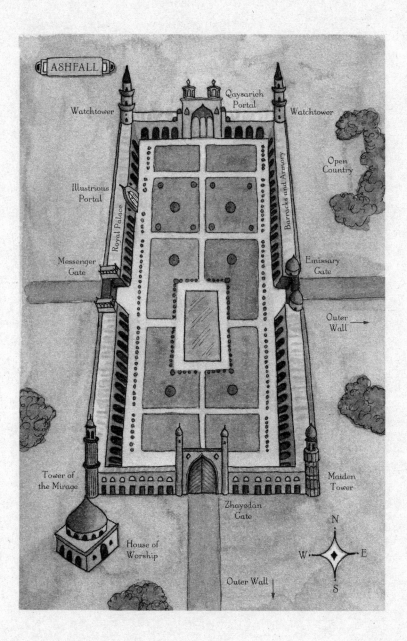

1

FROM THE NEAR HOUSE OF WORSHIP TO THE DISTANT HOUSE OF WORSHIP.

The Night Journey passed in a rush of wind. An eternity or an instant, an endless fall or a bright, buoyant skimming over enigmatic deserts and opulent green valleys—Arian couldn't define it. Her body wasn't fatigued; her mind was pliable and fresh. Yet she carried centuries of loss in the innermost parts of her soul as she was transported from the cavern of the Blue Eye to a city flattened by time, abandoned save for the deepest reaches of memory.

When she looked to her right, she saw Sinnia. And behind Sinnia, Daniyar and Sidi Yusuf, the Blue Mage, whom Arian had first encountered in the lands of the Negus. Moments ago, or a lifetime past, Arian had been at the center of the Blue Eye, a vast geological formation in the heart of an unforgiving landscape. She had stood on a stone plinth surrounded by tranquil waters that seemed to shift beneath her gaze, looking up through the roof of the cavern to a source of illusory light, Sinnia beside her, Daniyar and Yusuf at her heels.

There had been an orphan boy in her care, but now the boy was gone. He had vanished into the light. The same light that had brought them all here. All except Wafa, whom she couldn't find, no matter how she searched, the loss acquiring the painful weight of an ache.

Nor had she seen him at the other stops on the Night Journey. She'd been taken into a past that originated long before the wars of the Far Range. To ancient holy cities whose texts and ideologies had been lost to the encroachments of time. The Night Journey had shown her the extent of that loss.

Secrets had been revealed.

She had offered prayers for the dead at the site of a grave in the City of the Friend.

She had also witnessed the birthplace of the messenger of the Esayin.

She had been without her companions at these places of detour. How would she be able to explain her experience? Where she had been, and what she had witnessed, wasn't possible, the experience atemporal, outside of time that had meaning in the present—or the past as they had studied it. The cities she'd visited had been preserved, from the moment of the events that had given them their significance, rare and new, with untouched olive groves and lemon trees, the vales dressed in almond blossom. Her only reference to these places was her own sense of wonder.

As soon as Arian had given herself up to the source of the light that shone upon the Blue Eye, her consciousness of the physical world had altered. Her vision had fractured so that wherever she turned her gaze, she witnessed both the immediate, tangible present and the impossible, distant past of a world undamaged by war, where difference tinged each note of familiarity she tried to ground herself in. Even the words in her mouth had changed their shape, the vowels softer and sweeter, the consonants more pronounced, the Claim her mother tongue, its lexicon her place of birth.

But her name remained: Companion of Hira, First Oralist of Hira.

Most blessed of her time to speak the word. Most blessed to *apprehend* the word. For Arian, to read was to divine the deeper meaning within.

Language and light shimmered like a quicksilver fire in her veins, gilded the corners of her vision so that when she looked upon the world around her, she was seeing it with dual vision—with light upon light vision, keen as the lancing edge of Daniyar's silver gaze, pure as a note of Sinnia's rich voice, true as the heart of a lost and orphaned child.

She existed now between these three things—the penetrating look, the startling song, and the pure soul—in the immaterial, atemporal part of herself, the self that had undertaken the Night Journey to visit a place of myth, the City of the Four. To visit the holy city where the Adhraa had given birth to the miracle of the Esayin.

These were the gifts she had witnessed with the light upon light vision.

She drew a breath that shook with her sense of awe, felt her diaphragm move, and then she was back in her body again, feeling the weight of sinew and bone in her heels. Her heart slammed hard against the armor of her rib cage.

She was standing on a plateau just above the fissure of a ravine to the south. She gazed down, seeing it with dual vision—the gold-dusted sands, the sweeping curves of olive groves within the creases of tumbled hills whose climbing walls were studded with quartz that glittered with hidden sparks. And now, in her present, the same landscape abject and overthrown, the unbreachable divide of a yawning bereavement.

She shook off an unexpected despair. The dual vision didn't change, though she was no longer alone. Her companions were at her side again. Sinnia to her left, a brightness about her that seemed to flare from her circlets, Daniyar to her right, his hard shoulder brushing hers, and a little distance apart, the Blue Mage, to her surprise. He had relinquished his duty to guard the portal of the Blue Eye. Why he had done this she didn't know, but she wondered if he had been gifted with the dual vision as well. His turquoise gaze had never been so sharp, the cowl over his head ringed by a glowing aura.

Yet nothing about Daniyar was changed. Even with the dual vision, he appeared as she had always known him, his grave expression lightened by love as he turned his head and caught her gaze. He reached for her hand and squeezed it, his face shadowed beneath the hood of his cloak. He shrugged the hood from his head so that his coal-black hair tumbled to his shoulders. Though she tried, she couldn't discern that same aura of light around him that outlined the figures of the others. The connection between them remained the same, their bond pulsing like a heartbeat, deepened by the sacrifices that had cost them a life together.

He smiled at her, touching his forehead to hers. His breath drifted over her lips. She drew it into her lungs, a secret, silent caress.

"Where are we?" he asked. "Where did the Night Journey bring us?"

To the far distant house of worship.

She saw it with the dual vision, but in the present she was somewhere else.

She returned the pressure of his hand with her own. "I think to the outskirts of the Noble Sanctuary. But I *feel* it without seeing it."

His head dipped down toward the ravine where scuffs of faded clover grew. "After the wars of the Far Range, perhaps the Noble Sanctuary sank into the ground."

"No." The Blue Mage's warning was stark. "A holy city does not die. Its essence always remains."

His turquoise eyes cut through the falling twilight. "There." He pointed to a thicket of bramble that covered a flight of stone stairs. Light outlined his arm as he pointed. Light that bloomed without burning. Arian's breathing stilled, then picked up again when Daniyar's hand brushed her cheek, drifting to her throat with a tenderness that made her swallow.

"Shall we explore? Twilight is falling, and I'd like to find a place to pray." His words had the warmth of a caress on her lips.

The scent of a storm was heavy in the air, cold stone and rich mud mixed with the faint tang of oranges carried by the gust of wind that whipped their cloaks against their bodies. Sudden and precise, lightning strikes splintered the cobalt sky.

Arian glanced at Sinnia, a smile in her voice as she said, "The lightning must be for you. A reminder of the one who will come to claim you, as the Foxlord promised you in Timeback."

Sinnia glared at Arian, but their interplay was cut short as the Blue Mage strode ahead.

"Hurry," he urged them. "We've a long night of rain ahead of us."

At the top of the short flight of stone steps was a qanatir, an arcade supported by slender columns with marble patterns that had faded over the years. Daniyar joined Yusuf at the head of their party, but he came to a halt as they crossed under the qanatir into the open space of a courtyard. To their right was a small shelter, a dome with a fourteen-sided arcade, open to the elements. No one paid attention to the outlying shelter because what stood before them was a structure that reached to the sky, dominating the platform on which it had been erected. At its pinnacle was a dome that dwarfed the surround, built on a high drum that rested on a bridge. Like the slender ribs of the dome, its gallery of windows was smudged over with black lead, so that the dome hung over the esplanade like a baleful, portentous eye. The dome and the bridge that supported it were poised above a massive structure in the shape of an octagon. The eight-sided facade might at one time have been ornamented with decorative plaster and tile: broken bits of crystal shone in unexpected glints, a faint echo of the jewel tones of stained glass. But the lower half of the white stone walls was calcified with ash, while the upper portion had been stripped of its calligraphy, leaving the giant structure with no secrets of the Claim to share.

Its proportions suggested an edifice of singular purpose and grace. What remained was an approximation of its period of glory. Its porticos had collapsed, its outer columns damaged by the weapons of long-forgotten wars.

Arian tried one of the structure's heavy doors. It refused to budge, even with Sinnia's help. Then she tried the Claim. Still the door remained either locked or wedged in place.

The winds of the Night Journey whooshed in Arian's ears, pushing her head to the right to view the shelter that stood in the shadow of the black lead dome. Her vision retained its strange duality—the silhouettes of Sinnia and Yusuf were outlined in flares of gold, as they spread out around the smaller structure. She focused on the shelter, capped by its dusty dome, its columns chipped and, in the case of one, listing away at an angle from the dome it was meant to uphold. The shelter's ornamentation had been stripped away, exposing the wooden frame beneath. Naked and forlorn, it stood in the shadow of a much greater structure, reduced to its present state by centuries of war and neglect.

But the dual vision showed Arian something else: a bright silver dome resting atop coral and emerald columns over a hexagonal drum, the upper platform adorned with turquoise tiles, the outer arcade of columns glistening in shades of blue. On one side, a prayer niche was etched into a wall. The dual vision faded, leaving the present, catching Arian off guard.

A man was standing before the niche. Daniyar drew his sword. On the opposite side of the arcade, the Blue Mage did the same. The man at the prayer niche turned to face them, and Arian saw that he was dressed in robes of stiff white satin, embroidered with sheaves of wheat. Broad gold bands lined with red borders formed the cuffs of the outer robe. On his chest were two emblems: one of a woman whose face was obscured by a halo, her form gowned in a subdued blue, the other of an indistinct figure whose face was also disguised. These were symbols of the Esayin, whose holy scripture was a precursor of the Claim. If Najran had not stolen the treasures of the maqdas in the city of Axum, she and Sinnia might have seen similar depictions in the texts preserved in the city's sacred ark.

Some part of Arian had expected that the man who met them at the dome would be an elder. She saw that she was mistaken. Despite the splendor of his garments, the man's face was smooth and unlined, his head well-shaped, his hair clustered with curls, his tawny skin glazed by the sun, his eyes reflecting the kind of peace that must have been cultivated by the spiritual practice of a monk. Yet he was not an ascetic. Not when he was dressed in those robes, matched by a high-domed hat on his skull.

She would have guessed that he was close to Daniyar's age,

except Daniyar bore the weight of his years as the Guardian of Candour in the fine lines that crept from the corners of eyes that could change from soft gray smoke to purest silver.

She glanced up at Daniyar, who was standing at her shoulder, his body angled to shield hers. The cloak he wore over his battered armor was frayed, his sword ready in his hand, the cool silver of his gaze trained on the man who stood before the prayer niche.

He slid his sword back into its sheath and bowed his head.

Had the Night Journey graced Daniyar with the same dual vision that Arian now possessed? Was he seeing something she couldn't?

The man in the elaborate robes bowed his head. His hat dipped on his skull.

"The Custodian of the Holiest House welcomes the Guardian of Candour." His hands swept out before him. "If you wish to pray, consider this your house."

He spoke in an ancient language that was a sister to the High Tongue. Arian had studied the language at Hira, but its pronunciation had remained uncertain. It took her a moment to pick his words apart, and she wondered whether Daniyar could understand them, so she translated the greeting for the benefit of the others.

The Custodian's eyes drifted to her circlets before they closed. When he opened them again, he pressed his right hand to his heart, then extended it in her direction.

"Daughter of the Haram Sharif. You are welcome to pray, as well."

The Custodian moved aside to expose a prayer niche carved from white marble.

Arian considered his words. The term "Holiest House"

couldn't refer to this small domed structure with its humble mihrab. The Custodian was speaking of something greater . . . a place of grandeur that encompassed the Noble Sanctuary and the house of worship that presided over it, but also the atrophied city beyond, its walls sundered, its gates in disrepair.

To Arian's surprise, Daniyar spoke to the Custodian in the High Tongue, betraying a trace of the accent of his native city of Candour.

"I thank you for your welcome, but is this not your house? If I were to trespass with my prayer, the trespass would have weight."

Arian's dual vision fractured again, spilling lustrous silver light down upon Daniyar's head and across his shoulders. The hilt of his sword pulsed with it. The ring he had given to Arian throbbed with the same insistent rhythm.

There was an echo in Daniyar's words that reminded Arian of the histories she had read at Hira in search of deeper knowledge of her calling to the Claim.

In the time before the wars of the Far Range, a caliph had come to the Noble Sanctuary to treat with a patriarch of the Esayin. The patriarch had been dressed in his full regalia, a man of immeasurable learning whose dress impressed upon his acolytes, and on the caliph himself, the importance of his station. But the caliph, despite his own noble rank, was dressed in the travel-worn robe he had journeyed to the holy city in: the Commander of the Faithful come to the city as a pilgrim. The patriarch and the caliph had addressed each other with courtesy, when the matter under discussion between them was the patriarch's surrender of the city. Before terms could be agreed, the time of prayer had come and the caliph had wanted to pray. The patriarch had invited the caliph to pray inside the Esayin's sanctuary.

The caliph had refused, praying some distance to the south

on a prayer rug set at his feet by the patriarch himself. After the prayer, the caliph had confided that his actions carried such weight among his followers that the Esayin would have been forced to relinquish their holiest sanctuary because the Commander of the Faithful had once prayed beneath its dome.

Arian shivered as she understood the import of Daniyar's words.

If I were to trespass with my prayer, the trespass would have weight.

An honorable course set by a man whose actions deepened the dimensions of her love.

At the heart of the Noble Sanctuary, she dared to risk a new thought.

In the time before, the split time of the stolen and lost past, Daniyar would have been a sahabah. He would have been a Companion of Hira, at a time when both men and women served as Companions to the Messenger of the Claim. There was no proof more striking than the risks he took for her now.

He must have caught something of her emotion, because he turned to study her, his smile a gentle curve against the shadow of his beard, reawakening her to his love.

"We begin as we mean to go on. Claiming only what we have rightfully inherited."

The same sense of history weighted his voice, for he had studied the manuscripts of the Library of Candour.

When the dazzling glare of the silver light that spilled upon him had faded, Arian's dual vision became clear. In the set of Daniyar's head, she beheld the dignity of the caliph in his travel-worn robe, negotiating the terms of a city's surrender without transgressing the rights of its inhabitants. So would Daniyar have governed Candour, if the Talisman had not come to rule. A stark contrast to the One-Eyed Preacher, who would have burned the Noble Sanctuary to the ground after defiling its holiest of holies.

But despite her vision of the caliph and the patriarch, this modest shelter at the heart of the Haram Sharif was not a house of worship of the Esayin. The Noble Sanctuary had been established by the people of the Claim.

As if he'd read her thoughts, the Custodian turned to her.

"You wonder why I alone remain as the guardian of your holy places."

His hands moved to the wide gold belt of his robe, from which he unlinked a set of keys, heavy and ornate, the long spears terminating in a ring forged from iron.

Arian's dual vision shifted. Brightened. The same man in the same regalia, the depths of his knowledge reflected in his eyes, the weary lines of his face imprinted with years of sacrifice in pursuit of that knowledge.

When he spoke, the dual vision transported her to a forgotten past so that the ring of keys was outlined by a brilliant band of fire.

The patriarch had given the keys to the Esayin's house of worship to the caliph, who had answered, "I give you my word that as long as I hold the City of Faith, your places of worship will be under my protection. No one will trespass here."

The keys to the sanctuary had passed into the safekeeping of a trusted attendant of the caliph's. At dawn and sunset, the attendant had opened and closed the house of worship himself, and so the tradition had passed down through the centuries to members of his family, who honored the trust placed in them by a caliph who held himself above no law, and whose word had never been forsworn.

The dignity of a monk deepened the emotion in the Custodian's eyes. As Arian watched the moment both in the past and the present, he pressed the ring of keys into Daniyar's hands.

Daniyar tested the weight of the two keys before he spoke, regret sounding in the words. "I have no gift to offer in exchange."

"The gift was in the keeping of our house of worship. In return, I have kept the keys to yours. And now I relinquish that trust into the hands of the Guardian of Candour."

"Why?" Daniyar's head bowed under the weight of burdens he had borne too long. He had turned away from Arian to keep her from seeing the toll it had taken. "How have you judged me worthy?"

The Custodian posed a question of his own. "Will you pray while the daughter of the Haram Sharif enters the Blind Dome to complete her journey?"

He meant the dome covered in black lead, but the words stirred a memory in Arian.

"No," Daniyar said, his decision swift.

He reached for Arian, shifting the weight of the keys into his other hand. He pulled her close to his side, and when she fitted herself to his body without protest, a warm look of approval transformed the Custodian's face.

"You wished to pray." A reminder. "And you have come to a place of prayer."

Daniyar didn't ask how the Custodian had known this. The mysteries of the Night Journey were still being revealed. His arm fastened around Arian's shoulders, though he was careful with his far greater strength.

"She ventures no danger I do not venture first. As a servant of the One, this is my form of prayer. When there is time for reflection, I will reflect."

"I'll wait for you," Arian said. "If you need time, take it."

She touched his jaw, turning his head so that he was looking into her eyes. It was rare for him to ask for anything for himself; there had to be a reason for his request.

"Take the time you need," she repeated. "This is your journey too."

The Blue Mage interjected. "Wherever the Companions must venture, my sword will be at their side. Observe your prayer as you will."

The Custodian nodded at the black lead dome. "*From the Near House of Worship to the Distant House of Worship*. The journey of the Companions is complete. Where they must go from here, there is one man who may follow."

Yusuf strode through the arcade of columns into the shelter of the miniature dome. When he came to stand beside Daniyar at the prayer niche, his turquoise eyes were so piercing that even with the dual vision, Arian had to look away. She shaded her eyes with her hand.

The Custodian's eyes flared in shock as the Blue Mage came to stand before him, undeterred by his caution.

"Azraq," the Custodian accused him. "*You* cannot cross the threshold of the Noble Sanctuary into this house of worship. You are among those who will be assembled to plead on the Last Day, their eyes dim with terror."

"No!" Arian was stunned that the Custodian had some knowledge of this little-known verse of the Claim. "This is the Blue Mage, Guardian of Timeback. Look at him—perceive that his vision is unaffected." She moved closer to the Custodian, her green glance covering him. "From your interpretation, *I* could also be azraq. You mistake the meaning of the Claim."

He had understood the word and the verse to refer to those who were blue-eyed or green-eyed, destined to an afterlife of torment.

The Claim would not offer such judgment upon any part of the One's creation.

The Custodian looked to the Guardian of Candour, who nodded.

"The First Oralist is telling you the truth. You have nothing to fear from the Blue Mage."

Instead of bowing, the Custodian offered his hand to the Blue Mage, who grasped it at the forearm to accept his unspoken apology.

"Go," the Custodian said to their party. "I have given you the keys to the house of worship. One opens the outer door. The second . . ." He hesitated before pressing on. "The second is for you alone, daughter of the Haram Sharif."

But Arian knew she would not be leaving her companions behind. Even if she'd thought of doing so, Daniyar would refuse to part from her. She didn't share this, instead asking the question that concerned her: "Did any other approach before our arrival? A boy with brown hair and blue eyes?"

In the next minute the Custodian was standing far away from her, on the opposite side of the courtyard. Even with the dual vision, she hadn't seen him move. She stepped outside the shelter of the smaller dome to follow him, just as the sky was fractured by lightning. Electricity crackled through the open space as thunder rumbled overhead.

Daniyar called her back, but she moved to the black lead dome. The others followed.

"The one who came will not be the one who returns." The Custodian's voice sounded in her ears. Her head jerked back. The dual vision showed her the older monk of the past, imposed upon the young man of the present. "No one returns in the same form after the Ascension. The daughters of the Noble Sanctuary will ascend, as will the Guardian of Candour. I cannot speak of the one you named as the Blue Mage."

Yusuf's reply was brief. "The knowledge meant for me has already been revealed."

The ominous clouds emptied themselves. Rain pounded the courtyard. Arian found her hand grasped by Daniyar's as she was hurried from the miniature dome to the damaged portico of the black-domed house of worship.

"But have you seen a boy?" Arian shouted across the expanse of the courtyard. She blinked to clear rain from her vision, but the Custodian was gone, along with her opportunity to gain information.

Where was Wafa? How had he ascended? What had the Custodian meant by saying he would not return?

And how did a Custodian of the Esayin *know* of the Ascension?

What power did he possess to determine who had the right or the ability to ascend?

What would Ascension entail, when all along she had believed that both the Night Journey and the Ascension were metaphysical rather than material journeys?

Behind her, Sinnia engaged Yusuf, echoing Arian's unspoken questions. "When you said the Sana Codex wasn't what we imagined . . . when you guarded the portal of the Blue Eye, did you ascend? Can you tell us about the Ascension?"

Rain gilded the pure line of her profile, catching on the tips of her lashes. Yusuf tracked the path of a drop that trailed from the edge of her eyebrow to the corner of her fine-boned jaw.

"No, Companion. My knowledge is mine to guard, as yours must be, as well. I have brought you as far as I can. There is little more I can tell you."

"You left the portal of the Blue Eye unguarded." It was more a question than an accusation, though Sinnia was still wary of the secrets the Blue Mage had kept.

Yusuf responded in kind. "If Najran or his lieutenants breach the portal, you will need more than the Silver Mage at your back."

The name gave Sinnia a jolt. She had forgotten their enemy, Najran. A lieutenant of the Rising Nineteen who had pursued them across the Rub Al Khali to the Blue Eye, and who might even now be at their heels. Her gaze swept the courtyard as sheets of rain slanted against the horizon, all but obscuring her vision.

Yusuf bent close to whisper to Sinnia, "Don't be afraid. I won't allow him to harm you."

Sinnia's hand tightened on the haft of her whip.

"I'm not afraid." His promise had disarmed her. As had the concern mirrored in his shining eyes. She found that she could brave the clarity of his gaze, though he had discarded his trick of clouding it. Yet Arian had been forced to raise a hand to shade her brow.

"No, you wouldn't be." He seemed to be speaking to himself. "The way you fought beside me at the entrance to the portal . . . small wonder you were chosen to defend the First Oralist. But I've always known you were worthy."

Before Sinnia could respond to this, he had moved up to assist the Silver Mage as he tried the key to the door that opened the house of worship.

Daniyar's free hand fit one of the spear-shaped keys in the lock that sealed the house of worship. The key turned under protest. Heavy timbers shuddered as he put his shoulder to the door. It didn't budge. Yusuf edged up beside him to help, both men putting their weight behind the effort to enter the noble house. The door remained in place.

Soaked through by rain that leaked into the broken portico,

Arian laid her hand on the door. She offered the incantation known as the Opening. For the second time, her powers failed. Sinnia joined her voice to Arian's. The door remained stiff and unresponsive.

Then Daniyar echoed the verse, urging the others away. He laid his hand upon the door, and it swung wide without a trace of stiffness, beckoning them into the chamber's dark interior.

"Guardian of Candour," Arian whispered to him, as she brushed past his body, "or Commander of the Faithful?"

He caught her by the elbow, his black hair shedding diamond drops of rain. "What do you mean? I returned the Sacred Cloak to the Black Khan. I hoped it would help him hold Ashfall without our aid."

Something in his voice caught at her. The echo of a promise, the need to honor his word.

Arian set the thought aside. "Is your vision at all affected? Are you seeing anything beyond this moment or place?"

"Nothing has changed for me, Arian. Did the Night Journey alter *your* perception?"

He held her in place as Sinnia and Yusuf moved past them, his grip warm and firm around her waist, a touch she welcomed. She'd said very little, and yet, he'd understood. Guardian of Candour. Trusted with the keys to the house of worship at the heart of the Haram Sharif.

His beard brushed her temple. She turned her face up so that she was speaking almost against his lips, her breath sighing into his mouth. She felt his instant response in the hardening of his arm around her waist, but all he did was stand before her to listen.

"I'm affected with a kind of dual vision. As though I'm seeing the past as well as the present. Or if it isn't the past, I don't know *what* it is I'm seeing."

His mouth brushed hers, sparks of sensation striking all her nerves at once.

"What you're meant to see," he guessed. "What the First Oralist is meant to see."

She didn't tell him that the dual vision had showed him to her as the Commander of the Faithful: one man carrying a mantle worn by others before him—others whose names were so honored that they had passed into legend, myths rather than men. Those secrets were for another time, another place, when they chanced to find themselves alone.

This moment was for the Night Journey. And the secrets of the Israa e Miraj.

2

THE SPACE WAS TOO DARK TO SEE ANYTHING, BUT SINNIA MOVED AHEAD under a cascade of hanging lanterns, breathing a word into each as she passed. The word was *nur;* in the High Tongue it meant "light": the kind of light that transcended materiality or simple illumination.

Together they advanced into the chamber that opened up beneath the dome. Here the state of disrepair was less. The carpets beneath their feet were eaten away, so all that remained were a few threadbare traces of patterns in red and gold. But the interior of the structure was intact. Between the outer wall and a circular arcade beneath the great dome stood an octagonal arrangement of piers and columns, the piers built of stone, the columns irregular but retaining some sense of their brightness with their capitals preserved. Perhaps the interior had not collapsed because of the tie beams that supported the arches of the inner sphere, resilient enough to allow stonemasons and artisans to move about as they ornamented the interior of a dome of indescribable beauty. The decorative motifs that covered the beams were worked upon a gleaming bronze. The beams created a series of passageways that led to the circular arcade, an architectural pattern that directed attention inward.

The ceiling of the interior was undamaged, shielding their heads from the rain that pounded the dome. In the outer arcade, molded plaster formed the ceiling; in the inner ambulatory, wooden coffers were carved with bronze and gold vegetal motifs.

Sinnia advanced to the very center of the arcade, where a protective railing had long since fallen away. She stared up at the interior of a dome whose drum was built of firm, warm-hued stone, with windows beneath arches that appeared at intervals around its massive circumference. The windows were dark now with the storm lashing panes that had somehow remained intact.

The light from the lanterns illuminated patterns of such intricacy and beauty that Sinnia caught her breath, her head tilted back so she could view their dizzying pinnacle.

Just above the arches, a band of decoration had been peeled away, leaving a blank black canvas. Higher up the inside of the dome, where reds gave way to a profusion of gold leaf and paint, another band had been painted over, leaving a blank gold space.

What had been there that needed to be erased while the rest of the pattern was unspoiled? Sinnia deferred to Arian. She noticed with a start that although Yusuf and Daniyar had imitated her posture and were staring skyward, Arian had not been captured by the soaring beauty of the dome. Her attention was fixed on the clearing surrounded by the broken rail.

Yet there was nothing there to engage Arian, at least nothing that compared to the splendor of the cupola. She was looking at a misshapen stretch of rock that seemed carved out of the earth, with layers of silt on a craggy surface that was elevated at one end. Faded marks upon the surface of the rock were still visible.

But there was something . . .

Despite the fact that the windows were clouded over and the heavy lead dome allowed no other source of light to penetrate from above, a slender pillar of light illuminated the rock, piercing through its center so that the light trickled beneath the rock to a darkened space below that Sinnia had failed to notice. She heard the sound of water, a steady and gentle murmur, distinct from the rain that battered the dome like a drum.

But she still couldn't see what held Arian rapt.

"There's a pool of some kind below." Arian pointed to the surface of the rock.

Following Arian's gaze, Yusuf said, "It's a portal. It brought us to the distant house of worship. The light from the column on the stone reflects upon the pool below."

Yet the Night Journey hadn't taken them *inside* the house of worship. Seeing her puzzlement, Yusuf nodded at Daniyar. "Perhaps we needed the Guardian of Candour to turn the key. Or we needed the Custodian's permission to enter a holy place."

Daniyar peered across the railing to stare up into the light. The moment he did so, the brilliance of the light expanded, sharpened to such a point that he was forced to turn his head away. He bent his head so that his vision was limited to the rock.

"Do you know where we are, Arian? Do you know why this structure is oriented around this rock?" He studied the interior walls before adding, "This isn't a house of worship, as we thought. Look how many entrances there are. These octagons aren't arcades, they're ambulatories. There's no mihrab to indicate a direction for prayer. There's no space between the ambulatories for worshippers to observe prayer undisturbed."

Arian turned away from the unyielding source of light. She touched the bare surface of the rock with one hand, drawing in a breath as she made contact.

"This is the Sakhrah," she said. "This is the place where Ascension begins."

Her words were whispered with a reverence that made the Sakhrah holy.

Her eyes found Sinnia hesitating at the perimeter of the rail that had once protected the rock from the trespass of intruders. "Join me."

Arian vaulted onto the surface of the rock, just outside the reach of the pillar of light. She held out her hand to Sinnia, who approached with caution. Sinnia's senses told her there was nothing to fear, yet her heart pounded in her chest. If she took Arian's hand—if she stood upon the rock and stepped into the hallowed source of light—she would be transformed into someone other than who she was. She knew this with unshakable certainty. The process that Salikh had begun inside her prison cell at Jaslyk would be complete. Salikh had forced knowledge of the Claim upon her as a means of delivering her from the tortures of Jaslyk prison. But it had meaning beyond those walls. Meaning that now shone before her.

She hesitated as she contemplated the road that had led here. Sinnia had been sent to Hira as a novice by the Negus of her people, in the hopes that she would be accepted into the Companions' ranks. The High Companion, Ilea, had selected Sinnia as Arian's sole protector on the dangerous Audacy Arian had been assigned.

But touching the Sakhrah . . . climbing the rock . . . yielding to a source of light she couldn't comprehend—that would be *Sinnia's* choice. No one else could make it for her.

She looked up into Arian's eyes shining with inner contentment. Arian had made her choice. Whatever the Ascension was, whatever it was comprised of, Arian didn't fear it. She welcomed it. She aspired to it.

And the warmth of Arian's gaze conveyed that she believed that Sinnia was meant to ascend at her side, though Sinnia's doubts were many, her questions unfulfilled.

And then she thought she knew why Arian's expression reflected such contentment. Her inner certainty wasn't certainty at all. Arian had decided on faith.

She had trusted herself to the One.

A sigh eased out of Sinnia's body. She grasped Arian's hand and swung herself up onto the rock. But instead of stepping into the column of light, she stepped around Arian to the highest point of the rock's elevation. She slid down onto her knees, bent her forehead to the rock, to an irregular mark that shone beneath layers of silt. Tears slid down her dark brown cheeks. She touched the mark with her lips.

A fresh breeze stirred the curls at her temples. It stilled her inner trembling.

Sitting up, she wiped her cheeks with the back of her hand.

"I'm sorry," she said, looking up at Arian, whose expression was marked by tenderness, tears glowing in her eyes. "I know we aren't meant to venerate anything except the One, but I couldn't help myself."

In Arian's place, the High Companion would have delivered a stern rebuke, perhaps even called Sinnia's qualifications as a Companion of Hira into question, invoking a stringent interpretation of the Companions' code that held shadings of the Talisman's beliefs.

Instead, Arian sank down beside Sinnia and kissed the same shining mark. Then she smiled at Sinnia and said, "Is there anything but light in your love?"

She looked to the two Mages, who watched them from the perimeter and asked, "Do you know the legend of the Qubbat-as-Sakhrah?"

They shook their heads, one man watching Arian, the other Sinnia, whose hand was still pressed to the mark she had kissed.

"It holds that the rock—the Sakhrah—is elevated on one end because it tried to follow the Messenger of the Claim on the Israa e Miraj. The Messenger told the rock that its duty was to remain behind as a threshold to mark the journey. The imprint is from the Messenger's hand." She smiled again. "Or perhaps it's a footprint, as the Messenger of the Claim is said to have begun Ascension by climbing a staircase of light."

She came to her feet, bringing Sinnia with her, tasting cool, clear air, though neither the thunder nor the beating of the rain had slackened. Arian pressed both hands to her circlets and waited for Sinnia to do the same, her glance never straying from Daniyar's shadowed face.

"I must leave you now. My time has come to ascend."

She had anticipated Arian's conclusion, yet Sinnia was still unsure of the role that she was meant to play. *Ascend what?* she wanted to demand. *Ascend where?*

But now the Silver Mage was speaking.

I should be at your side."

Arian shook her head. "The Custodian told you. This part of my Audacy, I must complete alone. And Sinnia and you must do the same."

Daniyar didn't want to accept this, but each time he ventured close to the rock, the column of light erupted into a blaze that separated him from the Companions. The same was true for Yusuf, who had confirmed that though he was more familiar with the

Ascension than Daniyar was, he, too, had been unable to trespass beyond the boundary of the rock.

It took everything Daniyar had to allow Arian to venture into a place where he could not protect her. Not that the choice was his to make. Nor did he begrudge Arian the choice. Their denials were behind them now; they knew what they were to each other. He understood her calling to the Claim as he hadn't before, because he shared it. And now he would do nothing—*could* do nothing—to stand in Arian's way.

But he admitted to a fear of the unknown. He feared the loss of the completion he'd gained. He belonged to Arian as he'd never belonged to anything in his life, not even his vocation as the Silver Mage.

"You're not afraid?" Daniyar kept his own voice steady. "What if you cross a boundary from which you cannot return? As Wafa did."

What if you are lost to me forever?

He refrained from speaking the words aloud. He knew Arian had sensed his fear, and his expectation of grief.

"Trust me. Trust that I am yours in this life and the Akhirah. And know that I will wait for you to undertake your own ascent."

"The Overturner of Hearts knows that mine is steadfast."

Arian caught the echo of an ancient vow, and a fragile smile settled on her lips. He moved to the rock to reach for her, or at least to kiss her in farewell, but the fire that didn't burn—the clean, clear fire that spilled from the Sakhrah—sprang up as a barrier again. He raised a hand to touch it. Immaterial, insubstantial yet impossible to pass. As it touched him, he felt his irises brightening into pure, metallic silver, his vision so keen that when he glanced up at the summit of the dome, the bands that had been stripped of their ornamentation glowed with traces of calligraphy.

He tipped his head back, raising himself to his full height, the words just coming into focus, when his reverie was interrupted by the sound of a solid thud against the entrance to the dome. The door had closed behind them, heavy and impassable. The sound he heard now was the brazen thump of an axe.

He whirled around. His sword slid free of its sheath, the Blue Mage ahead of him at the door, bracing it with a powerful shoulder. The axe missed Yusuf by inches. Daniyar threw his weight against the door. He cast a look back at Arian and shouted, "Go! Find Wafa. Find the Sana Codex. But return to me, Arian. Don't leave me to fight this war without you. Don't leave me with empty hands."

He couldn't see her face, blinded by the column that had expanded now to cover the entire surface of the Sakhrah, no longer solid and pure, but shimmering and evanescent, its borders tinged turquoise and gold.

The axe fell again, this time its blade cleaving the door so that its wicked edge was lodged in the broken timber. The tabar's black steel blade was inlaid with gold decoration, a weapon as merciless as the Iron Glaive once wielded by Najran. But Daniyar had broken the Iron Glaive into pieces in their battle over the sands of the Sahel. This was a different weapon. And yet, through the damaged timber of the door, he saw that the man who wielded it *was* none other than Najran, the Angel of Blood. An enemy to the Companions of Hira, and to those who were their allies.

The Blue Mage hacked at the axe with his sword, trying to pull it out of the grip of its wielder. But Najran jerked it back, and it was Yusuf's sword that flew free. He chased after it while Daniyar continued to brace the door, yielding to the pressure in increments. He had time for a last look at the Sakhrah; his vision faltered as the column of light narrowed.

He saw Arian astride a horse.

Was it Safanad, Arian's horse?

He blinked. Arian's mare reared up on her hind legs, her neck arched so that her mane fell free in a series of long black tresses. From just below her perfect crest, in line with her elegant shoulders, a pair of white wings flared outward in a blindingly beautiful arc. Arian's hands caught at the mane and brought up the mare's head. The hooves of the mare were no longer touching the ground.

The curved head of the tabar just missed Daniyar's head. He rolled aside as the door gave way. When he looked at the Sakhrah again, the column of light had vanished.

Arian and Sinnia were gone.

3

Seven. Eight. Six.

When Arian slid from the back of her mount, she was standing on a cool surface in a space that had no dimensions and no color. In the far distance, the sky was molten lead, the blurry outline of hills like tufted flakes of wool, a world torn asunder, silent and removed. It seemed to her that the bright face of the moon had been darkened in a sky without stars, the sun and moon hanging so low on the horizon that they were at a point of collision, close to eclipsing each other. With a gasp she realized she couldn't command herself to move. Her arms were weighted by her sides, her head facing forward so that all she could see in the distance was a sky of liquid flame poured over the ruins of the world.

She was neither cold nor warm, her physical consciousness removed from her self-knowledge. What remained was vision, thought, and spirit, and then even that was gone, until the thoughts in her mind coalesced to reduce her to a string of words. But each of the words had weight. They had meaning she had never thought to reflect on.

There is no one but the One. And so the One commands.

Her circlets pressed down on her upper arms, binding her heart to her tongue, her tongue to her thoughts, and her vision to a line of calligraphy etched with ascetic grace.

In the name of the One, most Gracious and most Merciful.

She felt a presence on either side of her and tried to turn her head without success. Her eyelids grew heavy, her thoughts dull, her body so fatigued that she couldn't raise her lashes. A hand on either side of her wrapped around the circlets that bore the opening words of the Claim.

Sensation returned with a shock. The touch upon her circlets was bright and ennobling, an incendiary heat that struck all the way through to her essence, a lashing of fire as though she was being destroyed and created in the same instance, her impurities burned away. All that remained was her unflagging will, and the gift that bound her to the Claim.

Linguist, visionary, conqueror of the Word. A thing unknown to Hira before her coming.

She tried to speak, to call out. The figures on either side of her were unviewable. From the corners of her lowered eyes, she caught the brilliant flare of wing tips, just as Safanad, her mare, had flown on gilded wings to this lowest of seven firmaments.

The pressure on her arms altered. The figures were pulling at her, pulling her apart by the circlets, pulling in opposite directions. She tried to scream, a cry that betrayed no sound spilling from her throat, coarse and without the refinement with which her tongue had been trained.

Sobs racked her body as her limbs were pulled farther apart, until the vault of her ribs was split in two. She was being sundered. She was shaking, shivering, *dying,* the agony of her physical self a curse that none of her gifts could cure. She couldn't protect herself. She couldn't defend herself. Yet she didn't think of

Sinnia; she didn't even think to look for her. She didn't remember Daniyar, nor any of those she loved.

She thought of herself, her innermost core with its flaws, jealousies, uncertainties, and selfishness exposed for all creation to see. Exposed for the One to see.

Her cry reverberated across the igneous reds of the sky.

And then the fire that singed every nerve ending, the scalding heat that peeled her skin from her body and turned her inside out, dissipated as if it had never been, leaving no residue of pain. In this innocuous state, she felt her ribs shift and expand, her chest open and exposed.

A basin of light poured over the empty cavern of her chest, overflowing from her ribs until her entire body was bathed in light—in light upon light that pierced her skull, her eyes, her senses, her thoughts, and the essence of herself, where she was Arian, First Oralist of Hira. Friend, sister, beloved, and the fulfillment of prophecy.

"What prophecy?" she dared to ask.

From her right, there was a voice that produced no sound.

What will the Claim be in your hands?

From her left, it said, *What will the Claim be in your voice?*

"Glory. Power. Destiny. Tyrants brought to their knees. Punishment meted out. The Talisman wiped from the earth, the Companions of Hira ascendant. All will bow to our rule, as it should always have been."

She drew a triumphant breath.

"All shall bow to me, conqueror of the Claim, for none are more knowledgeable than I."

The light inside her chest turned sour.

The red sky was torn asunder, the sun shrouded in darkness, the stars scattered and blind, the mountains vanished, and the seas aboil—the truths of a world at endless war with weapons that sowed such complete annihilation that a millennium would have to pass before anything could stir upon the surface of the earth again.

Judgment upon judgment.

It seemed she had learned nothing, she possessed no wisdom or humility despite her years at Hira, believing herself infallible, cherishing her superiority, exploiting the privilege of her calling to the Claim.

The pain that had flooded her senses returned, firing her nerves with agony. Her lungs were starved for air even as they were exposed to it, her voice rasping in her throat in a series of heartrending pleas. How long it continued, she couldn't measure. It was an instant, it was infinite, it peeled her skin like the bark of a cedar, it realigned her ribs, it wreathed her arteries in fire, it froze the core at the heart of her like a cliff of ice at sea, impervious to fracture. It dismantled each narrow thought that had ever risen to her mind, stripping away the veils of herself, daughter of Armaghan and Saya, sister of Lania and Hudayfah, beloved of Daniyar, friend and guide to all the Companions, bonded in sisterhood to Sinnia, guardian of the orphan Wafa . . . and at her essence, First Oralist of Hira. The pain that racked her body and mind left her with a simple truth.

She was a daughter of the Claim. She was a servant of the One.

But there were others, as well.

From her right, the voice asked again, *What will the Claim be in your hands?*

The left repeated, *What will the Claim be in your voice?*

"Justice. Equity. Peace."

The left pressed her harder. *Do you swear an unbreakable oath?*

"I swear it without reservation. But first pass judgment on me. Show me how to end this war. Show me the seven firmaments so that I have knowledge of myself and knowledge of all that exists in creation. Make me understand the Claim, make it more than a ritual practice, as it is at Hira. Make it mean more than Recitation."

She didn't know how to convince the voices, so she carried on.

"Forgive me if I fail. If I fail and fail again. I ask only to be like Safanad. To raise my wings and ascend."

The light that had curdled within her spilled out of her chest again, a waterfall of coruscating beauty, sealing the cavity behind it, so that she was both senseless with the totality of the experience, and herself in full again.

The voice from the right was gentle this time.

The firmaments are not your destination. The knowledge you seek does not reside there.

"Then where does it reside?"

Within the Sana Codex.

A book appeared in her hands—no, not a book, a fragile collection of parchment bound between two sheer gold plates fastened by a spine of turquoise. The book was suspended before her, so that she was free to turn its pages with her hands. She read each sheaf of parchment, a reading that should have taken months passing in the course of an instant.

The Sana Codex she studied now was not as the Blue Mage had described it. It wasn't even the same as the collection she had held in her hands at the portal of the Blue Eye.

There *were* no variants, no substitutions for words she already knew. There were no lower and upper markings of a palimpsest scraped of text and put to use again. Seamless lines of Hijazi calligraphy were easy for her to read, the gaps in the manuscript restored. The Claim thrummed through her chest without dropping a note or a word.

Pages sifted through her hands, turning at the speed of her mind's eye. She recognized each word, the arrangement of each phrase. Not a single consonant was misplaced; there was no verse that was unfamiliar, no rejection of impurity from her innate knowledge of the Claim.

Words and phrases flew by.

Over this are Nineteen.

Today we have perfected for you your faith.

Is the reward of good anything but good?

And repeated throughout . . . *In the name of the One, Most Merciful and Compassionate.*

The same words that were inscribed upon the Companions' circlets.

Those circlets throbbed with a golden rhythm around her upper arms, until the last page was turned, and she came to the end of the Claim.

What she had learned was too vast to be contained, too enormous to be grappled with by one mind alone. And though she had grasped it, it was fading from her memory as the Codex sealed itself away. Who would help her remember it? Who could understand?

She made a helpless sound of protest. "I cannot recollect the Claim."

You swore an unbreakable oath. The rest will be determined by you.

A trace of insight followed from revelation. "You could have given me the Claim in any form. Why the Sana Codex?"

The new form must be congruent with the old. Then you will accept.

"Then why not the Bloodprint? I would have known the Bloodprint."

Heat seared her breastbone in a palpable touch of displeasure.

Do not use that name here; it sullies the gift of the One. The name is a reminder of an intolerable grief.

"Do you grieve the one whose holy blood was shed as he bent over a manuscript?"

No blood is holy. You are all creatures of the One.

She thought of the One-Eyed Preacher and rejected the claim. "How can a monster be a creature of the One?"

Through a series of choices, the same choices set before you.

"If I had chosen as he did, would I have forfeited an eye? Is clarity of vision the price of sacred knowledge?"

Do you in truth believe that something was taken from him in exchange for his gifts?

"He is One-Eyed. He is the One-Eyed Preacher. And he possesses more knowledge of the Claim than any other."

No gifts were offered to him, nor is his vision impeded. He suffers from no infirmity.

Arian was at a loss. What then *did* he suffer from? She couldn't perceive what the voices were trying to tell her when she had seen the truth for herself. The One-Eyed Preacher had appeared before her above the walls of Ashfall. Empowered by the Claim, his voice had sundered Ashfall's walls. He had killed luminaries of the court: the Nizam, the Black Khan's half-brother, Darius. And with a single bolt of magic, he'd struck the Princess of Ashfall dead.

His power was unparalleled, unprecedented. He had vanquished the cities of the south, bringing the Talisman to power and ushering forth the era of the Assimilate, the pitiless Talisman law. The Preacher *was* the Talisman incarnate. If he was a creature of the One, and not a devil of some kind, how was she to contend with him? How was she to bring him down?

"I have an enemy to destroy. An enemy who possesses the power of the . . . what shall I call it, if I am not to call it the Bloodprint?"

Know its name as the Criterion. The rest will be governed by you.

She could sense the voices receding with so few of her concerns addressed. She tried to hold them to her. There was so much she didn't know. So much they hadn't told her.

"How will I fight on alone when I am not a Hafiza? I do not know the Claim by heart."

You have never been alone. You have forgotten your teachers.

"They forgot *me*."

You must learn to see the Oralists when and where they appear.

If the Companions of Hira could have aided her in her quest for a written proof of the Claim, they would have done so by now. And if the truth could be found at Hira, why had the portal brought her here? Why had she taken the Night Journey if she wasn't meant to ascend?

The power of the Night Journey is yours to wield as you will. Why do you plead for the Claim when the Claim surrounds you, enshrined by the dome that was blinded?

"I don't understand what you mean. I see no calligraphy here; there is nothing for me to grasp. But I know I can solve these riddles if you permit me to ascend."

This is *your ascent, First Oralist. Your journey is suited to your needs.*

The voices vanished and the pressure on her arms ceased. She was alone on the material plane, the movement of her limbs returned to her. She found Safanad in the corner of her vision, graceful neck arched as she tilted up her head and whinnied for Arian to come. Arian spun around. She was in a cloistered room where moonlight spilled upon a porcelain basin. The room was small and self-contained, the air within tranquil and cool as it wafted through a set of arches.

A woman in a plain silk dress was standing before the basin, a cold stone gracing her finger. She pulled back her transparent veil to stare into the basin.

Let me raise my wings and ascend, Arian had prayed. *Let me find the knowledge I need.*

This was neither knowledge nor Ascension.

The woman in the white silk dress, the woman she was staring at across an invisible partition, was her sister, Lania.

The Khanum behind the Wall.

4

THE SCRYING CHAMBER HELD NO TRACE OF COLOR. STARS BLOOMED from lattices so fragile they seemed as if a touch would shatter them. Alcoves that led to four archways permitted entrance to the room. And above, beyond human reach, was a star-shaped window designed to spill light onto the floor. Moonlight upon light, but even so, it was the plainest room at the Ark, and nothing at all compared to the glories of the Tilla Kari, where the Khanum trained her doves.

A fountain stood in the center of the chamber, its basin a milky stone, water so pure in color it seemed the basin was empty. In daylight hours, the small room was dull, a leftover corner of the Ark. But beneath the shattering brilliance of the stars, white light played upon the water, and the subtle beauty of the lattices cast their patterns on stone.

Lania stood before the fountain, her face unpainted, her hair left long and loose, her body unadorned save for the oval moonstone that blazed from a finger on her hand. She was the former consort of the Authoritan. Her coup against him had left her the sole power in Black Aura, free of any man's demands.

She murmured a verse of the Claim with a twist of her voice that served to occult its meaning. The waters in the basin rose, forming an overlapping pattern. She thought for the briefest instant that the pattern revealed an image of her sister, Arian, in battle dress, worn and at the end of her strength.

Or perhaps the pattern was a reflection of the fountains of the All Ways used in the rites of Hira, and thus it showed Lania her sister. Just as Lania now wore the same plain dress favored by the Companions.

Not so strange, then, except that she had never seen Arian's reflection in the waters of the basin before. She dismissed the memory of Arian from her mind.

A cool wind carried the scent of Marakand loess. Honey-sweet and soothing, it conjured up the delicate perfume of wildflowers.

Lania snapped her fingers, and four women stepped forward, dressed in the same manner as their mistress, each wearing a moonstone ring.

"Khanum."

They offered Lania's title as an act of obeisance.

"Have you found her?"

Her green eyes searched the corners of the room for a fifth presence. When no one moved from the shadows, her voice lashed the doves like a whip.

"Where is she?"

Saher, the most valued of her doves, hastened to answer.

"The Ahdath are bringing her, Khanum."

"Was she taken to the Pit, as we thought?"

Saher hesitated, as if she would choose her words.

"Speak," Lania snapped.

Clasping her hands at her waist, Saher raised her chin.

"The Authoritan banished her to the Pit as punishment for allowing herself to be taken from the Gold House. She was sent here in lieu of the First Oralist, if you recall, Khanum."

At the mention of the First Oralist, the waters in the basin reflected Arian's image.

"I remember."

There was nothing patient or understanding in Lania's frozen glare.

"She wasn't left at the Pit long," Saher continued. "She was trained in the arts of the Gold House, a favorite there, I am told. So one of Nevus's soldiers claimed her for his own."

"Did he."

"I'm afraid so, Khanum."

In Saher's voice alone did Lania fail to discern a note of fear. Saher served her with diligence. It was even possible that Saher loved her, but Lania brushed the thought aside. She wasn't made to command love. Fear was what she wanted from those who served her, its ties bound to the bone, and it offered the sincerity of truth.

She wouldn't think of Arian. Or of Daniyar.

Perhaps her sister *did* love her—what of it? It meant nothing; it changed nothing.

And as for the Silver Mage—his sheer masculine beauty had made a mockery of her claim to indifference. His body a sculpture of clean carved lines, she had held him close and savored the dark male taste of him. The merest taste, that was all. He had offered nothing more; she had taken nothing else. The tenderness of his regret at hurting her meant nothing. She didn't think of Daniyar, or of herself in his arms.

How could she? He belonged to her sister. Just as Arian had stolen everything else from her. Their parents. Their brother. The Citadel. Her *rank*.

All of it claimed by Arian; it was Arian whose name was renowned throughout the lands of Khorasan.

First Oralist, indeed.

Lania didn't begrudge Arian her fate. She didn't envy Arian's purpose, or her adherence to tradition. She found it . . . troublesome. That with no skill at her fingertips save her use of the Claim, Arian had extended her influence to every corner of their lands.

How could one so unworthy—

But Daniyar had chosen her, hadn't he?

The waters rippled, showing her the torment on her sister's face. As torn and confused in her secret thoughts as Lania had been once.

"Khanum!"

She looked down to see that her hand was bleeding. She had pressed her moonstone ring into her palm with such force that it had cut into her skin. A single droplet of blood darkened her white silk dress.

She dipped her hand in the basin. The waters turned blood red, erasing Arian's image.

A knock at the door to the chamber heralded the arrival of the prisoner she sought.

"Wait."

The order was to her doves. She moved across the chamber, opened the door herself, and stepped outside. A fair-haired Ahdath soldier pushed the prisoner—Gul . . . Gul Nur—in front of him. Gul was dressed and painted in the style of the doves, but the right side of her delicate face was bruised. She kept her head bent low, her body trembling with fear in Lania's presence.

Lania questioned the soldier. "Are you the one who took her from the Pit?"

He brushed his hair back from his face, a sneer on his well-bred features.

"My name is Kiril, and I *rescued* her from the Pit. She did nothing to merit punishment."

Lania tipped up Gul's chin with a careful finger. She examined the bruise on the right side of her face.

"And this? She gave you trouble, perhaps."

The Ahdath laughed. "They all play coy at first. But we've come to an understanding."

Lania studied Gul's expression. "Did you share his understanding?"

Though she should have been afraid of the Ahdath at her side, the girl's response was bitter. "I wasn't given a choice. Either in the Pit or at the Tilla Kari."

"Is that so?" Lania dropped each word like a small detonation.

"Careful, witch." The Ahdath's menace was explicit. "You may have some skill at sorcery, but do not forget that my mother is Sovereign of the Sahirah."

The lift of Lania's brow was glacial. Did this pompous fool think to frighten her with his mention of an outcast heretical coven?

"Do you seek to shelter behind your mother?" If he'd had any sense at all, he would have dropped to his knees to beg her to spare him her wrath.

But he chose to feel slighted instead. "Do not insult me, witch. The recourse I have to the Sahirah should have you trembling in fear."

Poor, poor fool. Lania glided closer, moving Gul aside.

"You seem to forget, Ahdath." She chose not to bother with their names. "The Sahirah play at power, whereas *my* abilities brought the Authoritan down." She studied her fingernails. "Were the Sahirah there to assist? I do not recall."

"You underestimate my mother—"

An angry gesture of Lania's hand cut the Ahdath dead at her feet. A small scream escaped from Gul at the swiftness of Lania's action.

"He will trouble you no longer."

Lania snapped her fingers at two of the guards positioned along the hall.

"Dispose of him."

They hurried to obey, but one of the soldiers faltered.

"Khanum," he said with great care, "Kiril did not lie to you—he is the eldest son of the Sovereign. He was a noble. The Sovereign may be . . . displeased."

Lania pushed Gul into the room behind her, closing the door again.

"If you do not obey me at once, *I* will be the one displeased. Unless you wish to share his fate, I suggest you carry out my orders."

The guard lost his courage. He shouldered the burden of the dead man's legs without daring to speak again.

In the scrying chamber, Lania searched out the prisoner. Gul was standing near the basin, her dark head bowed, thick locks of hair shielding her from Lania's view.

"Position her."

Saher tugged at Gul's dress until she was standing in the spot where moonlight spilled down into the room through the star-shaped window.

"Look at me." Centuries of winter in her voice.

Gul raised her face again, this time into the light. The Khanum's doves gasped aloud.

Step by step, Lania advanced, until she and Gul were face-to-face. Her fingers traced Gul's features, running over her brow, her nose, her jaw, as Gul stood before her breathing in choked gasps, fearing what Lania could do.

When she could bear the suspense no longer, Gul begged, "Please do not give me to the Authoritan. I plead for your mercy, Khanum."

"I possess none."

Gul flinched at the words.

Lania's tone shifted. "The Authoritan is dead. You have nothing to fear from him." She looked into Gul's eyes, observing the pure green of her irises. The green of nephrite. And in a certain light, the green of persimmon trees.

"Then why——?"

Lania's lips stretched over her teeth. On anyone else, it would have been a smile.

"Because I can see how the ruse worked. You *do* resemble the First Oralist. But you are here in the Sihraat because you resemble *me*." She glanced at Saher, who was waiting for instruction. "Will it work?"

Saher took the girl by her shoulders to angle her face closer to her own.

"Yes. At night along the Wall? Yes, it will."

A cold delight sang through Lania's veins. "Then prepare her. Dress her, train her, give her a moonstone to wear."

Gul's eyes went wide, still not understanding what would have been plain had she not been suffering such fear.

"Khanum, if I am not to be punished, why have you sent for me?"

Lania's smile became cruel. "Did I say you were not to be punished, foolish child? You weren't meant for the Authoritan. I am sending you to Jaslyk."

The girl named Gul paled, swaying on her feet.

Lania pointed to three of her doves. "Take her. And take *care* of her."

When she was alone in the Sihraat with Saher, she thought of what else she required in order to further her schemes.

"Will the Warden of Jaslyk be deceived?" she asked.

The wrong response meant Saher would be punished.

"If she is trained." A moment's hesitation, then Saher gestured at the basin. "Why not scry the solution, Khanum? Your Augury could tell you more."

Lania dipped a finger into the crimson water. "I despise this color. Everywhere I look, I am forced to consider the Ahdath."

"The Ahdath serve *you*, Khanum."

"They would kill me in a heartbeat if they could. No doubt they plot against me as we speak." Studying the ripples she had created in the water, Lania addressed Saher. "There is something at Jaslyk that confounds my Augury. We will know the truth when Gul returns with her gift from the Warden."

"Do you trust Gul to protect the remedy you seek?"

Lania mulled the possibility. "She will be guarded by those whose loyalty I have Augured. She will also return with instruction on the uses to which the remedy may be put." She caught Saher's grimace. "Do you doubt my ability?" A lethal question.

"No, Khanum!" A quick shake of Saher's head, golden hair flouncing out in bright curls. "But I wonder about the properties of the remedy you seek."

She said nothing else until Lania gave a curt command. "Speak."

"What if the Warden discovers the deception? He might taint the remedy."

Lania shrugged, her silk dress slipping from one shoulder. "If Gul is unable to convince him that she is me, the matter will be moot. He will send no remedy at all." Her features tightened with impatience. "Enough discussion. It is time for the second pillar of my plan."

Saher waited for the rest.

"Bring me Temurbek the Axe."

"To assume command of the Wall?"

"To cleave like a virgin blade the Ahdath who would see me overthrown."

Emboldened by the Khanum's frankness, Saher ventured too far. "You *need* the Ahdath, Khanum. And what's more, there are Sahirah who back the Ahdath. Their sorcerous gifts empower a faction of soldiers on the Wall."

Lania's hand lashed out at this mention of the coven whose gifts were lesser than hers. Her nails gouged Saher's cheek in a crimson burst of blood, disfiguring the face of her dove.

"Has your Ahdath lover corrupted you?" Lania hissed. "See if he chooses to keep you now that your beauty is ruined."

Her hand to her cheek, Saher managed a choked apology. "Forgive me for my presumption. I thought to warn you, Khanum."

"I accept your apology this once, but do not mistake me again. Now do as I asked."

When Saher had gone, Lania braced her hands on the basin. A murmured spell, and the touch of crimson vanished. The waters were sterile and clear. The image Lania had sought to banish reappeared once more.

Throwing her head up with prideful disdain, she trailed her fingers through the water.

The image remained in place.

Lania leaned down toward the basin and spoke.

"What do you want, Arian?"

5

ARIAN STEPPED OUT OF THE SHADOWS INTO THE ROOM. THE AIR AROUND her was a moonlit shimmer that parted like a wave in her wake. She touched nothing, experienced none of the room's materiality, yet knew herself present in the scrying room with her sister, whose hands she wanted to take in her own yet feared to. Though Lania had spared her life and set her free after her confrontation with the Authoritan, she offered Arian none of the affection she longed for.

She brushed her troubling thoughts aside and gestured at the door through which Gul had been escorted away. "That poor girl's fate should have been mine."

Lania faced her across the basin. Her eyes seemed metallic in the glinting light.

"Would the First Oralist of Hira change places with a hostage to fortune?"

"I already did. Gul was sent to Black Aura in my place." A brief hesitation before Arian asked, "What do you seek from Jaslyk, Lania?"

Lania ignored the question. Careful calculation on the features that resembled Arian's own, like a mirror image distorted by tempered glass. One hand reached across the basin to pass through Arian.

The feline eyes narrowed.

"How do you come to be here, sister?"

The wondrous nature of her presence shone in Arian's eyes. "I took the Night Journey to the distant house of worship. From there I ascended to this room."

"*Ascended?*" Lania spat out the word. "You think this is a place of Ascension?" She raised both arms to indicate the Ark. "Bloodshed, madness, an abundance of death—that is all you'll find here." The sound of her laughter was brittle. "Do you believe Black Aura is a signpost of the Israa e Miraj?"

A sudden realization pierced Arian. Lania knew the ancient stories as well as she did. Perhaps Black Aura had nothing to teach her beyond pain, but Lania herself was a source of untapped knowledge, having once been a child of Hira. Her eyes began to blaze as shattering truths made themselves known. Hira was under threat. She was desperate to save Hira, and through Hira, all of Khorasan. She had imagined that the purpose of the Israa e Miraj was to return her to Hira supreme, her powers and knowledge prevailing.

Instead, she had come to Lania, and now she guessed why, her abilities with the Claim altered by the ascent, transmuted into something new. She could wield the Claim like a weapon with her voice; she could use it to penetrate truths that had been hidden until now; she could use it to soothe others, to calm them in the face of the storm, to deepen her bond with Daniyar so that a part of him was present within her thoughts, within her knowing.

And she could use it to communicate with others touched by the Claim. Her gifts were evolving. Her immersion in the truths of the Sana Codex meant they were growing stronger.

Your journey is suited to your needs.

Light spilled from her chest to flow down the outline of her limbs. She was a thousand insubstantial pieces of herself; she was whole with an iron will that would not be denied. Lania took a fumbling step back. She had made of her unpainted face a mask, and now the mask split open. Expressions chased across her countenance: horror, fury, outrage, loneliness . . . emotions as ephemeral as whitecaps on shifting waves.

A corresponding awareness arose within Arian of what the daughters of Inkwell had lost, their tragedies distinct, the possibility of their redemption a candle flame tended in secret against the heart of a tempest.

You must learn to see the Oralists when and where they appear.

"I need you at Hira, Lania."

"Why." Pallid lips pulled up at the edges as Lania forced herself to speak, to stand without trembling under the impact of the light that had spread to suffuse the corners of the room.

Hira's light?

No, no, it was impossible that a place of the vilest treachery could blaze in her mind's eye as a beacon guiding her home.

The Khanum of Black Aura had no home.

Except for that which she *claimed* for herself, clawed from the wreck the Authoritan had made of her, with no one to aid her, no one to deliver her from torment. The Sahirah could have used their sorcery to help her, yet they'd never chosen to do so.

"You know that isn't so."

She put her hands to her ears to block Arian's voice, reading her thoughts with such certainty that rancor boiled in Lania's chest, rose like bile from her throat.

"You cannot magic me, Arian."

"I do not seek to."

"The light . . ."

"Isn't mine. It belongs to Hira."

But as Arian spoke these words, the light faltered and went dark. Lania drew a trembling breath. A wild glee bubbled in her veins at the sight of Arian's confusion.

"It would seem your assumptions about the Ascension are mistaken. Can it be that some forms of knowledge are denied even to such a personage as the First Oralist of Hira?"

Arian flinched from Lania's contempt.

"How did you learn to hate me, Lania?"

A smooth indifference gilded Lania's countenance.

"You stole the life that should have been mine, but what does that matter now?" Her hands wove a subtle pattern. "You have seen the empire I rule. You ask me to trade it for the ascetic comforts of a life at Hira, yet do not tell me why."

"Hira is at risk. The Citadel is at risk, along with all our sisterhood."

"Why should that matter to me?"

"You know why," Arian said. "You've always known why."

Calligraphy appeared along the circumference of the basin and began to glow.

Arian read the words aloud. "'I seek refuge from the temptation of Shaitan, the devil.'" Humor sparked in her eyes, lightening the rhythmic cadence of her voice. "I am not a devil, Lania. I am your sister, Arian." Her words became quieter still. "Is Hira a temptation to you?"

Lania closed her eyes. When she opened them again, her face

was blank, her voice an iron barrier that crushed any hint of closeness.

"I have never found much sisterhood in women. Hira was the cause of all my degradation. Should it fall, my tragedy will be requited."

A wave of emotion battered Lania's defenses. Pain. Dark as the ridge of a mountain at midnight, warm as the dissolution of darkness at daybreak.

I seek refuge in the Lord of Daybreak.

The wayward prayer canted into Arian's mind, blossoming at the arid edges of defeat. Pain and beauty mingled together as she experienced Lania's grief. She took it into herself in a succession of golden pulses until she asked, "What of Hira's scriptorium, Lania? What of the Khorasan Archives?"

Though the light no longer outlined Arian's form, its echo lingered in her eyes, making it impossible for Lania to hold her gaze. Lania's eyes fell to the basin. She read the runes to herself, her lips whispering without a trace of sound. The words had always heartened her before; she configured the runes as a shield against any who dared to strike against her. This recitation was different. As she sought the shelter of the words, luminescence spilled from her tongue to her chest. A tenuous connection formed between herself and Arian, light that arrowed from her heart to Arian's, lustrous and many-layered, offering a warmth she hadn't known since the day their house had fallen. The pain of it was intolerable, brushing her with brightness, a chisel struck against the marble of her corruption. Betraying no sign of the damage it was inflicting—*undoing?*—she drew upon her innermost strength to deny it. To outflank it. She didn't *want* it. She didn't want anything it promised.

"Our history," Arian persisted. "Our legacy. What we hold in trust for future generations. Would you see it destroyed by the One-Eyed Preacher?"

"Does he come?" Words drawn from Lania without conscious will.

Arian touched her circlets, then her chest. "He has risen, I feel it here. He will burn the Citadel to the ground, and the scriptorium with it." Their eyes met as Arian added, "You were apprenticed to the scriptorium. In time you would have become the Custodian of the Archives. Could you see the treasury despoiled? Could you watch the archives burn to ash?"

Arian stood across from her sister, placing her hands on the cool stone of the basin so that their fingers touched. Lania snatched back her hands before Arian could encroach farther. Before she could finish binding Lania with her surreptitious gifts.

Weary now, she said, "You have your battles, Arian. Know that I have mine."

"You seek vengeance upon the Authoritan's men? Or perhaps upon these Sahirah your unfortunate dove described? Is that why you send an innocent girl to Jaslyk?"

"As you sent Gul to Black Aura," Lania rejoined. She made a bleak, dismissive gesture. "You will find no innocents behind the Wall." She clutched the rim of the basin at the compassion in Arian's eyes. "Do not pity me."

"May I not love you, Lania? May I not repay the grace you once bestowed on me?"

Through stiff lips, Lania demurred, "Do not test me in this manner. I spared your life once. I will not do so again."

"So you will not tell me what Jaslyk portends?"

Lania stepped away from the basin, her movements lacking their customary grace. She found a spot out of the glare of moonlight, seeking comfort in the shadows.

"If you had ascended," she said with subtle cruelty, "you would already know."

The light in Arian's eyes dimmed. Self-doubt was her unrelenting weakness, knowledge she guarded even from herself.

She strove for calm. "What you seek from Jaslyk is beyond my purview to pursue. I need you at Hira." She felt the rightness of her conclusion settle in her bones. "You must come. You *will* come. I cannot stand against the One-Eyed Preacher on my own." She hunted for the words that would persuade her sister, that would turn Lania from her fatal course. "I've come to claim you for Hira. It's time that you came home."

Lania's moonstone glowed from the shadows. She raised her hand and turned the stone toward Arian. The room began to shimmer before Arian's eyes. Its perimeter shrank until she was viewing Lania through the narrowest of prisms, under an icy light.

The mirror image distorted before her eyes until Lania's face became a concavity of shadows, her lips a snarl of rage.

"Even should you ascend to the heights of knowledge through the Israa e Miraj, you will not see my face again."

6

SINNIA'S ASCENT WAS PEACEFUL. QUIET. CONTAINED. FOLDING HER IN worlds of warmth. She rose on the back of a glittering steed whose wings were composed of the ribbon of stars that shone above the city of Axum—her home. Her senses were stroked by the fronds of palm trees, the air sultry with heat, the indigo richness of the sky leavened by a starlit glow. When she touched her circlets to assure herself of her own existence, she found herself within a garden at the center of a group of trees flung like a green mantle over blue indigo hills.

Tributaries rustled beneath the grounds, silver braids of water that trailed down gentle slopes. Sinnia gazed at the trees. As she drew closer, she recognized them. Acacias of infinite variety, sycamore figs, redwoods and junipers native to the lands of the Negus, dry date palms and rich-plumed fans, lush coral trees in bloom, their flaming petals said to spring from the blood of fallen warriors. All these Sinnia knew. The tree-garden felt like her home, layer upon layer of belonging lying on her heart like moonlight quiet on a secret glade.

She followed a slope that climbed higher past the circle of

drifting trees. She skipped over silent streams that sparkled like links in a chain. At the top of the slope, a single tree spread its beneficence over the glade. It was wide and flat-bottomed with thick nettles, a tree she didn't know. It did not grow in Axum. Nor had she seen it in the lands of the south.

As she looked at the tree, it seemed to multiply itself, an emerald expanse touched with starlight at its pinnacle, leaves dancing in a lightning-green embrace. At the base, its shade was endless—covering a world, a universe, a continent of unexplained questions, a space of interminable unknowing, a galaxy swallowing itself without a dimming of stars.

As she stood beneath its limitless shade—or was it light?—the arms of the tree reached out to enclose her, and the Claim began to unfurl its limits through the tendrils of her thoughts, like delicate coral shoots searching through beds of seagrass.

This tree she hadn't seen before, all light and shade at once, was the Lote Tree of the Utmost Boundary. She had crossed the Garden of Refuge to the tree's outermost limit. She put up a hand to shade her eyes from the clarity of its light.

The Verse of the Throne rose up in her mind, infinite and glorious, and then intimate and personal, as if it were a message destined for her ears alone.

Her comprehension was instant, the Claim unraveled by Salikh's subliminal teaching. The base of the tree was the base of the same throne described in the Verse.

The utmost boundary was the boundary between two worlds: the world of that which was known, and that of the mystical unknown . . . not just the Verse of the Throne, but the *universe* of the throne, the mystical knowledge beyond it, the screen between creation and its source, the unknowable realm of the One.

She could not ascend beyond it. She did not even try.

She was made immobile as a voice spoke from her right.

You are humble, Companion from the lands of the Negus.

Sinnia sank to her knees.

"I am privileged to kneel before the Lote Tree of the Utmost Boundary. I am honored to kneel before the throne."

Are you a servant of the One?

"Always."

Will you deviate from the path laid before you?

She felt a flicker of confusion.

"What path?"

Your Audacy, sahabiya. Will you honor it to the end?

"To defend the First Oralist of Hira? Such was my vow. I will not abandon it."

To defend the First Oralist is to defend Hira. There is no difference.

"I understand."

You must. An instance of doubt will end it.

This she didn't understand. The fate of Hira, of all of Khorasan, could not rest upon her shoulders. She had grown in knowledge and ability since her first days as a Companion of Hira, she had grown into the Audacy the High Companion had entrusted to her, but she alone could not stand against the One-Eyed Preacher's power. No matter what Salikh had taught her, there were limits to her skill.

With some caution, she asked, "Is this my Ascension? Are no secrets to be revealed?"

What would you wish to know?

"How to protect Arian. How to defend Hira."

The voice fell silent, the silence lasting for so long that Sinnia was moved to stir from the giant tree's embrace. Its nettles whispered over her upper arms. When they touched her circlets, she experienced a jolt, as if lightning had dispersed from her heart down through each of her veins. Her lips felt singed and blue, her dark irises spangled with spots of blood. An amber veil was drawn over her face. She looked through it to a spacious chamber that was filtered through the glow. A long and narrow room sectioned by arched windows overlaid with mosaics picked out in opals and pinks. Along one wall was a magnificent fireplace glazed with tiles in minutely expressive geometries, though its porcelain basin was hollow. No fire would ever be lit in this upper chamber of Hira's precious scriptorium.

Giant lanterns were dotted about a carpet woven of silk threads so fine that the surface seemed translucent: at the heart a crimson medallion, at the borders a pageant of blues. Long cushioned banquettes were placed beneath the windows. And to one side, across from the fireplace, a stand called a rahlah, fashioned of pale green nephrite on an iron mount painted gold.

Resting on the rahlah was a book. A manuscript of miniatures illustrated by lapis lazuli ink on sumptuous fields of gold. A breeze turned the pages one by one. She saw a steed with glittering wings arched above a barren rock. Not a horse, not a mule, something other, grander in scope and design. She saw blank faces beneath a resplendent dome, its gold so shattering, she thought it would render her blind. On another page, there was a double-bladed sword from which leapt two lines of fire. The sword had a name, the dome also, but she recognized neither, though each had weight, had heft. Each slanted a spear through a chamber of her heart.

A lote tree on one page. In the foreground, the wide expanse of sheltering leaves, beyond it a transparent veil shimmering silver and gold, and far beyond that an infinite partition. She couldn't look, her senses wrung dry, her eyes overwhelmed by the radiance of the cosmos. But the hand, the materials, the exotic luxury of the manuscript . . . these she could identify.

The manuscript was the Miraj Nameh, a book of the Israa e Miraj. It was held at the Citadel of Hira, where she had once spied it. A stolen moment in a chamber when a Companion of senior rank had brought the manuscript to the reading room and left it there unattended.

A chance moment when Sinnia had experienced the joy of gazing upon a bifolium.

A line appeared beside an illustration, sheer simplicity of form balanced by elegance of script. It rang against the inside of her skull. It made her irises blossom. Her hair grew out in silky loops to whisper down her shoulders. Her palms grew bright, and the color of her lips ripened. When she had finished gazing at the book, the Axumite suns of her dark brown irises were rimmed by circles of blue.

Script appeared between the illustrations, a language she didn't know.

She was on the cusp of comprehension, on the cusp of knowing how to defend what she cherished most in this life.

And then it was gone. Stolen away with swiftness and secrecy, removed in both distance and time. Forever lost to her. Forever beyond her grasp. An instant of uncanny knowledge, a lifetime of blankest ignorance. Three sets of words upon a page.

The Buraq.

The Blind Dome.

The Bladebone.

What did these words mean?

And how were they linked to the charge that had been laid upon her shoulders: *To defend the First Oralist* is *to defend Hira.*

The arms of the lote tree enclosed Sinnia again.

Is there no knowledge you seek for yourself, here at the Utmost Boundary?

She wanted to know many things. If the Age of Jahiliya would ever come to an end. If the Bloodprint was redeemable. She wondered if the code that bound the Companions of Hira was at all mutable, and whether the Companions might one day be released from their vows of allegiance. This thought was more for Arian, though an image touched her mind like a page preserved within a book: a proud, dark face with eyes as blue as the river that bounded from a mesa into a golden sea.

But none of this mattered now. None of her curiosity about the world beyond the veil between known and unknown, or about the Companions who had gone before her, mattered if she didn't try to ensure the safety of Hira. Of the First Oralist—her sister, her partner, her friend. So she asked what was of greatest importance, the questions that would aid her to this end.

"We were sent here after the Sana Codex. Is there anything in the Codex that would aid me against the Preacher? And if there is, how should I understand its teachings?"

Does your faith exist without knowledge? Has your will been suborned, Companion?

Sinnia set her jaw. "My will is my own, my submission to the One given with purpose." She hesitated. "I don't submit to the Assimilate. I don't believe that faith was meant to be a prison. I know we are better than this."

You are wise, Companion. You must take what you need from the Sana Codex.

"Teach me," she whispered.

You already know.

Yet the voice chose to oblige her. It murmured verses in her ear. *There is no coercion in matters of faith. The way of truth is distinct from the way of error; thus, those who reject the powers of evil and believe in the One have taken hold of a support most unfailing, that will never give way.*

Sinnia held the verses close, enlightened by their lucidity. Tears formed in her eyes as she felt the voice recede. She tried to hold on to it.

"Don't leave me."

You are the best of Companions. Know this and Ascend.

A singular sweetness broke over her, a mesmeric, cushioning warmth that offered recompense for hardships she had suffered, and that promised a future less bleak than all their options would suggest. A lack of *aloneness*. The sense that the battle being waged would no longer be fought by two Companions of Hira cast into a wilderness of war.

She was so uplifted by the sensation that she sought to make it permanent. She reached up to touch a leaf of the magnificent tree, the tree of indefinable limits.

"What are you called?" she dared ask.

Sidrat al Muntaha.

The whisper had no sooner reached her ears than she was a world away, her fingers gracing the outermost limit of a branch, a touch of green life surging, singing, before the garden fell away, and she found herself in a place of bitter cold, at the very precipice of war.

No need to ask where she'd come. Ten lifetimes could pass and she would still remember the Citadel of Hira.

A junior soldier of the Citadel Guard brushed by her. She wondered at his lack of greeting, but when she put out her hand to attract his notice, he moved past her without seeing her. Perplexed, she stepped out of the shadows onto the catwalk that linked the outer ramparts. Some distance ahead, she recognized two Companions of Hira, women of the first rank.

One wore the attire of the Companions, a white silk dress, accented by the gold circlets on her arms. Her hair was bound in a simple twist above her nape. She was an older woman with eyes that had seen far too much. The other woman was dressed in armor that made her strong body seem more formidable, a deep frown marking her brow as she held a spyglass to her eye. The spyglass wasn't necessary under the high full moon, but the woman was tracking the movement of Talisman forces who were advancing upon the Citadel.

The night was so cold, the air felt as though it might break into solid squares, the stars frozen in a sapphire void, crisp against Sinnia's skin. She was *at* the Citadel of Hira. She could sense it, touch it, feel it. Enfolded in the clasp of the night, she saw soldiers at the towers and walls, felt the chill from the absence of watchfires, yet no one remarked upon her presence.

She offered a greeting to the two Companions: Psalm, the General of the Citadel, and Ash, the scholar who held the rank of Jurist. She expected a warm cry of welcome, but the silence echoed. The two Companions took no notice of her.

She touched Ash's shoulder, the material of her dress silky against Sinnia's palm. Ash didn't stir. Her full attention was on Psalm. Then Sinnia understood.

This was part of her ascent. Not as she had expected, the firmament a plane of knowledge beyond her reckoning; rather, as the result of her plea.

Show me how to protect the First Oralist. How to defend Hira.

She wondered again at the power of the Claim. An indecipherable majesty that was almost a source of fear due to its remoteness. She brushed her questions aside. Talisman forces were camped below the ramp that led to the Citadel Gate, the small party a forerunner of greater numbers to come.

Soon the siege would begin. If the One-Eyed Preacher joined it, the Citadel would be overrun. She tugged the invisible reins of the ascent—seeking freedom, seeking to return to Hira in truth. She was needed here; she couldn't wait for Arian.

But the voice of the Ascension whispered a reminder.

To defend the First Oralist is to defend Hira.

She'd been sent here to discover how to achieve that end.

7

"TELL ME WHAT YOU'RE WAITING FOR, PSALM."

Psalm's granite-flecked eyes flicked to the Companion Ash.

"You called this meeting, Ash. Perhaps it is you who should speak."

Ash sighed. "Have we come to this? Are we reduced to playing games?"

Psalm set her spyglass on the wall and held out her powerful arm. Within moments, a falcon dropped from the sky to settle on her gauntlet. She snapped a tiny roll of parchment free from its talons. She read it to herself, then buried it inside her armor. From a pouch at her waist, she extracted a piece of meat to feed to the falcon, stroking her fingers over its head, a gesture of tenderness from a woman without weakness.

She turned to face Ash, grim decision in her face.

"The Talisman have not attacked, but I've no doubt they will. They've scouted our defenses, and they've summoned reinforcements. They perceive our vulnerability. Soon their siege will begin."

Ash murmured a quick imprecation, her slender shoulders

hunched. "Then it seems that despite the efforts of the First Oralist, we've reached the same bitter end. There is to be no freedom
for any of our sisters."

Psalm thought of the refugees the Citadel had taken in, and of
her recent consultations with the Companions who were Hazara.
Neither she nor they discounted Arian's efforts. She'd made the
same case to Ash. Other Companions could proclaim defeat, but
she needed Ash at her side, determined to hold the Citadel, no
matter the scarcity of their defenses.

"It's too soon to despair. Our war has just begun." She raised
her arm. The falcon sped off into the blue oblivion. "Why did you
want to speak to me? And why in secrecy, Ash?"

Ash wrapped her arms around her torso. She faced the Talisman camp. "Where is Ilea? She should have returned from Ashfall
by now. We will soon be under attack, and we are missing *both*
Ilea and Arian."

And Sinnia, Psalm thought. Though Sinnia was young, Psalm
valued her skills and missed her cheerful presence. She'd brought
life to the Citadel when she'd been sent to Hira from Axum. A
breeze touched Psalm's ear. She glanced beyond Ash, and for a
moment, she thought she saw another figure. She thought she saw
Sinnia arrayed in a dress of gold as a bold, young queen of the
Negus. A deception, no doubt summoned from the depths of her
need.

She patted at the place beneath her armor where she'd tucked
away the message the falcon had delivered.

"The High Companion was drawn into the defense of Ashfall.
Her message heralds her arrival. We will be safe until she comes."
The tension in her face eased as she touched her circlets. "Have a
little faith in my skills, Ash."

Ash ran her fingers over the script on her own circlets. Like

Psalm, she was measuring the Talisman's preparations. "Let's pray that she sets the Citadel to rights. The new recruits to the Guard are eager, but some of them appear rather too slow to learn."

Psalm nodded and waited, knowing that Ash would not have been comforted by news of Ilea's delay.

"What of the Bloodprint?" Ash spoke of her uppermost concern. "Why hasn't Arian returned? Why hasn't she brought it to Hira as directed?"

"She must have her reasons." Psalm took the opportunity to probe the Jurist's loyalties. "Do you doubt her?"

Surprised at the question, Ash said, "I *miss* her."

Again, Psalm waited. Would Ash declare her loyalty? Would she aid Psalm in her plans to ensure the Citadel's defense?

"I miss Arian *and* Sinnia. When Arian is here, the Citadel feels invincible. Her presence alleviates our fears."

Psalm couldn't deny it. She, too, felt steadied by Arian's presence. But more than that, Arian was strong enough to hold the Citadel's secrets. She was very much Psalm's equal.

To the southeast, a Talisman chant began, underscored by the hollow sound of drums.

"In Arian's absence, can you recite the benedictions? Can you shelter Hira in the Claim?"

The question was deliberate, designed to push Ash into thinking of her responsibilities while Psalm unraveled the rest of Ilea's message. She didn't think the Companions were strong enough to hear its truths. The One-Eyed Preacher had seized the Bloodprint from the stronghold of Ashfall—the worst possible outcome. But more demoralizing was the fact that Ilea had made allegations against Arian, claiming that the First Oralist had renounced her vow of chastity, and thus abandoned the Audacy that held their fate in the balance.

She left me no choice, Ilea's message read. *I had to expel her from the Council. She chose to renounce us.*

Psalm weighed these claims against what she knew of the politics of the Council.

She made a swift decision. She would tell no one of Arian's expulsion from the Council. It served no purpose to weaken the Council at a time when the Companions needed to accept that no one would be coming to their rescue. They would have to rely on themselves.

Psalm stood at the helm alone, but she needed Ash on her side.

"Arian will be here soon enough. We must not let her down."

She faced the other woman, reaching out to press the circlets on her arms. After a moment, Ash emulated the gesture, murmuring the benediction Psalm had asked for.

"In the name of the One, the Compassionate, the Companions will stand firm."

Psalm felt the strength in the other woman's grip. Ash spent most of her time in the scriptorium, a slender form bent over manuscripts she sought to study and preserve, but she hadn't let the study weaken her. More, though Ash's voice was soft with the cadences of a thousand recitations, it was still firm and alive.

Ash moved closer to Psalm, feeling the cold of the night. Shivering under the impact of all that was still to come. Two Talisman soldiers approached the ramp. Their cloaks pulled over their faces, they kept their weapons at their sides. Two more of the soldiers carried a sturdy staff. Glaring up at the Citadel's walls, they planted it in the ground. The wind shifted and the flag on the staff whipped open to disclose a bloodstained page.

In a voice that was rich and eloquent, one of the men proclaimed, *"There is no one but the One, and so the One commands."*

His words were echoed with force by the men in the Talisman camp.

But when the party retreated, there was no other sound than that of the wind ripping at the Talisman flag.

The Companions on the wall repeated the same prayer with a different inflection. Then Ash pointed to the Talisman flag.

"Arian was right. It was always coming to this."

8

ILEA SLIPPED INSIDE THE CITADEL WITHOUT ALERTING THE GUARD, using the Claim to mask her entry through a tunnel that ran beneath the Council Chamber, just as she'd used the Claim to penetrate Talisman lines. Her talent was such that she'd stolen a horse to ride as far as the outskirts of the Citadel. But instead of riding up the ramp, she'd used a private entrance to the fortress, and now she emerged in an antechamber that led to her personal quarters. There she bathed and changed before donning a cloak to climb to the Citadel walls.

She took in Psalm's preparations for defense. She noted the Talisman flag planted at the gates of the Citadel with a frown; a wave of her hand scattered it to dust, leaving the Citadel's motto to frame its gates.

Never to be altered by the encircling tremors of time.

Yet soon enough they *would* be encircled, and the Citadel would have to make its stand.

She'd learned enough of the Claim that even without Arian at her side, she would be able to hold back the insignificant Talisman party at their gates. And if it transpired that she couldn't—if the Preacher saw her as an enemy, despite her careful plots—there were other ways to appease him. Her tactics had kept his focus on Arian, leaving the Council free to work its will. The Preacher deemed Arian a greater threat to his efforts than all the Companions combined—Arian's doing again, an insult to be remedied in time, though it served her purposes now.

Now she frowned as something intangible stirred. Psalm was at her post above the Citadel Gate with Ash. Two commanders of the Guard stood beside them, listening to Psalm's instructions before moving off to carry them out. Was someone else standing by Psalm's shoulder? A figure dressed in gold, wearing a coronet of coins?

Ilea murmured the Claim. A distortion rippled through the air to unmask the image. She found nothing, a flight of fancy, then. The cost of dabbling too long in the secrets of the arcane. There was always a price to be paid.

Psalm raised her head as Ilea approached, her gray eyes wary. "High Companion. We welcome your return to Hira."

Ash gave Ilea a warmer reception, moving to embrace her. "Thank the One," she said. She looked past Ilea's shoulder, puzzled. "Where are Arian and Sinnia?"

Ilea studied Psalm, her senses stirring with the knowledge of her deceptions. "Haven't you informed the Companions of the news? I did send word."

Ash looked from Ilea to Psalm, a frown sketched on her forehead. "Psalm gave us your message. We know you were delayed at Ashfall, but I thought Arian and Sinnia would return at your side with the Bloodprint."

Ilea's wrists flexed, resonating with remembered power. She could use that power against Psalm, but Psalm was a tool she still required. The Companions might rise up in revolt if she played her hand too soon.

She leaned against the wall, surveying the party of Talisman who lingered at the causeway. Disperse them now and risk drawing the Preacher's notice, or wait for the assault?

Questions she would put to Psalm when the Council was assembled. She would appear to yield to Psalm before she raised the matter of Arian's status. If Arian returned, Ilea wanted the Council on her side. Best to begin with Ash, by revealing what Psalm had concealed.

"The One-Eyed Preacher captured the Bloodprint in Ashfall, but I studied it before he seized it; part of it is in my possession." Her lips curved, cold and beautiful. "I'm surprised Psalm didn't tell you. Just as it seems she didn't pass on my message that the First Oralist abandoned her Audacy. I had no choice but to banish her from the Council."

Ash's hands jerked together. In a reflexive movement, she touched her circlets, her eyes wide with horror. She was shaking her head, looking to Psalm.

"*That* was the message the High Companion sent?"

Psalm whistled to a contingent of the Guard, redirecting them to another part of the wall. "It served no purpose to alarm the Companions when war is at our gates. The High Companion was due to arrive—better for her to explain her decision herself." Her face hardened. "As you know, Arian would never betray us."

Ilea's hands clenched within her cloak. "Arian has taken the Silver Mage to her bed."

Psalm surprised them with a laugh. "I wouldn't blame her if she did, but how do you hope to prove that?"

Ilea drew herself up, her bearing fiery and proud. "My word should be enough."

Psalm opened her mouth to speak, but Ash cut her off. "If you are accusing a Companion of Hira, and not just any Companion but the First Oralist, then your word does *not* suffice. You must supply four witnesses, or the First Oralist must confess. Do you expect that she will?"

Ash was the Jurist. Of course she would insist on adherence to the law.

Ilea whipped her cloak over her shoulders, letting the other women see the brilliant fire of her circlets. Power roared through her veins.

"Do you see her here? She abandoned the Council of Hira in pursuit of her lover."

"Impossible." Psalm snorted in disbelief. "Did she take Sinnia with her as a third?"

Ilea's golden eyes began to glow, her power demanding release. Arian's influence was unraveling the Council. It had begun with the parents who had raised both their daughters to become Companions of Hira. The Council's power structure would have been usurped. So Ilea had made her calculations. She had done her best to ensure that such a fate would never come to pass, control remaining in her hands. The supremacy of the daughters of Inkwell had not been permitted to flourish in the past; nor would it do so now. The blow she struck would be fatal.

Psalm stared into the strange miasma of her eyes, unperturbed, but Ash took a step back.

"What's happening to you, High Companion?"

Ilea's senses heightened. "It's nothing. It's the aftereffect of the Conference of the Mages. My eyes will dim in time."

No, they wouldn't. Because she wouldn't allow it.

She was kindling her power as she spoke. She focused on persuading Ash, knowing that in this matter, it was Ash who would influence the others. If Arian returned, she would rise or fall depending on Ash's verdict.

"You were there when the Silver Mage came to ask for a dispensation on Arian's behalf. You *know* the two of them are bound."

Ash's face was shuttered. "Arian cannot be exiled in the absence of her testimony."

"And if she chooses *not* to appear before the Council? As she seems to have done."

"Then we'll have more to worry over than Arian's divided allegiance." Psalm's interjection, cutting and precise. "How long can we hold the Citadel without Arian's assistance?"

Ilea considered the men who were camped at the end of the causeway. A small enough party. She could burn them with a word. She fastened her cloak against the chill of night, her plan of attack decided. With a contemptuous nod at Psalm, she gave an order to Ash.

"Summon the Companions to the Council Chamber." Her eyes narrowed to two gold slits. "It's time for you to rule on Arian's status as a member of our Council."

She stalked off, her cloak whirling behind her. Members of the Guard followed.

Sinnia expelled a shaky breath. On the plane of Ascension, she had sought to learn how to defend Hira, how best to protect Arian. She hadn't anticipated that she would need to defend Arian from conspiracies hatched *at* the Citadel.

The danger to the Citadel did not arise just from the Talisman camped beyond their gates. Before she and Arian returned, they would have to anticipate that Ilea would do her worst.

9

THE BLACK-AND-GOLD TABAR SHATTERED THE DOOR WITH ANOTHER heavy stroke. Najran wrested it free with careless strength, and then he was in the room. The whoosh of the axe stirred the hair that fell to his shoulders. He twisted aside as the Blue Mage pushed him back. The blade of the tabar swung in a wide, calculated arc. It struck hard against the Blue Mage's solid cuffs. Sparks spangled out from the clash, striking the runes etched in the metal.

Najran read the runes. He spun away to a spot near the elevated point of the rock. He covered the ground inside the sanctuary in a few decisive strides, keeping the rock between himself and the Mages as he searched for the First Oralist of Hira.

Yusuf and Daniyar advanced on opposite sides, swords held high and battle-ready, despite Daniyar's instinctive sense that blood must not be spilled beneath the dome. Najran tried to evade them by leaping onto the rock. But the same cold fire that had divided the Companions from the Mages formed an impassable wall, thin as a veil of ice, unbreachable as a passage sealed by the shudders of the earth.

Najran paused, the axe gripped in both hands. The lieutenant of the Nineteen had lost his taunting composure. Fury darkened his well-formed features, his eyes a blank tapestry on which the dancing flames of the ice-fire were reflected.

"What is this? Why did she come to a temple of the Esayin?"

Daniyar masked his surprise, mirroring the Blue Mage's movements as he advanced inch by inch around the rock. Why did Najran believe the Qubbat-as-Sakhrah was a temple of the Esayin? What did he know that Daniyar and Yusuf didn't?

He stayed quiet as Najran taunted him, the axe describing a steel-tipped path from shoulder to ground and back, the blade's kiss as light as the fingers of a seamstress working a panel of silk. His display of skill was meant to intimidate the Mages, to cause them to give ground. He'd retreated because he'd thought he could strike at them from higher ground by climbing the heights of the rock. With grim satisfaction Daniyar realized that Najran hadn't witnessed Arian's ascent, or Daniyar's inability to follow her.

Seeking Najran's measure, he asked, "Do you enjoy killing for its own sake, or is there a reason you pursue the First Oralist to the point of madness?"

From the corner of his eye, he caught the Blue Mage's subtle nod. Both men edged up another inch. The blade of the axe whirled out, the tabar incising a line across Daniyar's ribs. As he absorbed the blow, part of Daniyar's mind recognized the gold decoration on the blade. It was writing in a somewhat familiar language. Not the High Tongue, but a shadow of it, perhaps.

Ghayb, he thought. Vanished. And ghayb, the mystical knowledge that lay beyond the veil between two worlds. Between the wonders of creation and the One who created all there was in existence.

"There is purpose in it." Najran flicked the axe. If the Blue Mage's sword hadn't caught at the edge of his cloak and unbalanced him, it would have marked the place between Daniyar's brows. It nicked the edge of a dark brow instead before it fell away.

"The First Oralist's inversion of the Claim seeks to deny the supremacy of the Nineteen. Such heresy cannot be allowed."

"You don't strike me as a man of faith. Nor as one who would bow before the vagaries of numerology."

"Vagaries?" The tabar flew back to Najran's side as he reflected on the charge. "Numerology is a precise science." His unreadable gaze contemplated the contours of the rock, the lethal mind considering its options. "Its results are measurable . . . certain . . . assured. A man can depend on it when mysticism fails."

"What of a woman?"

A sleek smile from Najran. "The Rising Nineteen operate within a hierarchy. The First Oralist accepts no master. She refuses to yield her gifts on behalf of the greater good."

"The greater good?" Daniyar scoffed at the words. "A servant of the One would not seek to twist the Claim in pursuit of his own power. He would seek no such mastery over a Companion of Hira."

He leapt forward, his sword a glinting thrust. Najran pivoted so that Daniyar's sword was caught in the folds of his cloak. At the same time, Najran's axe glanced across the turquoise-studded pommel of the Blue Mage's sword, carving a line through stone, as hard-edged and bleak as a whisper from the dead.

Though Yusuf shoved the axe back with some force, Najran's feet remained planted. He drew the axe away, then let it fall again in a lazy, suspended arc. Despite his adroitness with the axe, Najran had boxed himself in. As the Mages pressed forward, there was nowhere for him to retreat. He began to chant in an unfamiliar tongue that Daniyar wondered if he somehow knew. Yusuf's expression mirrored Daniyar's confusion.

Then they experienced the impact of the intonation. The chant slowed their movements to a ponderous stillness, as if they were armored soldiers whose boots were trudging through mud. The next swing of the tabar would unbalance them. The one that followed after would slice across their necks.

An electrical arc fired a path through Daniyar's half-formed thoughts. A rapid inventory of the Candour, of the pages he had glimpsed in the Pearl of Timeback . . . lessons, descriptions, forewarnings, runes . . . lexicons that borrowed from one another.

Over this are Nineteen. The nineteen guardians of the denizen of the hell of Saqar, if the Akhirah was a reality, and not a place of foreboding.

The secrets he glimpsed, his recognition of Najran's source of power, permitted him to turn it back against Najran, trapping him within his own recitation, in the strength of a language that Daniyar would never dishonor.

"Hold him," he said, freeing Yusuf as well.

This time, when he leapt through the veil, he landed upon the rock.

He was in a room in the Library of Candour, a pale apricot light gilding its luminous walls. High ceilings hung over carpets that gleamed a ghostly green, silvered at the edges. On dark tables of carved walnut wood, manuscripts were stacked; on others, unrolled scrolls overflowed with script. Words, sentences, paragraphs, arguments, philosophy . . . a treasury of literature.

Histories and geographies. Myriad analyses of the catastrophes that had befallen Khorasan in the wake of the wars of the Far Range. Requiems for empires, litanies of loss. Language like a medicine snake coiling through barren hills.

He looked down at his hands and saw that he was unscarred by battle, dressed in the fine regalia that befitted the Guardian of Candour, his silver sword polished at his side, the ring he had given to Arian scattering its light on each manuscript he read.

A room full of books but at the center, a naked space on a table bereft of words.

A small stone stand with embellishments of silver that matched his sword and his ring had been placed on the table, its leaves open like two hands grasping at an empty sky, the basin of morning vacant.

The absence of the Candour was a familiar ache, a part of him that would never be recovered. The Authoritan had burned the Candour with a word. And before it had been reduced to ash, two haunting letters had hovered in the crimson fire.

حق

Together they had formed a word in the High Tongue that summarized the Guardian of Candour's trust: Truth and Right. He had interpreted those words to the best of his ability, guided by a Guardian's compassion. But he had not been able to save the book that had imparted to him the wisdom of those who had come before him.

What would you give for its return when you abandoned it twice?

The voice that challenged him was no more than curious; something in its intonation made him appreciate that by stepping onto the Sakhrah, he'd begun his ascent.

"Twice? It was burned by the Authoritan. I did not relinquish it by choice."

The first time at the Cloud Door, the second in Black Aura.

Then he understood. In both cases, his hold upon the Candour had been threatened by his commitment to Arian.

"Love is a gift more sacred than any scripture."

GUARDIAN OF CANDOUR!

The words poured into his ears like the strident notes of a trumpet, disparaging and harsh.

He didn't flinch from them.

"I did what I judged was necessary."

So sure of your judgment, then?

"No man can claim certainty. It is no secret I struggled, but I hoped to be taken on faith."

You have killed many men.

"Yes." For how could he deny it when the faces of the dead visited him at night?

You allowed the library to burn.

Tears clouded the shine of his eyes. He knew these crimes. He'd held himself culpable before any had thought to accuse him.

"I remember."

You ignored the rise of the Talisman because you counted them your own.

"No! *No.*" And then, contradicting himself under the weight of a pain he knew he deserved yet hadn't learned to bear, "They *are* my own. How can I deny who they are? How can I deny who I am?"

Silver Mage, Guardian of Candour. Your time is at an end.

He went still. A violent grief rocked his frame.

"I do not yield. I *will* not. Arian and I still have time."

Is that all you are, Guardian of Candour? A creature of yearning and bereavement?

He stumbled to his knees, his hands braced upon the Candour's empty stand.

"*Is* that what I am? Have you judged me and found me wanting?"

No reaction to the question that tore away the veil. That tore at the heart of him. He thought of Arian, of Sinnia and Yusuf, of friends whose trust he had gained, and of the orphans he had tried to protect. A man on his own against an army devoid of mercy.

He bent his head, felt his hair sweep over his forehead to fall upon the empty place where the book should have been.

The Ascension was a harrowing source of confusion. It left him without guidance; it shrouded him in sorrow.

You think yourself abandoned?

"I offer no complaint."

You wore the Sacred Cloak.

"Yes."

You took it because the Cloak was meant for you. There are other things you hold dear, things that are meant for you, just as you will know when it is time to yield them.

His head jerked up at this construal of the purpose of the Cloak. "How can that be?" He struggled to find the right words, truth surfacing from the darkest parts of his soul. "I was unworthy even to lay my hand on it."

Something settled in the library—a graciousness of space. Ordered rows of parchment, like the stones the people of the Everword laid upon the graves of their dead.

Would you fulfill your trust, Guardian of Candour?

"To the end. To my last breath on this earth. Make me worthy with the charge you would lay upon my shoulders."

Stained glass lay in shards upon a marble floor. Smoke and

blood painted over a silhouette of a city in ruins. He caught his breath. It was Ashfall. Ashfall in its last hour.

Reclaim the child of Hira from the dark. This is the purpose you will serve.

Strange to make this request when his devotion was plain.

"I will not leave Arian again."

But the light dimmed in the room, the wind whispering over pages he had traced, and he knew he'd misunderstood. It wasn't Arian he was meant to save.

He watched the Maiden Tower fall, the Qaysarieh Portal collapse. He wrenched his thoughts around. If not Arian, then—

Candour burned in his vision, a city swallowed whole by the vindictiveness of the One-Eyed Preacher, a man he hadn't faced. The silver sword blazed in its sheath, stirring at his side.

Regain the city of Ashfall, and let your trust pass on.

His whole body shuddered, his sinews rippling with strength. He surged to his feet again.

"I do not understand. *Candour* is my trust."

The wind whipped against his cheek; he turned his face to shield it.

And there at the far end of the library stood the orphaned boy Wafa.

10

NAJRAN'S AXE DANCED LIKE A LIVING FLAME, EACH BLOW DEFLECTED not by Yusuf's sword, but by the use of his heavy gold cuffs. The axe struck hard at the cuffs, yet failed to rend them, their runes unmarked by the tabar's unblunted steel.

They had fought each other to a standstill, and now both men stood panting beneath the dome. Yusuf's build was stronger: his musculature far outweighed Najran's. But Najran's lean body was exercised in battle, his speed shifting the balance. He drew his tabar back just as Yusuf raised his sword to shoulder height, the fine edge of the blade held parallel to the ground. Both men had tried to use the Sakhrah for leverage; neither had been able to penetrate the veil of fire.

Nor did either man have enough breath to taunt or threaten the other. Najran's pupils split as he positioned the axe. Thin gold threads spread out over the midnight irises in a pattern that reflected the decoration that gilded the axe.

Yusuf shifted so that his front leg bore his weight.

"What is that? What have you done to your eyes?"

The axe whirled between Najran's shoulders.

"You cannot win this battle, Mage of Timeback. The tabar and I are one."

The axe whistled down. Yusuf blocked it with his left cuff.

Najran nodded, feinting back. "Those cuffs cannot be gold. My axe would have shattered your bones otherwise. Are you an alchemist?"

Yusuf parried another blow. "Perhaps."

Najran uttered a phrase in a thick, evocative tongue.

Yusuf supplied an invocation of the Blue Mage.

His pacing was thrown off a fraction, but he said to the Angel of Blood, "Aramaya cannot harm a Mage of Khorasan. It is a sister-speech to the High Tongue."

Najran hadn't been expecting him to know it. The blade flew, arced, *sang* . . . and caught him across his chest. The ripple of movement scored a trail of red, a crimson splash against bronzed skin, a swipe of calculated pain.

They lunged at each other, blades flying and meeting. The point of a sword caught. The handle of the axe was chipped. Steel met steel with a fiery scattering of sparks, hot blue tipped with orange. The gold pattern overspread Najran's eyes. The two-headed tabar began to fall in a series of rhythmic strokes, slice after slice, to the right and the left, though not in a discernible pattern. Yusuf alternated between lunges with his sword and defensive maneuvers with his cuffs. But in time, he guessed wrong and the tabar caught him in the shoulder, driving deep and pushing him to his knees, his blood spraying in a scarlet curve.

Najran's laugh was soft.

"You may know my speech, but none are exempt from the gifts of the Angel of Blood."

The axe fell again, a second blow hammering home the first. Yusuf grunted. He raised his right cuff to shelter the wound in his opposite shoulder, blood draining from his body. His blue eyes found Najran's. "I see you no longer call yourself by the name of the Iron Glaive."

Najran ran his fingers along the scalloped head of the axe with a subtle, indifferent shrug.

"I possess a multitude of weapons. If one is riven from me, another comes to hand." The axe played between his wrists. He glanced over at the Sakhrah. "Were it not for the veil of fire, I would leave your body as an offering upon the rock as my gift to the First Oralist."

Gasping now, Yusuf said, "Blood should not be spilled beneath the shelter of this dome."

Laughter like a scimitar. "Too late for that, I'm afraid. You are spent, Sidi Yusuf. A fine repayment for the schemes you over-turned in Axum."

Yusuf replied in Aramaya, "You speak words in the world." And in the High Tongue, he added, "You sow corruption in the land."

Both hands fell to his thighs, the right cuff smeared with his blood.

Najran frowned down at him, his hands stilling on the axe. The Blue Mage accused him of spreading falsehood. And of greater import, of iniquitous deeds. The words should not have concerned him, but uttered by a Mage of Khorasan, they weighted his hands with lead.

"You have to come to death on your knees, Sidi Yusuf. Your curses do not disturb me."

The turquoise eyes of the Blue Mage did not dim. He raised the index finger of his bloodstained hand to point to the black lead dome.

"The Rukha d'Qudsha will not see me wasted."

A throb of terror pulsed through Najran's blood. How had this Mage on his knees summoned a holy name in Aramaya?

From the corner of his eye, he saw that the fire-veil that guarded the rock had dissolved, and he faltered. He took a step closer to the rock, the axe loose in his hand. The Blue Mage did not rise to stop him, weakened by the loss of blood. The roof above their heads split open, a high dome composed of light that shone like the shimmer of a pearl.

Najran gaped at the sight. The limestone rock beneath the dome now blazed like the heart of a ruby, full of secret fire. A rainbow of red and green danced in the space above it, illuminating a . . . flight of stairs? Or a ladder? From beneath the rock, four rivers spilled into the chamber, their waters cool and soft. He shook his head twice, and the fantastical image vanished.

A white-gold cataract roared into the chamber, pouring forth light, peeling the lead from the gallery of windows, and from the dome itself. Sunlight canted through the aperture, reflected in great gold plates that outlined the outer surfaces of the dome, so that from a distance, a halo shone on a desecrated land.

A tracery of lines crept around the dome's interior, a diaphanous calligraphy, a delicate geometry that traced a promise of the One's.

Verily the sanctuaries of the One will be maintained by those who believe.

In place of a barren rock, a flight of stairs ascended a zenith that pulsed with white-gold light. The axe fell from Najran's hand. He moved to the ladder. His hands faltered on the rungs, then he was thrown back by a swelling wave of sound. It was the Claim as he had never heard it, given voice by two of the Companions.

His head hit the bar of a wooden beam with force. He found himself on the ground, within reach of the Blue Mage, who had collapsed inside a circle outlined by his blood. The last thing he saw before he closed his eyes was the First Oralist, her hands clasped to the wounds on Sidi Yusuf's shoulder.

11

When Yusuf came to consciousness, he was in the company of friends. The First Oralist, Sinnia, the Silver Mage, and the boy Wafa, who was something more—something other?—than a boy. The blue eyes that had seemed so unusual on a child of the Hazara were outlined now with a nimbus of silver. They brought to mind the intermittent light that pulsed from the ring of a Mage. The Silver Mage. And the blue had brightened to the color of Yusuf's startling eyes.

The anointed boy who looked back at him was as curious as the child Wafa had been.

"Are you well?" he asked, his speech reflecting a new maturity.

Yusuf tested his wounded arm. Though the eviscerating ache was gone, he could not move it. One of the others had bandaged it and bound it with a splint.

Wafa now edged down to rest his hands on the Blue Mage's runes.

Yusuf looked to the others to see if they would object. Sinnia's beautiful features reflected her apprehension, her concern for him, while the Silver Mage stood aside, near the First Oralist, whose face was somber with regret.

For the wound he had suffered in taking on Najran?

No. Her gaze was on the boy who wasn't just a boy. She mourned the loss of the child she had taken as her own. Who the boy was now, she would have to learn anew.

Yusuf glanced down at his cuffs. The runes carved into gold denoted his origins, his gifts, the secrets he still held. With Wafa's touch, the black markings silvered over. The runes became as clear as the fluency of script upon a page. He sensed a contained power in the boy that would develop a rhythm over time.

"You were called to ascend."

"You knew I would be." Wafa spoke without fear.

"In the care of the Companions of Hira and under the protection of Mages, I thought it possible. But your call to the Ascension rests upon your own merits."

The boy flushed, the soft rise of color in his face as delicate as a girl's.

"I was . . . blessed." Self-consciousness from one who was yet a child.

The Silver Mage helped Yusuf to his feet. As Mages of Khorasan, they recognized the nature of the boy's blessing. As servants of the One, they had chosen not to shirk their duty, but in doing so, neither had known peace. Wafa's fate would be similar.

He murmured to Daniyar, to prevent the others from hearing. "Do you know what happened to the boy?"

A troubled nod in response.

Najran lay unconscious beneath the ribs of the dome, the axe dismantled at his feet.

Daniyar's head tilted up to the calligraphy that laced the interior of the dome like the outgrowth of flowering vines, each trailing tendril bright with a spark of knowledge.

"Najran thought this a temple of the Esayin. But this temple was new to the Esayin, a new beginning altogether that heralded the coming of the Claim."

"You have acquired comprehension," Yusuf noted.

"A gift of the Ascension." Daniyar turned his head to indicate the others. "We should speak of the Israa e Miraj while we can."

They gathered in a circle beneath the dome, the Sakhrah bare and cool in their midst, its ruby fire abated.

"I am called to Hira," Arian said.

"And I." Sinnia's quick echo. "The summons is urgent; we cannot delay."

They waited for Daniyar's response. He glanced at Yusuf, then at Wafa. His silver eyes dull, he reached for Arian's hand.

"I do not want this; I would rather be at your side. But I have a duty to acquit. I must make my way to Ashfall to fulfill my trust."

Arian shivered under the impact of words he hadn't yet confessed. "Your trust?"

"My trust as the Silver Mage for a city poised to fall." His hands tightened on hers. "I *must* leave you, Arian. I wish there was another way."

The light from the dome rained down upon their heads, a harsh reminder of Ascension. The sacrifice demanded of him wasn't one he understood, but his decision was made. Sinnia would stand with Arian until the end. His gifts were needed elsewhere.

He refused to look at Arian, afraid to see the accusation in her eyes.

"We part here, then." Yusuf nudged Najran's body with his foot. "What of the Angel of Blood? He cannot be left alive."

"Nor can life be taken in the precincts of the Noble Sanctuary. I suggest we leave him to the mercies of the Custodian." Daniyar paused. "If Ashfall comes to ruin, the people of Khorasan are lost. Will you offer your aid? Should the tide turn, and the maghreb be in need, I would not hesitate to come."

Yusuf sheathed the sword that had taken a battering from Najran's axe.

"I do not challenge the wisdom you gained upon ascent. My sword will be at your side."

Daniyar surprised him with the shadow of a smile. "I would rather have your return to the Conference of the Mages."

Alert and aware, the Blue Mage considered Wafa.

Alarmed, Arian held out her hand, Wafa's name upon her lips. "He goes with me. He will be safest at the Citadel."

Daniyar dropped his head, muttering a bleak curse. She *knew*, he thought. The tears in her eyes told him that she knew.

"My love, Wafa is in my charge. He must go with me to Ashfall." He thought for a moment, considering how to tell her. "And from there, perhaps to Candour at my side."

"That is not his place!" She jerked her hand from his. She strode across the circle to Wafa. She grasped hold of his shoulders and pulled him into her embrace. "You cannot go with the Silver Mage—you *must* not. Your place is with me and Sinnia. You are a ward of the Companions. You are a child of Hira, *my* child."

Wafa hugged her, blinking back his own tears.

"You must let me go, sahabiya. My fate is no longer in your hands."

"Don't call me that!" She was shaken by the change in him, the growth.

Wafa took one of her hands and pressed it to his cheek. "My

lady, Arian. No one knows better than I what the Talisman in-flict. I cannot let the Silver Mage stand against them alone, when you were the one to teach me what it means to be loyal."

She appealed to Daniyar. "I do not want this for him. I know what you have suffered, what you endured in Candour. If Wafa goes with you . . ." She was crying in earnest now, and Daniyar drew her away from Wafa, away from the concern of the others.

He took her to the outer ambulatory.

Fear clawed at her. "I will lose him. I will lose the boy I love like my own."

Daniyar held her tight, letting her absorb the hard support of his body though she tried to break free, letting his love for her whisper through every limb. And still her sobbing did not ease.

Because her tears were not for Wafa.

Her eyes were like diamond-scattered jade, her grief scoring him like the edge of a dagger poised in delicate hands.

She pressed her lips to his chest, one fist punishing him in a senseless rhythm.

"Israa e Miraj was meant to be a deliverance. Instead it will steal you away!"

He pushed aside a lock of her hair to whisper in her ear, to put an end to her pain.

"My love, I must do my part to fight the One-Eyed Preacher."

"No! This is something else. I *feel* it." Sobbing the words, she struck at him again.

He silenced her with a kiss, giving her time to taste the truth. To know it from a place where lies were not possible between them.

When he sensed the easing of her panic, he brushed her cheek with his lips.

"Nothing could make me leave you. But how will I hold myself worthy of you, if I ignore the truths of the Ascension? What would you do in my place?"

She ignored the question, gazing at him with bleak intensity. "The Ascension showed me my duty. This is the end. This is the last stand. Either the Citadel holds or the One-Eyed Preacher wins. If my task takes me to Hira, and yours to Ashfall, what if we never meet again?"

His breath escaped in hot surges against her lips.

"Then you will be my companion in the Akhirah."

She stamped her foot in a rare display of temper.

"I want to be with you in the Damson Vale, not in a sphere that we must die to reach! And what if you forget me in the Akhirah?"

"I am yours in all lifetimes, Arian. On every surface of this earth, and every plane thereafter. How could I forget you?"

She smoothed her palms against his chest, raising her face to his. Instead of kissing him, she let the warmth build between them, her body absorbing every nuance of his strength with a pleasure so deep it was a permanent ache, a star verging on nova in a perfect binary system. If he left, she would be swallowed by the void that pulsed between the filaments of galaxies.

"Did the ascent hurt you?" she asked, her fingertips touching the strong cords of his throat. He stirred beneath the touch, silver eyes heating, but he let her hands wander at will.

"Rather, it showed me the end of the world—"

"It showed me the end of *all* worlds," she interrupted.

"Did you experience hopelessness?" His hands touched her with fluency, aligning the fit of their bodies so his voice was closer to her ear, low and rough, and richer than the Claim.

"I experienced purpose."

"As did I. So you see—"

She pressed a finger to his lips. "Do not say it again. Let me learn to accept it."

"As you wish."

She was held close against his heart when she asked him, "How is it possible for Wafa to be so changed?"

"The dominion of the One is over all things." His bright eyes moved over her face. "Did you *see* the One? Do you know what the One is?"

"The dominion of the One is over all things," she echoed. She told him of the voices that had held her in place, light at the edges of her vision. "They must have known that I couldn't bear a fuller glimpse. The One did not speak to me, though there were lessons for me in the Ascension." A sweet smile touched her lips. "And I gained the Sana Codex."

Daniyar's eyes closed, gratitude enfolding him like a mother's embrace, warm and profuse in forgiveness.

"Then we have hope." A roughness in his voice. "Hope to overcome the darkness."

Her hands reached up to hold his face, and he gave in to the encompassing temptation, opening her mouth with his kiss, drinking deeply from her lips. When he pulled away, his breathing harsh, she caught his face in her hands, affected by the sorrow in his eyes.

"What are you not telling me? Is it to do with Wafa? Does the change in him affect you in some manner?"

How not to lie to her while denying the truth?

"I am to be his . . . mentor."

"He could ask for no better." Uncertainty beneath the staunch belief, some part of her wandering close to the precipice of truth.

Imperative that he pull her back.

"He was brought to himself by your love, Arian. He will never be enslaved again."

"Will you be able to keep him safe?"

How to tell her, how to accept this final duty . . .

"Or he will do the same for me, as he is wont to do."

"Keep your promise to return."

"Keep *yours*. Do not let the Preacher harm you."

She brought her palms together over his heart. "That wasn't a promise." The innocence of her inquiry was tinged with the kind of foreknowledge that would haunt her. He couldn't let that happen, so he found a way to make the vow.

"From the foundations of this earth to the Akhirah, my soul is in your keeping."

Something in the words was off, something in his voice, in the fading glory of his eyes . . .

"Daniyar—"

"Arian," he coaxed, "don't make it hard for me to go when calamity approaches Ashfall."

The warning jolted her.

"What do you know of Ashfall?"

"The city is on the verge of apocalypse."

The urgency of the moment called to her, even as his hands held her wrists in a somber farewell that neither was willing to end.

"How will we make our way from here?" he asked her.

"There is a portal . . . a system of portals. If I had only known."

One strong hand smoothed over her hair before he gathered up the long tresses to let them slide between his fingers.

"These discoveries were part of your Audacy; they were an answer to your need. Do not blame yourself for things beyond your control. Where is the portal?" His voice was gruff.

"Beneath the rock, there is a cave that contains a pool. The cave is called the Bir al Arwah. If you look at the surface of the Sakhrah, there is a hole that shows the opening below. There must be stairs nearby that lead down into the cave."

He glanced around, her hair still caught in his hands.

"The Well of Souls?"

"You know of it?"

"It was mentioned in the Candour. There was a drawing . . ."

He glanced back at the Sakhrah, counting the number of alcoves behind the outer ambulatory. "It's there." He turned her in his arms until her back was pressed to his chest. He aligned his right arm with hers, raising it to point. "There, do you see it?"

Engulfed by his steadfast strength, she nodded. "We should go."

Something hot and wet stung the side of her neck. "Yes, we should."

She tried to turn in his arms, but he held her fast, both arms caging her ribs.

"Wait," he said. "Don't look at me. There's something I want to say to you."

Her heart lurched. Then it plummeted like a stone flung into a bottomless pool.

His cheek nuzzled hers, his breath hot against her skin.

"This day you perfected for me my faith. You completed your grace upon me."

His lips touched the tears on her cheek. He released her from his embrace to lead her to the top of the stairs.

"We will see each other again, Arian."

But this time he made no mention of his promise of the Damson Vale.

12

THEIR PARTY DESCENDED THE STEPS THROUGH A PASSAGE CARVED FROM a shaft that resembled a ruined chimney. Water whispered over stone in an ever-present murmur, while the bedrock below extended pale fingers of supplication to the Sakhrah above.

As they moved beneath the Sakhrah, they passed a niche carved into the wall, a flat white mihrab robed in marble, with a prescription beneath the arch: *There is no one but the One.*

And beneath this, a small, black paving stone was inset in the marble, inscribed with the pleas of the faithful.

I seek refuge in the One.

At the bottom of the stairs, they found themselves in a small, square chamber crowded with stalactites that framed a pool of ultramarine blue. As Arian descended the stairs, splinter-sharp crystals from the pool reflected the light with thousands of sparkling fragments.

To the right of the pool a turret of rock formed a pedestal wide enough for two or three to climb. But a column of stone formed a barrier between the base of the stairs and the plinth.

Their small company gathered at the bottom. Arian studied

the barrier that prevented their access to the plinth. Mineral deposits had dripped down from the ceiling of the cavern to build upon deposits on the ground. She didn't touch it, examining its corroded patterns.

She offered a verse of the Claim. The column seemed to shift. She considered it, frowning, and then realized that though the surface appeared as porous as dripstone, it was solid all the way through.

She and Sinnia chanted the Claim together. Then Yusuf lent his voice.

When the stone remained unyielding, Wafa cast a sidelong glance at Daniyar. He nodded at a portion of the column that curved inward like a nave. Daniyar approached it, brushing past Wafa. When he placed his hand on the stone, a tiny notch appeared.

He bent his head, reflecting on his choices. Each moment he delayed was a moment that worsened the people of Khorasan's need. But each moment of delay was also the postponement of a separation he couldn't face.

"Daniyar?" Arian's gentle voice asked a question.

He looked up, ignoring the others, seeing only Arian's face. Fear had begun to bleed into the beauty of her eyes. Before it could take root, he brought out the keys the Custodian had given him. He held up the second, untried key and gave it to Arian to slip into the notch.

The harsh stone of the column dissolved into sand at its touch, the pathway to the pool left unobstructed. He took Arian's hand and led her to the base of the plinth.

In the unnerving silence that followed, Sinnia cleared her throat. "There are many different legends about the Well of Souls." She approached the pool with an air of nonchalance. She dipped a hand into its cool blue waters. The pool began to froth with furious whispers, a noise that subsided as she withdrew.

"The people of the Everword claimed that the Sakhrah covered an abyss. The abyss contained the waters of a flood that drowned the entire world."

Yusuf held his hand just above the waters of the pool. The light from the crystals danced on his golden cuffs. "Better not to disturb the waters than to call forth another."

Sinnia measured the clear span of air between the surface of the pool and the ceiling of the cavern that lay beneath the Sakhrah.

"The people of the Claim believed that this pool was a river of paradise. A palm tree was said to spring from its depths to balance the weight of the Sakhrah on its fronds."

Blue crystals sparked in the tiny rivulets that flowed like draperies over cool stone.

"If the weight of the world above depends upon an invisible tree, perhaps we should hasten this along." Yusuf's urging made the others hurry. Arian and Sinnia climbed the plinth. Arian waited for Daniyar, her face drawn into despairing lines.

Why had he taken a verse of the Claim and transformed it into a pledge? Why did his movements seem beleaguered and reluctant? Arian searched for words to encourage him.

"The Commander of the Faithful recognized this turret. He gave it a greeting of peace; the rock returned it with a greeting of greater generosity: 'Peace be unto you, and the mercy of the One.' He named the speaking rock the Tongue. I think it will uphold you."

And for a moment she thought she glimpsed the Sacred Cloak upon Daniyar's shoulders. With an effort, she kept her voice from trembling.

"Give the people of Ashfall our greetings. Tell them our prayers are with them."

He could not find it within him to offer a greeting more generous than hers.

"Be safe," he said in farewell. "Be *free*, heart of my heart."

13

A DAWN LIKE RETRIBUTION. LIKE RECRIMINATION, THE SKY A SILVER-blue shimmer above a haze of ash and smoke. The air dry enough to choke on. To die on, though the spears of jeweled light that broke through the glass wreckage of the scriptorium reminded Arsalan that he was very much alive, standing in the midst of incalculable destruction, the Princess of Ashfall at his feet.

The Princess had burned the scriptorium. She had murdered the scholars who studied within its halls. She had killed the Zareen-Qalam, a man of such great learning that his like would not be found again. Not in all the lands of Khorasan. Not for many lifetimes to come.

She had slain the Zhayedan who had tried to stop her, with no more than a grazing of her wrist. With obscenity pouring like a cataract from her once-innocent lips.

He caught the pale flash of the wings of hawks against the black and gold sky, the sun rising in an arc of fire, as pristine and promising as if nearly everything hadn't already been lost. The hawks were carrying messages from Zhayedan captains across the field of war. Their urgency reminded Arsalan that the time for

98

grief would come later. This moment had been purchased at precious cost when there was still something of Ashfall left to save. Left to burn if the Talisman had their way. Or if the ghul that ruled the Princess were to appear again.

"Commander Arsalan."

He waved away the soldier who approached, anxious for his return.

"Please give me a moment, Esfandyar."

His voice was raw from the smoke he'd inhaled, but his courtesy, his calm, remained. Esfandyar nodded, backing away, his stance one of battle readiness. His eyes drifted to the figure of Ashfall's princess, clothed in a webbing of silver fronds, unable to move her slender limbs. Her head was turned to the side, eyes the color of twilight pulsing like bruises in her face.

The Commander of the Black Khan's army gestured to the Assassin, who knelt at the Princess's side, watchful behind his steel mask. It was the Assassin who had spun the web that had saved the Princess from her fall. In a moment of sanity, Darya had perceived the destruction she'd wrought at the ghul's behest. Then she had tried to end the ghul's violence by throwing herself from the palace walls to the square where the battle raged.

A creature of poisonous secrets, the Assassin had brought Darya back. He had saved her. For this moment, this purpose. That Arsalan might kill her himself. That he might take his revenge. Avenge his brothers, his people. Those he grieved, as he would not grieve for himself.

Soft and considering, he said, "Release her. Bring Darya to me."

He slid his sword from the jeweled sheath that was a gift from his Khan. His Khan, who had given him an order as he strode from the scriptorium, from the ruins of Ashfall's glory.

Do not repeat your mistake. Kill the ghul before she wakes.

Had he ever refused his Khan?

Had his Khan ever considered what it might cost him to bend to his will?

"Better not to release her, if you intend to take her life." The Assassin. Smooth as he conceded the Princess, untroubled by the consequence to Arsalan of carrying out Rukh's order.

The flex of powerful arms as Arsalan unsheathed his sword, refusing to look at Darya. Refusing to *see* who she had been. What she had meant to him, a sparkling, dark-eyed child whose unaffected laughter had echoed through the palace. Her innocent conversation had enchanted the Zhayedan. She had bound Arsalan's hands with a garland she'd fashioned herself, aglow at what she'd believed was his proposal. She'd tracked his footsteps along the walls, her entire being lit with joy when he spared her a little of his notice. A girl who loved a brother who refused to love her in return. The brother *he* also loved.

And so they had come to this. This triangle of love, betrayal, and despair.

How would that betrayal be repaid?

Arsalan's hair was powdered with bits of glass. He breathed the remnants of burnt vellum through his lips. The metallic taste of the blood of men he had loved . . . honored . . . trained . . . was in his mouth. And yet, and yet . . .

The blow he struck would be grievous, the injury immense. To take the life of the girl he had cherished . . . cared for . . . protected. To come to a moment in Ashfall's fortunes when he could protect her no longer.

Do you believe you will not be tested as those before you were tested?

Here, then, was Arsalan's test. He motioned to the Assassin without giving away his inner turmoil. His suffering.

"I will execute the prisoner, but not while she is bound."

He raised his gleaming sword, balanced it with effortless strength. His voice without inflection so the others would not know.

The soldier who waited for him stifled a gasp, though he did not question his commander. Neither did the Assassin, who rose from the ground, bringing the Princess with him. A liquid movement of his hands over the Princess's body caused the webbing to fall away. She stood exposed, clothed in the blood she had shed, the long, dark trails of her hair imparting a measure of modesty. The Princess raised her chin. The ghul's eyes gleamed at him with hatred. Arsalan remained expressionless. His sword thrust forward in an arc of brutal grace. The ghul leapt back in a shudder of movement, its bones broken and reset, each time with less coherence, with less consideration for the tenderness of the spirit they enclosed.

The Assassin stood aside, refusing to assist.

"This is your choice, not mine."

A painless conclusion when the Assassin was the one who had used his sorcery to corrupt Darya's sweetness. Conjuring a ghul from a girl whose heart had been filled with grace.

But when all other choices were extinguished, what did that matter now?

The soldier behind him drew his sword with a grating whisper of steel. Arsalan said, "No," without turning his head.

Where there had been love between Arsalan and Darya, there was now the cold hollowness of loss, her betrayal a chasm that stretched between them, one he couldn't overcome, one he had no wish to bridge. The cost of killing her would be measured when the turn of battle permitted. A moment to reckon with the hard-won truths that peeled away slices of his soul.

Darya had loved him.

But Arsalan loved only Rukh.

The consummation of his betrothal to Darya had been an act of ruin, a presaging of other losses, for Rukh would take a queen, just as he had taken one lover after another. He had bedded the High Companion while manipulating Arsalan's affections. He'd allowed the intimacy of Arsalan's kiss, but scorned the depths of his love.

He'd assumed that Arsalan's affections wouldn't change—that he couldn't be broken.

When Rukh had permitted Arsalan's kiss, had he done so out of genuine desire or as a matter of inquiry? Had he wanted to know about Arsalan the one thing that remained outside his grasp, forever beyond his control?

Wheels turning within wheels. The intrigues of Ashfall's court, Rukh's ceaseless machinations. The Black Khan's determination not to yield. His insistence that Ashfall was the glory of an age, and that he alone could raise it to greater heights. His refusal to admit his mistakes. His certainty that his wrongs would be forgiven, should he think to ask forgiveness.

But there was also the companionship, the solidarity, the *history* . . . Rukh's unflinching reliance on Arsalan, his certainty that of those he ruled, those he governed, Arsalan would not betray him. A trust unlike any other, a bond unlike any other. And beneath the endless scheming, the laughter . . . the effortless seduction that underlined every breath.

For all these reasons, Arsalan loved him.

For these reasons, Arsalan was *willing* to be governed, though Rukh had not demanded that he yield all of himself. His judgment, his integrity, his faith were all intact. These were the things that Rukh loved in turn, the things he wouldn't change, the crux of who Arsalan was, a friend he wouldn't weaken. A friend of the heart, a brother.

But not a lover, never that. No matter that Arsalan craved it. *Burned* for it. Ached to hear a whisper of love in return, to feel a strong hand upon his own in more than a brother's caress, in defiance of all propriety. Yes, Rukh had shielded him, but why had he never made it possible for Arsalan to stand as who he was, unshielded? Why had he preferred to keep Arsalan in the shadows, tied to him by a thousand separate strings of duty and obligation?

Perhaps for a moment like this. Where he could expect Arsalan to carry out a command to execute the Princess of Ashfall without compunction or regret.

An act of calculation, not love.

The thought tormented Arsalan, until he found a way to make it palatable to himself. Was it not a reckoning of love? Did the demand not pulse with it? For who else would Rukh trust to make such a sacrifice? Who else could he entrust with Darya's life *and* death? There must be love in that. Broken and bent, perhaps, cruel and self-sparing, hypnotic and irresistible . . . much like Rukh himself. A weakness in Arsalan's blood. A weakness so fundamental that if Rukh sought a dagger to use on him, Arsalan would place it in his princely hands himself.

Who then was the corruptor, who the corrupted?

He didn't know, didn't want to know. He'd been tangled in Rukh's web since boyhood. He neither sought nor wanted freedom. All he asked for was respect.

Which until this moment had been Rukh's unequivocal gift.

His mind shied away from the confrontation in Rukh's chambers when Rukh had seen his lust and named it in the presence of the First Oralist, a woman Arsalan esteemed. A betrayal of inexplicable cruelty, though the First Oralist had not judged Arsalan or found him wanting.

But there was also the fallout to consider. Rukh's terror that the insult had sundered their bond. His uncertainty. His sincerity when sincerity had always been a game. His love when love was what he chose to withhold.

That was something to remember at this moment of decision.

Arsalan encroached upon the ghul. His blade went wide as the ghul undulated. Sinew danced away from steel, bones shifted and re-formed. He tried not to look, but Darya's unexpected gasp drew him in. The ghul spat at him, a red foam coating her lips. But the eyes were Darya's, drowning in pain, as she tried to put herself in his way. As the ghul's power collapsed, Darya fell to her knees, pushing her dark hair aside to bare her neck to his blade.

No colloquy between them at the last, just steel whispering over fragile skin, fissures in a wall of smooth, warm flesh, the seething silence reframed.

A hot veil of blood covered the nape of the girl he had loved as if Darya were *his* sister instead of Rukh's. Until she had taken him to her bed. For there, in the quiet of her chamber, she had lain like a fallen gazelle in his arms, her eyes bleak with the knowledge of coercion, a knowledge she couldn't escape when he wore his pain like a shield.

Her head turned up at the last moment, and she whispered in the sweet intonations that had chased him through the years, "Please, Arsalan. You must see this through. I can't control the ghul. She won't rest until she kills you."

The tip of the sword wavered, the pressure easing.

She had made the mistake of looking into his eyes. Of speaking to him as Darya. For the ghul he could have killed—*would* kill. But Darya, his guileless shadow, Darya, the sister he knew Rukh loved, *that* task would see him undone.

The Assassin did not interfere. He was no more than a breath away for the sake of Arsalan's safety. Yet not close enough to take up his sword.

It was for Arsalan to choose.

Do not repeat your mistake, his prince had said. *Kill the ghul before she wakes.*

He had made mistakes with Rukh. Was this to be another?

"Please."

Another soft entreaty. Darya holding the ghul at bay with the tattered shreds of her will.

"Commander."

The soldier Esfandyar reminding him of his duty. Of the war that cut away at Ashfall, piece by devastating piece, gates sundered, walls aflame, catapults booming through the night, a crimson cast to the clouds, to his thoughts . . .

The metallic sound of the Assassin's voice, even and measured. Even as it measured him.

"The Nineteen are pressing the Messenger Gate. Will you wait for them to rise? Will you allow the Princess to distract you?"

The wrong words to persuade him.

For what had Darya been all her life, other than a distraction? A girl at the periphery, unwanted by her suitor, no matter her sweet persistence. She'd been ripe for the ghul's taking because of how she'd been unloved. And in the flush of a dawn that might well be Ashfall's last, there was one choice he could make that would honor his beliefs.

She was a child of Hira. He was a man of faith.

He quenched the seeping line on her nape with the filaments that clung to her skin.

His words pierced like arrows through stained glass, sharp and tinted with light.

"Near the entrance to Qaysarieh, there is a cistern where the Begum Niyousha used to pray." He sensed the Assassin's surprise. "Yes, Darya's mother. It is the one place I can think of where the Princess might overcome the ghul. She used to pray there with her mother." He hesitated, considering the man he was assigning the role of Darya's protector.

A brief dip of the Assassin's mask, a silent gesture of respect.

"I know it, if you would have me take her there."

"And your dark arts?" A harsh question. "Will you use them on her again?"

Both men watched as the silver laces that draped Darya's torso began to expand, knitting back bone and flesh, sealing the gaps between her ribs.

"They have their place." No comfort from the Assassin, then. But Arsalan had mistaken him, for he added in a voice as heavy as boulders hurtling down into a river, "But I should not have applied them to the Princess. I thought her stronger than this."

Arsalan's sword tipped down. He passed it to Esfandyar to clean, for he would not return it to its jeweled sheath with Darya's blood upon it.

She knelt quiescent before them, her body racked with shudders as she waged the battle within, a bruised twilight in the eyes that lighted on his face with nameless yearning.

"She was strong enough to bear her brother's rejection, and to endure her isolation at his court. She watched her dreams die before her eyes." For Darya had witnessed his stolen moment with Rukh. "The Princess has borne more than any woman should have to bear. That you encouraged her fall is a mark for your soul to carry. I cannot kill her. I *will* not."

He removed his glove so that his hand passed over Darya's head in the whisper of a caress. The ghul remained quiet. She didn't raise her head to gnaw at his knuckles with her teeth.

The sword slid back into its sheath in a seamless motion typical of Arsalan's grace.

The Assassin covered Darya's shivering body with his robe before he lifted her into his arms. The mask dipped toward Arsalan again as he posed a final question.

"And the Khan's order?"

Arsalan flung up his head, a dangerous glitter in his eyes.

"I am not a pawn to be played in this game between you and the Khan. I am Commander of the Zhayedan. Let no man who sees me forget that Ashfall's fate rests in *my* hands."

A slight softening at the edge of the Assassin's eyes. A sign of satisfaction because the Princess had been relinquished to his care, obliged to him for her existence.

Perhaps because this was what the Assassin had schemed for all along.

Too late for Arsalan to disavow his choice. To recant or express regret. To acknowledge his betrayal. For what would Rukh think of him if Darya struck at Ashfall again?

14

Dawn slid down walls pierced by thousands of arrows. Cries of war stormed their flanks. The Messenger Gate buckled, a stone buttress that had stood for centuries, its timbered doors sheathed in the protection of double layers of steel, painted with scenes of historic conquests. Daylight pushed for an entry that would herald the beginning of loss.

The Nineteen lurched forward again, pushing their ram before them, under the protective cover of a shed. Teerandaz arrows hurled fire across the shed's roof, but the ram mounted on ropes remained secure, its iron head indifferent to arrow and flame alike.

A second thrust, a third, a fourth and the gate collapsed, enemies pouring into the heart of the Black Khan's capital, the Zhayedan's shock troops engaged on their own ground at last. A cannonade of fury in their ears, the sheer scale of the noise deafening the square. Clashing steel, the shouts of men, the splintered whistle of arrows. And muscle and bone against the weapons meant to rend them, waves of men breaking beneath blunt force, the heels of armored boots grinding skulls into the ground.

From the Maiden Tower, Arsalan sent a message to Rukh. The Black Khan accepted his warning by spearing fire into the square.

"No!" Arsalan's fractured cry stopped him, a roar echoed by others in the square. Rukh's voice was rough and raw in his throat; the power of the Dark Mage faltered when the smoke cleared and he saw that he couldn't contain the fire, couldn't protect his forces from it—he had slaughtered his own men.

The Cataphracts staggered under the twin assault, saved by the fact that the Nineteen's ram lay in ruins. The soldiers of the Nineteen who had survived the Black Khan's attack backed away from the source of the fire. Chaos beyond measure, bodies beyond number, the Cataphracts regrouping. No sign of Maysam, their commander. A quick look and Rukh found him: his fiercest fighter's head impaled at the end of the ram, his earlier miscalculations paid for. Rukh's breath caught. He coughed and the magic within him fell silent, biding its time, waiting for him to recover, to sort through the terror and fury of his thoughts. He whipped out his spyglass to better survey the flattened grass in the square, crushed beneath corpses arranged in gruesome thrusts. Death in all its guises, the Cataphracts hacked and disemboweled, their chests torn open, their bodies headless and maimed wherever the Nineteen struck. Blood upon bone upon blood.

And the stench, by the grace of the One, the stench, the excruciating scent of burnt flesh, the iron taint of blood on the air, poisonous fumes of smoke hanging above it all with no wind to clear them away. In the square, his fighters were choking on it, peeling off their helmets to breathe, while men who were his enemies for reasons he didn't know wielded scimitars and pikestaffs, their loose robes swirling, their habitual recitation on their lips.

Over this are Nineteen.

The chant of fanatics who could not comprehend beauty—

who would destroy a millennium of grace if it meant their creed would flourish.

I'll see them all dead before I let them take my crown.

The magic stirred in his veins, a furor of fire and silk.

And then Arsalan's influence surfaced as a different thought came.

I'll send them into the fire before I let them harm this empire or its people.

A delicate lancing of the magic now, scarlet-tipped and eerie in its patience. Stunned by the enormity of its own potential. Chastening somehow.

But how to summon it? How to guide it, *direct* it with subtlety and precision?

His soldiers were waiting for him to act. He narrowed his search to the environs of the gate. If Maysam was dead, where was Khashayar? The spyglass swept around.

There. The younger soldier had assumed command, the edges of his cloak burned, a line of fire racing up one arm. He battled on, ignoring it, as another member of the Khorasan Guard leapt forth to suffocate the flames. Their training stood them in good stead. When one man fell, another moved to replace him in the fluid choreography of the Zhayedan, perfected by thousands of hours of rigorous instruction and put to the test by many battles fought.

They were shocked by their Khan's misdirection of the fire, but they were not undone.

He realized he couldn't help them in the square. And he was too far away to be of any use to the soldiers at the Messenger Gate. The Talisman pressed him from the east. He couldn't abandon the Emissary Gate, when they were the greater threat.

Regroup, regroup—but how?

Trust yourself.

His head snapped toward Arsalan. That was Darya's voice. *Darya's,* not the ghul's. The magic crept toward his heart like a panther padding on its paws. Prowling, steadfast, persistent. A cat whose head was cocked in curiosity. Or in bewilderment.

He had ordered his sister's execution. Once dead, she could not penetrate his mind. The powers of the ghul could not live on after Darya had died.

Darya's voice contradicted his certainty.

Arsalan couldn't do it. He couldn't kill me. He loves you too much to allow you to harm your own soul.

Warning flashed in his mind, his anger scented with blood.

Do not speak of Arsalan to me. Do not presume to know what he is to me or what I am to him.

I cannot speak of you, brother. Your heart is so closed, it has always been closed. But Arsalan I know. I have loved him all my life.

A blinding arc of his magic slipped through his hands like fire, illuminating a path to the Qaysarieh Portal. He glanced around him with care, then across to the Messenger Gate. No one else had seen it. Even Arsalan was immune.

Petal-soft and accented with tears, Darya's voice spoke again.

Just as he loves you. Won't you forgive him this trespass? Will you not grant him my life?

His magic turned, restless and churning, vivid with realization. Spinning. Spinning the truth in its manifold forms.

Arsalan had refused to kill Darya. He had released the ghul, had left it to torment Rukh when Rukh could bear anything but this. Agony gnawed at his insides, his certainties suspect, his judgment—his *faith*—in others called into question again. After the Nizam's betrayal, he had vowed never to trust again. He would not be weakened by affection.

I will not tolerate betrayal, ghul. No matter the source.

It couldn't be countenanced from Arsalan. It couldn't be *thought* of from the friend he loved more than he loved any other.

Arsalan would sooner betray himself. Do you not know him at all? Do you not trust me to know him?

Noise from the courtyard battered his ears. He struck the spyglass against his head, gnashing his teeth, trying to block the insidious lies.

Trust me, Rukh. Trust yourself.

A wild roar left his chest, magnified by the magic, tearing his vocal cords apart.

"You are not my sister! The Princess Darya is dead!"

Arsalan's head jerked toward the agonized sound. Rukh was still holding the spyglass. Across the distance of the square, Arsalan had heard his cry. He watched as Arsalan dipped his head in concern.

A soldier called to him, and Arsalan turned away, but not before Rukh had seen. Not before he had understood the meaning of Arsalan's gesture. The apology for having refused his order offset by his certainty that he had made the right decision.

Rukh doubled over, trying to focus through the pain. If betrayal had come like a thief in the night, he loved the one who held the blade.

The magic became a bewitching frolic, persuading him to relent. It rippled through his veins, thickened with each breath, an elixir sweeter than blood.

At the back of his thoughts, a familiar current flowed. Arsalan's voice, his patient commands, orders flowing in an undisrupted rhythm as he adapted to the variables of battle. The Zhayedan had praised Rukh in the war room, but Arsalan was the fixed center of a world spun into war; he was the center of Rukh's life.

And like himself, the Zhayedan would die for Arsalan. They would die for his ideals.

They would leave no battle unfought; they would give their lives on the field because Arsalan had taught them that Ashfall was worthy of the sacrifice.

Grace, glory, dominion, a future promised from a history of such distinction that empires had risen and fallen while Ashfall remained, a single candle burning in the face of a storm that would not die.

Ashfall was alchemy.

Ashfall was everything they were.

The men who had poured through the Messenger Gate fought with their own rhythms, with the dignity of the cultures they had sprung from, but what were they against Ashfall?

Who were they against a prince?

Who were they against Arsalan?

Rukh raised his arms with effortless grace, feeling the magic touch him, hearing the echo of Darya's soft voice.

Trust me. Trust yourself.

What if the ghul takes you again, sweet sister? What if you are speaking for the ghul?

A hitch in the voice that whispered through his mind. The taste of fear, slippery and cool, silky and skeined with doubt.

I cannot promise you otherwise, Rukh, as I cannot promise myself. But I believe in you as Dark Mage. I believe that in your hands Ashfall will not come to harm.

His hands moved in multifaceted patterns. He allowed himself to dwell for a moment on the things Darya *hadn't* said, the blame she had *not* laid.

He had let her come to harm, not once, but twice. He had denied her love all his life. And then he had stolen the one man she yearned for despite not desiring him himself. This was the cruelty of having everything he wanted before he thought to ask for it, the cruelty of excess.

Such was his legacy as Darya's beloved brother.

A punishing smile edged his lips.

Given the same set of circumstances, none of his actions would change.

Rukh's magic bolstered the gate, perhaps another hour won. Another hour to soften the ache of Arsalan's betrayal. To wonder when the ghul would strike at his empire again. Would strike at him, its heart churning with hate. An agony Arsalan's refusal to obey would force him to relive.

He turned back to the Talisman to vent his wrath upon their ranks.

"Excellency!"

The alarm came from the Maiden Tower, fire licking up white stone, holes punched through massive blocks of masonry by some unknown weapon the Talisman had brought to bear. Projectiles that burst into fire upon contact, collapsing their iron shells. A row of Talisman archers took out the Zhayedan who guarded the tower from the turret. No help in defeating the weapon could now be offered from the watchtower that also served as an armory.

The base of the tower was on fire. If the fire spread, the tower would crumble, and the arsenal within would set off explosions that would bring down the curtain wall.

Soldiers raced to the Maiden Tower in response. Rukh raised

his arms again, his voice hoarse with exhaustion, torn between the Emissary Gate under siege and the imminent collapse of the tower. His power as Dark Mage stuttered in his throat. He was able to direct fire, he didn't know how to extinguish it. He sent his magic deep into Talisman ranks instead, sweat breaking out on his forehead, as he tried to distinguish the weapon that had launched the iron projectiles from a battery of other munitions.

The fire began to spread. He heard the ominous groaning of mortar, as masonry began to shift. He tasted sulfur and charcoal on the air. Could he wrap the tower in a form of protection before the flames swept the pinnacle? Cries of terror escaped from soldiers trapped inside. The stairs—if the stairs were damaged, none of the Zhayedan would be able to stand the watch.

He aimed one hand at the Emissary Gate, the other at the door to the stairs. Divided, the magic faltered. The door to the turret erupted in flames, and the shrieks of immolation from within were cheered by the Talisman below, as the Zhayedan struggled all along the wall.

In the name of the One, what could he do with his powers as Dark Mage?

The Messenger Gate was just holding. There was overwhelming pressure from both the east and the west, and all-out war in the square below. With the magic at his fingertips, how had it come to this? Ashfall was on the brink. His empire would come to naught, his name dishonored for all time. But who would record the empire's losses, and where would the records be kept? The scribes had been slaughtered by his sister, the scriptorium reduced to ash.

And as for the Companions of Hira, or the other Mages, there was no means by which they could return in time to help push back the assault.

He made the decision to let the tower fall. The Emissary Gate had to hold or the Talisman would pour into the city. Nor had he made the decision to evacuate, as there was nowhere that he knew of that his people could flee to safely. Too assured of their superiority, the Zhayedan had not planned for such comprehensive defeat.

He sent a message to Arsalan. This was the endgame. The Zhayedan would continue to fight, but Ashfall would not survive. Arsalan would have to decide when to admit as much.

He was just about to turn his back on the Maiden Tower when he caught sight of a figure racing along the wall. The soldier wore an armored helmet pinned with an arrowhead aigrette. An aventail made of iron hung from the helmet's back, protecting the soldier's neck above a massive quiver that carried a steel-tipped arsenal. The soldier was a Teerandaz archer.

She stopped some ten feet from the base of the tower. She knelt and tipped her head back, pulling arrow after arrow from her quiver and firing them in a zigzag path up the courtyard-facing flank, just above the path of the flames, into the narrow joints between the blocks of stone.

While the arrows were still quivering, the archer jumped to her feet, retreated a dozen steps, then approached the tower at a lightning-fast run. A half-step before the reach of the flames, she vaulted up the side of the tower, using the shafts of the arrows as stepping-stones for her climb. In fifteen paces she was at the top, swinging herself over the wall to land within the pinnacle's protection. She dropped her bow to the ground and pulled out a pair of curved blades. She ran the circumference of the tower, cutting the ropes that framed the turret, slashing open thick leather pouches the ropes held fast in their grip. A weighty white substance hurtled down, as the archer above shouted down a single command.

"Masks!"

The Zhayedan at the base tightened the masks they had donned under their helmets. The archer above did the same. A curious reaction occurred when the powder reached the fire. The flames tunneled upward in a furious, heated rush. The Talisman cheered again. But then the flames were muffled. They surged in a final choked effort, then subsided, spent. Clouds of white smoke coiled up from the catwalk and dissipated in the cool chill of the air.

The archer ran the circumference of the tower again, slashing a second set of ropes that held a heavier set of bags. Water tumbled down in gleaming rushes. The cloud cover was broken, leaving freshness behind. The Zhayedan erupted in cheers.

The archer at the pinnacle called out, "Teerandaz, here!"

A dozen or more Teerandaz archers leapt over the stone debris, the line of figures winding like a serpent up the spiral stairs. At the pinnacle, the archer who had doused the flames issued a series of instructions.

The Teerandaz took up positions.

Their captain shouted a command.

A hundred arrows rained down upon a halfway point between the Maiden Tower and the Emissary Gate. They struck the sturdy wooden mount of the Talisman weapon that had launched the projectiles.

The captain of the archers fired three arrows. The first set fire to the arrows the Teerandaz had aimed. The second propelled a sack into the air above the mount. The third vented the sack, which contained a phosphorous mixture. The launcher hissed before it exploded, its apparatus detonating the weapon's remaining missiles. A giant ball of fire engulfed the Talisman army to the east. Soldiers fell back from the Emissary Gate.

Another hour won.

The archer sped down the Maiden Tower in the same manner she had climbed up, racing to the Black Khan's side, to the thunderous accompaniment of cheers. She ripped off her mask and bowed before her Khan, her ebony eyes ablaze.

"Captain Cassandane returning to duty, Excellency. Where do you want me now?"

15

THERE WAS NO TIME TO RETREAT TO THE WAR ROOM, SO THEY HELD A quick council on the wall, where Rukh and Cassandane met with Arsalan and Khashayar, and a second rank of captains who had filled the holes in the command structure. Zishaan, Niyal, and Shayan were the most senior of these. Niyal was a born negotiator, Shayan a counterintelligence expert, and Zishaan promoted to the post of Captain of the Khorasan Guard.

Cassandane's lieutenant Katayoun, a springy willow of a woman with double-jointed arms, had also been called to consult. She'd welcomed Cassandane's return with open relief and now stood by to listen.

"A spectacular effort, Captain." Arsalan's praise made Cassandane's spine snap straight.

She held his gaze for a moment, a quiet pride in her eyes. Then she bent her head with regret. "I should have been more tactful in my dealings with Captain Maysam; then I would not have been absent from my duty."

Arsalan waved this aside, though his face was set in harsh lines at the fate of the captain of the Cataphracts. "We will grieve when grief is due. We haven't yielded the city, nor *will* we. That must be our focus now."

The younger captains looked at him with something close to awe.

"We need to regroup. Cassandane, you'll command the defense of the Maiden Tower, but I want Katayoun at the Tower of the Mirage."

Katayoun saluted. "I will not fail you, Commander."

He nodded. "Niyal, find two dozen of your best men to accompany the archers." He looked at the young captain. "Their job is to shield the Teerandaz at any cost. We cannot afford to lose a single archer."

"Depend on me, Commander."

"Where do you want me?" Khashayar asked. "Shall we continue as we were at the Messenger Gate, with you at the wall, and me on the ground with the Cataphracts below?"

This was the dilemma. Most of the captains of Khashayar's rank and experience had been killed on the field. He needed someone as seasoned as Khashayar to hold the Emissary Gate. He glanced over at Rukh, whose expression awoke a strange sense of unease. Was it deceptive? Mistrusting? Or disconsolate? He noticed Rukh's fatigue, as he noticed everything about Rukh.

"Are you well, my Prince?"

Rukh's head tilted at an arrogant angle.

"Well enough, I imagine, until treachery strikes from within."

Stillness descended upon Arsalan. The others glanced at him in surprise. He kept his face immobile, his heart beating fast in his chest.

Rukh had said "until," and not "unless." Just as he'd thought, Rukh had guessed that Darya was still alive. He knew that Arsalan had chosen to spare her, in direct defiance of his order. But Arsalan refused to apologize, as he was not the one at fault.

Ignoring Rukh's resentment, he said, "Then I will reassign Khashayar to aid you."

"Will you, indeed?" came the silky response.

Arsalan frowned. This was not the time for games.

Matching Rukh's arrogance, he said, "Unless you think you can hold the gate on your own. In which case, I have more need of Khashayar than you."

Khashayar cleared his throat, but did not interrupt. The Teerandaz archers found that their weapons required their attention.

"You decide," Rukh drawled. "You are Commander of the Zhayedan. You know what is best. After all, your judgment is superior to mine."

Arsalan grimaced, knowing what Rukh accused him of, but out of patience with his Khan. He snapped out orders without taking his gaze from Rukh. "Cassandane and Katayoun, to your posts. Shayan, I want you at the Zhayedan Gate, in close contact with Cassandane and Kat. Zishaan, take your troops to the Emissary Gate. You will assist the Khan. Even a voice as powerful as his cannot reign forever. Khashayar will stay with me."

Rukh's eyes flared at the subtle jab, but a small smile played about his mouth.

He gestured for Arsalan to continue. Arsalan made quick work of reviewing the strengths of his remaining captains.

"Niyal, you will also serve as liaison between the gates. Coordinate communications between the gates and the towers. Be unsparing with the Zhayedan. If one man falls, a dozen must be ready to take his place."

"Commander." The young captain departed without further instruction.

Zishaan cleared his throat. Arsalan turned to the captain he'd assigned to the Emissary Gate. Zishaan's eyes were an inky shade of black beneath the lustrous arches of his brows, his movements supple and expressive. As sleek and lethal as any of the Zhayedan, he often served as Khashayar's personal guard. Well aware of his strengths, he offered his advice.

"Our losses have been heavy, Commander, but there are others we could call upon."

Startled, Rukh asked, "Who? The Zhayedan are the last defenders of this empire."

Zishaan bowed. "Excellency, there are Talisman defectors within the safety of our walls. It is past time for them to be called to assist with our defense."

"No." Arsalan spoke for Rukh. "We are not yet that desperate that we would risk their treachery. Keep them confined as they are, unless I order otherwise."

Zishaan opened his mouth to obey when the Black Khan cut him off.

"Those men came to us under the banner of the Guardian of Candour—the Silver Mage. With all he risked to defend Ashfall, I do not suspect him of treachery."

"Nor I," Arsalan agreed. "But he cannot guarantee their obedience to his call in his absence from the city."

"Do you think me incapable of judging that for myself?"

Arsalan jerked his head at Khashayar and Zishaan. "We will resolve the matter of the Talisman later. Carry out my orders."

He was left alone with Rukh. He felt his anger dissolve at the obvious signs of Rukh's weariness. The battle had not spared him. Like Arsalan, his armor was stained with sweat, smoke, and traces of blood. His features were cold and severe in the opal light of dawn. As compelling as a lightning storm, he was seductive in any guise he wore. Arsalan was shaken by a tremor of response. But this time Rukh didn't smile, didn't tease. When Arsalan tried to grip his forearm, Rukh jerked his arm away.

"Your assurances will not suffice to erase your deceit."

A faint band of color crested Arsalan's cheeks.

"How did I deceive you?"

The color on his cheekbones deepened as Rukh raised a sardonic brow.

"Apart from the obvious, you mean?"

A small part of Arsalan was relieved to hear the humor that undercut the slight.

"There is a war going on," he said with heavy patience. "Might you berate me later?"

Rukh's humor fell away.

"I want those Talisman to fight."

"Why? To punish me for defying your command? Your pride cannot be so feeble that you would punish Ashfall, as well."

Rukh's entire body tautened, dark flames leaping in his eyes.

"Be careful, Arsalan."

A brutal slash of a smile. "As you were careful of me? Again and again, unto a world without end? You expect me to abase myself by falling to my knees—"

"What an apt metaphor for your desires."

Arsalan lunged at Rukh. He gripped the back of Rukh's neck and jerked him close.

"Will you throw my lust in my face whenever we disagree? Is that how you intend to triumph in every contest?"

"I thought it love rather than lust." Rukh studied Arsalan.

His breathing labored, Arsalan demanded, "Then why do you demean it?"

Rukh mirrored Arsalan's gesture and gripped his neck with one hand. A curl of his powerful magic held Arsalan in place.

"Does it demean you to want me?" The magic warmed Rukh's hand, but his eyes were fragments of ice. "I thought I could trust you. I thought I would always be able to trust you."

Arsalan's throat rippled as he swallowed.

"How has anything changed? What have I done that merits this castigation?"

Rukh spat out his sister's name. And then he let Arsalan go, the noise of the battle returning to him in full force.

"The ghul did not die. She spoke to me again."

A whistle came from the tower. Arsalan jerked up his head and nodded at Cassandane's signal. The Teerandaz were engaged in restringing the ropes that bound the pinnacle. New defenses would soon be fastened into place.

Hoarse and discomfited, he asked, "What did Darya say?"

Rukh's mouth was a bleak line of pain.

"She asked me to forgive you. She asked me to take your love on trust."

"Then why don't you?"

Rukh gestured at the ruins of the scriptorium. At the wounds Darya had wreaked upon their bodies and armor, wounds that had been given cursory attention while the battle raged.

"Strange, isn't it? That I tried to kill my sister for you? But you who claim to love me could not do the same to spare me these agonies now."

"What agonies?" Arsalan's attention was riveted on Rukh.

"The agony of battling on *both* sides of Ashfall's walls. The agony of deciding that Darya must die. If you love me as you claim, you should have killed her on command."

Arsalan put a hand to the back of his neck, searching for a lingering trace of Rukh's warmth. But all he felt was cold.

And now the battle called him: he had nothing more to give.

"If you love me as *you* claim, Rukh, you should never have asked."

16

THE CISTERN WAS STAINED WITH BLOOD, ITS SANDSTONE COLUMNS PIT-
ted with marks that were the outcome of a skirmish between the
Assassin and the ghul. For now he held her bound by the webbing
that renewed its tensile strength whenever the ghul struggled.
Two voices raged at him: the ghul inside his mind, and the Princess Darya begging him to end her life. He could not say he wasn't
considering it. If he couldn't contain the ghul, the Princess would
have to die.

Her tear-streaked face was clammy with sweat, her eyes
crimson-tinged and wild. The turquoise lanterns that hung between the columns shadowed her face with the blue cast of death.
Using the webbing like a leash, he edged her closer to the prayer
niche. Perhaps—as Arsalan had suggested—the magic he had
awakened within her might find balance in a place where Darya
had prayed.

The ghul redoubled its efforts to break free, spitting and hissing in his face. He cleared his mask of her spittle and jerked her
forward again. Her fingers bent into claws, scrabbling for an unprotected surface on his body.

"Quiet," he told her, and imbued the word with the majesty of the Claim.

The ghul began to whimper, self-pitying, inhuman sounds as her claws dug grooves within her palms. He stopped. He unwound another length of lace to bind her hands. Taking advantage of his momentary distraction, the ghul jerked free of the leash and leapt away to the colonnade that surrounded the cistern. Water dripped down into the pool in increments, a hush against the wailing of the ghul.

The Assassin used the Claim with perfunctory skill. The ghul contorted her limbs under the weight of his words. She yanked at Darya's long hair. The Assassin snapped at her to stop, so she tore at the webbing instead.

Hudayfah addressed the Princess. "Continue and you will find yourself shorn of any pretense to modesty. If you *wish* to undress before me, that is another matter." He shrugged to make his indifference plain.

The ghul came at him with claws bared, teeth hungry for his throat. He caught her by the wrists and bent her hands at an unnatural angle. A little more force and her wrists would break.

"Stop!"

An urgent request from someone Hudayfah knew. Moving with haste, he spun out skeins of the webbing until the ghul was immobilized, her mouth covered, her fingers bound together, her hands stiff at the wrists.

When she was secured, he glanced back at the cistern. Three figures stood near the pool. The Mages were familiar, the third was a boy he didn't know. They made their way over, aghast as they gazed at the ghul.

"The Princess?" the Silver Mage asked. "Or the ghul who suborned her?"

"When she communicates with her brother, she seems to be herself. But the ghul can reappear without warning—she isn't able to control it."

He was conscious of a burning hostility from the boy with the strange blue eyes. He looked again, with a sense of recognition. Was it the same boy who had accompanied Arian on her quest? He was enlightened at once.

"Free her!" Wafa demanded. "There is no spirit here more innocent than hers."

The boy moved to seize the Princess from Hudayfah's grasp. The Assassin dodged him, holding him back with the dagger that appeared in his hand.

With some haste, Daniyar explained the risks the ghul posed. And then, deciding to trust the Assassin, he told him of events that had transpired since their last meeting. To his surprise, Hudayfah seemed relieved. He made a quick report in turn that described the current state of battle. The Mages exchanged a glance. There was little time to spend in the cistern, then.

"The Princess is a child of Hira—" Daniyar began.

"I told you as much," Hudayfah interrupted.

"I was shown the truth at the Sakhrah. What I'm less certain of is how to free the Princess from the ghul."

"You think them separate?"

Daniyar watched as Wafa took hold of Darya's hands, trying to give her comfort in her state of near suffocation.

"If you know otherwise," he said, "you should tell me now."

The Assassin tipped his mask at the Blue Mage. "He is the one who knows."

Yusuf frowned at the Assassin. "You meddle where you shouldn't."

Hudayfah deflected Yusuf's charge. "It was a fair trade, Mage of Khorasan. I gave sanctuary to many of your manuscripts during the Harrowing of Timeback. And there was one book that intrigued me."

"What book?" Daniyar demanded, with a touch of forewarning. In Timeback, he had asked the Blue Mage the same question.

Yusuf met his eyes, the Blue and Silver Mages linked like pearls on a fine strand of silk. And in conjuring the image, Daniyar realized the truth.

"The Pearl of Timeback." A book similar to the Candour, filled with the rites and knowledge bequeathed to the Mage of the Blue Eye. A book of secrets and magic.

Yusuf nodded. "I sent it to the Fortress of the Assassins. It seems the Assassin took liberties with it."

"Knowledge is power." The Assassin bowed his head. "But I do not intend to misuse it."

"So do all men say." A wry glimmer in Yusuf's eyes.

The three men had fanned out to form a circle around the Princess. They watched one another, rather than the Princess, whom Wafa had now gathered in his arms to defend her from the others. Daniyar turned to Hudayfah.

"You learned something from the Pearl. So tell us, tell *me,* that I may fulfill my charge."

The Princess whimpered again, the noise intensifying, and as it did, Wafa's eyes began to blaze, the irises expanding to bright silver clouds.

The Assassin studied the boy for a moment, then nodded to himself as if he'd just confirmed a long-held suspicion.

"The Mage of the Blue Eye knows the Pearl better than I, but there was a rite mentioned that speaks to the condition of the Princess."

Yusuf shrugged off his cloak, motioning to Daniyar to do the same. And all the while, Wafa watched them, anger and confusion in his eyes.

"The rite of Infisal." Yusuf wondered if the Silver Mage would understand. "A detachment—a separation of the soul from the ghul."

"An exorcism, in fact. How is the rite conducted?" As Daniyar asked this, the silver sword stirred at his side. He put his hand on its hilt in an effort to contain its energy, to calm it, yet the magic worked in reverse. From his doubt and indecision, *he* was calmed.

"Through the recitation of a charm," the Assassin said. "We must call the Princess from herself. Better that there are two of us here to fulfill the rite's requirements."

Yusuf shook his head at the Assassin's explanation. "*Three* Mages are required for the Infisal to be fulfilled."

But the sounds of the catastrophic battle beyond Qaysarieh penetrated the cistern, cutting off further argument.

Daniyar knew of Hudayfah's intense loyalty to Rukh, though he didn't know what lay behind it. What concerned him was that the Assassin's considerable skills could have been placed at Arian's disposal, and served to protect her.

"Will you call the Black Khan from the walls?" A blunt query.

A subtle lift of the Assassin's shoulders. "The Khan's efforts as Dark Mage are needed at the gates. But even if he could be spared, he would not come. The ghul destroyed the scriptorium. And she attacked Commander Arsalan and the Khan. He gave the order for the Princess to be killed."

Darya's piteous cries intensified at the words. Her body shook with tremors. Yet the claws of the ghul did not retract.

"Be gentle!" Wafa snapped. "The Princess can hear you."

Behind his mask, Hudayfah's expression lightened. Of course

the boy would defend her. The Princess had once shielded him from the Black Khan's wrath.

"The Princess destroyed the scriptorium?" A whisper bleak with sorrow from the Silver Mage. A whisper that carried the memory of the Library of Candour.

"The ghul burned it to ash—nothing survived the blaze. She also murdered the scholars of the scriptorium, and the Zareen-Qalam."

A shocked silence fell. The Princess moaned in denial.

Yusuf muttered a prayer. His gaze probed Daniyar's. "Can you confirm that she *is* a child of Hira? Are you certain this was your charge? If you are wrong . . ."

The lessons of the Ascension weighed on Daniyar. He hadn't anticipated the extent of the ghul's malice. Of her raw need for power and control, stolen at her brother's expense.

If she had murdered the Zareen-Qalam and the scholars he had trained, how *could* she be a child of Hira? *Was* she a child of the Claim?

A stirring like the brush of wings against his shoulders.

A word dropped into his mind like a rounded marble, hard and cool to the touch. A word that warned against judgment.

Rahem.

Mercy.

And the construction of a phrase that flowed from it.

In the name of the One, the Beneficent and Compassionate, with mercy in all things.

With the eyes of the others on him, he resisted the words.

Darya's cries became pained.

The phrase inside his mind hardened.

Judge not lest ye be judged.

If this was his charge, if Ashfall's survival depended on it . . .

He found himself looking into Darya's eyes, their beauty shrouded by bewilderment.

Why? she seemed to ask him. *Why, when all I wanted was the freedom to study at Hira?*

"Yes," he said aloud. "She is a child of Hira, and she must be delivered. We must conduct the rite as best as we two can, if her brother will not aid her."

A sob from Darya made him regret the reminder. But he was hungry, aching, and tired, aware of a growing cold that expanded from his core. He needed this to be done.

The Assassin pointed to the small gold carpet beneath the prayer niche. He slipped between Wafa and the Princess, dislodging the youth with a brief touch at his wrists. He gathered Darya in his arms and placed her body on the carpet.

"No one must stand between the Princess and the direction of prayer." He indicated the painted mihrab, an arch of turquoise and gold.

The Blue Mage and Daniyar stood on opposite sides, an empty space in the middle for where a third Mage would have stood. Yusuf recited a phrase in the rich, throaty rhythms of his voice, pushing the phrase back and forth like an abacus bead on a string. Daniyar practiced the phrase, turning its nuances over in his mind.

Humanity. Sincerity. The Dawn.

Verses of the Claim blossomed under these names.

Yusuf raised his hands. Daniyar mirrored the action. His right hand moved in a line from his heart up to his throat, and from there to the top of his head. The webbing that bound the ghul disintegrated. Darya's body jerked. The ghul's claws spiraled out. Her hair began to lengthen, turning white at the crown. Teardrops spilled from her eyes as her claws sank into the mihrab. She tried to peel it from the wall, but in the face of the chant she failed.

Humanity. Sincerity. The Dawn.

The ghul began to wail, Darya's body thrashing at the confinement of the rite. When she could not vent her fury on the mihrab, or on the men who sought to contain her, she slashed at her body with her claws.

"No!" Wafa shouted. "It's not working!" He turned to the Assassin, his eyes burning through his skull. "Do something!"

The Assassin's hands were twisted together, the first sign Daniyar had seen that he was touched by events beyond his control.

The Assassin's voice was laced with menace. "It is *you* who must do something. You who must choose to act."

Yusuf's voice faltered, and Daniyar, too, fell silent, as the ghul leapt and writhed.

Wafa became quiet and composed. "You *know,*" he said to the Assassin.

His eyes found Daniyar's. "And you know too." Wafa's irises had divided like flat-bottomed clouds, the base a pure blue, the nimbus a rising silver.

"Hurry!" the Assassin insisted, as the ghul clawed at Darya's skin.

Daniyar extended a hand to Wafa with a profound sense of sorrow.

"I did not wish this for you."

Wafa gripped the hand that reached for his with a depth of love he couldn't voice.

"All will be well, Guardian of Candour."

He filled the empty place between the two Mages. The three of them clasped hands. Power flowed down the length of their connection, tripling the effect of the chant of Infisal. Vibrant turquoise and silver threads wound about each other to form a visible netting that drifted down upon the girl whose fragile body shook with involuntary spasms.

"We are your protectors in this life and the Akhirah."

The ghul's wailing ceased.

"Therein you shall gain all that your soul desires, all that you should ask for."

The ghul's talons snapped, the claws receding back into the Princess's delicate hands. But fighting the Infisal's power, the ghul's head tossed from side to side—its power not entirely contained. A shriek tore from her throat. And then the Princess began to falter, her skin drained of color, her body of the vestiges of life. She collapsed in a heap on the prayer rug, a stream of blue air issuing from her lips. If the ghul was meant to die, she would take the Princess with it.

Yusuf raised his voice in a new verse of the Infisal.

"Nor can a soul die except by the leave of the One, the term being fixed as if in writing."

The ghul turned her eyes on the Blue Mage and spat forth a stream of vitriol.

But three voices now amplified the closing rite of the Infisal.

"NOR CAN A SOUL DIE EXCEPT BY THE LEAVE OF THE ONE, THE TERM BEING FIXED AS IF IN WRITING."

The power of the chant bloomed to fill the empty cistern, stirring the waters of the basin. Light poured down on the mihrab, its emerald tiles shining like the tail of a peacock, like a bird poised on the verge of flight . . . or a winged guardian at the apex of ascent.

This time, it was enough.

The cobalt stream of air assumed the shape of a sharp-taloned creature that drifted up to the vaulted ceiling. It hung there suspended, its limbs distorted, its hair ragged and wild, its claws pointing to the girl collapsed on the carpet below.

Then the smoke shape broke into pieces and floated away in eerie silence.

The Mages dropped their hands. The Assassin wove between them to catch the Princess in his arms. Her eyes opened, their deep brown color lightened to a smoky topaz deckled with traces of gold. Color returned to the pale skin of her cheeks, the midnight tresses of her hair leached of gray, save for a single white lock.

She looked down at her hands, seeing for the first time with a cry of dismay that the webbing had fallen from her body. Needing no explanation, the Assassin covered her nakedness with his cloak, wrapping it around her and setting her on her feet.

She wobbled a little before she found her balance, the Assassin's hand warm at the center of her back. She looked up at his mask. "How did you free me from the ghul?"

He nodded at the others. "The Silver Mage named you a child of Hira. The others found that reason enough to help."

Yusuf contemplated Darya's transformation, seeing the gentleness beneath the marks the ghul had left on her spirit.

"I did not know whether we would succeed." His gaze slid to Wafa, whose eyes were now like his own.

Then Wafa did something unexpected. He knelt beneath the mihrab, tracing its arch with the fingers of both hands, then touching his fingers to his forehead. In his kneeling position, he reached for the Blue Mage's hand and pressed it to the same spot. He repeated the gesture with the Silver Mage's hand, ignoring his slight resistance.

Wafa rose to his feet, a new light in his eyes.

"I hope you will guide me," he said.

Neither Mage could dispute his right to ask.

"The third Mage." The Assassin's conclusion brought Wafa's secret out into the light. "Though *which* Mage, I cannot say."

A strange ache in his chest because Daniyar knew he could.

17

WHEN THE MAGES HAD LEFT THE CISTERN, DARYA WANDERED OVER TO the pool.

"I prayed here many times," she told the Assassin. "Yet somehow I failed to notice the properties of this pool. Is it a portal?"

When the Assassin hesitated, she concluded the truth for herself. "Of course, it is. The Qaysarieh *Portal*. I should have realized long before now."

She knelt, clad in the Assassin's cloak, to trail her hand through the pool. The waters rippled with a diamond-hard light that bounced off the pool's silver rim.

She felt a peaceful stirring, the faintest trace of a promise. When she glanced down at her reflection in the pool, she ignored her pallor and the smudges beneath her eyes. She focused on the image that had come to mind of a girl-turned-woman wearing a white dress, two circlets on her upper arms. On one hand, she wore a silver and onyx ring that canted on her finger. She twisted the ring into a new shape, and Darya gasped in surprise. Strange filaments of magic shivered over her skin. Her fingers flexed in response, as she heard an echo of the First Oralist's voice, promising her the magic of the Claim.

I will recite it for you, Darya, until you can read it for yourself.

The First Oralist had held her as she cried, and then she had announced, *You are a child of Hira. You belong to us.*

Did she? Aloud, she mused, "I wonder where this portal leads."

She touched the water again, and the image of the woman in the white dress disappeared.

Darya rose to her feet. Unhindered by the costume of the Princess of Ashfall, the movement was limber and graceful, like a swan untangled from the rushes of a swamp.

"I feel lighter. Freer. I suppose I have you to thank for that."

"Do not thank me, Princess. My actions have served you ill."

The light dimmed in Darya's eyes. "Then it's true? The burning of the scriptorium? My assault upon Arsalan? The attack on my brother? They happened?" She shook her head, impatient with herself. "They didn't just happen—*I* did them, didn't I?"

The Assassin bent his head, neither judging nor excusing her.

"I didn't mean to," she said. "I didn't *want* to. But that doesn't change things, does it? I am still responsible for everything I did."

"I am answerable as well."

The curve of her mouth turned down. "You couldn't have guessed what I would do. You thought to serve my brother, as you have always done. You wished to spare him pain."

"You judge yourself yet absolve me of blame. My motives were not so selfless."

The deafening sound of a mortar attack broke through the quiet of the cistern, the end of an interlude that was almost peaceful.

"You should retire to your chambers, Princess. You need food and rest."

She tugged at the single white lock of her hair, unaware that he followed the gesture.

"While the city suffers the ravages of war? Does no one expect more of me than that?"

"What will you do, then?"

"Lend myself to our defense."

Another rare hesitation from a man of the Assassin's will. "Your brother would have you shot on sight."

A tear spilled from the corner of Darya's eye. She wiped it away with a grimace. "I cannot remain in my chambers."

"What skills do you have to lend?"

She knew what he was saying, what everyone said: that her purpose was to be idle, as she lacked the talent for anything else. She was meant to be decorative, an ornament of the court. But freed from the ghul, and awoken by Hira, she knew she had more to offer.

"I must beg my brother's forgiveness, then we shall see." She hadn't shed her wariness of the Assassin, but she had learned to keep her counsel. "Will you aid me in that?"

He bowed. "I would not leave you regardless."

Because he feared the ghul would resurface? The thought was plain on her face.

But what he said was "Because I am the one who brought your brother's wrath upon you." His gaze swept over her in a manner that made her blush. "But you should dress before you approach the Khan."

Her blush deepened, her eyes sliding away from his mask. "Yes, of course."

He bowed again, indicating that she should precede him from the cistern. She tightened his cloak around her as she did.

Neither noticed the shadowy figure that appeared behind them at the pool.

18

AN EARSPLITTING CRY DROWNED OUT THE DULLNESS OF TALISMAN drums at the base of the Citadel. It caught Arian and Sinnia on the far side of the Talisman camp when the portal that was the Well of Souls should have transported them to Hira. Perhaps to the blue-tiled fountains in the open courtyard inside the walls of the Citadel.

Instead, what shielded them from the Talisman advance party was the small rise of a grass-covered hill to the rear of the camp. As the party of Talisman was smaller than the vanguard of the Nineteen that Arian had lulled with the Claim, she could also cover their passage to the Citadel with the use of her magic.

Or so Sinnia thought before two giant birds of prey flamed out of a midnight sky, their cries erupting on the wind. The Talisman took shelter in their tents. On the exposed upper ridge of the rise, there was nowhere for Arian and Sinnia to do the same.

The agonizing, compulsory cries beat down on their heads. Not even the clarion call of the Akhirah could be as destructive as this.

"Drop!" Sinnia flattened herself, and watched Arian do the

same, both of them covering their ears. She struggled with her use of the Claim. She couldn't feel its rhythm, when the stridency of the cries blanketed her thoughts. She peered up at the star-scattered void, trying to see what approached.

Two giant shapes detached themselves from the margins of night, the span of their wings extended above talons spiked like the masts of seafaring ships.

The birds flew over the Talisman camp—once, twice. Sinnia heard the alarm from the ramparts of the Citadel. Adrenaline pumped through her veins. Her heartbeat slammed against her ribs in a jittering rhythm that made her movements propulsive. The piercing cries of the birds made communication between herself and Arian impossible, but she signaled Arian to stay low. She pulled her bow into her hands, rolling onto her back.

The giant shapes dropped into the lower half of the sky, sweeping past the Talisman camp with a graceful turn of their wings. Relief swept over Sinnia when the screaming stopped. Her pulse jumped in her throat as a low boom of thunder followed. The wide belt of grass that divided them from the Talisman caught fire.

Sinnia tilted her head up to see two enormous fire-tailed birds with large reptilian heads open their razor-sharp beaks. A cannonade of fire lashed the vale, burning a path to the hills beyond, smoke rising in great gold plumes above a veil of red rain. The birds wheeled and dipped and scanned the plain below with giant obsidian eyes.

Their tails split and dipped low, their feathers braided like skeins of colored silk, but spiked and abrasive, skimming Arian's and Sinnia's heads. The great talons clutched on emptiness as the birds cried out their fury at having missed their prey.

Sinnia rolled into Arian. "Firebirds! Rukhs from the legends described in the Glory of Kings. But in our legends, the rukh is a noble bird in service to ancient prophets."

Arian put her mouth to Sinnia's ear. "The same phoenix that gives the Prince of Khorasan his name, but I do not think *these* rukhs are given to nobility. Look there." She turned Sinnia's head to the camp. "Their tents remain safe. These creatures are directed by a greater force."

She felt Sinnia's nod, her long, loose curls soft between Arian's hands.

The rukhs wheeled back, wind ripping through the plumes that feathered their heads. In the surreal gloaming that lightened the sky, they caught sight of their prey. The mouth of one opened. A pale green stone dipped to the edge of its tongue.

"Go!" Sinnia pushed Arian away from her body and rolled to the opposite side.

The stone descended with a boom. Fire shot up in a spray from the place where they'd lain. The rukhs' cries were like the screams of dying souls. Neither she nor Arian could summon the Claim in response. A thought flashed through her mind: they needed to work harder at the defensive properties of their magic, when circumstances *didn't* allow for forethought.

She could only pray they'd have time to do so.

The firewall leapt higher, but she could still see Arian. Just as she could see that the Talisman had become aware of their presence. Orders were shouted from the plain, just as the rukhs struck again. The firebirds concentrated on Arian, encircling her with their fire. Then they dropped lower in the sky. The plumes that covered their heads were different colors, one emerald, one a flaming scarlet, though their flat obsidian eyes were the same.

Arian tried to tamp down the fire while dodging the falling stones.

Sinnia ran back twenty paces in the opposite direction. She tucked her hood and cloak around her body, then she picked up speed like the spotted cats of her homeland, gathering herself in a burst of velocity to vault over the firewall.

She landed at Arian's side, the borders of her cloak aflame. She ripped the cloak from her body, freeing her bow and dropping to one knee. Her head angled up, she aimed at the rukhs. Their cries became ferocious as arrows bounced off their plumes. The ears of the Companions bled. The rukhs armored their bodies with their wings, reducing the span of their flight. They flew higher and higher, Sinnia's arrows bouncing away.

Both rukhs converged on Sinnia. The stones they dropped were aimed at her head. Her timing was critical: she moved, danced, fired, and leapt away, the firespray edging closer to her body, as Arian tried to give her cover. But Arian was not as skilled at archery as Sinnia.

"Arian." Sinnia was down to her last few arrows, and the rukhs began to streak down from their heights. "They're not trying to kill you; they're trying to contain you. Give me the arrows you have left. Crouch down beneath me."

As soon as the transfer was made, she balanced one knee on Arian's back and waited for the rukhs' approach. Their lolling tongues rolled back. They knew they couldn't attack without killing Arian. But it seemed they had other weapons. Their hind legs lowered, their blade-sharp talons extended. In the first pass, they came so close that Sinnia's curls tangled in their claws. She didn't waste ammunition. She waited for the next sortie, her knee braced on Arian's back.

"Help me if you can." But Arian's attention was directed to the group that had broken from the Talisman camp, tracking them across the ridge. She tried a subvocal murmur of the Claim. The mournful shrieks of the rukhs speared through the sky, shattering all sound.

The emerald rukh descended first.

Sinnia counted her arrows. When the emerald rukh expanded its wings for its final approach, she fired three arrows into its breast. Two broke off without penetrating, but the third found its mark. A bright crimson stain began to spread. Blood spilled down from the sky. Sinnia dropped her bow and flattened herself on Arian's back, rolling them both to one side.

She grunted as she felt the blood spray drip down one of her arms. It scored a trail of fire from her shoulder to her circlet, and there the injury stopped. Her circlet blazed with a fire of its own, swallowing the slick of blood. The emerald rukh's body thumped down inches from their heads, convulsing the ground like an earthquake.

When the tremors stopped, the scarlet rukh rose again.

"Sinnia!" Arian struggled out from under Sinnia's body. "Sinnia, where are you hurt?"

She reached for Sinnia's arm, about to touch the deep gash on her shoulder, when Sinnia yanked her arm away.

"No! It's poison. Don't let it touch your skin!"

The scarlet rukh's cries filled the sky. The Talisman took cover, as it soared to the heavens then turned and plummeted down.

Ignoring the searing pain in her shoulder, Sinnia shoved Arian a little distance away to give herself room to fight. She discarded her quiver and bow. She balanced her limbs in a warrior's stance, legs apart, eyes aimed at the rukh. She uncoiled the whip at her waist, her teeth gritted against a staggering noise, her ears bleeding.

She knew it from her tortures at Jaslyk. It was a reading—a *rending*—of the Claim that came from the One-Eyed Preacher.

The cries of the rukh were a subversion of the call that heralded the Akhirah. The systems that governed the earth would sink beneath its fury.

Thus assuring his reign.

Arian stood with her sword in one hand, ready to lunge up under the firebird's talons.

"Wait." Sinnia's calm resonated. "The rukh is coming for me."

It sang like a stone flung from a catapult in a magnificent arc.

Closer, faster, deadlier, as Sinnia's keen eyes judged the distance.

At last, its talons extended out, its scaly hind legs together. But before Sinnia could react, the talons turned outward, revealing a padded underside. The rukh dipped low and gripped Arian by the shoulders. Its huge wings flapped twice; it rose with Arian in its grip.

Arian's sword flailed as the rukh shrieked with delight. Her eyes and ears bled, as she rose high above Sinnia's head, her sense of balance lost.

Though Sinnia cursed herself for misjudging the rukh's target, she was quick to adapt. Her right arm flew back. The whip coiled and arched, an instrument of defeat. Grounding herself on the ridge, her strong thighs braced, her powerful arm leaping and flicking, she wound the whip around the rukh's talons just above Arian's hairline—over, under, around and around—and then she jerked with all her strength, bending back the rukh's legs.

"Jump!" she shouted to Arian. "There!" She pointed to a patch of grass.

The firebird tumbled. Arian ripped herself free from its claws. She hurtled toward the ridge, bracing for impact.

Falling from the sky, the rukh shuddered and crashed to a halt, skidding to the ground, its talons scraping Sinnia's throat. It lay gasping for breath, its scaly spine broken. Gemstones spilled from its beak until, at last, its eyes rolled up inside its head.

Winded but unhurt, Arian cleared the distance. She plunged her sword into the rukh's breast. Panting at the effort it took, she drew it out and wiped the blade clean.

She turned to Sinnia to praise her effort when lightning fractured the sky.

SO.

A voice of pure horror boomed inside their heads, louder than the firebirds' cries.

YOU HAVE THE AUDACITY TO ASSASSINATE MY RUKHS.

They quailed beneath the dominion of that voice, terror firing their thoughts.

Puncturing the canopy, a powerful force descended. Cloaked in black smoke, a head with a single piercing eye appeared beneath a towering turban, the face of the shape expanding to fill the sky. The smoke drifted lower, and the shape reached out its hands.

Sinnia measured out each beat of her heart. Beside her, she saw that Arian's head was pushed down beneath the force of the assault, made to bow to the One-Eyed Preacher.

A cry of grief tore through her chest.

The Preacher raised one finger. Sinnia fell to the ground like a minaret toppled by a giant.

Arian struggled to speak through the terror that froze her thoughts. Her trials with the Authoritan were magnified a thousandfold in the presence of the One-Eyed Preacher.

"Self-defense is not assassination."

WHY DO YOU NOT SUBMIT.

It wasn't a question, its purpose to ensure obedience.

Blood-tears began to drip from Sinnia's eyes, the poison in her shoulder scalding.

"I submit to the One," Arian managed. "There is no one but the One."

ACKNOWLEDGE MY SUPREMACY OR DIE.

His voice reached under her rib cage and began to separate tissue from bone, peeling her like a hunter fleshing a deer. She bled and broke and tried to remember the lessons of the Miraj.

Suffused with weakness, she whispered, "You *cannot* kill me, Preacher. I am a daughter of the Claim."

THEN I WILL KILL THE OTHER.

The Preacher closed his hands. A vise tightened around Sinnia's ribs until she felt them crack. She began to pant for breath.

Arian caught Sinnia's arm. Her fingers slid up to Sinnia's circlet. Rhythms of love and sisterhood flowed between them, a feeble replenishing of each. Their circlets glowed, and Arian used their ambient power to fight.

"We are *both* daughters of the Claim. *Which of the One's favors will you deny?*"

A hand reached out. It flung their bodies from the safety of the Citadel.

YOUR PRESUMPTION KNOWS NO BOUNDS.

I AM THE MASTER OF THE CLAIM.

Everything inside her torn, Arian choked out, "The Claim has no master. It belongs to all of us, as does the Criterion."

The voice thundered again. Agony pounded her skull.

WHO TAUGHT YOU THAT NAME.

Help me, she thought. *Please. There must be something that can help me.*

And in making the plea, words came to her mind, words from the Sana Codex.

"The One who created all there is in existence. The One who will see us to the Citadel."

Arian found her way to her knees again, reaching out to clasp Sinnia to her side.

Again, Sinnia shielded Arian from the arm that was smeared with poison, though she leaned against Arian for strength. They held each other close, trying to sustain each other's hopes, each other's gifts. But they couldn't hold out for long.

The One-Eyed Preacher had studied the Bloodprint, and he'd used it to bolster his sorcery. His voice could flay the skin from their bones; he could unravel them with pain.

Now he flicked their bodies over the ridge like pieces of parchment on a wind of ill omen. They landed in the midst of the Talisman camp, surrounded by soldiers on all sides.

The stone that had replaced the Preacher's natural eye turned toward the Citadel. A white light arrowed from the stone to the walls of the Citadel. A dozen fires rose along the ramparts to be met with cries of alarm. A warning bell sounded—late, far too late.

The stone eye did another sweep. The torches that hung from the Citadel's braces were snuffed out. In their place hung a dozen Talisman flags, the symbol of the bloodstained page rippling on the wind.

THERE IS YOUR CITADEL. THERE IS YOUR CRITERION.

Arian and Sinnia exchanged a desperate glance. Help should have come from the Citadel by now. The Companions should have gathered at the walls to face down the One-Eyed Preacher. What were they waiting for?

"No." Arian held on to Sinnia to beat back the pain, each vein and artery stripped of blood, the chambers of her heart tender. She called on an oath from the Codex.

"Over you are watchers. Honest witnesses who know every-thing you do."

The Preacher's voice fell silent at the charge, the briefest re-spite.

The Preacher took a new form then, the figure of a younger man dressed in the clothing of the Talisman tribes, a pagri wound about his forehead, eyes like quarried hematite burning in a skull obscured by the thick shadow of a beard. The smoke dispersed, and the harsh, handsome angles of the skull became clear.

Arian's breath escaped on a sob. Because she *knew* him, his eyes bright and clear, the pupils streaked with rust.

"You—you are from *Candour*."

The pain eased, making it possible for her to think.

"You fought in the earliest phases of the Talisman's ascent. To *liberate* women and children. How—*how* can you be that man? You were on our side . . ." She flung out a hand to the Talisman camp. "And now *this*? This is all your doing. How can that be possible, Preacher?"

She remembered something else, horrible and wrenching, something she couldn't reconcile with her knowledge of the Claim or with the benedictions of the One.

"You won their loyalty at the Shrine of the Sacred Cloak. You wore the Cloak upon your shoulders." Her body was shivering, and now her teeth began to chatter. "You recited the Claim with the Cloak upon your shoulders; you promised the deliverance of Candour. *But you lied*."

She rubbed both hands over her face. Her palms came away wet with blood.

The boom of thunder ceased. The voice of a man spoke in a plain and unaffected dialect. His use of it was *authentic*.

"I did not lie. Do you not remember the history of Candour as it reemerged from the wars of the Far Range? The Russe left us to decades of war, and then there was what came after. If you know me, you know why I rose to leadership in Candour. To put an end to bacha bazi."

The shameful words made Arian sob. The practice of bacha bazi was the reason Daniyar had refused to give up his guardianship of Candour. He'd protected the boys of the city from sexual servitude to warlords, as the practice resurfaced from the old world.

"Of course, I did more than that," the man continued. "You may remember the outrages practiced by the ruler of Lashkar. Every child of Candour knows the story of Helai and Husay."

Arian's sobs shook her body. Helai and Husay, two young girls who had been kidnapped, raped, and mutilated by a warlord from a province east of Candour. This man whose face she recognized had set out to rescue the girls with a group of followers. A violent confrontation had taken place, but in the end the rescuers had triumphed. The warlord's broken body was hung from a minaret, a public denunciation of his crime. And then Helai and Husay had been taken back into their families at their rescuer's insistence. When they'd reached the age of consent, their rescuer had offered them a choice of partners from among the ranks of his followers.

When the girls had refused to marry, their rescuer had described them as innocents and promised his protection for life. Arian had heard the tale as a child, and she had often seen this man's face in manuscripts that recorded Candour's history, before the Talisman had burned them.

"You cannot be that man," she said at last. "That man would never have proclaimed the Assimilate. That man was a protector of the innocent, just like the Guardian of Candour."

"The Guardian of Candour." The Preacher considered this. "His time is at an end."

Arian's heart turned to ice. She felt the truth of it in her bones. She had seen it in Daniyar's eyes, but blinded by the glories of Ascension, she had refused to admit it.

"No." The word was forged from steel, broken from her innermost self. "No, I do not yield him. And you do not hold the power you seem to think you possess."

DO I NOT.

Lightning danced in the sky. The thunder boomed again, the image of the younger man's face vanished, and the smoke shape expanded to cloud over the lightning, the stone eye piercing her skull. He set her arteries aflame, he made her deaf and mute, he blinded her, he wrenched her limbs from their sockets.

She had never known such pain.

She burned and bled and broke. She was subjugated and unmade.

Then Sinnia's arms crept around her, and golden circlets touched hers with a soft, metallic clink. Their circlets aligned, the delicate calligraphy entwined in loops and strokes, and then the words vanished from the circlets and began to drift free, a tracery on the air that rose higher and higher, expanding across the stone-eyed skull. Leaf-thin pages of a manuscript turned. A page opened on a new chapter, and a series of verses from the Codex fell from Arian's lips like drops of honey melting in her throat until . . .

Magic condensed in her veins. It poured from her fingertips in thin gold streams that wove around the image of the skull. The verses were not addressed to Arian, First Oralist of Hira. They weren't meant to be her solace, yet she took them as her own, because the Claim had ever been her solace. It had always supplied her need.

> *Did We not soothe your heart?*
> *And lift from you the burden*
> *That weighed down your back?*
> *And raise for you your reputation?*
> *With hardship comes ease.*
> *Lo, with hardship comes ease.*
> *When your work is done, turn to devotion.*
> *And to the One, turn for everything.*

Fireworks erupted in the sky. Arrows rained down on the Talisman camp. Voices chanted a welcome from the walls.

The Citadel had joined the battle.

When Arian looked again, the One-Eyed Preacher was gone.

19

ARIAN CALLED DOWN THE CLAIM ON THE TALISMAN, CLEARING A PATH to the Citadel of Hira. Sinnia's voice echoed hers, as men screamed and died.

The Claim was a furnace in Arian's mouth, and she used its fire without mercy. Her lips curved in triumph. Talisman soldiers broke beneath the words, a dozen or more at a time. *This* was what the Claim was meant to be. Thunder in her heart, power beyond containment.

She relished the strength it gave her, shamed by her feebleness before the One-Eyed Preacher. The Claim had stripped her weakness away. She could rend the skies with her voice, immolating anyone who dared to stand in her way—

"Arian!" A cry of fear and uncertainty from Sinnia.

What will the Claim be in your voice?

All will bow before me. All will tremble at my recitation.

No!

Her forgotten oath resurfaced.

Justice, equity, peace.

They were inside the Citadel, and once inside Hira's walls, the fury of the Claim was calmed, a power held in abeyance, for the next time, and the next.

The handsome guard who had accompanied her once before met her inside the gate.

With an effort she remembered his name.

"Captain Azmaray, why was the Citadel late to come to our aid?"

He seemed struck by her transformation, or perhaps he struggled to accept the use she had made of the Claim as the Talisman camp burned.

"The Companions have been in Council. But when the General became aware of the attack, she called us to your defense." His glance flicked to Sinnia, and he murmured a courteous greeting.

She answered him in kind, then asked, "The Council remains in session? When we are under threat of attack?"

A frown marked Azmaray's brow, and with it a trace of doubt. "The High Companion convened the Council to debate matters of defense. After calling the Citadel Guard to your aid, the General returned to Council as a matter of expediency."

Arian pondered Psalm's actions. "Do you know what the General found so pressing?"

He smoothed a wing of dark hair from his forehead. "The workings of the Council are closed to the Citadel Guard." With a slight reproach, he added, "As you well know, sahabiya."

Arian accepted this without question, though her sense of urgency remained. "Please return to your post on the wall. We have no need of an escort."

"The High Companion asked me to report on your return."

Thunder cracked all around them, and Arian raised her brows. "I'm on my way to see her, so there's no need for you to come."

Azmaray made no apology, his hard features acquiring a subtle edge, his voice shedding its deference. "I serve at the High Companion's pleasure."

Arian brushed past him. "The Citadel Guard serves the *Citadel*. I suggest you remember that before the Citadel falls."

His face closed down, and he left them with a curt bow.

Sinnia caught Arian up at the tower that led to the Upper Citadel, describing her vision of Ilea during her experience of the Ascension. As Arian listened, the waters of the hammam were quiet, the playful fountains still. The use of torches was limited, the Citadel Guard at the walls, except for a small contingent at the door that led to the scriptorium.

They had been climbing the tower stairs, but now Sinnia came to a halt, as she considered their reception by Ilea. "If the Council is convened, should we take a moment to dress?"

"Given what you've just told me, this can't wait. It worries me that the Council should be in session now."

She glanced out along the walls. Guards were in position above the gate, but along the walls the battlements were deserted, arrangements that augured poorly for the Citadel's defense. But she paused as she realized other measures had been taken. Harmonies of the Claim were arranged in subtle rhythms above the Citadel Gate. She touched the harmonies lightly with her thoughts and recognized the Companions had tried to do their part.

"Help me, Sinnia." She cast both arms out, the Claim a shuddering power she had only just contained. Sinnia lent her gifts to the effort. They vocalized verses of terrible import, draping them over the barricades. Their long, low lament settled along the ramparts.

"This will have to do for now, though without the full strength of the Companions, these wards will not protect us for long." She jerked open the door to the tower.

Sinnia's footsteps echoed Arian's as they climbed, the air inside the tower stifling. They passed into the Council Chamber, where the Companions were in some form of battle dress, including the High Companion, who was wearing her golden armor.

The Companions were arguing back and forth on one side of the fountains of the All Ways, with the High Companion on the other, seated on the White Throne, her posture reminding Arian of the Begum of Ashfall: a queen accepting the homage of courtiers, except that the Council was a consultative body, and not—as Ilea wished—a docile and fawning court.

Arian and Sinnia descended the tiers of the chamber. At first no one noticed, so intense was the discussion. But gradually Companions gasped in recognition as they passed. When they reached the All Ways, the fountains' intricate patterns collapsed, the turquoise waters falling quiet. When Sinnia would have crossed the boundary, Psalm reached out to pull her back. She addressed the Council at large.

"My contention has proven true: this is the wrong time to rule on the First Oralist's standing. Let us deal with the threat at our gates. Then, if you still deem it necessary, the Council can be resumed with Arian and Sinnia present."

With a sense of shock, Arian realized that this wasn't a consultation over matters of defense: *she* was the reason the Council had been convened. She turned back to Psalm, who gave her an oblique glance.

"Your trial in absentia has advanced," Psalm said in a lowered voice. "Ilea has rendered a verdict of expulsion even though that is for the Jurist to do. We are contending with these . . . anomalies." A careful description of Ilea's personal animus against her. Psalm took in Arian's expression and added, "If you could vanquish the Preacher, you have nothing to fear from Ilea."

Arian's concern was for the Citadel. "The Preacher will return! This reprieve won't last."

"Then be quick about stating your case. Ilea perceives you as the greater threat."

"She underestimates the Preacher."

"You underestimate Ilea." The Citadel's general grimaced. "This farce of a trial could mean the end of Hira. You cannot let that happen, Arian."

Beneath Psalm's customary calm, Arian detected a tremor of relief. An old loneliness had been assuaged with Arian's return. She had been Psalm's confidante, the two of them aligned in their bleak understanding of the Talisman's endgame. Her backing at the Council would strengthen Psalm's position, ensuring that Ilea would be forced to hear their concerns.

Arian pressed Psalm's hand in gratitude. It was Psalm who had held the Citadel against the Talisman this long: the rest was up to Arian.

She crossed the boundary of the All Ways. Ilea rose from the White Throne to meet her, her greeting cold and unequivocal.

"You dare to trespass in this chamber."

Arian had been expecting rage, even condemnation. Instead, she was met with this cold disapproval, as if Ilea had gained an advantage and was certain her judgment would prevail.

"How could I be trespassing when I am a Companion of Hira?"

A banked fire in her eyes, Ilea continued. "You were stripped of rank and banished from Hira because of your transgression of the law. The verdict has been rendered. You have no standing here."

But from the muted whispers of protest, Arian could tell the Companions were not as certain of that in light of her return.

Their anxious queries filled the chamber. The Companions

named for the Mothers of the Believers—Saw, Moon, Ware, Rain, Zeb, and Dijah—held themselves aloof, as if the allegations were so dire they couldn't bear to look at Arian. But could these women who had taken her in, and raised her up as First Oralist, so easily credit her corruption?

Her gaze moved through the chamber, searching for Ash. Ash nodded coolly, and Arian's breath caught. Had Ilea also managed to persuade the Citadel's Jurist against her? Psalm had spoken of the *forms* of justice, not of the Companions' support. She passed a hand over her face to shield herself from the thought.

Turning back to Ilea, she crossed her arms and pressed her hands to her circlets. They flared to life, the script on the golden bands aglow.

"Strange. My belonging to this Council does not seem to be in doubt."

Nervous laughter rippled up the chamber's tiers.

The Jurist came forward. The waters of the All Ways rose to greet her. She dipped her head and touched her circlets. "Peace be with you, Arian."

"And with you, Ash. Have you ruled on my expulsion in my absence?"

The silver lanterns burned bright in response to the richness of her voice.

Ash contemplated the tips of her long fingers. "In your absence, the matter was out of my hands, but as you have arrived in time, you have the right to be heard." She directed this last at Ilea. "The accused has returned. This hearing must be reopened."

Arian and Sinnia exchanged a glance. How long had Ilea been planning this? Though the question perturbed her, Arian asked calmly of Ash, "May I know the charges against me?"

Flustered, Ash's hands twisted together. "The High Companion has accused you of abandoning your Audacy." She met Arian's eyes, her own unreadable. "You have also been accused of renouncing your vow of chastity. The High Companion submits that you gave yourself to the Silver Mage in a flagrant demonstration of lust." She paused, choosing her words. "And it is known you share a history with the Guardian of Candour, who came before this Council at one time, to ask us to release you from your vows."

Ilea pointed to Arian's hand in triumph. "They share much more than history! The First Oralist wears the ring of the Silver Mage—what further proof do you require?"

The ring's lustrous radiance spilled into the chamber, lighting the Companions' faces. They gaped at it in surprise. They may have been disposed to discredit the accusations, but the truth of the ring was undeniable. Several of the senior Companions expressed their disapproval, but a stunning Companion of mixed Hazara and Shin War ancestry offered Arian an opening. Her name was Mask, and Arian had entrusted her with the care of the Hazara who had fled to Hira weeks ago.

"Is it true, Arian? I would gladly hear your account."

Comforted by her compassion, Arian took a moment to inquire, "Are your people well, Mask?"

"If you think to win Mask over with this show of concern for the refugees you forced her to take in, know that your schemes will not succeed!" Ilea accused. "The judgment against you stands!"

Ilea's fury froze the waters of the All Ways. The chamber was now quiet. Then Arian waved her hand in a delicate display of strength, and the fountains resumed their dance.

"The well-being of the Hazara isn't something I would exploit."

No one doubted Arian's sincerity when the truth rang like a warning bell from the heights of the Citadel Gate.

Mask ignored Ilea's outburst. "They are indeed well, First Oralist. Half-Seen and I thank you for the risks you took on their behalf."

"I caused more harm than I wished. Sinnia delivered them to the safety of the river, and *you* received them at the Citadel." She faced the senior Companions. "The rescue of the Hazara will have been in vain if we do not make ready to face the One-Eyed Preacher. You must have witnessed his arrival."

There was a cry of assent from the junior ranks, and Arian looked to Ash.

"Look to *me*, First Oralist!" Ilea made the Claim an imperious demand. "The *Companions* will attend to the Preacher once we've dealt with the threat within."

She means me, Arian thought. *But how could I raise my voice against the women of this Council? How do my convictions threaten them? And why does the High Companion see this darkness in me?*

But she bit back her anger and said, "Then may I address the allegations? If I recall the rules of Council, it is *Ash* who must render a verdict as our Jurist." In an undertone, she advised, "Do it quickly, Ash."

"What possible defense could you offer when you flout your defiance of our laws?" Her face ablaze with anger, Ilea moved to seize the ring of the Silver Mage. A blinding light pulsed from the ring, and Arian pulled her hand away.

"Isn't that the purpose of a trial—to allow for proof of innocence? Though I can hardly think it auspicious with the Talisman hammering our gates."

Ilea whirled to face the Companions. "The First Oralist seeks to avoid your judgment, as she knows there is no proof that would justify her desertion. She insults this Council with her divided allegiance."

"Desertion?" Arian echoed, grim fury in the single word.

Her eyes gleaming with a canny light, Ilea resumed her seat. "Did I miss your return with the Bloodprint? Or do I need to remind you that you were told to bring it to Hira? In your lust for the Silver Mage, you freely abandoned your Audacy. The only matter that occupies you now is how to gain dispensation."

Ilea's manipulation of the Claim was nearly imperceptible: it stirred embers of loneliness within Arian, taunting her with the neglect of her sisters in pursuit of a hopeless Audacy, while lewd insinuations were distilled to members of the Council.

Ilea's execution of her tactics was flawless, its effect on the Companions stark. But in the wake of the trials of the Israa e Miraj, its impact on Arian was slight.

The unmaking of the world . . . the clarion call of the Akhirah . . . the terror-stricken reckoning with the darkest parts of her soul—the cataclysm of Ascension had steadied Arian's sense of herself, preparing her for this confrontation.

She directed her answer to the Council.

"I have not surrendered my allegiance—why would I return if I had?" She touched the ring on her finger, swept by a wave of love, of comfort when it was most needed. "But I do not deny I am bound to the Silver Mage, an attachment I willingly formed." She shook her head at Ilea's malice. "That you would reduce a consecrated bond to little more than lust—"

"No!" The desolate cry came from Dhiya, a Companion from Tanah Melayu. "No Companion of Hira may be bound to a man. The High Companion was right to accuse you—you *have* renounced the Council. We looked up to you, Arian," she said in anguish. "How could you do such a thing?"

Attempting humor, Sinnia offered, "Have you *seen* the Silver Mage?"

"Sinnia!" The pained rebuke came from Dijah, a Companion whose authority and standing were such that Sinnia bent her head before her. "Please do not mock our traditions by coveting a man's beauty, no matter that he *is* the Silver Mage."

Sinnia made a sound of distress. "Forgive me, Mother, but is it covetous to mention beauty when all beauty derives from the One? If you knew the Silver Mage, you would know his character is as noble as his bearing. How else should we judge a man?"

"This Council was not convened to debate the qualities of men!" Dijah's conflicted gaze turned to Arian. "The Silver Mage could be a prophet of the Claim, and still that would not extenuate the infringement of your vows. You know these tenets bind us all."

Arian raised her head. Dijah's sorrow was painful to bear, but she held the eyes of the woman who had comforted her childhood terrors. Though she had grown frail, age had not diminished the Mother of the Believers; it had only enhanced her stature.

She reproached herself for being the cause of Dijah's unhappiness, but it was imperative the Companions know the truth. "I give you my word that I've held to my vows. Nor did the Silver Mage seek to persuade me otherwise. Yet the High Companion accuses me while concealing her own indiscretions."

Dijah's indrawn breath was audible. She turned her face away, as if Arian's allegation was a great source of shame. Ilea seized the opportunity to step into the breach.

"Arian *confessed* her transgressions; this counteroffense is nothing but a ploy!"

Ash interceded swiftly. "Arian did not confess to *sexual* transgression—in fact, she expressly denies it. She merely spoke of an attachment. And I would hasten to add, to accuse chaste women of sexual transgression without producing four witnesses to the act is a violation of the law. If such a course were to be pursued, the accuser's testimony would be discounted hereafter." The line of her mouth tense, Ash glared at Ilea. "You have not been able to summon *any* witness to misconduct, and I will not permit a misreading of Arian's admissions." She turned to Arian. "I would say the same to you, First Oralist."

The tightness around Arian's heart eased, even at this reprimand. She had underestimated Ash—she *hadn't* been convicted in absentia. "I'm afraid I would not be able to call four witnesses to a similar charge against the High Companion. But I ask you to consider *why* she accuses me, given her intimacy with the Black Khan, the man she admitted to these very chambers."

A concerted gasp sounded from the Companions. Dijah murmured a prayer that sought forgiveness from the One. It was echoed by Rain and Saw, who had withheld their approval of the Black Khan's presence in their midst. The Companions whispered to one another in confusion.

Ash frowned at Arian. "You make a serious claim. As I have warned you, if you cannot produce evidence to support it, you should not make it either."

Arian called Sinnia to her side. "I would be guided by your counsel, Jurist, but in this instance what I have to say calls into question the High Companion's motives for wishing to expel me. She conspired with the Black Khan to deliver me to the Authoritan. Though she sent me after the Bloodprint, she never intended to allow me to deepen my knowledge of the Claim—not when it might challenge hers. Her naked desire for power in the face of all this"—Arian indicated the thunder that rattled the Citadel's walls—"would see me exiled from Hira at the moment my gifts are needed most." She sought out Dijah again, gentling her words with the Claim, a mark of her deep respect. "Why should the High Companion do this? Why dispossess the Citadel of *any* weapon in its arsenal? The timing of this trial is ill-judged. We must turn to the Citadel's defense and commit to the fight against the Preacher. If the Council should rule against me in the aftermath, I will accept the judgment. But if the Citadel should fall—"

"Enough!" Ilea thundered. Seething with jealousy, she charged, "You have always tried to usurp my role, and now you would challenge my command! I will not say it again: *You have no standing here.* It is not up to *you* to accept the verdict. My judgment on you is final."

Anticipating Ash's protest, Ilea gripped the Jurist's throat with the savage power of the Claim. The Companions were stirred to protest this abuse, but it was Dijah who raised her voice.

"You do not have the power to enforce your judgment. You insist on adherence to our laws, and are right to do so, but the *benefit* of the law applies equally to Arian. She has the right to a defense, and if you continue to deny her, we would need to consider not only the validity of your ruling, but your decision to move forward with these proceedings at this time."

The Companions' approval of Dijah's argument was vocal, catching Ilea off guard. Her thoughts raced along a well-worn track, simmering with bitterness and rage: If the Council were to turn against her, her larger aims would be thwarted. And it would be Arian's doing.

Dijah now turned to Arian. "I appreciate the urgency you speak of, but I warded the walls myself when we were summoned to Council—"

"We strengthened those wards," Sinnia put in, and Dijah's shoulders slumped with the weight of her relief.

"You were wise to do so, my child."

Arian rallied. "The wards won't hold for long against the One-Eyed Preacher."

"Arian, we do understand the danger." Dijah's reproach was mild. "What we do not know is whether you abandoned your Audacy, or how you would justify your bond with the Silver Mage. If you expect us to follow you in ignorance, how is that any different from the High Companion's demands?"

Ilea's eyes flashed at the charge, but Dijah continued gravely, "If you would have our trust, Arian, give us the same in return. We deserve an explanation, so the only question that remains is whether you will submit to the Council's demands."

Arian bowed her head, abashed. Dijah could not be faulted for her gentle admonition; it was Arian who had chosen to disregard her duty.

A catch in her voice, she said, "Forgive my lack of humility. My thoughts have been preoccupied with the battle at our walls—"

Dijah held up a hand to stop her. "Do not make excuses for yourself."

"Then where would you have me begin?"

Dijah's conference with the senior Companions was brief. "If we are to believe your account of your Audacy, we must trust in your integrity. Tell us of the Silver Mage. If he did not lead you astray, there is no question of expulsion, nor any reason for us to doubt your word."

Arian swallowed a hasty reply. The question was more than warranted; it was the insult to Daniyar's honor that was painful to bear.

"I fear the High Companion has given you the wrong impression," she said with quiet dignity. "The Silver Mage asked to pledge himself to me in an *honorable* bond, without lessening my status as First Oralist. I promised him that if the time should come—if the future we dream of for Khorasan should come into being—I would ask for this dispensation."

A shocked murmur ran through the ranks of the Companions. Saw and Rain were shaking their heads. Moon muttered her flat refusal.

Silencing the others, Dijah asked for clarification. "The Silver Mage would wed you?"

"Yes."

"And you would take him in turn?"

"If he should return to me. He has joined the battle of Ashfall. But if he survives—if *we* survive—I would take him as my own." A thought occurred to Arian, a truth of the Claim that she wanted Dijah and the others to hear. "I would be his garment, just as he is mine."

Dijah's expression didn't change, but the younger Companions stirred at this echo. Their faces softened with appreciation for Arian's dilemma, for her words were a declaration of an abiding love.

Ilea's cold laughter cut across the chatter. "The First Oralist implicates herself without the need for witnesses. Is anything nearer to a woman's body than her garment?"

Arian faced her without flinching. "You would know better than I."

Scandalized whispers filled the chamber. Then Mask cried out, "Stop this, please stop this! We will not be able to undo the damage we are doing to ourselves. We are tarnishing the name of the High Companion, and slandering our First Oralist."

In the silence that descended, Half-Seen asked to be heard.

She was younger than the other Companions of senior rank, yet she was held in great esteem as the Collector of the Claim.

"I fear you have misunderstood the verse in question, High Companion, and perhaps this is why you accuse the First Oralist. The garment is a metaphor for closeness. Those who are joined in an honorable bond have no secrets from each other; they keep each other from harm, they serve to enhance each other's dignity." She gave a modest cough. "As any close study of the Tradition will reveal."

Psalm shot a glance of triumph at Arian. More than anyone, their general understood the need to return to their walls, and now things were moving in their favor.

Ash walked over to press the Collector's hands. "Thank you, Half-Seen. We are grateful for your wisdom, as always." She took a moment to collect herself, having never ruled on such a matter before. "But though I appreciate the sentiment, the Companions must be exempt from these considerations. We cannot subvert centuries of tradition."

"You permitted the Black Khan to address this chamber," Sinnia reminded her. "That was quite a subversion."

"As per the needs of circumstance. There is a difference between our personal desires and our roles as members of this Council." Ash took no pleasure in the distinction, but it was this abstention from sentiment that made her own Audacy so powerful. She turned back to Arian. "I'm sorry. Anything else would weaken us. But in the absence of evidence to support the charges against you, you cannot be expelled from the Council. That said, I regret that I'm unable to rule on the matter of dispensation. I studied our histories at the Silver Mage's request, but the High Companion refused to grant him a hearing."

And though Arian deeply desired that dispensation be approved, she did not disagree or speak to oppose Ash. The survival of Hira had to be her first concern, whereas Ilea was fiercely driven to use the trial to rid herself of a First Oralist whom she saw as her rival.

"The matter was plain to me," Ilea said now. "I may *choose* to ask the Jurist for a ruling, but if I am self-guided, I am not bound to do so."

Melati, a young and lovely Companion from Nusantara and a specialist in the arts of the book, who often studied with Half-Seen, now spoke. "Forgive me, Exalted, but in my understanding, that would require you to establish *evidence* of self-guidance."

Half-Seen nodded her approval. "Melati is correct. You cannot assert a right without establishing the basis for that right. And to address the question of the Tradition, ours is a living tradition, meant to flourish and expand. It was designed to adapt to new realities. That its development was arrested before the wars of the Far Range is a crucial loss to us all." She pointed to the fountains. "The significance of the All Ways is that we consider *all* ways."

"It's what separates us from the Talisman," Sinnia said quietly to Arian.

Arian nodded grimly, her thoughts still attuned to the battle coming to their walls.

The Companion named Saw, who had not yet spoken publicly, now objected to the point Half-Seen had raised. A descendant from the Najjar tribes of the holy cities, she was one of the few Companions who wore a veil, and in the tradition of her people, she had wrapped her veil tightly around her forehead. Learned in the history of the holy cities, she was familiar with the Claim's jurisprudence. Her talent for simplifying complex matters had earned her the Council's respect.

"You speak of innovation in matters of faith, Half-Seen. What Arian asks of us would be an innovation, and all innovation is forbidden. As Collector, surely you know this."

Half-Seen stood her ground. "Unless the act considered to be an innovation should, in fact, have a precedent. But even if a new practice *is* an innovation, as long as it does not violate the spirit of the Claim, it is open to our consideration."

Saw shook her head. "If a precedent existed, the question would be moot."

Melati wasn't as intractable. "Much of our history was lost after the wars of the Far Range. We know there are gaps in our knowledge of how the Tradition was construed."

Saw mulled this over. "Are you aware of a precedent, Collector? Or do you support a new practice?"

A beautiful smile settled on Half-Seen's lips. "Only the precedent of the first Companions. They were not known to be celibate; many were bound in marriage. Could *their* example be unlawful?"

"Most of the early Companions were men," Saw pointed out. "And do not forget that the Mothers of the Believers were held to a different standard. The same would hold true now for Companions senior in rank."

"So again, men obtain an advantage that is denied to women. Is that what our Council stands for?" Half-Seen's glance touched on the senior Companions. "Not all of us were named for the Mothers of the Believers. And wasn't there a time in our history when even the Mothers of the Believers were honored by a sacred bond themselves?"

The Companions were thoroughly engaged by this discussion of their history. They were ready to continue in this vein, but Ilea silenced the chamber with the static thunder of her voice.

"Enough! You debate niceties of law while the Talisman prepare to invade. The First Oralist's desire to be granted dispensation is the least of our concerns. *The question before us is one of Arian's allegiance.* The Silver Mage would demand the First Oralist's loyalty, an allegiance due solely to us. If it is given elsewhere, how could this Council trust Arian with its future or survival?"

Such dark rage underscored the question that Arian knew Ilea would compel the Council to agree. There was one path forward for the Citadel, a path Ilea had determined according to her own calculations: to hold power and hold it without accountability. She was cutting short the debate as it turned in Arian's favor, using Arian's plea for urgency against her. An act of desperation on Ilea's part, but also an illustration of her ominous command of the Claim. So much so that the Companions failed to notice Ilea's swift change in tactics.

Her thoughts moving quickly, Arian focused on Ash. "The High Companion cast these charges as a matter of my character, but if she is judging my *loyalty,* it is easy for me to answer. During the course of my Audacy, I came to view the question of allegiance in a different light. Sinnia and I found refuge with the Negus, and the Queen of the Negus taught me to see that the fidelity we owe is not to the rules of Council, *but to the All-Seeing One.* In an honorable bond between two partners, the One is always the third. And if these bonds are blessed by the One, how can the Council deny them? How can the Council view them as the basis of disloyalty?"

Mask sounded uncertain. "Do you say this, Arian, after everything we have seen men do to the women of Khorasan? Have men honored these bonds by respecting the guidance of the One? Based on your own encounters, could you make such a claim?"

Mask came to Hira from Maze Aura. She had seen the worst of the Talisman, and knew their cruelties well. She couldn't know why Arian's position had altered. But to speak to Mask's concerns, Arian posed two questions. "Do you think of women as victims? Do you see us as powerless, Mask?"

Mask hesitated—she sensed there were nuances she might have overlooked.

Arian offered her own conclusion. "I know that I don't. Nor do I count all men as among those who would enslave us. This Council asked me to share the outcome of my Audacy. If I have your consent to continue, I will answer your questions."

Cautioning Ilea not to interrupt, Dijah nodded at Ash.

20

ARIAN BEGAN WITH THE STORY OF ALISHER, THE POET WHO HAD SAVED her from gruesome violation in Black Aura. She described Arsalan, the Commander of the Zhayedan, who had defied his Khan to protect her from being blooded. And Khashayar, the soldier of the Khorasan Guard who had risked his life to escort her on her quest, leaving the city he loved as it faced apocalypse. She spoke of the gentle equality between the men and women of the Cloud Door, and of their Aybek Zerafshan, who had accepted without quarrel her refusal of his offer of marriage. She told them of Illarion, a captain of the Ahdath, who had assisted in Sinnia's rescue from Jaslyk. She expressed her admiration of Salikh, the teacher of the Claim who inspired the followers of the Usul Jade, and of a man named Ruslan who had sacrificed himself to her cause. She gave them her account of the First Blood of the Bloodless, who had shown her such respect in relinquishing the Bloodprint to her care. Of the Alamdar who had sheltered them in the lost city of Firuzkoh, and the Hazara who had wept with gratitude for the prayer she had offered for their dead.

Tears slid down her face when she told them of Turan, killed before her eyes in Marakand, giving his life to save a boy he knew she loved. She made herself speak of the Hazara boy Wafa, who had no reason to trust a woman from the tribes that had massacred his people. Defying his Talisman masters, the boy had killed to save her. He'd known the cruelty of whip and cudgel, yet had learned to trust her. He'd taken Arian and Sinnia as his own.

Her words caught them all in a trance as, more than anything, Arian wanted them to realize how narrowly they had conceived of the greater world beyond their walls. Answering the questions they had posed, and speaking through the Preacher's thunder, she told them of Daniyar. His rescue of her at the Shrine of the Sacred Cloak. His killing of his own cousin to save her in Firuzkoh. His escort along the dangerous route to the Sorrowsong. His tortures at the Ark, where he had offered himself to the cruelty of the Authoritan in order to save her from worse. She described her duel with Najran, the duel she wouldn't have survived if Daniyar hadn't found her at Jabal Thawr. She spoke of his self-denial. She told them of the battle at the airship, and how he had lain feverish and broken in her arms. And that when he'd come back to himself, she had decided to relent. She had tried to bind herself to him, but *he* had spoken of her vows. He'd insisted her consent be purposeful, and given to him without regret. He had valued Arian's honor at the moment she'd chosen to forsake it.

A ripple of understanding whispered through the chamber.

"He wore the Sacred Cloak. He walked alone into the heart of the Talisman to persuade their commanders to end the attack on Ashfall." Arian's voice faltered at the memory. At the unbearable loss that had gripped her. She thought about everything Daniyar had done, everything he *was,* and she gave them the one truth that mattered above all others.

"The Guardian of Candour yielded the *Candour.* He offered

it up at the Cloud Door; he bartered it for safe passage behind the Wall. He did this to further my Audacy. He did it for me *as* First Oralist of Hira. If the time ever comes to speak of dispensation, I would ask that you remember his sacrifice. And I hope this Council will not think to impugn his honor again."

Ascendant on the White Throne, Ilea clapped her hands. "A pretty recitation!"

Arian tilted back her head. "Do you doubt his character when he strengthened your gifts during the Conference of the Mages?"

The thunder battering their walls grew louder, but Ilea persisted. "*You* are the one I doubt. Despite this tender account of your travels, you failed to return with the Bloodprint, the sole purpose of your Audacy."

Wearily, Arian answered, "I did not say I was invincible against the One-Eyed Preacher."

"Ah." A catlike smile flicked across Ilea's face. "And does that not answer the charge?"

Sinnia bristled, her spine prickling with warning. "To founder against the Preacher does not establish desertion! We may not have recovered the Bloodprint, but that doesn't mean we failed. Tell them the rest, Arian."

"You didn't abandon your Audacy, you didn't offend your vow of chastity. In fact, you did nothing wrong," Ilea mocked. "Yet the only defense you are able to conjure is the dubious one of your character. Despite the intimate encounters you have described at such length." She drew herself up in triumph. "You neglected to mention the time you spent in Ashfall, or to explain your relations with the prince of the city himself." She infused the words with innuendo.

"I leave the Black Khan to you," Arian said coldly. "Though treacherous, your acquaintance is deeper."

Mask's soft protest recalled her to herself—to the purpose of the Council. Seeking comfort, Arian came to stand beside Sinnia, her palms turned up in supplication. Sinnia placed an arm around Arian's shoulders, and slowly, her anger subsided. It was time for the Council to decide how they would judge her in the end, so she offered the one defense Ilea could not refute.

"The High Companion defames me." Breath held, she glanced around the chamber, allowing the silence to build. Then quietly she asked, "How can you doubt my honor when I was chosen to ascend?"

Dijah's face crumpled, the string of her prayer beads pulled tight around her wrist. She leaned closer to the All Ways, her voice the merest thread.

"You were chosen *to ascend*?"

Arian's eyes touched upon each Companion in the chamber.

"I completed the Audacy I determined for myself. I fulfilled the Israa e Miraj."

Dijah stared at her, speechless.

"Both Sinnia and I were chosen to ascend, and so I ask you to honor my service to this Council, and to remember who I am. It is who I have always been—your First Oralist."

Ilea's voice shattered the White Throne. She yanked Arian around to face her. "How *dare* you tell us these lies? How dare you debase Sinnia in the telling? Who do you imagine will believe you?"

"I will stand as witness," Sinnia shot back. "To my own ascent and Arian's."

"I demand proof of these claims!"

Ilea's cry of fury extinguished the light in the chamber.

Arian freed herself from Ilea. With a soft incantation, she redeemed the darkness.

When the Companions looked back at the dais, she was holding a leather-wrapped bundle in her hands. She raised it to her lips and kissed it, certain of herself to the core.

Her glance at the Companions was a benediction, echoed by the opening she offered.

"All praise belongs to the One, the One who governs all worlds."

21

THE WRAPPING FELL AWAY. THE COMPANIONS SCRAMBLED TO THEIR feet for a better look at the golden plates in Arian's hands that were bound by a turquoise spine. Arian let the book fall open.

Half-Seen approached, her brow marked with consternation.

"What is it?" Ilea snapped, shards of the White Throne lying at her feet.

Ilea doesn't know. Though her connection to the Claim runs deep, it is not the knowing of Hira's High Companion. And again, Arian wondered at her motives for insisting on this trial.

Arian passed the book to Half-Seen, who leafed through its pages with care. Though she was soft-spoken, the extent of her scholarship, and the wisdom that sprang from it, meant that her words carried weight. She looked up at the Companions, stunned.

"Proof that the First Oralist *did* fulfill her Audacy. This compilation is *older* than the Bloodprint." She positioned the book so the gold plates were balanced lightly on her hands. Radiance filled the chamber, an aura hovering over Half-Seen's head. Arian's sight altered. With the light upon light vision, she saw an image from the past. A Companion of Hira named Hafsah, whose dignity was such that Arian had to turn her eyes away to concentrate on the present.

"I don't know how to believe it," Half-Seen whispered, "but this is the *Sana Codex*. Where did you find it, Arian? How did it come to you?"

"It was a gift of the Israa e Miraj."

"Legends," Ilea spat. "Folktales cherished by children."

"*I* cherish this legend," Half-Seen said as she studied Ilea. "Do you disbelieve our Tradition, Exalted? Is such a thing possible for our High Companion?" Pity touched her voice.

Seeing that she had erred, Ilea amended her response. "I would not wish you to be misled by a Companion who uses the Israa e Miraj as a means of persuasion."

Psalm cut in. She'd had enough of waiting while war trembled at their gates. "Arian gave this Council ten years of her life. To pursue the Audacy you assigned, she gave up the man she loved. *She* is not the one preoccupied by power; she thinks only of this Council."

Arian was warmed by Psalm's defense, by a bond that her years away had not diminished, but she admitted, "I am also thinking of the future the people of Khorasan must share."

"That is your duty as First Oralist. No one here would fault you for it." Psalm moved closer to the High Companion, stepping around the ruins of the throne. "You've called your session, Exalted. You've made your case and failed. I refuse to permit any further delay. If you allow the Citadel to fall, I will think Arian right to have questioned your motives." She glanced over at Ash. "Have you ruled?"

Ilea flicked a hand, and Psalm went reeling back. "How *dare* you subvert the workings of this Council?" She let loose her fury on the Companions. "Neither the General nor the Jurist can determine this matter! If my judgment is to be overturned, each of you must have a say! Each of you must cast a vote!"

Psalm exchanged a glance with Ash; they were both susceptible to Ilea's manipulations. Ash nodded slowly, straightening where she stood, her gaze bent on Ilea.

"As Jurist, I am obliged to call the vote on the charges brought against the First Oralist of Hira, a judgment that would see her stripped of rank and banished hereafter from this Council. Who votes in favor?"

The Companions were constrained in place by Ilea, but not a single hand went up.

Ash looked to Ilea, struggling against her distortions of the Claim to give voice to the judgment. "There, you have your answer. The First Oralist will retain her rank and her place at this Council."

But Ilea had come too far and risked too much to give way. She inflicted the Claim on the Council, pieces of marble funneling her fury as they rose in the air behind her head. Bladelike fragments flew around the chamber, embedding themselves in the walls.

"That was not the only charge! The Council will rule on the issue of dual allegiance *now*. One woman alone cannot wipe away our history, or undo our traditions to satisfy her own desires! You will vote on the issue of dispensation in the absence of precedent."

Arian used the Claim to shield the Companions from the detritus whirling over their heads. "I do not *ask* for the ruling while the Preacher is at our gates! My personal desires have no relevance when I may not live to fulfill them!"

"You do not command the Council!" Ilea's jealousy and outrage shattered the basins of the All Ways. The chamber's lanterns began to shiver in the grip of their stanchions. "*Take the vote and rule!*"

Ilea's hand curled into a fist, and Ash cried out, gripping her temples in pain.

Her voice dull, and her movements deadened, Ash called to the chamber, "The Council will vote on the matter of whether dispensation will be granted."

Ilea hissed the Claim at her, and painfully she added, "Raise your hand if you agree that Arian may remain First Oralist while bound to the Guardian of Candour."

There was nothing more Arian could offer in her defense. She looked up at the faces of her sisters. Women she loved and respected, women she would die to protect. They held the future of Khorasan in their hands through the vote that would outlive them.

None moved until Ash called again, sounding more like herself, "I call the vote."

Hands went up around the chamber, and Ash counted out loud, naming the Companions who'd agreed to grant dispensation. None from the first rank, save Psalm. Dijah, Rain, Moon, Saw, Ware, Zeb, and the others—of these, none voted in Arian's favor, and though it was not a vote against Arian as First Oralist, their judgment was decided. The junior Companions were more generous, however, and as Ash completed the roll call, the tension in her voice eased. The chamber had come to a tie. Sinnia had voted in Arian's favor; neither Arian nor Ilea were permitted a vote.

"Again." Ilea's command was gravel and fire.

"Again, please," Ash repeated.

She studied the Companions, wondering if any would choose to reconsider. They raised their hands with more confidence this time, but the outcome was the same.

The Council had come to a tie.

Ash kept her thoughts to herself. She weighed Arian's arguments against the history of the Tradition and considered the account Arian had given of her Audacy. She spent a moment recalling the stir the Silver Mage had caused when he'd come to bow his head before the Council. She thought of secrets kept and intrigues explored. Of the absence of the captains of the Citadel Guard as the Talisman pressed their assault. Of the frequent presence of the Black Khan in the High Companion's chambers. A presence she had always questioned, if only to herself.

She thought of the decade Arian had spent dismantling Talisman slave-chains, on a quest to recover a sister who had once been destined to be Custodian of the Archives.

She thought of Half-Seen's appeal, her insight into precedent, and of the precedent the Collector had cited to give her argument substance.

And she thought of the child Arian, delivered into her care by a gentle captain named Turan, terrified and broken by the murders she had witnessed and the loss she had borne. She thought of the mausoleum in the Citadel's garden, where Arian's parents were buried. She remembered her search of the archives at the Guardian of Candour's request.

She met Arian's eyes and smiled. "Mine is the deciding vote."

"Ash, I warn you—" Ilea's caution was brutal.

"You insisted on the vote." She battled Ilea one-on-one, their struggle quiet and intense. And then, bolstered by her conception of the Claim, the Jurist of Hira fleetingly prevailed. She called out to the chamber with conviction.

"Mine is the deciding vote."

The Companions went still.

"Mine is the deciding vote and"—she took Arian's right hand and pressed it to her heart—"I grant you dispensation."

22

"No." Ilea's voice reflected an unalterable purpose. The Companions would not take this moment from her. Arian could not be allowed to override her authority, or to gain a victory that disputed her right to govern. Arian's vision of dual allegiance would unravel Ilea's campaign for the future. The Council of Hira would rise. The Council of Hira would *rule*.

"I reject the verdict."

It was Ilea's choice to silence the waters of the All Ways, to keep them placid as she spoke. There would be no purifying ritual that gave power to the judgment.

Waves of displeasure rolled down the tiers of the Chamber. Dijah slowly came to her feet. She had voted against dispensation, but she had not agreed to overturn all the rules of Council. And Ash's agitation was also plain. She motioned to Dijah to wait. This matter belonged to her jurisdiction. She would be the one to resolve it.

She confronted Ilea. "Who are you to reject a verdict of this Council? Hira's High Companion is not above the law. And as per that law, as Jurist, *I* have ruled."

Ilea's smile was unpleasant, marring her pristine beauty. "There is a higher authority than yours *and* mine."

Now Dijah added her voice, her censure evident. "Do you refer to the One? Do you *presume* to interpret the will of the All-Seeing One?"

Ilea flicked her fingers, a dismissive gesture that provoked a cry from the Companions, a warning Ilea ignored. She turned to the page who had appeared, a clever young novice named Mei Lai, apprenticed to the Council from Shin Jang. She delivered a scroll to the High Companion, then stood to one side, flashing a guilty look at Sinnia.

Ilea unrolled the scroll with a snap.

"I have no need to interpret the will of the One, when it is plain on the page."

"What page?" Psalm demanded.

Ilea's nod was condescending. "How could I forget, General? Your knowledge of the Claim is scant compared to mine."

From the corner of her eye, she caught the flare of anger on Arian's face. Good. A small victory, but one she could use. When Arian tried to speak, Ilea turned to Ash.

"Am I not entitled to a rebuttal of the First Oralist's claims? Do you see how she would forestall me from stating the Council's law?"

Though she was angry herself, Ash had no choice but to uphold the forms. She waved for Ilea to continue.

"Allow me to read you a page from the Bloodprint, the very page I risked the journey to Ashfall to collect. Copied from the original by my hand."

She moved into the space opposite the All Ways. She recited the opening formula with such power that the Companions' heads were bent low.

She turned the words on Arian, flinging them like knives.

"*O you who have believed, obey the One and obey the Messenger, and* obey those in authority among you. *And if you disagree over anything, refer it to the One and the Messenger, if you believe in the One and the Last Day. That is best for you and fairest in the end.*"

She had been practicing the verse since her return to the Citadel, drawing from it the meaning she needed, heightening the strength of her compulsion. The waters of the All Ways rose in two parallel streams, jetting up in pale blue spikes to form the bars of a cage.

"You don't know this verse, do you, Arian? Neither did your mother, for all her learning. She didn't teach it to you or your sister. Perhaps her fate would have been different if she *had* gained this knowledge. But you claim to have been gifted with Ascension, and if your claim was righteous, I would have no power over you."

Arian couldn't evade the meaning of the verse when it was rolling through her mind. She sensed its potential for glory, just as she understood its capacity for ruin. And she was shocked by the mention of her sister. What did Ilea know of Lania? Why would this verse speak to Lania?

Why would Ilea *think* of Lania at this moment?

Echoing her thoughts, Ilea repeated, "*Obey those in authority among you. I* am the authority here."

Thin lines of blood stippled Arian's face across both cheeks. The Companions gasped at the sight. The verse *did* have power over Arian, just as it held them powerless and enthralled.

"Exalted!" A shocked protest from Ash. "The meaning of the verse is *lawful* authority."

Ilea waved one hand to the right, expanding her focus to Ash. The words began to cut, pushing Ash away from the All Ways.

"Do you question my lawful authority? Would you strip us of *all* our customs?"

"You accuse me of doing so when you yourself are using the Claim to override our will?"

"You overestimate my skill, Ash. And insult your sisters' autonomy. How you receive the Claim is a matter of your own inclination. It may even be one of disposition. You must learn to hold *yourself* responsible."

Dismayed by this logic, Ash stared at her.

Ilea waited no longer. She recited the verse again, and Arian lurched away, powerless. The foundations of the chamber began to shake, the waters surging up above the boundaries that had been designed to contain them.

"Arian!" Sinnia cried, reaching for Arian's hand.

Ilea blocked the move, motioning Sinnia back. The diadem on her forehead cast a raging light. It suspended all activity. She had molded the verse to her needs, and now she turned its raging intensity on Arian.

"When you fail to serve the purposes of this Council, or when you overthrow an Audacy I assign, you no longer act as First Oralist. You no longer serve Hira when you refuse to accept my authority." She struck at Arian's circlets, but they were tightly bound to her arms. "I divest you of the rank of First Oralist. You are banished from Hira for all time."

Arian opened her mouth, but Ilea had concentrated all her strength on this single attempt, passionate authority throbbing in every word. Used like this, the verse was even more powerful than the Verse of the Throne. Arian's eyes rolled back in her head; there was no defense she could mount.

She managed to gasp out Ilea's name, the Council watching in horror. And as a part of the theater for her audience, the High Companion intoned, "This Council brooks no disloyalty, and this judgment is passed by the Claim."

She shoved Arian hard into the path of the All Ways. The waters rose to cage her unresisting form. Though she tried to force her throat to call on the strength of the Claim, she could not find a way to overcome the verse's overarching dominion.

"No!" Sinnia's cry of horror resounded in the chamber before it was flattened by the verse. "If you banish Arian, you must also banish me. Wherever she goes, I go."

She made to leap into the All Ways, but the Claim-verse arrested her in place.

Ilea narrowed the verse, parsing its syllables so that the layers of Sinnia's mind were peeled like the bark of a birch.

"Of all the Companions, Sinnia of the Negus, *you* cannot disobey me." Ilea rolled up the scroll. She entrusted it to Mei Lai, who shuddered at its power. Then she turned on Sinnia, gripping her by her circlets. "Why do you think I assigned you to Arian? I chose you for your habit of obedience to your Negus and his queen. You were *destined* to obey my authority."

Ilea's inflection altered the meaning of the verse: it was whetted like a dagger's edge, weighted like a Zhayedan mace. Sinnia's thoughts faltered beneath its staggering compulsion.

Blood-tears forming in her eyes, she choked, "May you use your newfound knowledge of the Claim against the Citadel's *true* enemies."

She could say nothing else, offer no condemnation of the High Companion's actions. Ilea had not lied: Sinnia was bound to obey the oath she had sworn because she had never before questioned the High Companion's authority.

For how could Sinnia have guessed that *this* was what Ilea wanted? To banish the only Companion who could rival her in power, when together they might have been able to rout the One-Eyed Preacher. She was pricked by a memory of Ascension.

The Sidrat al Muntaha had given her guidance; it had suggested a different outcome. To defend the First Oralist *was* to defend Hira. But how did that help Sinnia now?

Her circlets burned beneath Ilea's touch, a searing pain that clawed at the edges of her sanity. Then Ilea released her, her golden eyes triumphant at seeing Sinnia's weakness.

Ash fought against Ilea's compulsion and stumbled to the waters of the All Ways, but there was no trace of Arian to be found. Psalm struggled to help her, her gray eyes clouded with grief . . . with traces of fear, something Sinnia had never seen from the Citadel's steadfast general.

"Such misuse of power," Ash whispered. "Why would you do such a thing? Why would you do it *now* with enemies at our gates?"

"Do you dispute my authority?" The Claim-verse underlined the strength of Ilea's rebuke.

Ash went pale, trembling. "I cannot. I *dare* not. The Claim speaks for us all."

Psalm shook her head, that gesture from their general conveying a depthless wound.

Satisfied, Ilea studied the faces of the Companions, drawing her power in to give them some sense of autonomy, when, with the verse on authority, they were firmly within her control.

"The survival of the Citadel does not depend on the gifts granted to one woman. If you fear the Preacher, I have long had his measure. I will face him with your help: together we will defeat him. As for the First Oralist—our traditions will not be rewritten for the sake of her lustful desires. What price our victory against the Preacher, if we forfeit who we are? Men may hold sway over Khorasan, to our great cost, but they have no say within these walls. They have never governed the workings of this Council, and so it *must* be evermore."

But the suspicion in the eyes of the Companions had not dimmed—not even for those who had voted against granting dispensation.

"You were wrong to do this," Dijah forced out between her teeth. "The First Oralist obeyed the rules of Council; she did nothing to lose our respect." Her brittle hands gestured at the scroll Mei Lai had tucked to one side. "We convene in these chambers as a shura—you *must* consult with us, just as our voices must be heard!"

Saw spoke up when Dijah could say no more, her fragile body failing.

With no less anger, she said, "You cast the ruling of the Jurist aside, and in doing so dishonored us. *Munafiqah,*" she charged Ilea, before she was silenced by the verse.

"Munafiqah?" Ilea echoed with an icy tilt to her brow.

The Companion named Rain had escaped the more harrowing effects of the verse because of her previous silence, but now she added her voice.

"You did not answer Arian when she asked you about the Black Khan. And I have seen him wander this Citadel at will—even to the doors of your chamber. It would seem you condemn her for transgressions you are guilty of yourself. And that *would* make you a hypocrite."

Melati spoke up bravely. "Arian was granted Ascension. She brought us the Sana Codex, but more than that she came to the Council with the light of truth on her face. The celestial light upon light—a light that would not shine if she was trying to deceive us." With an anxious sigh, she finished, "How could you doubt her, Exalted? What do you really fear? Don't you see that we can best defend the Citadel with Arian at our side? No one's use of the Claim could be truer. Why else did we raise her to the rank of our First Oralist?"

The Companions began to stir, lending strength to Melati's defense.

Ilea burned with the furious impulse to strike Melati down. But her rule of Hira was dependent on their notion of her legitimacy, so she began, "These are spurious allegations—"

There was a hard knock on the chamber's outer door. A thunderous crack shook the foundations of the Citadel. The walls of the chamber rippled.

"The Preacher!" Sinnia cried. "He's here. The Citadel is under attack."

The knock sounded again, the door thrown open by a young captain of the Citadel Guard. His expression reflected his knowledge of the severity of his trespass, for no member of the Guard was permitted to enter the Council Chamber, but the depths of his panic propelled him.

He stumbled halfway down the stairs.

"Exalted! I beg clemency. The One-Eyed Preacher has appeared . . . *above* our walls, I know not how." His voice caught in his throat. "But I have other news to report—dire news. There is treachery within our walls: Captain Azmaray has defected to the Talisman. He leads a contingent of the Citadel Guard in an assault upon the archives."

An uproar broke out in the room.

"Enough!" Ilea pointed to Psalm. "Take the Companions who are skilled in recitation to the walls. Position them as you deem best. I will guard the gate." She pointed to the Companions. "Ash, Half-Seen, to the scriptorium. Nothing else will matter if the archives burn."

Sinnia freed herself from the chains of the Claim-verse. "They are scholars, not soldiers. Let me go in their stead."

Psalm was already moving to the stairs, shouting directions to the others. Companions fell in line behind her.

Ilea gave Sinnia a regal nod. "Do not think to betray me. You cannot act against this Council to save the First Oralist now."

"I am thinking of the *archives*. There's no time for anything else!" Sinnia reached for Ash, tugging her along, still affected by the Claim-verse. Half-Seen had not waited. She was already at the door, impatient to rescue the archives she had tended with such scrupulous care.

"Hurry!" Half-Seen shouted.

Sinnia's circlets were charged with a sudden bolt of heat; then Ilea released her.

"Go, and do not fail."

Sinnia flew down the stairs, the Jurist at her heels. As they descended the tower to the main courtyard, they bypassed skirmishes between factions of the Guard. Ducking around the mausoleum, Sinnia pulled Ash along with her, doing her best to keep up with Half-Seen.

"The reading room." She thrust the words at Ash. "Are any manuscripts on display?"

In a reading room opposite the tower of the Council Chamber, two flights above Hira's scriptorium, manuscripts were often studied by senior members of the Council.

"I don't know," Ash gasped, trying to keep Sinnia's pace. "But all that matters is the treasury below. We must protect our legacy!"

She staggered to a halt as they ran right into the Citadel Guard. Sinnia's whip cut a path through the fray, Ash hovering behind her.

They'd lost sight of Half-Seen in the clash. Then they heard a high-pitched scream.

Some forty feet ahead, Half-Seen lay sprawled, a soldier of the Citadel Guard standing above her with his sword raised to attack. Sinnia ran ahead. She leapt up against the trunk of a palm tree, then bounded down, her whip uncoiled in a lingering flick that wrenched the sword from the arm of the guard. The sword tumbled through the courtyard, clanging against stone, but before Sinnia could jerk back her whip, its tail end was caught by the guard, who used it to haul her closer. When she stumbled into arm's reach, he coiled the whip again and dropped a loop around her neck. Then he began to tighten it.

Her hands scrabbling at her throat, Sinnia looked up into his face.

It was Azmaray, one of the Guard's captains, his ambergris eyes wild and unfocused, his face clammy with sweat.

A voice boomed out above the Citadel's walls, the roar of the One-Eyed Preacher. It seemed to inflame Azmaray. He yanked harder at the whip. Sinnia gave up her feeble struggle to wrest it back, frantic for air. Instead, she reached for the daggers on her back. Bringing both hands up at once, she sliced Azmaray across the torso.

The wounds she'd caused were deep, but his strength didn't falter in the slightest.

His dark-amber eyes were blood-tinged now, and all at once she understood: the Preacher's voice controlled him, strengthened him like a ghul of legend, divorced him from the reality of his limitations.

A blood-spotted darkness at the edge of her vision, she called to her lips a verse she had heard Arian sing to Larisa, the leader of the Basmachi resistance. A promise of fealty, of the solidarity of sisterhood wherever the battle was waged.

"Azmaray." She called his name, hoping to awaken him to himself, as the whip cut deeper into her flesh. "Azmaray, *come unto that tenet that you and we hold in common*."

She crooned the words again, with the last bit of breath she had left.

Then she heard it echoed by other voices. Half-Seen, who tried to pry the whip free from Sinnia's throat, and Ash, calm and certain, with no other weapon than her voice.

Sinnia could have severed the whip with her sword, but some instinct told her not to. She could have plunged her blade straight into Azmaray's heart, but that same instinct told her that Azmaray was not lost to them: his eyes began to focus. She read the horror behind them, the staggering weight of dread, and she redoubled her efforts.

"Come unto that tenet that you and we hold in common. Azmaray, come."

His breath coming in great gulps, his hands released the whip. He wheeled away, his chest bleeding, as his injuries made themselves known. She couldn't spare him another moment, though she felt the pain of it deep within. She had struck down a member of the Citadel Guard; she, a Companion of Hira, and he sworn in loyalty to defend her to his last moment of life. The horror in his eyes held her as he collapsed, blood burbling from his mouth.

But Ash had more presence of mind than she did. She called to a Companion she had spied in a corner of the courtyard, Maryam from the Valley of Five Lions. Maryam was a healer.

"Help him if you can. We must get to the archives."

The women passed one another, thunder shaking the walls,

the sky afire with a blinding, unnatural light. Talisman arrows rained over the parapets, falling into the courtyard, and the three Companions swerved to avoid them.

Across the distance, Sinnia could see that guards Psalm had assigned to the scriptorium were still of the Citadel's ranks. They hadn't been turned. They hadn't been planted by the Talisman, but they battled others who had.

Nothing else would serve, Sinnia thought. She and two scholars could not cut through the fray to reach the door to the scriptorium.

There was still one weapon within Sinnia's reach, but Ash and Half-Seen couldn't help her because they didn't know.

If Arian was with her, how easy it would be.

But Arian was the reason she needed to reach the scriptorium.

Their fight couldn't end here. Arian would find a way back to the Citadel, and in the meantime, Sinnia had a duty to defend the scriptorium. More than that, she'd been given a charge upon Ascension. She'd been shown the Miraj Nameh, and she needed to find out why before the scriptorium burned. In their battle against the One-Eyed Preacher, the manuscript was significant, a truth she'd managed to keep from Ilea.

She would break free of Ilea somehow, and fulfill her charge.

Unable to break past the Citadel Guard, the defectors to the Talisman grabbed torches from the braces in the walls. They launched them at the Citadel Guard, who used their shields to block the fire. But one sailed through to its target. The door of the scriptorium erupted into flames, and Half-Seen's cries of agony filled the courtyard.

Sinnia took a deep breath, massaging the muscles of her damaged throat.

Giving it everything she had, she called out the Verse of the Throne.

23

SINNIA ROARED THE VERSE. SHE WATCHED FLAMES LICK UP THE DOOR TO the lower Citadel. Smoke slid over the beauty of ancient timber like a forewarning of death . . . of incomprehensible loss, Half-Seen's desperate cries sounding in her ears.

With one arm she pushed the other woman back. Half-Seen's devotion to the scriptorium had robbed her of any care for her safety; she would burn in an effort to save the archives. With the hand that wasn't holding on to Half-Seen, Sinnia massaged her larynx to magnify the sound of the Throne-verse, casting it out so that it hung like a veil over the gardens. A mantle over the men who were eager to bring down the Citadel in their Preacher-inspired haze.

But Half-Seen's frenzy was disrupting Sinnia's efforts. Forced to use more of her focus to restrain Half-Seen, the Throne-verse faltered in Sinnia's throat. Gaping holes pierced the veil of protection she had flung out over the courtyard. The flames began to spread, the door that led to the scriptorium swallowed whole by fire.

"Half-Seen—"

"Let me." A man's voice sounded behind her. Keeping hold of Half-Seen with one arm, Sinnia's head swerved to look. A warrior with a dark beard and thick sable hair grabbed hold of Half-Seen's arms. His eyes burned blue in his brown face, and she recognized that the man was a Talisman tribesman, though he was dressed as a member of the Guard.

"No!" she gasped. She released Half-Seen to reach for her daggers, then stopped when she saw that the man had pulled Half-Seen back against the hard wall of his chest, one strong arm around her waist.

"Continue," the man said. "Do what you were doing to protect us. I'll keep her safe." His dark head swiveled. He caught sight of Ash on Sinnia's other side, shielded by members of the Citadel Guard. He wrapped Half-Seen in his arms, subduing her frantic struggles. "We have them, Companion. Give your voice free rein."

"Let me go!" Half-Seen's nails dug into his arm. "The manuscripts are all that matter!"

Both Sinnia and the stranger ignored her.

Sinnia used the Throne-verse again.

"There is no one but the One, the Living, the Everlasting." Her chant was certain and fierce. The veil began to seal itself, but the fire spread from the door to the stairs to the lower Citadel. The Preacher's recitation thundered overhead.

"Sinnia, please!" Half-Seen begged, trying to free herself from the stranger's grip.

Sinnia aimed the verse at the stairs.

Summon it, she told herself. *Control it. Rescue your legacy; rescue your sisters in the Claim.*

Without knowing how she did it, she spread her voice like a blanket thick enough to suffocate the moon.

"To the One belongs all that is in the heavens and the earth."

Half-Seen's cries disappeared. The sound of clashing swords faded.

Another deep breath and Sinnia warned, *"Who is there that can intercede with the One, except as the One allows? The One knows what lies before you, what lies after you."*

She felt a wetness. The One-Eyed Preacher using the power of his recitation to shear through her use of the Claim. Cool streams of blood dripped from her ears to her neck.

She tilted her regal head back and shouted up at the sky, shaking in every limb, *"You comprehend nothing of the One's knowledge, except as the One wills."*

The Preacher's response was like the crushing of mountains, the terrifying power of the Claim grinding against Hira's walls to cries of despair from every quarter.

Unbowed, Sinnia accused him again. *"The throne of the One comprises the heavens and the earth."* And then in her own words, "All this is ours. Under the One's protection."

The sheer conviction in her voice smothered and swallowed the flames. Thick curls of smoke poured from the opening to the stairs. Sinnia waved her hand. A dense white powder sank down over the smoke. The curling plumes disappeared.

"Let me go to the manuscripts!" Half-Seen wrenched at the stranger's arms.

When she was released, she stumbled. She whirled around to glare at him, and he put up his hands in feigned dismay.

"You *dare* to restrain a Companion of Hira!"

"It seemed preferable to letting you burn alive." His sharp smile was full of mockery.

Half-Seen couldn't think of a response, so she vanished down the stairs, Ash following in her wake, with a troubled glance at Sinnia.

"Go with them," the man said. "They need your protection. I'll do what I can up here." He jerked his chin at another group of fighters, where a man as tall as himself led a handful of soldiers to the tower above the causeway. "My brother, Hamzah, will help as well."

Sinnia caught the flash of green eyes as the soldier named Hamzah called down to the man with Sinnia, "Take the other tower."

Concerned, Sinnia said, "You're both Talisman. Warriors from Khyber is my guess."

"Are we?" The stranger's blue eyes seemed to burn through her. "You're safe, Companion. Go. Go help the others." He paused before continuing, his voice deepening. "Who was she?"

"She?"

"The one who would have died to rescue parchment and ink."

In the urgency of the moment, Sinnia used Half-Seen's name. "There's a reason Hafsah was willing to risk her life on behalf of our scriptorium. She is known as the Collector."

"A beautiful name," the stranger said. "For a beautiful woman."

Sinnia blinked at this. How in the heat of battle had the man had time to notice? She assessed him, hoping she was right to trust him with Hafsah's name. He could have killed all three of them. Instead, he'd told her to call the magic, and he appeared undamaged by the Claim, at least on the surface. But she didn't have time to test his loyalty.

She touched his arm in thanks. "If you should see the First Oralist, please do what you can to help her. Tell her where I am." He wouldn't know who Arian was, she realized. "She is from the south. She has long hair, and she is green-eyed like your brother. She—"

The man cut her off. "Hamzah will know." His voice went soft for a moment. "Both of us will recognize the First Oralist if we see her. Call for me if you need me, my name is Qais, Companion. May the One keep you." He dipped his head and was gone.

Just as well. She might have no choice but to accept his help, but she was loath to trust him with the secrets of the scriptorium. But there was no more time to consider the motives of the two brothers she suspected of being from Khyber.

Furling her whip, she chased after Half-Seen.

24

Sinnia was greeted at the heavy double doors to the scriptorium by two members of the Guard. She recognized them as senior soldiers, and murmured a prayer of relief.

"Some of the Guard have turned traitor. They're trying to burn the scriptorium. Do what you can to make sure the fire doesn't spread down here."

They saluted her, weapons braced in their hands.

She pushed her way through the doors, searching for the others. She found the Jurist and the Collector on the far side of a great hall whose sweeping, book-lined walls reminded her of the soaring cliffs of a canyon. She rushed over, skirting tables where manuscripts lay in stacks, past alcoves where hundreds of books were collected. On one side of the hall, names were etched above the alcoves that led to recessed rooms. Inside the rooms were tables, chairs, and a handful of manuscripts, set aside for specific Companions. When Sinnia and Arian had first met, Arian had been engaged in the act of writing, an act Sinnia had never before witnessed, though now her own knowledge had dispelled her bemusement with Arian's skills, if not with the craft itself.

She hurried past Arian's alcove to join the other Companions.

"What is it? What are you doing?"

Half-Seen rubbed her arms, as if she still felt the imprint of Qais's powerful hands.

"We have to protect the scriptorium," she told them. She turned her back and began to sort through the books on the shelf behind her, beautiful lines of script indicating their titles.

"Half-Seen, take a moment. Your mind is clouded."

Sinnia's concern was reflected in the deepening lines around the Jurist's eyes.

Half-Seen ignored them, continuing to rummage through the books.

"What are you hoping to do?" Sinnia demanded. "We will secure the safety of the treasury by the means we have at our disposal, but beyond that, what more can we do? Where else would the manuscripts be safe?"

Half-Seen turned back to face her, one brow raised, so that for a moment she reminded Sinnia of Arian. "There's a mechanism in this alcove. We can seal the scriptorium before they set fire to it again."

Sinnia shook her head, spiral curls whipping against her temples. "No, Hafsah. We would suffocate in here. They would burn us alive."

Half-Seen turned back to her work. She seemed to be counting under her breath, pushing books aside in reckless haste.

"You don't understand, Sinnia. The mechanism won't just barricade us inside the scriptorium. It shifts the walls of the scriptorium: every alcove and nook will be safe from the assault."

She glanced back over her shoulder, just as her hand closed on a thick metal rod with a tulip-shaped head. "If one of us has to die to rescue the archives, it should be me. You two should go, you're needed at the walls."

Ash tugged Half-Seen away.

"You intend to *bury* the scriptorium? And yourself along with it?"

Half-Seen pushed back damp tendrils of hair from her forehead. She nodded.

"It will be safe from the Preacher. And Arian knows . . ." She paused. "I've never quite trusted Ilea, so I told Arian how to reverse the process. That's why I haven't done it before now—I needed to be sure Arian would return. She will, won't she?"

"Of course she will." Sinnia was firm in her conviction. "Release the mechanism, and we'll go to the walls where we're needed."

"It won't work like that. Someone has to hold the rod until the scriptorium sinks."

Half-Seen moved to act, but Sinnia yanked her back.

"Wait! We can debate this in a moment, but I have a far more pressing task. I need your help, Half-Seen. Yours, too, Ash. I can't search the scriptorium on my own."

"What are you looking for?" Ash gripped Half-Seen's hand. "Will it help defeat the One-Eyed Preacher?"

Sinnia's agreement was vigorous. "Yes! It's a manuscript I was shown upon the Israa e Miraj." She made a cutting movement with her hand at their doubtful expressions. "It doesn't matter if you don't believe me about the Miraj—the point is the manuscript can help us. You were studying it once in the reading room, Ash, perhaps you know why."

Neither Companion responded to Sinnia's claim about the Miraj, but Ash asked, "Which manuscript, Sinnia?"

"The Miraj Nameh. I don't remember much about it, except that its pages were filled with drawings."

"Drawings?" Half-Seen sounded offended. "The Miraj Nameh is a priceless manuscript *because* of its illuminations. But why should it aid you now?"

Sinnia hesitated.

"We can't help you if you don't tell us," Ash pointed out.

"I'm worried that you might find it hard to believe me."

"Tell us," Ash insisted. "We learn the same Tradition, why should we disbelieve?"

Sinnia let a breath escape from her lungs. In wondering tones, she described the nature of her ascent, faltering at her description of the Lote Tree of the Utmost Boundary.

"It was magnificent. Shade everywhere at once, yet it gave the gift of illumination. I was shown a page of the Miraj Nameh, an illustration. There were words on the page that I could read, but they had no meaning for me." Realization struck her. Outside of Arian, who else was as knowledgeable as the Jurist or the Collector?

"What were the words?"

Sinnia's hope sprang back to life. She remembered that feeling from the Ascension . . . knowledge pouring from her heart down through her veins to be carried away from her deepest essence. She was meant to share it. That was why she was here.

She repeated the script she had read on the page. "It was just a series of words: the Buraq, the Blind Dome, the Bladebone. Do they mean anything to you?"

Half-Seen echoed the words. "The Buraq, the Blind Dome, the Bladebone."

Sinnia nodded, grateful that the revelation had drawn Half-Seen's focus from the mechanism in the wall.

Ash shared what she knew. "The Buraq is familiar." She looked at Sinnia, choosing her words with care. "When your Ascension took place, did you not ride the Buraq?"

And then Sinnia remembered. The Buraq was the winged steed that had borne the Messenger of the Claim upon the Israa e Miraj. Her voice shaking with excitement, she said, "Yes! And I saw Arian's ascent. She was riding her mare. That must be what it means." Her voice throbbed with excitement. "What of you, Half-Seen? What can you tell me about the Bladebone?"

But Half-Seen didn't know. "Let me think on it for a moment."

There was no time for reflection, with the voice of the Preacher reaching each corner of the Citadel, so Sinnia urged Half-Seen on. "You have to help me find the Miraj Nameh."

All three women turned to stare at the walls of the scriptorium.

"There are three places where it might be kept." Half-Seen gazed around.

Sinnia interrupted. "Ash, when I first came to the scriptorium, you were studying the Miraj Nameh in the Upper Citadel. I saw it for a moment on your rahlah."

"I returned it to Half-Seen's care months ago."

Half-Seen waved to attract their attention. "The Miraj Nameh has three classifications: it could be among the books on art, history, or faith."

Dismayed, Sinnia said, "Those are the three largest sections of the scriptorium. Do you know which one it's stored in now?"

Half-Seen massaged her temples. "I've been reorganizing things down here." But her silent contemplation yielded no solution. "There are too many manuscripts for me to remember—we'll have to search all three sections." She made a gesture of appeal. "There's a way to narrow down the search. A book of that caliber would be kept on one of the upper shelves."

"Why there?" Sinnia gauged the distance. Due to Half-Seen's possessiveness over Hira's treasures, there was only a single ladder in the scriptorium. They would need to be creative in terms of gaining access to those shelves.

"The most valuable manuscripts are kept behind glass to preserve them from dust."

"We must hurry," Ash said. They could hear the thunder rumbling above. And beneath it the sound of booted feet, tramping across the courtyard to the stairs.

The Companions separated, Half-Seen's plan to bury the scriptorium forgotten.

Ash stopped in the alcove of the arts. She pulled a table to the wall and climbed on top. Half-Seen used the scriptorium's ladder. Sinnia ran down the length of the hall to where Half-Seen had pointed to the manuscripts associated with the Claim. The glass cases that held them ran the length of the hall. Sinnia didn't wait for the ladder. She spun out her whip to catch the braces on the walls that held the lanterns. When she was certain they would hold, she flicked her whip from brace to brace, using them to swing around the room.

"Sinnia, the manuscripts!"

She ignored Half-Seen's protest. "I'll be careful."

The whip poised in one hand, her leg muscles braced, Sinnia opened the cases with her free hand, hearing the sounds of the other Companions' search with half her attention, the rest claimed by the sound of boots trudging down the stairs.

Pausing, she drew her daggers from her back.

"Catch!" She flicked them at the other Companions. Ash caught one at the hilt. The other landed at Half-Seen's feet.

Sinnia swung open another case. "They're coming. You need to be ready."

When Half-Seen looked as though she would abandon her task, Sinnia called, "Don't use the lever! Help me find the manuscript first!"

The boots thudded closer. Sinnia picked up speed, script blurring before her eyes.

"Anything?" she called to Ash. The Jurist shook her head, treading between the cases in her section.

"It's not in the history section, Sinnia." More familiar with the arrangement of the manuscripts, Half-Seen had finished her search, and now moved to help Ash.

A loud thump sounded against the door. The clash of steel followed.

The glass cases flew by, Sinnia's whip cracking at lightning speed.

The doors to the scriptorium were thrown open.

"Sinnia!" Half-Seen's warning was accompanied by a dash to the rear.

The whip between her teeth, Sinnia choked out the words, "No, Half-Seen!"

Talisman sympathizers bolted inside, followed by a single Citadel guard, one man against six. None of the Talisman were carrying torches, but it wouldn't take them long to upend one of the lanterns and use it to light a blaze.

She cracked the whip so that it coiled around Half-Seen's waist, pulling her away from the alcove at the rear. "You'll kill us all if you don't wait!"

The Citadel guard battled hard, but when he fell, he was stabbed by a brace of swords, his low moans of pain a counterpoint to their thrusts.

With little hope of being heard, Sinnia started shouting the name "Qais!" Her whip lashed out in fury; she caught Talisman swords, delaying two as the rest rushed the Companions.

"Ash!" she screamed. She took a running leap, bounded over three of the tables, and somersaulted to land in front of the Jurist, the whip leaping as if it had nine tails instead of one. She heard Half-Seen fumbling at the shelves, her hands scrabbling for the lever that would seal the scriptorium off, and all of them within it.

"Stop her!" she shouted at Ash.

Hating herself for doing it, Sinnia grabbed a priceless book and held it before her like a shield. Not a moment too soon. A Talisman soldier stabbed through it. She dropped it and let the whip fly, throwing him back. Then she grabbed another, to the sound of Half-Seen's scream.

"No, Sinnia, no! Don't harm the manuscripts!"

Battling six men at once, the whip biting, streaking, tearing, Sinnia drew another weapon from her hip, a short, sturdy sword. She retreated from the Talisman in a dual-handed dance. But she no longer had a hand free to use as a shield.

A blow to her shoulder made her bite back a curse. Another deflected off her circlet.

"Qais!" she shouted again, knowing neither Companion would be able to help her fight. She heard a scuffle behind her, knew Ash was trying to hold Half-Seen back, to gain them another moment, just one more . . .

A clean-shaven Talisman slashed at Sinnia's knee, and she went down, the Talisman following in a tangle of limbs. The whip was useless now. She called the Claim, a temporary barrier between their swords and her twisting body, one ear attuned to the desperate skirmish between Half-Seen and the Jurist. If the lever moved, saints of the earth and sea, what could she do to stop the destruction of Hira? She knew the Miraj Nameh was critical to their stand against the Preacher. If she lost access to it, if they lost the archives—

As she felt the Claim-barrier give, she whispered to herself, *"The throne of the One comprises the heavens and the earth."*

She heard a strangled cry as the face of a Talisman soldier hove into view, felt a sword strike at bone, but whose?

"Forgive me that I failed you, Arian." She used the blunt thrust of her sword as a shield.

"Don't give up, Companion!"

Bodies flew away to crash against the walls. A case shattered. Shards of glass rained down. Her leg was trapped in the coils of her whip; she couldn't roll away.

A heavy male body flung itself over hers until the glass rain stopped. When it did, the man jumped to his feet, shaking off bits of glass from his hair like a lion flinging water from its mane. He pulled Sinnia up. With brusque efficiency, he ran his hands over her limbs.

He stepped back at once. "You're not hurt," he told her. "Nothing serious, at least." He shook his head in disbelief. "I've never seen a woman fight like you—"

Sinnia's brows went up. She looked at the bodies of the Talisman, and then back at the man's sword, its blade scarlet with blood.

"You killed six men with one sword, Qais."

"You held off six men with a *whip*."

They grinned at each other in mutual appreciation.

Then Sinnia heard the sound of the lever. Jolted from her state of bemusement, she cast about for her whip. Qais moved faster. He drew a dagger from his waist and pitched it end over end. It buried itself in the shelf, jamming the lever in place.

boots were steeped in dirt. Of his app...
Cloak was all that remained clean.
s expression said more than his dishevel-
that had raged unabated was explanation

Khan, slipping around the Mages to the
e crumpled at the sight of the Talisman's
gnored him for the moment.

he said to Rukh with some amazement.
imaced. "A temporary fate. We were close
the Mirage, and the Messenger Gate has
And you see what's happening to the east."
indicating the Talisman's unspent forces.
r, his face falling. "Where is the First Oral-
to return with you."
ack, so I came in her stead." He made his

his eyes as he listened, Rukh addressed the
d to join the Conference of the Mages."
he charge. "Nor did you offer your assis-
rowing of Timeback. We each did what we
ople."
d. "None of that matters now. Tell us how
sidered the armillary sphere. "How are you
"
ayed his plans. "When my brother was Dark
here to harness the power of the stars. This
e the burning of the scriptorium that the sky
n determine how to awaken that power, I can
mies, but the window is small. I must unlock
ybreak."

"Is that what you wanted, Companion?" His clear blue eyes hadn't missed a moment of the interaction between Sinnia and Half-Seen.

Taking her first breath in what felt like years, Sinnia laughed. "Call me Sinnia. You've more than earned the right."

Still burning off adrenaline, she moved to take Half-Seen in her arms, calming her deep-rooted tremors.

"I'm sorry, Hafsah, believe me, I'm sorry." She kissed Half-Seen's forehead. "I know this isn't what you wanted, but please have a little faith in me. And if not in me, then in Arian."

Shame and fear drowned Half-Seen's beautiful eyes. "I'm sorry too. But my first duty is the preservation of the archives."

Sinnia nodded. She glanced at Qais, pushing Hafsah in his direction.

"Watch her in case she changes her mind. Don't let her seal us in."

Qais's eyebrows formed sharp black angles. "You'd let yourself die for these books?"

Half-Seen looked through him. "I don't expect one of the Talisman to understand."

"If you expect me not to understand self-defeat, you're right. My brother and I will go on fighting until there's no one left to fight." He took in the halls of the scriptorium. "But I see why you love this place." His voice gentled in the rough-soft vowels of his native dialect. "I have some sense of why you'd choose to die for it."

"Sinnia." Ash broke into the discussion. Sinnia whirled to face her. The Jurist was carrying a book, a weighty tome with a dyed-indigo binding, the leather supple and rich. Even in the dim light of the lanterns, its deckled edges shone like amber.

"You found it." Joy erupted in Sinnia's veins as Ash pressed the book into her hands. She touched it to her forehead, feeling its power sing through her before she'd even turned a page. She sensed an overspreading shade, felt her limbs caressed by the softest of nettles, heard a clarion call in her ears that drowned out the Preacher's fury.

"This *is* it," she told the others. "We've found the Miraj Nameh. And now, perhaps, we might find a way."

"A way?" Qais questioned.

"To end this war. And put an end to this madness."

THE NIGHT THAT
loss, the Zhaye
walls. But a ch
nized the Silver
the Black Khan
no longer guard
was either with

The Black K
Mages. He'd bee
lary sphere. It ha
looked the Talis
hand extended,
ther man ackno
But then Daniya

Rukh's face
matted, his armo
visible at his thro
the skin on the
collar so the ony

collarbone. His e
and armor, the Sa

The wearines
ment could. The
enough.

Wafa avoided
terrace. His your
strength, but Dan

"You held the

The Black Kha
to losing the Tow
been breached tw
He threw out a h
He looked past Da
ist? She was suppo

"Hira is under
explanations brief

A glint of ange
Blue Mage. "You
Yusuf counter
tance during the I
could for our own

Daniyar interve
we can help." He
planning to use th

Sighing, Rukh
Mage, he used the
is the first night si
has been clear. If I
use it against our e
the sphere before d

Yusuf strode out to the terrace to join Wafa. The Talisman's forces extended as far as the salt plains. The Zhayedan had done some damage, but nowhere near enough to push the Talisman back. The Emissary Gate was under pressure, the Zhayedan Gate as well.

"What target have you chosen?" Yusuf couldn't envision how a single strike could repel an army of this size. He accepted the Black Khan's censure. He *should* have lent his strength. The Harrowing had desolated Timeback, but Ashfall was poised at the edge of extinction.

The other Mages joined him. Rukh gave his spyglass to Yusuf, pointing to the salt plains.

"They do not tire, they do not rest. They're animated by the One-Eyed Preacher, whose power is stronger than before. But they do have a point of weakness." He tilted the spyglass up. "Do you see that bank to the north of the salt plains?"

Yusuf focused until he found it. "What of it?"

"The caravan just under the bank is where they store their supplies. How long could they hold out, if we were able to destroy it?"

Yusuf passed the spyglass to Daniyar, who swept it across the plains. "An army of this size wouldn't limit itself to a single storehouse."

Rukh had considered this. "They've grown arrogant. They haven't dispersed their caravan because our tactics are defensive. They don't think there's anything to fear."

"Not quite." Daniyar made a small adjustment to the spyglass. "They've surrounded their caravan with prisoners from your outlying villages. They've considered the possibility of a strike. If you hit the caravan, you'll be killing hundreds of your own."

Lowering the spyglass, Daniyar saw the shadows in Rukh's

eyes. He wasn't telling the Black Khan anything he didn't know; Rukh had made these calculations.

"Ashfall must survive."

"He's right," Yusuf agreed. "This isn't like the Harrowing of Timeback, when we had time to send civilians into the desert. There's no retreat possible with the Rising Nineteen to the west and the mountains to the north. The battle for survival will begin and end here."

A murmur of protest from Wafa despite his loathing of the Talisman. This was death on a scale the boy could not imagine. The Silver Mage attempted to soothe him. Something passed between them that made Rukh pay closer attention.

"Why isn't the boy with the First Oralist?"

"Wafa has his reasons."

Rukh paused before he shrugged this off. "Will you assist me?"

"How?" Daniyar knew nothing about how the sphere might be used, the Candour had never spoken of it, and the Dark Mages of Ashfall had held its secrets close.

"I tried to channel my gifts through the sphere. When I recited the Dawn Rite, the stars remained silent. Even among the metaphysical, Ashfall has no allies."

The First Oralist had left the city to burn. As had the High Companion, who had more cause for concern about his fate. He reminded himself that the Golden Mage worked her schemes according to her own ends, but at least these two Mages had come.

"The Dawn Rite is for the dawn. Come morning, Yusuf and I will aid you." Daniyar's eyes touched on the boy, their brightness dimming. "And perhaps Wafa, as well."

Rukh gave a mirthless laugh. "We won't make it to morning."

He moved away, and Daniyar noticed how his movements were ponderous and slow, his bitterness plain, as if they had already lost. He was nothing like the careless prince who had taunted him at every turn.

Daniyar raised the spyglass back to the field of battle, judging for himself the soundness of Rukh's fears. Bolstered by their second flank, the Talisman were spread out over the grasslands between the walls and the outer ramparts, so numerous that there was overflow between the Zhayedan and Emissary Gates, with entire brigades positioned at the base of the south wall's towers. The Talisman had weaponry to spare, judging from the caravan that all but obscured the hills that rose behind the salt plains. Their forces were fresh for the attack, despite the losses they had taken and the defection from their ranks. He counted more than thirty tribes under the Talisman's banner, and he couldn't guess how many of those soldiers had been conscripted or how many were believers in the One-Eyed Preacher's cause. From this distance, they all appeared inspired by the same fanatical devotion.

Yusuf turned his back to the Talisman. "It is not the Dawn Rite you need."

Rukh's body tightened like a Teerandaz bow. "Tell me what you know."

"You seek to strike a sudden blow? A defining one?"

Rukh gave a regal nod.

"Then you need the Rite of Qari'ah." Yusuf brushed past Rukh to the armillary sphere, judging its orientation.

"Teach me." Rukh followed him to the sphere.

Daniyar added his voice. "And me, for I do not know it either."

"Let me adjust the sphere, then I will teach you both."

Yusuf's lean fingers slipped through the rings to the globe at the heart of the sphere. The unmarked globe was surrounded by three graduated rings: the meridian, the equator, and the ecliptic horizon that charted the path of the sun across the sky. The colure that circled the sphere represented the fixed position of the stars, and Yusuf drew his fingers along it.

"What are you doing?" Rukh demanded. "The sphere was in position."

"Not for the strike you want." Instead of judging the distance to the salt plains, Yusuf glanced up at the sky, then positioned the meridian perpendicular to the horizon, parallel to a line that ran from north to south. It was clear that he was orienting the rings around a specific point. He adjusted the second ring to intersect with the horizon to the south.

When the rings were aligned, he pointed to the sky with a long forefinger.

"I've never tried it with an astronomical device, but to use the Rite of Qari'ah, you must fix the position of the Al Mintaka star."

"Al Mintaka?" It wasn't difficult to read Rukh's hope. Ashfall needed a miracle. Perhaps the star would provide one.

"The Belt." The name of the star stirred a memory of the Candour. Daniyar's sword stirred at his side, its light flaring before it dimmed. The connection he'd thought of vanished as he focused on the Blue Mage.

Yusuf taught the other Mages the verses of the Rite of Qari'ah against the backdrop of Talisman drums, the one balancing out the other.

"Are you ready? Once we lose sight of the star, we will lose the rite's power."

Rukh and Daniyar nodded. Yusuf positioned their hands, his own on the central sphere, Daniyar's on the ecliptic ring, Rukh's on the outer meridian.

"Hold fast."

With the barest trace of hope, Rukh muttered, "Hold fast to the Belt . . . to the rope."

Yusuf called out the incantation that opened the Conference of the Mages. His voice hoarse with exhaustion, Rukh followed along.

And then the Qari'ah began, brought to life by the flagrant power of three Mages.

"What will make you know what the Qari'ah is?"

The armillary sphere began to vibrate. It shimmered to life then subsided.

"Raise your voice," Yusuf told Rukh. "Let's begin again."

Rukh struggled to comply. He'd been wielding his powers as Dark Mage since he'd brought them to life. Every part of his body ached; his vocal cords had unraveled like a skein of carded wool. But he kept going, his head thrown back, his onyx eyes fixed on the hot blue points of the Belt, shining like Ashfall's last hope.

The armillary sphere caught fire, light transmitted along the arc of its rings.

The Mages continued to chant.

"The Qari'ah will occur on the Day when humanity will be dispersed like moths, when mountains are tufts of wool. Then for those whose weight of decency is heavy in the balance, their joy will be assured. But those whose measure is light shall be engulfed by the abyss."

The fire consumed the sphere, the black point of Al Mintaka agleam. As the intensity of the light grew, the rings began to burn. The Mages ignored their discomfort and held firm.

They chanted the final verse of the Qari'ah.

"What will make you know the abyss? It is a fire hotly burning."

The light from the armillary sphere arrowed through the night. From the fixed point on the meridian, it connected to a star in the sky like a beam. A moment passed as the chant hummed in their throats. The Talisman raised their heads.

The star in the sky caught fire. A blazing corona spread across the firmament, higher, fiercer, hotter. Then it sliced down like the stroke of a sword that split the field in two, brutal and precise, sowing destruction to the south of the salt plains.

The Talisman's caravan erupted. Explosions gathered force, mirrored in greater and greater blasts. Commands shouted into the chaos were undercut by the screams of soldiers and civilians alike. The rearguard turned back to salvage what they could of their supplies, only to run into their own destruction.

The light from the star shut off, its echo an eerie shadow. A suffocating silence descended on the plain. From the terrace above the field of war, the air seemed to be sucked from all around, swallowing movement and sound. The Mages' hands were welded to the sphere, their vocal cords squeezed to silence. The Talisman began to regroup.

"What's happening?" Rukh demanded of Yusuf.

The Blue Mage shook his head. When he tried to call forth the Qari'ah again, his larynx was seized by a fist. The Silver Mage had also been silenced.

Brother.

And then Rukh knew, his sister's whisper in his head.

The ghul—the ghul had struck *again*, shutting off the beam from the sphere.

This isn't the way. You must not wield this destruction.

"Get out of my head!" Rukh roared. The sound came out as a croak.

Think of our people. Would you kill them without cause?

Mute now, he spoke to the ghul in his head, desperate to persuade her.

What people? This strike is against the Talisman.

The Talisman use them as shields, and you gave your word to defend the citizens of our empire—

MY *empire.* He cut her off, terrified by the thought that the ghul's awakening had given her the power to command the intensity of Al Mintaka against the efforts of three Mages.

Your empire, then. But my people, as well. Let me help you, Rukh. Let me do my part.

I don't need your help; the Mages are more than enough.

The ghul feigned sadness.

Get out of my head, ghul. Let me call Al Mintaka again.

You do *need my help.* The ghul's insistence was piteous. *Don't you see the shadow of Al Mintaka?*

Bewildered, the Blue and Silver Mages watched him cast his head up at the sky, at the eerie shadow illuminated by the dim glow of the Belt.

Mute with horror and fear, Rukh closed his eyes against the sight, against the knowledge of why his solo attempts to direct the sphere had failed. For hadn't Darya always been their half-brother Darius's shadow? When Darius had used the sphere, Darya must have aided him. As she claimed to want to aid Rukh now. Fury underlined the horror he felt, at those he held closest. The Assassin and Arsalan; they had conspired to this end. He begrudged them his forgiveness, if he chose to forgive at all.

And *Darya*—he knew what Darya wanted, guessed at what she thought she could do with the power she'd awakened.

Darya knew that Al Mintaka wasn't a single star. It was a bright giant locked in orbit with a fainter sequence star, an orbit completed every six days. What he was seeing now was the shallow eclipse of a star whose magnitude had dimmed. And somehow Darya—somehow the *ghul*—was able to control the eclipse.

Calling upon his deepest reserves, he forced his voice from his throat. "Hurry. We must try the Qari'ah again."

The Mages made the same dire effort, their voices tinged with pain.

The star giant burst into flame, and triumph roared through Rukh's mind. The ghul couldn't stop them. The Qari'ah *would* work.

The air on the plains roared back in a brutal, furious burst, and fire came from all sides as the star-beam lanced across the rear of the Talisman, burning a path across the plains.

No! the ghul cried. *This kind of killing is madness!*

The shadow-star shone. The beam looped back around the paired stars, its power enhanced tenfold. Both stars began to burn.

The Qari'ah faltered and died.

Rukh held on to the sphere with all his strength, fighting the power of the ghul, keeping the Qari'ah at the forefront of his mind. The reinforced star-beam cut through Talisman lines. Elation throbbed in his veins, his dark hair plastered to his forehead.

Brother, stop this! I cannot be a party to murder. There must be another way!

Leave me be, ghul! There is *no other way!*

The sphere began to move, the outer meridian shifting. The path of the star-beam altered, swinging to the city walls.

"No!" Rukh cried.

Al Mintaka's fury was unchained. The path of fire that had cut through the Talisman now roared toward Ashfall unchecked.

The Mages tried to recalibrate the rings, but Al Mintaka's gravity was a force too great to contend with. They struggled to move as if their limbs were weighted by chains, pushing the rings to and fro.

Darya! Rukh shouted. *Stop this madness before you destroy us all!*

No, she sobbed. *Brother, I'm trying to help!*

The armillary sphere caught fire, the Mages thrown against the stone balustrade. Wafa cried out in fear.

Unchecked and undirected, the star-beam focused on Ashfall. Burning, blistering, scalding, soaring, it swallowed the Zhayedan Gate. Fire raced along the southern wall, spreading toward the watchtowers.

Cries of horror and alarm sounded from every quarter.

No! Darya sobbed in Rukh's mind. *No, I meant to* help! *I am the* twin *of the shadow-star! Darius told me so!*

The Mages couldn't move, couldn't speak, such was Al Mintaka's potency. Rukh would have killed Darya with a thought if he could; her despair meant nothing when her actions had doomed Ashfall. He watched the Talisman surge through the gate and set his city on fire.

It was over.

The ghul had killed them all.

And still the star-beam burned.

With a wild cry, Wafa raced down the terrace. A frantic look in his eyes, he tore the Sacred Cloak from the Black Khan's shoulders and threw it over the sphere, covering its rings.

The star-beam switched off like a snuffed candle, a dull fire roaring in its wake.

The Mages found themselves free of Al Mintaka's power. Of the ghul's recalibration.

The Black Khan staggered to the ledge, watching the Teerandaz fight to contain the fire before it crumbled the towers.

A chasm had opened beyond their walls, creasing the field of war. To the south of the crease, the salt plains burned, the Talisman depot destroyed. The chasm had divided the Talisman's army in two: fire continued to burn the rearguard, while closer to the city walls, forward troops raced to the Zhayedan Gate.

Rukh heard Arsalan's roar, saw the Cataphracts re-form to face the new offensive, Khashayar lending his aid, Cassandane and the Teerandaz readying a counterattack.

Now the ghul was quiet, with the city's destruction assured. Or perhaps some other force had constrained her. Rukh found he didn't care. There was nothing left in his heart to hate his sister with. What more could she do to destroy all that Ashfall had been? No doubt the Talisman would take her as their queen.

He watched with disinterest as the Silver Mage pushed himself up from the wall. Stumbling before he found his gait, he made his way to the sphere. Ignoring Rukh's cry, he swung the Sacred Cloak around to settle on his shoulders. With three decisive movements, he repositioned the rings.

"Wafa, help me." He called the boy once before Wafa leapt into action, holding the sphere in place.

The Silver Mage whispered the Qari'ah to the sky as Rukh watched, knowing there would be no miracle to oppose their certain fate.

The star giant lit up. The shadow-star stayed dim.

Light flared from the fixed point on the meridian out into the sky to a point beyond his vision, catching the dominant star. The star-beam switched on again, its power altered somehow.

As Wafa gripped the sphere, the Silver Mage drew his sword and touched it to the beam. The color of the star-beam altered from purest gold to cool silver. The tip of the sword split in two, its edges limned with light. The Silver Mage used the sword to guide the beam.

Rukh's thoughts cried out for vengeance. He opened his mouth to command the Silver Mage, to tell him where to strike.

But Daniyar turned his head and smiled at Rukh, a bone-deep weariness etched into his face, the brightness of his silver eyes dulled.

He didn't wait for Rukh's instruction.

The sword drew a line of silver-blue fire along the perimeter of the southern wall, a fire that didn't burn, didn't spread. A shimmering ice-blue veil dropped from the sky, separating the Talisman from the Zhayedan and Emissary Gates. When they tried to push through the veil, their bodies were incinerated. Cries of horror sounded through the Talisman's ranks.

The Silver Mage called down to their army, his gift magnifying his voice.

"Again the One offers you the chance to refute violence and send your army home. I give you this final warning as Commander of the Faithful."

He drew the sword close to his body and held it up from the waist, both hands closed over its hilt. The bifurcated blade gleamed. He completed a complex gesture with the sword, almost as if he was using it to write in a calligraphy of the stars.

What he wrote was the name of the sword.

The Bladebone. Daniyar's sword was the Bladebone.

Rukh read the word in the High Tongue, but he saw it flare across the sky in dozens of other tongues. It was called the Bladebone, the Spine-Splitter, the Belt of Celestial Stars. The words hung suspended in the stars, then their imprint vanished.

Daniyar sheathed his sword, the silver-blue veil still in place.

There was utter confusion from the Talisman in response.

Daniyar's glance encompassed Yusuf and Rukh.

"The veil will hold until morning."

Rukh nodded, thinking of what he and the other Mages could do on this side of the veil.

Fire might take the towers.

The Cataphracts could lose the battle in the courtyard, but no one else would advance.

And a few hours hence, the Dawn Rite could alter the city's chances again.

26

THE COLOSSAL POWER OF AL MINTAKA STILL SIMMERED IN RUKH'S veins, his limbs trembling, the column of his throat ransacked. The Blue and Silver Mages had fared no better than he. Along with the boy Wafa, they were taking rest and refreshment in the war room, lost in their own thoughts, silent and unspeaking.

A massive battle had been fought in the courtyard before the Zhayedan declared victory. No Talisman had been left alive within their walls; the Cataphracts had pushed them through the Zhayedan Gate into the incinerating star-veil. Arsalan had managed to put out the fire that had engulfed the southern wall, but their fortifications were hours from crumbling. The southern wall would not hold. And sooner or later, the watchtowers would fall as well.

Now efforts were being made to bring the last of the Zhayedan's defenses to bear in the southern half of the square. The armory was depleted, while around the gates, legions of Zhayedan lay dead. Khashayar continued to issue orders for the defense, though he had fought through the night and could have little left to spare. Called from his defense of the Messenger Gate, his fierce will had wielded the Cataphracts like a battering ram against the Talisman.

Now in an act that neared obscenity, he was ordering his troops to pile bodies around the Illustrious Portal to cut off access to the palace. The Talisman deserved no better, the soldiers thought, but it was a grave dishonor to the Zhayedan who had fought to keep their city safe. Khashayar disagreed. He had argued that this was one more service the city's defenders could perform. A grim smile played over Rukh's lips: the Zhayedan were fighting as if they would be pinned with glorious honors and named to the Order of Khorasan.

But too few had survived to fight the next day's battle to hold their crumbling walls. Rukh's voice was ruined, his power in remission. Even if he could gather himself again, how long could the Mages of Khorasan stand against two armies intent on annihilation?

He glanced back at the armillary sphere as a prelude to joining the Mages.

No one had altered the position of the rings, and no one would until dawn peeled back the darkness. The power of Al Mintaka was too unpredictable, and no matter how Darius had wielded it, Rukh couldn't do the same. Not with the ghul working against his efforts, though the ghul had remained quiet through the night. The Assassin was also absent, and Arsalan was still in the thick of preparations for the morning, as if he feared to come to Rukh after what the ghul had done. He *should* be afraid, Rukh thought. If Arsalan had carried out his order, none of this would have come to pass. The southern wall would still be standing, the Zhayedan Gate intact. And thousands of his soldiers would have survived slaughter.

He stirred, making his way to the table to join the others. A page held his chair, while another hastened to serve him refreshment.

"What happened?" Yusuf asked, after Rukh had taken his first few bites of a meal he didn't taste. "Why did you lose control of the beam?"

Rukh reached for the chalice that was always brought to his hand, the cup studded with gemstones that paled beside the fire of the star. A furious pulse of anger burned inside his chest.

"The power wasn't mine alone. Al Mintaka has a twin, it seems—a sequence star open to interference, in this case the ghul that corrupted my sister. When the ghul usurped the power of the stars, I lost control of the beam. The consequences, you've seen."

Yusuf set down his cup with a frown. "When we arrived here, we found your sister with the Assassin—we exorcised the ghul. The Princess is free of it now."

Rukh's lips drew back over his teeth in a snarl. "You've just had ample evidence that your exorcism failed."

Daniyar joined the conversation. "Are you certain?"

Rukh scowled. "The ghul spoke to me. It seized control of Al Mintaka's orbit through the power of the sequence star."

Daniyar weighed Rukh's words. "I meant, was it the ghul who tried to redirect Al Mintaka, or was it the *Princess* who interfered?"

Wafa had told him of Darya's intercession during his interrogation by the Nizam. And he'd witnessed Darya's independent turn of mind for himself during the Black Khan's banquet.

"They are one and the same to me."

Rukh thought of the people he'd failed to protect, and felt something hard settle on his heart, closing off other possibilities. If he could summon Al Mintaka again, he would wipe out the Talisman to a man.

The next night would be clear, but before he deployed the star-beam again, he needed to see to the ghul. He snapped his fingers at a page.

"Find the Assassin. Tell him to bring the 'Princess' to me."

A runner came to the door of the chamber as the page departed. "Excellency," he panted, his shortness of breath suggesting he had covered some distance at speed. "The Messenger Gate is under attack again. We can't hold it much longer."

The Mages scrambled to their feet, their meal forgotten.

Rukh set down his chalice. "Where is Commander Arsalan?"

The runner's eyes flashed with fear. "On the ground, organizing the defense. But he asks for your aid. We lost too many men in the last attack." The deep breath he took turned into a sob. "Captain Khashayar's troops are covering the palace with assistance from the Teerandaz."

Rukh cursed, his thoughts scattered. The Blue Mage called him back.

"You need to evacuate the city."

"There's nowhere for them to go. The tunnels below Qaysarieh would lead them into the arms of the Nineteen. The Talisman are to the east; there's no passage north through the mountains. The inner walls are the city's last defense." He tried to sort through tactics, but tactics were Arsalan's gift. He jerked his head at the runner. "Tell Commander Arsalan we're on our way." He looked to Daniyar for counsel. "Will the veil hold without your presence on the wall?"

Daniyar nodded, his head tilted toward renewed sounds of battle. "Until dawn," he reminded them. When the runner had taken his leave, he addressed a different issue. "You need soldiers in the square."

"My men are dead in legions. What would you suggest I do?"

The Black Khan touched the onyx rook at his throat to reassure himself that it wasn't over yet.

"The men who carried my banner into the city—why haven't you let them fight?"

The Blue Mage interrupted, calling Wafa to his side. "We'll assist your commander while you decide this."

Wafa looked back at Daniyar, whether for guidance or permission, Rukh couldn't tell. The Silver Mage bent his head, and the others left.

Rukh didn't hold back then. "I don't trust your Talisman. They could do as much damage to our chances of survival as the ghul did to our walls. A second betrayal"—he grimaced—"or a third, if you consider my Nizam's defection to the ranks of the One-Eyed Preacher—Ashfall would not survive it. We cannot fight enemies on both sides of our walls."

A stern voice interrupted before Daniyar could respond.

"Your sister is not your enemy, Excellency."

Rukh found himself facing the Assassin.

27

Up until that moment, Rukh's relationship with the Assassin had been characterized by mutual convenience, and by some measure of trust. Rukh had said nothing upon the Assassin's disclosure of his identity. He hadn't blamed the man for bringing Darya back from the dead because the act had awakened Rukh's powers as Dark Mage. But this was a step too far. Nothing could excuse Hasbah, or Hudayfah, as he now knew him, for allowing the ghul to survive after Darya had razed the scriptorium.

In all the years of their association, Rukh had never touched the Assassin. Now, as the Silver Mage watched, he grasped the other man's arm to drag him to the terrace.

It said a great deal about their relationship that the Assassin didn't resist. He gazed at the ruins of the southern wall, his attention captured by the star-veil.

As the Assassin continued to examine it, Rukh said, "Look at my sister's work. We are hours away from extermination. Darya is not just my enemy, she is the enemy of Ashfall. Of all of Khorasan, given time." His lips became a bitter line. "Though, of course, our enemies may well count her a friend."

The Assassin's response caught Rukh off guard. He raised Rukh's hand to kiss his onyx ring.

"The ghul is dead, Excellency. The *Princess* was trying to aid you."

Rukh snatched his hand away, a hot flush rising to his face. "I thought you loyal to me."

"Do not doubt it." The Assassin's voice became soft. "I did not know the Princess could reach into your mind, or the extent to which she shared your gifts."

Rukh sputtered with rage at the Assassin's delusion. "She shares nothing of mine! Her gifts are Ashfall's curse!"

The steel mask gave nothing away. Doubtless that was why the Assassin wore it.

Rukh grabbed him by the shoulders, his ring striking the mask. "I look upon their army and am reminded of a proverb. A man has three enemies: his enemy, the friend of his enemy, and the enemy of his friends." He counted off on his fingers. "Darya. You. And the Talisman."

The Assassin's gloved hands grasped the Black Khan by the forearms, impenetrable mask to dark, tempestuous face.

"The kindness your father did me is written in marble on my soul, the injury you do me now, in dust to be forgotten. I am not your enemy. Nor would I ever stand with anyone you counted as an enemy. The Princess hurt you. She harmed this city, perhaps beyond recall, but not because of any loyalty to the Talisman. You know she is led by her heart. Yes, she is impetuous, even unwise. But who has spared the time to teach her otherwise?"

"Then she should have done nothing! Her whims have doomed the people of Ashfall."

The Black Khan tried to release himself from the Assassin's grasp but found he couldn't. Without exerting undue pressure, the Assassin held him firm. "She is trying to make amends. You would do well to let her." He nodded at Daniyar. "Just as you must permit the Talisman's defectors to fight. As Authenticate, the Silver Mage will confirm that they are loyal, and his motives, at least, you have no reason to distrust."

Authenticate.

Rukh had forgotten the Silver Mage's gift, if he had ever known it.

Unable to wrest free from the Assassin, he twisted to face Daniyar.

"Does the Assassin speak the truth?"

A troubled look from the Silver Mage. "There is no lie in his words. That just means *he* believes them."

What choice did the Black Khan have? Swamped by a feeling of recklessness, Rukh said, "Then go, my lord. Call your Talisman to fight." And when Daniyar had gone, he surged forward and touched his face to the Assassin's mask, willing to cling to any last bit of hope.

"How does my sister seek to make amends?"

Warmth inflected the Assassin's toneless voice. "You asked where your people might go when the city is overrun. I offer sanctuary at the Eagle's Nest."

Rukh rocked back on his heels. "How would they reach this sanctuary? Every route out of the city has been barred."

Now, at last, the Assassin released his grip. Stepping away from Rukh, he pointed north.

"As a gift to your father, the Assassins carved out a road between the Eagle's Nest and Ashfall. It leads from the tunnels beneath Qaysarieh to the mountains. I have shown the Princess the way; she oversees the evacuation as we speak. But we must hurry."

Rukh's heart stopped, then stuttered back to life. "Do this and you shall have anything you ask." Then caution pulled him back, tempered the immoderate vow. "Darya has no authority. Who would listen to her?"

"Commander Arsalan issued the order to the city's inhabitants."

His fury boiled over. Darya, Arsalan, the Assassin. Each conspiring against his authority to keep him in the dark. But whether it was anger he felt or wounded pride, he refused to let it rule him. Arsalan would never act against Ashfall, and the Silver Mage had verified the Assassin's account of his plans. It was Darya who threatened the empire.

"Kill her," he ordered. "If we hold another day, I'll be able to use the armillary sphere without risking her intervention."

The Assassin paused. "She understands. She knows what she's done, and now I know better than to leave her unattended."

"She is unattended *now*." A crushing rejoinder. "What does Darya's self-knowledge matter when I must deal with the consequences?" He moved back into the war room, where he pointed to the page who was clearing away his meal. "Bring me the Shahi scepter and my cloak."

It occurred to him then that he was not in possession of the Sacred Cloak. He and the Silver Mage had passed it back and forth, as necessity demanded. The Silver Mage had departed for the Zhayedan's barracks still wearing it.

He'd done so in order to persuade his defectors to fight, Rukh argued to himself. But a prickle of unease suggested there might be more to it. The Cloak had curled around the Silver Mage's body; its folds had clung to his hands. And there had been a darkness in the silver eyes when he'd conjured the star-veil . . . but there was no time to think of that now.

The Assassin made as if to check him. Rukh stilled. The Assassin did nothing without purpose, his movements always controlled.

"What is it?"

"I will do whatever you ask in the interests of Ashfall, but I will not deceive you. I do not intend to kill the Princess." He was quick to forestall a rebuke. "The power that awoke within you belongs to your sister as well. She may be able to use it to further enhance your abilities."

Rukh's response was outraged. "I've relied upon your assurances before, to the detriment of Ashfall!" Another slight shift of the Assassin's body, and he was awakened to the prospect of danger. No matter his oath of loyalty, the Assassin was a threat. Tempering his anger, Rukh said, "I don't need Darya. I have the other Mages."

Hard chips of jade looked back at him through the mask.

"I offer you my fortress. I send my men to die in your name. I fight at your side without flinching. I will do all that you ask, but this I will not do. I will not kill the daughter of the man who rescued me from death."

"*My* father." Though defiance colored his response, Rukh felt a sudden chill.

Soft and low, Hudayfah warned, "And *my* father in all but blood."

The Shahi scepter was brought to Rukh's hand.

Both men's eyes fell on it. Cold fear blossomed in Rukh's chest. He curled one hand under the head of the scepter, sweeping it to his heart.

His concession came at the cost of his pride.

"Very well. I will ask another to carry out my order."

The clarity of the diamond that topped the scepter was obscured by clouds of smoke. The Assassin's metallic voice became the voice of a man again, low and harsh in its timbre, as if his throat had been ravaged by flames.

As Rukh now knew it had, for Rukh's father had rescued a youth named Hudayfah from the aftermath of a fire. His life had been saved, but not before the fire had done its damage. Yet Rukh knew that the Assassin could alter his voice at will. That he didn't trouble to do so now suggested his depth of feeling.

"I have indulged your every whim, Excellency, but I will stand against you in this. If you harm the Princess, I will seal off the route to my fortress."

The diamond hardness of the scepter bit into Rukh's palm until it bled. The Assassin touched a gloved hand to the orb, and the smoke within its depths cleared.

"You are a prince who pays his debts, and your debts to me are many," he pointed out.

Eyes narrowed, Rukh inclined his head. He waited for the rest with arrogant disregard.

The Assassin tapped the scepter. "I do not want this. I do not want your city or your empire. I want nothing of your riches. I will allow no harm to come to you, but the moment has come to pay the debt. To honor the promise you made."

Rukh moved the scepter out of the Assassin's reach.

"What *do* you want in payment of the debt?"

"The Princess. I want you to give her to me."

The power of the Dark Mage surged. Rukh's onyx eyes bled crimson. He was shaken to realize that he still felt protective of Darya.

Scowling, he asked, "For what purpose? I won't allow you to practice your sorcery when your dark arts have served her ill."

The oppressive air in the war room eased, a lightness behind the mask.

"I wish her bound to me. I would take the Princess as my bride, as you know I would never take the ghul." He watched the Black Khan's grip on his scepter ease. "You need not fear any insult. I require no dowry, and my settlement upon the Princess will be worthy of her rank."

Rukh looked past him to the columns of the Talisman's army.

"She is promised to Arsalan." This debate was pointless, but he was uncertain whether to accept the assurance that the ghul had been expelled.

"The Commander does not want her."

"Arsalan will do as I ask. He is loyal to me." The betrothal was meant to honor that loyalty, to bind Arsalan in the one way he knew he could.

"No more so than I."

Rukh motioned to the pages to leave the room. Afraid to approach the armillary sphere, he rested one hand on the table, taking a moment for himself.

"My sister loves Arsalan. The betrothal was my gift to her."

The Assassin was shaking his head. "The marriage would be a travesty. Would you wish that for her?"

Rukh's head jerked up. "What would it be with you?"

"Whatever we choose to make of it." A bow and then the Assassin added, "Excellency."

A runner from the Emissary Gate appeared. And Rukh had no more time to waste on a fate that was anything but certain.

"Take what you will, if there is anything left to take." He dismissed the matter from his mind. "But do not leave her side. I fear what else my sister may choose to visit on me."

28

"Rukh?"

Of course, Arsalan would be the one to come and find him. His general appeared as tired as Rukh felt, though he'd found a moment to have his armor repaired.

"Was that you?" Arsalan came to lean against the balustrade beside Rukh, surveying the damage to the Talisman, eyes of obsidian picking up the glint of stars.

"The Mages lent their assistance. I suppose you've come to reprove me for having the arrogance to assume I could wield the power of a star."

Arsalan sighed. He slung an arm over Rukh's shoulders, his body radiating warmth.

"I'm not your conscience, Rukh."

If not Arsalan, then who? The tenderness in his eyes meant Arsalan knew full well that he curtailed Rukh's more outrageous tendencies.

"I beg to differ. I would have run amok without you long ago." Rukh's smile was fleeting. "But for now we hold to the east."

A temporary reprieve was still a reprieve.

He realized he was waiting for Arsalan to praise him. Arsalan must have reached the same conclusion, for his affection was plain in his voice. "You did well. You did all that could be expected as Prince of Khorasan, and more."

Rukh feigned unconcern. "You needn't flatter me."

"Needn't I?" Such warmth beneath the teasing.

He wouldn't give it up, Rukh decided. Not for anything. After all, a prince was entitled to an indulgence or two with his world burning down around his ears. He felt Arsalan pull away.

"You're not still angry with me?"

Rukh wasn't ready to offer reassurance, so he asked a question of his own. "What of the Messenger Gate? You asked for reinforcements."

"The Blue Mage is there now, and Khashayar assists him. I needed a moment."

Arsalan's arm fell from Rukh's shoulders. He braced both arms against the railing, the movement stretching lean bands of muscle all along his torso. He wore his sable hair longer than most of the Zhayedan, and now he brushed it from his face.

"The Messenger Gate can't hold. There's been too much damage. And the Zhayedan are spent, so it's good we've begun evacuation."

"The Talisman will take it all, regardless." Rukh did his own inventory of the damage. "They've burned the Shah's house of worship because we didn't hold the outer defenses. What comes next? The palace, the throne room—the *throne*. The scriptorium is gone." A reminder of the damage Darya had inflicted, though without the acrimony of his earlier accusations. "They'll bring our towers down, they'll rip the written word from our walls. They'll force me to watch the violation of the women of my family, and then they'll stake my head at the Zhayedan Gate."

He let himself taste defeat. He wallowed in the bitterness of the words, but as he'd come to expect, Arsalan didn't indulge his melancholy.

"If it comes to that, I'll fight at your back myself. You've no reason to be afraid." Together, they watched the Talisman's maneuvers, their numbers and machinery vast. "Not all that much reason," Arsalan amended. "I'm still here. Khashayar, Cassandane, many of our captains. They're loyal to you. They'll fight until there's nothing left to save, so don't despair, Rukh. Your gifts are many. They will see us through."

Rukh turned to look at him, trying to penetrate his self-assurance. "And what of you?"

Star-pricked eyes settled on his, the hint of a question in them.

"Do you doubt my loyalty, Rukh?" He brushed a bit of debris from Rukh's shoulder, his touch lingering. "Because I could not kill Darya?"

"No." Rukh gripped the hand that Arsalan had raised to his shoulder. "You were right, you didn't deserve that. And I should not have asked you to compromise who you are, or to carry out an order I could not carry out myself." Humility was unfamiliar on his lips, the apology a little strained. He glanced at the destruction to the south. "Though ethics come at a cost."

Arsalan looked staggered by the charge. "The ghul brought down the wall?"

"Or Darya." Rukh shrugged. "Well-meaning as always before the injury comes."

Arsalan started. "She's involved in the evacuation. I should go and supervise."

Rukh caught his arm, feeling the strength of the tendons beneath his touch. "The Assassin is there to mind her."

"Would that he had minded the wall."

"Indeed."

There had been too many mistakes. But fighting a war was not a matter of strategy falling into place. There were variables that affected the outcome, though Rukh had not expected that his sister would be one of them.

"I should return," Arsalan said again. "I wanted to be sure you were well." The velvet rasp touched him like a caress. And in those star-touched eyes, Rukh caught sight of a vast loneliness.

He dealt with it as best as he could. He told a page to bring Arsalan some refreshment, and then he hooked an arm over his shoulders. "Stay with me awhile, I would spend some time with you. Who knows what the morning may bring."

Their heads knocked together, the star-veil casting blue shadows over their skin.

"I hope it will bring deliverance. But for now, I am with you, my Prince."

So for a time they talked of other things than war.

29

THE DOUBLE DOORS THAT LED TO THE ZHAYEDAN'S BARRACKS WERE barricaded by two soldiers of the Khorasan Guard. Daniyar had given no thought to how he would persuade them to step aside, and now he spoke to them with the weariness of a man who felt his power draining from his body like a river emptying into the sea, silver strands separating and fraying, even as the hours of night wore away to hasten the dawn.

"Soldiers are needed to hold the Messenger Gate." He indicated the doors. "Including the Talisman prisoners."

"We are under orders," the younger of the pair said, as a loud boom echoed through the square. All three men froze.

"I understand." Then Daniyar said, "But the gate cannot hold without more men. As it is, we may not reach the gate in time."

The other soldier was older, and he took the time to appraise the Silver Mage, his gaze drifting over the Sacred Cloak. The soldier strode away, down the long hall of the armory and barracks, calling the other with him. With a last reluctant glance at the barred doors, the younger member of the Guard followed.

Daniyar unlatched the doors and stepped inside the cavernous hall. The barracks were well-proportioned, designed with the same artistry found throughout the corridors and palaces of Ashfall, with large windows looking out upon a slender strip of greenery that separated the barracks from the eastern wall. The windows were more than decorative, allowing light into a space that at night was lit with hundreds of copper lanterns. They were also fortified, with arrow slits on both sides and portable wooden stairs positioned beneath each. At intervals, the stairs led to a second floor with dozens of exits connecting the barracks to the outer wall.

Members of the Khorasan Guard barred access to the wall from the stairs. They stared at Daniyar in surprise, but none moved to draw a sword. They knew him too well by now.

Daniyar adjusted the Sacred Cloak.

"You are needed at the Messenger Gate." The sound of a piercing horn underlined his words. "Your commander summons you."

The Khorasan Guard began to file out, recognizing the summons. One man stopped to warn Daniyar. "You cannot hold the men in the barracks on your own."

Daniyar's glance swept the hall. Rows of narrow cots ran the perimeter on both sides, leading to a soldiers' mess. The kitchens at the rear were silent, the Talisman gathered in a group nearby. With two armies poised to break through the gates, none had chosen to rest. His eyes found Toryal, the young Talisman soldier Daniyar had promised safety.

"I don't need to hold them," he said to the last member of the Khorasan Guard. "They'll be fighting at your side."

When the barracks emptied of the Guard, Toryal moved to meet him, carrying the Silver Mage's standard in one hand, a black rook smudged upon his forehead, as if he'd tried to erase it.

Daniyar made a swift count of the men who followed Toryal. Fewer than two hundred men had defected from the Talisman's ranks.

"More would have come, if they could have reached the gate in time."

There was nothing for that now. "The city will fall soon. Will you help us fight?"

Tears burned behind Toryal's eyes, but the young soldier was too proud to let them fall.

"You promised us safety."

A fist of regret seized Daniyar's heart. Pressing Toryal's shoulder, he said, "I promised you a choice." His gaze swept over the other defectors, these lost boys of Candour who had trusted his word at such risk to themselves. "The choice to decide where you stand, and what you are willing to fight for. You must know that none are safe within these walls, and so I ask you again: Will you fight at my side?"

Another man spoke up, this one wearing the weight of years of hardship on his face. He was as tall as the Silver Mage, but not as strong, his movements fluid, his pale eyes bright. Daniyar remembered him out of hundreds of men, remembered crossing his path in Candour. The soldier's name was Uwais.

"Does the Guardian of Candour ask us to take up arms against our own?"

Daniyar reached for his standard. He found himself leaning his weight against the staff. He forced his head up to hold the other man's gaze, piercing it with silver clarity.

"How could they be your own if they brought you to this?" His fingers caressed the green pennant of his standard. He read its white script aloud. "'Defend the truth in the face of all dishonor.' That is what I ask you to do."

Uwais stood firm. "To defect from the Talisman's war is one thing. But it would be an act of grave dishonor to take up arms against our kin."

Toryal interrupted before Daniyar could say more. "Are the women of your family safe, Uwais? Can you promise them safety if the Talisman should win?"

Uwais's face hardened. With lethal swiftness, he gripped Toryal by the throat, his fingers digging into the scars at the younger man's neck.

"A man asks to forfeit his life if he speaks of the women of my family." But he released Toryal once he'd delivered the warning, his eyes on the Silver Mage.

"You're Qabail?" Daniyar asked. "From the mountains, is my guess." Qabail referred to the outlying tribes of the southern territories who'd held out longest against the Talisman.

"Khyber," the other man said.

The Khyber chieftains had come under the Talisman's flag over the course of the years. It would take more time than Daniyar could spare to convince Uwais to set his allegiance aside.

He touched a gentle hand to Toryal's throat, admiring the young man's fortitude.

"The army of the Nineteen is at the Messenger Gate. That is whom I ask you to fight. The Zhayedan may be soldiers, but this city is home to civilians. I seek a way to save them."

Daniyar didn't prod Uwais, didn't taunt him for lack of courage. Uwais's pale eyes blazed with intelligence; he was someone the other men would follow. Now Uwais measured the Sacred Cloak. His hand twitched toward it, a gesture he contained.

"Is this a trick?" he demanded.

So much pain in those ice-blue eyes, his suspicion brutally earned.

Making an instant decision as the sounds of battle grew louder in the square, Daniyar drew the others into a huddle. The folds of the Sacred Cloak enclosed them.

"No trick." His voice was husky from continuous use, from the power he had drawn upon during the Rite of Qari'ah. "Do you not remember me as Guardian of Candour?"

Uwais brushed the folds of the Cloak with wonder. The heads of all three men touched, and Daniyar experienced a surge of power like a silver blaze through his heart.

Uwais nodded. "I remember." He signaled the rest of the soldiers. "We will fight the Nineteen. Do not ask more of us than that."

Daniyar pressed his fingertips to a point on his forehead, remembering the carnage that waited outside. He had to prepare them for that.

"The Talisman broke through the gates more than once. The Zhayedan fought them to a standstill. I would not give you pain, but many of your brothers lie dead in the square."

Uwais discounted this. "Such are the costs of war. If we are going to do this, lead us."

Passing Toryal his standard, Daniyar urged the defectors through the hall, brushing the black rook on each man's forehead as he passed, so that it glimmered silver in the dark. Each soldier passed his test. He drew a breath of relief.

Another boom shook the square.

The soldiers moved into formation.

Then they began to run.

30

THROUGH THE LAST HOURS OF THE NIGHT, THE TALISMAN DEFECTORS fought beside Daniyar. Their silver rooks glittered in the dark, the tide of battle sweeping back and forth through the monstrous clash of weaponry, and the occasional detonation of a charge that set new fires along the wall.

Far above the courtyard, a rush of arrows rained down on the Nineteen like the black waters of a flood. Firing down on both sides of the gate, Teerandaz archers led by Cassandane tried to slow the Nineteen's advance. The Blue Mage stood above the gate, his hands cast out in a wide arc, as rites from the Pearl of Timeback carved a path of flame through the enemy.

Pushing his hair from his eyes, Daniyar saw that Wafa echoed the Blue Mage's gestures, while serving as a liaison between Cassandane and Yusuf, coordinating their attack.

A sword clanged against his own, and he returned his attention to the battle, pushing soldiers of the Nineteen back. Their style of fighting reminded him of the Assassins. They leapt and whirled, turning on the smallest radius before bringing their swords to bear in agile, twisting thrusts that gutted flesh and shattered bone. The precision of their strikes was augmented by the chant that fell from their lips, a chant that seemed to slow the responses of the Zhayedan.

"Over this are Nineteen."

Daniyar's sword trembled in response.

Men fell all around him. Zhayedan, Talisman defectors, the blue-cloaked fighters of the Nineteen. And still the battle raged, sparks striking off swords, arrows catching at bare throats, pike-staffs delivering brutal blows to unshielded ribs.

The Nineteen were not armored. They had agility, the chant on their lips, and that was all. But the sheer weight of their numbers was pushing the Zhayedan back. Daniyar fought until he thought the muscles of his arms would lock. Arsalan, too, battled on, and wherever he made his stand, the Zhayedan rallied around him with their war cry: smooth and polished in the war room, blistering and bold on the field.

This night we hold.

None of it was enough.

A push from the Nineteen opened up a gap in the defense. Men streamed through to the Illustrious Portal, where Khashayar's troops did their best to hold the palace. Wiping sweat from his face with a fold of the Sacred Cloak, Daniyar glimpsed a dozen Assassins leaping over the bodies piled at the entrance to the palace.

The Assassins wove a sinuous pattern against the oncoming thrust of the Nineteen.

Thunder boomed overhead. The Nineteen rallied again. Daniyar thought of the star-veil that shielded the city to the south. Would it hold with his attention divided, his strength almost spent, and dawn creeping up on the horizon?

He dodged a blow from a mace, then glanced up and caught Wafa's eyes, far, far above him on the wall, an eerie silver-blue

Ausma Zehanat Khan

that resembled the points of the star-veil. Wafa waved down at him, and Daniyar's sword came alive in his hand. He handled it with rare fury, ending life after life, catching glimpses of Uwais, who fought with lethal grace, daggers in both hands; of Toryal, who was borne back against the crush of bodies; of members of the Khorasan Guard, who had yielded to his authority in the barracks; of Khashayar, whose skill with sword and spear he wouldn't have believed if he hadn't seen it with his own eyes.

Daniyar's silver sword obeyed his every command, cutting him a path clear through to the gate, where after a period of intense fighting, he found himself back to back with Arsalan, holding off the unrelenting flow of the Nineteen with little more than determination. It couldn't last. Unless the buckled gate was repaired, the Nineteen would continue to throw themselves into the Zhayedan's defenses until there wasn't a soldier left alive to resist.

His sword became tangled in the cloak of an enemy soldier. Another thrust a dagger at his throat. He lost his footing, and a dozen men were on his body; he was mired in blood and sweat and mud, using his forearms to block the heavy blows.

A haunting cry from the wall.

His sword began to glow, its power surging through his body.

The cry sounded again. Men rolled off his body, scrabbling at their necks.

A rough hand reached down and hauled him to his feet. Uwais. Who threw himself back into the fray before Daniyar could offer his thanks.

His sword began to pulse in his hand. An electric surge moved up from his wrist into his arm, forcing him to raise it high above his body.

The Sacred Cloak swirled around his shoulders, as thick as a suit of armor, its soft folds untainted with sweat or blood. His left arm moved of its own volition, drawing the Cloak over his leather breastplate like a shield.

The muscles of his arms had stopped shaking. His sword shimmered like a lance of fire, at once as heavy as a mace and as light as a skein of silk.

Thunder boomed again. Something shifted in his mind.

These fighters of the Nineteen were ensorcelled. They would never tire, never admit defeat, never withdraw from the attack. The chant upon their lips was infused with the One-Eyed Preacher's alchemy, and as long as that power persisted, the tribes from the Rub Al Khali would follow the Preacher to the end.

Daniyar muttered the name of the One. Whether as plea or protest, he didn't know. If he'd had a choice, he would have shown mercy to the warriors sent to Ashfall to be fed to the Zhayedan's steel. He would have shown them the same compassion he'd offered to Toryal.

But he could not afford mercy with the army of the Nineteen.

He understood what the cry from the wall had meant—what Wafa had called down to him, the boy forever altered by the trials of the Israa e Miraj.

Daniyar's right hand closed around his sword.

He raised his head, the roar of his voice a weapon that stilled everything around him.

"You think you bring hell to the people of Khorasan. You should tremble in your bones to usurp the majesty of the Nineteen Keepers of the Saqar, who do not descend from my line or yours, *and who do not exist in this world*. Know that I have taken arms against your cause, and for all your ignorance in naming yourselves the Nineteen, *this*"—he shook the silver sword, watched its shape change so that the tip split farther, close to cleaving the sword in two, both edges lit with flame—"*this* is the sword that will bar the gates of hell."

The Nineteen shuddered, faltered for a breath, then threw themselves at him again. Arsalan shouted a warning to him, but the blows of the Nineteen rebounded off the Cloak. His sword painted a glittering arc of destruction, blood spraying from but not adhering to its divided blades. Words came to life along the edges of the sword. One side bore the Guardian of Candour's motto. But a new line of calligraphy settled on the other.

Daniyar called out its admonition. "*There is no sword like the Bladebone, and none like the warrior who wields it.*"

He slashed in both directions, raising two lines of fire. Those trapped within the fire found their spines severed. A fierce sense of satisfaction took hold of Daniyar, for this sword had been known as the Spine-Splitter, and its legend had just proved true.

The sword fell in repeated thrusts. Its blows were met with agony. Blood-darkened bone littered the field, and still Daniyar pressed on to the other side of the gate.

"Rukh!" he bellowed. "Yusuf! Bind the gate with the Dawn Rite. It will hold back the Preacher's sorcery."

A faint wash of light began to sweep over the night. A golden haze tinted with crimson drifted across the city walls.

Daniyar didn't know where along the walls the other Mages might be, but he felt the power of the Dawn Rite surge over the army he faced. He couldn't contribute to the Dawn Rite, every ounce of concentration aimed at maintaining the star-veil. But Rukh and Yusuf didn't falter: verses were flung out with a splendor that broke like a flood, drowning all in its path.

"*Say I seek refuge in the One from the evil of those bent on occult endeavors.*"

Above their heads, midnight arteries were threaded with strands of gold. The Bladebone held high, Daniyar turned back to the Messenger Gate. Between the giant towers that buttressed both sides of the gate, Yusuf and Rukh had woven a turquoise web. It lacked the incinerating power of the star-veil, but it worked to fend off the Nineteen.

He caught sight of Toryal, his armor rent and body bloodied. The tears on his face echoed the hopelessness in his eyes. But why? They had won the briefest of respites, but a victory was still a victory, and now the Zhayedan, the Assassins, and the men who fought under Daniyar's banner stood a chance of clearing the square . . . at least until the star-veil dispersed.

Toryal fought his way to the gate, his body shaking with sobs. Their eyes connected through a forest of bloodstained spears, and Toryal cried, "Please don't leave us, my lord."

And then Daniyar understood.

He was trapped outside the gate, his sword his only protection.

One man alone against an army.

31

THE BANISHMENT CHARM UNRAVELED ARIAN. HER INSIDES ACHED, HER limbs were stiff, her skin a waxen mask imprinted on the bones of her skull. A dull ache throbbed behind her eyes, a band of pain fastened like a vise around her temples.

There was a terrible leap of fear through her veins, a bruising pressure beneath the fragile construction of her ribs. She rubbed a fist over her heart, felt the weakness of its response. It wasn't the banishment charm that had caused it—it was caused by the fading of a bond. The sundering of the vow she had made to Daniyar on their journey to Timeback.

"What would I bind you with?"

"Your hair. The beauty of your eyes. The sweetness of your kiss. The murmur of the Claim on your lips. Any of those. All of those."

"Then we are bound."

A sob broke from her throat. What had Daniyar done to cause this crushing sense of loss? Why did it hurt as though a silver star had burned into silence in the sky?

"Why do you cry, sister?"

Arian trembled with shock. Whatever Ilea had intended, the banishment charm had sent her back to Black Aura. She found herself in the scrying chamber, facing Lania across the basin.

Lania was beautiful in her scrying robes, a dress of pure white silk, a moonstone upon her finger, her hair left long and loose, the mask she had repainted hard with secret calculation, her eyes bright with hostility. In this moment, they could have been twins, though Arian knew that she brooked no comparison with her elegant sister. Arian's body was bruised all over, and she was still wearing the battered armor that had seen her through her Audacy.

She spread out the hand she had made into a fist and rubbed it over her breast.

"The Silver Mage." She forced out the words. "I think . . . I think Daniyar has fallen."

Lania's mask tightened. She dipped her hand into the basin. The water rippled out from the center in delicate circles.

"I warned you, little sister." She studied Arian's face, assessed the pain she made no effort to hide. "I warned you that your Audacy would cause you a suffering unlike any other." She took note of the dull gleam of Arian's circlets. "Is there more to your anguish?"

Arian shivered. Why did Lania make her feel so young and uncertain?

"The High Companion banished me from the Council of Hira."

Lania's lip curled back. "Ilea?"

Arian nodded, sensing the undercurrents of unfamiliar truths.

Lania snorted. "Look at how she holds to her insignificant kingdom."

Was Hira insignificant? Arian winced at the thought.

Lania drew one finger in a pattern through the basin.

"How do you come to be here, sister? I warned you that you would not see me again, yet your presence here makes me a liar." Her eyes darkened with anger.

Feeling cold, Arian rubbed her upper arms.

"There is . . . a system of portals. You must know it as well." She pointed to the basin. "This must be the source that connects Black Aura to the All Ways."

"Are there others?" A feline curiosity sparked in Lania's eyes.

For what Arian wanted in exchange, she knew she would have to offer undiluted honesty.

"The Blue Eye is a portal. And you already know of the Well of Souls. In Ashfall, there is Qaysarieh, I believe. These are the ones I know. There may also be others."

The clear waters in the basin had turned a milky white under Lania's attentions.

"Is use of the portals limited to the Companions?"

A harder question for Arian to contend with. Because if Lania learned how to use the basin as a portal, what would prevent her from transporting herself into the heart of the Citadel to fulfill her dreams of revenge?

"Lania." Arian needed to think, to find a way to persuade Lania to aid her, but all she could feel was the aching throb of her heart. "Please, I need your help."

My love, don't let me go. Hold on a little longer.

Her sister looked up. With her free hand, she motioned Arian closer.

"Tell me what I want to know, and I will grant you a boon. But choose with care, Arian, for I will not grant you another."

Arian fell quiet under the weight of that warning. Her body

ached with the aftereffects of the Preacher's assault and the sense of wrongness the banishment had produced.

"The Citadel is under attack. Soon the scriptorium will burn."

She searched Lania's face for a sign that would link her to a shared past. But the Khanum of Black Aura was very much in evidence now.

"Is that the boon you ask? The power to return to Hira?"

The painful vise around Arian's forehead tightened, and her heart . . . her heartbeat was slowing. She was weakening, losing her will.

She braced both hands on the basin. "No. No, that is not what I ask."

Bent over the basin, she drew in large gulps of air.

"What, then?" A cold note of amusement as Lania watched her suffer.

"Daniyar," she whispered, because he had always loved her, had always tried to honor her, and she had promised him she would hold no loyalty higher than her loyalty to him. His star . . . his star was *fading*, his years of service done. He would never have the chance to show her the Damson Vale.

"Stand up straight," Lania snapped. "Tell me what you want, and what you will barter in exchange."

If you knew what I have suffered, would you not show me kindness?

But the firmness of Lania's tone made her bring her reeling thoughts to order. No matter that Ilea had banished her, she was still the First Oralist of Hira.

"Tell me if Daniyar is safe. Tell me how I can help him."

A cruel smile graced her sister's lips.

"Do you ask me to Augur the future for you, sister? Will you join in the sorcerous arts though bound by oath to Hira?"

Arian hesitated, searching for a way through the trap. "I do not ask you to Augur the future. I wish to see the present."

"So clever." A cunning parry. "Yet what you seek in the end is divination. You wish to know what I know; you wish to see what I *see*."

If Lania demanded this concession, Arian would give it.

"As you wish. Please, Lania, I must *know*."

"So weak," Lania mused. "You have made yourself so weak, Arian."

The opposite was true. Her love for Daniyar had made her strong. She wanted to be worthy of him. The clarity of that thought in her mind, she dipped her right hand in the basin and caught at Lania's hand.

Lania's body jolted. The swirling waters boiled over the edge of the basin, the color molting from white to purest gold.

Lania tried to pull away. Arian held on, her earlier weakness forgotten. She felt it too—that electric jolt of connection, of vibrance, of *magnificence*. She wasn't fool enough to let it go.

"Tell me what you see."

Compelled by the strength of Arian's emotion, Lania did as she asked, her head forced down to the basin to the images that formed on the surface of the water.

"He's alone," she gasped. "Alone against an army."

"Is he hurt? Will he fall?" With her free hand, Arian fastened Lania's opposite hand to her circlet. *"Tell me."*

Lania couldn't raise her head from the basin, though Arian exerted no force.

"I cannot see." It was no more than the truth. "His future is unwritten. I do not see him on any plane I search."

Her entire body shook at the strength of Arian's reaction.

A fine line split the roiling waters, silver bisecting gold. And then knowledge came to Lania, and she lifted her face, her eyes pitying Arian.

Her fingertips hovered over the silver line. "This line connects the Silver Mage to you."

"What is it?"

Lania shook her head. "I'm not certain. I sense the interest of the One-Eyed Preacher."

"Daniyar has had no congress with the Preacher."

The waters changed again. "The Preacher knows him now."

Lania studied the images a little longer: a man alone on a battlefield, a gleaming sword in his hand, the brightness of his eyes ebbing, just as Arian's circlets had dulled.

"His star *has* dimmed." Frown lines creased her mask. "But I cannot tell you what that means, or whether the Silver Mage will fall."

The silver line in the basin intertwined with another color, this one a bright blue.

She glanced up at Arian. "It seems as though your lover ascended, yet there was more to his Ascension than he may have told you. Do not ask me to tell you more. His mysteries are not mine to share."

Seeing Arian's naked pain, her arrogance fell away. "Arian, why? Why do you open yourself up to such sorrow when your destiny is that of First Oralist? The Silver Mage must fight his battles alone, just as you fight yours."

But Arian thought of the sisterhood of the Companions of Hira. She thought of her own sister. Lania had released her from imprisonment at Black Aura. And she repeated the truth she'd learned upon her ascent.

"I have never been alone."

Lania tried to draw away. Arian covered the hand on her circlet and held firm.

Footsteps sounded in the hall. Lania's head dipped toward the basin. She broke free of Arian's grip.

"Be careful what you say now."

32

ARIAN RUBBED HER CIRCLET. FOR AN INSTANT, IT HAD BURNED HER, BUT when she slid her fingers beneath it, she found her skin undamaged.

With a slight knock, a young woman with a scar on her cheek entered the scrying chamber. She curtsied before the Khanum, both hands behind her back. She caught sight of Arian and flashed Lania a look of astonishment.

"What do you bring, Saher?"

The dove extended her prize to the Khanum: a stone jar with a sealed lid.

"From Jaslyk." She beamed with pride. "Gul delivered it as you asked."

Lania's fingers folded around the jar. Its weight was denser than she'd expected, and the jar slipped from her hand.

Arian stopped its fall with the Claim, the jar suspended in the air for an infinitesimal moment, before Lania's grip firmed again.

The two sisters exchanged a glance, and Arian said, "No, Lania. You *mustn't*."

The change in Lania was instant, the mask of the Khanum intact.

"You have no authority here. *I* command in Black Aura, and my course is decided."

"Lania—"

Lania turned in a whirl of silk, pointing Saher to the door.

"Go. These are private matters."

Arian admired Saher's courage when she stayed where she was.

Lania's hand shaped itself into a claw. "I gave you a command."

Swallowing hard, the dove said, "Khanum, I fear there is unrest among the Ahdath. They are gathering against you on behalf of the soldier you killed, the one who took Gul for himself."

"I Augured as much." A curt response. "That is no concern of yours."

"I would not wish any harm to come to you, Khanum."

Lania studied the dove's scarred cheek for a moment. "Foolish child, I believe you mean it." A quick gesture erased the scar. Saher stroked her cheek, but was wise enough not to speak.

"I am forewarned, you need not fear."

When Saher had left, Lania placed the jar on a pedestal near an archway that led into the room. Moonlight spilled over hair as dark as Arian's own, gilded the silk dress so that her movements became sylph-like, her head bent in contemplation over the sealed jar.

Arian was torn by indecision. She was needed at Hira, and even more so by Daniyar—she couldn't let him fight alone—but she also knew that she could not permit Lania to spread the contents of the jar. Lania's scheme to unleash the plague would bring about the end of the world.

She edged closer to the pedestal. Lania's head came up, her green eyes tinged with crimson as she watched Arian's approach.

"I told you not to come back here. I warned you I have no love for you."

"I don't believe you. You speak with cruelty but show me kindness."

"When I collared you and gave you to Nevus, was that kindness?"

"Yes! You did not give me to the Authoritan, or to the soldiers of the Ahdath. You gave me the chance to save myself."

"And I suppose it was compassion that had me torture the Silver Mage."

"You kept him alive while you bided your time to strike. Another gift."

"And when I kept Daniyar in my chambers for myself? When I kissed him so you could see, was that a kindness to you?"

A feral smile curved her lips until Arian said, "No, that wasn't kindness. You were driven by love. You love him as I do. I do not blame you for that. The man he is, the depths of his courage—you came to see that for yourself."

It took Lania a moment before she could say, "He was nothing more than a dalliance. There are men aplenty in this city."

"There are none like Daniyar."

They had reached an impasse. Arian placed her hand on the jar.

"Careful. Be very careful, sister."

Arian shivered at the smile that distorted Lania's mask. She realized she couldn't win like this. She couldn't use logic or persuasion against the woman who had deposed the Authoritan. She had to make herself vulnerable to find that same part of Lania.

She let her body soften, let her hand slip from the jar that contained a plague that Lania considered a remedy.

"If love is what you seek, Lania, know that you will find it.

Know that you deserve it. Not every man is like the Ahdath, or like the Talisman who stole you from our home."

Lania struck out with her hand. Her nails tore at Arian's face, leaving long scratches on her cheek. Arian didn't flinch.

"Look at me, Lania."

Bewildered, Lania did.

They stared into each other's eyes, Arian seeing with the power of the Claim, searching for Lania's secrets. Such sorrow and rage at her core, such dire self-loathing and shame.

"I was alone." A statement without inflection.

"I know." Arian touched Lania's cheek.

"Our parents and brother were dead, and for all I knew, you had been taken too. But I was the one to suffer, while you found refuge at Hira."

Arian thought of the night their house had burned, the weight of memory pressing deep. If she and Lania shared the burden, could their relationship change? How could it hurt to try?

"They beheaded our father. They ripped out our mother's throat. They burned our brother alive. He still bears the scars to this day."

Lania's mask cracked. *"To this day?"*

"He lives, Lania. Like you, he stayed hidden. He hoped to take revenge." She reached for Lania, pulling her close, harsh angles into softness, Lania's fury and pain against Arian's unchecked need. "I was a child. I couldn't save you. But every day since, I have prayed to reclaim the sister I love."

Lania hadn't known safety since the day she'd been stolen from Candour. She tried to pull away from Arian's embrace. Arian held her with the Claim.

Her slender limbs convulsed. "You would use the Claim against me?"

"To ask you for honesty, yes."

"You wouldn't survive my truths."

"Tell me, Lania, please. You need someone to hear you."

As no one had heard the helpless cries of the girl Lania had been.

There was a long pause before Lania spoke in the wondering tones of a child. "Did you know that Ilea knew? In those first days after I was taken, she was asked to send a force to rescue me. She refused on the grounds of neutrality—of keeping peace with the Talisman."

Arian fell to her knees, taking Lania down with her.

"No, Lania, *no*."

"I was in the hands of the Talisman for months before the Authoritan bought me. And what do you think happened to me before I was delivered?" She pressed her knuckles to her lips. "I opened the door to the Talisman, when our father warned us to hide. I *earned* this fate for myself. My actions destroyed our house."

"Don't take their crimes on your shoulders! You were *never* to blame!"

Arian was looking at a mirror image twisted by self-hatred, as Lania's poison spilled out.

your childhood, Arian,
oh, how I was puni

of men killed our mother and father. I
myself *much* more. And

Pain such as Arian had never known—had never wanted to know, but why else had she dedicated her life to the freeing of Talisman slaves, if not to forestall this very fate for the women of the south? If Lania possessed the courage to speak, Arian would listen.

And listen she did, as her sister whispered in her ear of the use the Talisman had made of her, until word had come from the Authoritan that he wished to purchase their prize.

Lania was crying, silent tears that streaked the painted mask. Lead stained Lania's robe and splashed across Arian's armor.

"I did not love the Authoritan—I *couldn't*. But when I told him what the Talisman had done, he hunted them down one by one. All he asked in return was for me to share my gift with the Claim."

Arian stroked Lania's back, wondering how she could have thought to judge her sister.

"It wasn't enough, Arian. It will never be enough." She rose to her feet, glaring down at her sister. "Do you understand now why I must use the plague? I do this for both of us. For the brother we lost. For our parents, Armaghan and Saya, founders of the Inkwell scriptorium, honored teachers of the Claim."

Her hands fastened around the stone jar.

"We have the same enemy, Arian. If I use this as I intend, Hira will be safe. The archives will be safe. And you will be protected from the One-Eyed Preacher. He will not touch you again." A cunning expression crossed her face. "He won't harm Daniyar."

At the mention of Daniyar's name, Arian's heart lurched. He couldn't fall. Not with the fate of Ashfall resting on his shoulders. Not with the vow he had sworn. No~~~~~~he was part of herself.

Don't give me up, my love. No matter w~~~ ~~ou learned *Ascension, for I learned you are mine. My sword, my shield, my destiny. My garment as I am yours.*

Her indecision cast aside, she made use of the Claim for herself. She didn't know if she could reach him, or if he could feel the bond between them, but she sent him her reckoning of the verse that had surfaced to her mind from the Codex.

The One created mates for us from our own kind that we may find peace in them, just as the One set between us love and mercy.

She would not allow him to yield. She would not allow him to turn from his vow.

Here, in these, are signs for people who reflect.

She could not give him more until she had dealt with the threat of the plague.

"The plague cannot be contained, Lania. It won't discriminate; its effects will not be limited to the Talisman. It will sweep over Khorasan, killing everyone we love."

"I love no one, sister."

Lania waved her left hand in the air, the gesture accompanied by a sibilant whisper. The lead mask restored itself, and from behind it, a stranger peered out.

But Arian had learned to see past the surface, and just as she refused to yield Daniyar, she refused to abdicate her responsibility to her sister.

"You love *me*, Lania. You love Hudayfah. You love the Companions of Hira. Lie to yourself, if you choose, you cannot lie to me."

The untapped power of the Claim began to throb in Arian's veins. Lania responded with a verse of enchantment. Fine white crevices appeared on the surface of the jar.

"Let them all die, then. These lands need a cleansing. This ugliness must be washed from the face of the earth. The Ahdath, my doves . . . you. And me."

Arian's response was unerring. She laid a gentle hand upon her sister's cheek, coating her fingers with the white paint of the mask.

"I know why you wear the mask, Lania. But you were never ugly."

She put both hands on Lania's cheeks and wiped off the paint. She continued to draw away the lead, until her palms were stained with it, her skin scented with its poison, her lungs drawing it in. None of that mattered against the power of the Claim, against the beauty of the truth. She tried to make Lania see, offering a new verse.

"Do not mix the truth with falsehood or conceal the truth while you know it."

"No!" Lania cried again. "The Talisman—"

"—do not own you. They can't hurt you anymore. The image you see in the waters of your basin isn't a reflection of their cruelty. It's *you*, Lania. It's only you. See yourself, as I do."

Lania snarled at her. "And what do *you* see when you look at me, little sister? What do your gifts perceive?"

Arian kept her hands on Lania's face, kept her gaze fixed so that green eyes looked into green. With the Claim she showed Lania everything she saw, and when it was done, and Lania was holding Arian's face in return, she murmured, "I see strength, I see courage. I see beauty beyond compare, and a light that shines upon light. I see love, Lania. And through it all, I see the Claim. These are your gifts also, bequeathed to us by the teachings of our house." Her grip on Lania's face became fierce. "The Talisman didn't steal your gifts. They could never take from you the essence of who you are. *'Do not mix the truth with falsehood or conceal the truth while you know it.'* Take this lesson of the Claim for yourself."

She sealed the fissures in the jar. Lania let it go, the tears she cried now cleansing the cruelty of her memories.

"I can never be the girl I was again." She said it as if she'd just realized it. She caught Arian close; she buried her face in Arian's hair, waiting. She had been waiting for judgment, and when the judgment had come at last, it wasn't anything she'd feared.

"You don't need to be that girl. Be the woman you are. Be the sister I love."

Lania held on for a beat. Then she released Arian. She left the jar on the pedestal alone and moved to rinse the lead mask from her face, and with it, the last of her tears.

Possibility pulsed through her, and alongside it, the truth. Unleashing the plague would not restore her innocence. She would lose the parts of herself that Arian had uncovered. Her spirit undimmed, the light upon light that was Inkwell's undying gift. The light of knowledge upon a receptive mind. And beyond that something richer and deeper that she couldn't move the veil aside to see. The truth of it was obscured, though she felt the stirrings of discovery.

She dried her wet face with a fold of her dress, as another truth speared out from under the vicious weight of the past.

There *were* things that were dear to her, things the Talisman had no right to claim. The Talisman's rights were forfeit, their lives were forfeit, but there were other ways.

She had dueled with Arian and fallen short, yet she was not defeated. The truth hidden in obscurity emerged a little further, fluttering at the edges of her mind.

She set it aside for now, the plague-jar forgotten. A confrontation she had Augured would soon come to pass. The Ahdath were at her door. She was on the cusp of a choice. She whirled to face Arian, noting the dull color of her circlets, and remembered the Silver Mage.

"Tell me how to help you, Arian. The Citadel cannot fall."

33

THE MAN NAMED QAIS HAD CALLED HIS BROTHER TO HELP HIM DEFEND the door to the scriptorium. Sinnia, Ash, and Half-Seen remained below, huddled around the manuscript.

Ash held a lantern aloft to aid them in their search, while Half-Seen located the manuscript's prolific index.

"What are you looking for?"

"The Buraq, the Blind Dome, the Bladebone." Sinnia repeated it by rote. "Something that will help us against the One-Eyed Preacher, and in doing so, help Arian as well."

The lantern jerked in Ash's hand. "Sinnia, when the High Companion banished Arian, your Audacy came to an end. You cannot challenge her authority—she was correct in her reading of the verse."

Sinnia's jaw jutted out. "What sense does that make, Ash? I'm a Companion of Hira, not a slave to Ilea's will. I have a mind of my own."

"Not in defiance of an oath sworn to the High Companion." Ash looked as if she herself had come to doubt that oath, given what had passed at the Council.

"You spoke of lawful authority." A haunting flash of awareness stole up Sinnia's spine. There had been something more to the verse that had been powerful enough to banish the First Oralist of Hira, and to hold Sinnia to an oath she had deeply come to regret. The prickling awareness altered. It stung like the scrape of nettles over her skin.

Ilea had insisted on a single point: *Obey those in authority among you.*

But Ash had mentioned *lawful* authority.

Sinnia calmed her mind, forcing herself to retreat into a memory of nightmare: her time in Jaslyk prison under the hands of the Technologist. The white needle had pierced her veins, but its poison had been transformed by a melancholy murmur from the cells nearby, the murmur from a fellow prisoner at Jaslyk, a formidable teacher of the Claim. Mudjadid Salikh, founder of the Usul Jade, the *new method* of teaching.

What was the new method?

Salikh had whispered a word into her mind to negate the toxicity of the needle: the word was *struggle*. He had urged her to struggle to a praiseworthy end: not just that of her own survival, but also of her duty as a Companion of Hira in the struggle against oppression. Then he had taught her the variations of the word, and as Sinnia parsed those memories, the variation of struggle that had made her spine prickle was the stem word *ijtihad*.

Ijtihad. Independent reasoning in place of imitation, for in the classical Tradition of the Claim that Sinnia had studied at Hira, the emphasis had been on conformity to that Tradition. Or to speak as a jurist, on conformity to precedent.

Ijtihad spoke of the opposite: of a jurist arriving at a solution to a question through a rigorous process of reasoning. The Talisman law had closed the door to this practice, the Preacher decreeing that all matters of law had been decided prior to the wars of the Far Range.

Salikh's conclusion was otherwise: he'd insisted on a scrupulous reexamination of issues on which the Claim was silent or open to interpretation—a method that defied authority, that defied customary rulings that authority was never to be questioned. The Authoritan's law behind the Wall, the spread of the Talisman's Assimilate, were designed to nullify freedom of thought, to abolish freedom altogether.

"Ash, might there be another reading of the verse Ilea used to banish Arian? As Jurist of the Council, could you not apply ijtihad?"

Ash set the lantern down. She grabbed Sinnia by her circlets.

"The door to ijtihad was sealed long ago. Who told you otherwise?"

Sinnia recounted her experience at Jaslyk. She shook her head to herself. Her heightened awareness of the Claim wasn't due to the teachings of Salikh alone. There was also the effect of the Israa e Miraj. It underscored her challenge to Ash.

Then she asked, "Who told you that door was closed?"

The Jurist kept hold of Sinnia's circlets. "It has always been so, and it was reaffirmed—"

"By the Talisman law of the Assimilate."

"Yes."

The two women looked at each other.

A sardonic glint in her eye, Sinnia said, "I am no Jurist, but the meaning of the root of ijtihad is to struggle. To struggle against our own base impulses, but also to struggle for a righteous cause. In all this"—she glanced around the scriptorium—"our desire to preserve knowledge, our desire to liberate our women, our *peo-*

ple, what cause could be more honorable for the Companions of Hira?"

The Jurist's eyes filmed over. "What are you asking of me, Sinnia? You saw me humbled by the High Companion. If her knowledge of the Claim supersedes mine, how can I defy her?"

Sinnia's jaw firmed. "This would not be defiance. I'm asking you to *reason* through Ilea's reading of the verse she used to banish Arian. I think you may be able to do so through the principle of ijtihad." She cast a wry glance at the stairs that led to the courtyard. "Unless you think we can hold the Citadel without Arian's help?"

Ash breathed out. "No. No, I do not think that." Another breath. A far-seeing look came into her eyes, as if she was flipping through the pages of a book, a little of her pride restored. She dropped her hands from Sinnia's circlets and began to pace. She stopped to pin Half-Seen with a glance. "Ilea warned that we are bound to obey those in authority among us. She drew her power from that verse. That power compelled us all—it was virtuous, I thought."

Half-Seen paused in her search of the Miraj Nameh's index. "I remember."

Sinnia's reply was grim. "We have also seen the Preacher make liberal use of the Claim. There is no virtue inherent in its use, only in how we understand it."

Ash resumed her pacing. "*Obey those in authority among us. And if you disagree over anything, refer it to the One and the Messenger . . .*"

"Have you ever done so?" Sinnia motioned to Half-Seen to continue her search.

"In my prayers, but those prayers have not availed us." A frown creased Ash's forehead, the lines etched there by worry deepening. She began to reason aloud. "Obey those in authority among us, those we have chosen to place in authority, as the Council chose the High Companion. Chosen from among ourselves."

Sinnia fought the urge to take Ash by the shoulders and hasten her conclusions. The sounds of battle were growing more intense.

Ash came to a halt. She grasped Sinnia's circlets again.

"Perhaps there *is* another possibility. Why didn't I think of it sooner?"

Sinnia pretended calm. "No matter. Tell us now."

"Those in authority among us are those we have *entrusted* with authority. Ilea claims that we must obey those in authority among us, and so we obey the edicts of the High Companion." She murmured to herself, trying out alternative translations. "Yes! Yes, I think I have it. 'Pay heed to those among you who have been entrusted with authority.' Sinnia, it is possible that when that trust is betrayed, so is that authority."

Sinnia's senses came alive. The rightness of Ash's conclusion burned away her uncertainty. Her features set in grim lines, she said, "What could be a greater betrayal of trust than to banish the First Oralist from Hira in the name of absolute power?"

Ash stared into her eyes, her doubts a reflection of her modesty. She was the Jurist of the Claim, yet she hesitated to arrogate all knowledge of the Claim to herself. She was willing to be corrected, and humble enough to allow for the prospect of being wrong. Each of her past rulings had come after hundreds of hours of study. She may have doubted herself in the face of Ilea's manipulation, but now she brought up her hands. She cupped her palms and raised them before her face. She tilted her head, her voice shaded by uncertainty. "With the sincere desire to uphold the truth, I base my ruling on my knowledge of the Claim, and on the unjust outcome of what transpired at our Council. As our trust *was* betrayed, I believe I have no choice but to rule that the High Companion's authority is unlawful. Arian's banishment was unlawful."

The walls of the scriptorium shook. The pages of the Miraj Nameh fluttered, disturbed by an unseen wind. Sinnia's scalp tingled. From an impossible distance, and under the cover of thunder, she heard the murmur of the fountains.

"Do you feel that?" she asked the others.

It was Half-Seen who replied. "Something has happened to the waters of the All Ways. They no longer form a barrier." Frightened herself at the notion of challenging Ilea, she marveled at Ash. "You've undone the banishment. I didn't know you held such power."

Ash rubbed her palms over her face, from her forehead to the tip of her chin, still anxious yet reassured by the murmur of the All Ways. "All power belongs to the One."

And Sinnia and Half-Seen reaffirmed, "All glory belongs to the One."

Half-Seen cautioned Sinnia. "We may have found a way to help Arian, but *you* are still bound by your oath. You swore personal allegiance to Ilea. You won't be able to defy her."

Sinnia cast about. At the time she had been assigned her Audacy, Ilea's authority had been both legitimate and lawful. Salikh's new method of reading the Claim could not assist her with this. But if she was the one bound, could she guide others to act in her stead?

Every part of her resisted the notion that these two scholars should take her place at the forefront of a war. *She* was meant to serve as Arian's sword arm. *She* was meant to defend Arian with her life. How could she gainsay such a trust? How could she make herself strong enough to overcome the oath she had sworn?

Her eyes fell on the pages of the Miraj Nameh. As she floundered, the memory of her ascent pricked her with new urgency. Turning the words over in her mind, she repeated what she had been told upon Ascension.

"To defend the First Oralist *is* to defend Hira."

What she had experienced at the limit of the Lote Tree of the Utmost Boundary became real to her in ways she hadn't grasped in that place between two worlds, where she'd been too overawed to search behind the veil.

Is there no knowledge you would seek to empower yourself with at the Utmost Boundary?

She'd asked to be shown the secrets of the Sana Codex. She had asked if the Codex contained anything that might aid her. An audacious truth now ripped the veil aside, her freedom rooted in a verse long stripped of its context. A truth newly gained. Because now she understood the context of coercion as antithetical to her free will. Ilea's subtle control lessened before it slipped away altogether.

"Ilea will compel me no longer. My actions are my own."

Half-Seen shook her head. "I know you've proven yourself, Sinnia, but the High Companion's power is of a kind you cannot comprehend."

"Can't I?" Sinnia smiled her bold, dazzling smile, the veil of stars reflected in the ebony gleam of her eyes. She shared the truths of her Ascension with the others.

"*There is no coercion in matters of faith. The way of truth is distinct from the way of error; thus, those who reject the powers of evil and believe in the One have taken hold of a support most unfailing that will never give way.*"

Ash contributed her own knowledge, her wisdom overtaken by Sinnia's light. "*For the One is All-Hearing, All-Knowing.*"

Half-Seen's hand stilled upon a page of the Miraj Nameh that depicted an illustration of a horse-like creature flying above a gilded dome.

"Sinnia, your words undo our truths. They undo our allegiance to the High Companion, to the Council of Hira itself." Half-Seen's doubt was clear. "Is this blasphemy, Jurist?"

Love for the mother of her people spilled from Sinnia's heart. The Queen of the Negus had shown her the way, when she had offered a simple truth to two Companions of Hira who should have known it for themselves.

"As Arian said, the allegiance we owe is not to the High Companion, but to the All-Seeing One. Examine your own heart, Half-Seen, and tell us what it reveals."

Ash shook her head in warning. "It won't work for others, Sinnia, as it does for you."

"Why not?"

"You ascended, as we did not. Your understanding of the Claim is superior to ours."

Sinnia's dark skin heated with a blush. She put up a hand to object. "You are the Jurist of our Council, and Half-Seen is the *Collector*. I could never claim the knowledge of two as learned as you. I am a novice in these matters."

Ash's smile was generous, uncomplicated by envy.

"You have seen beyond the veil. You and Arian both. So the two of you have the ability to contend with the High Companion. Now tell us what we must do."

The three women turned their attention to the manuscript again.

Another burst of thunder shook the walls. The three Companions winced.

Sinnia muttered to herself, "Whatever stroke of enlightenment awaits me, it needs to find me soon." She cast a dark look at Half-Seen. "But don't even think of entombing us again."

Half-Seen's blush was visible.

"I'm sorry. All I could think of was what we would lose, what all of Khorasan would lose, if the archives burned. Our three lives against lifetimes of learning? How could you ask me to weigh that? My duty as Collector is to put the archives first."

"You think the written word is more important than lives?" Sinnia asked the question without judgment.

"Yes," Half-Seen whispered. "I alone of all the Companions *must* think that, for this is the Audacy to which I have been sworn."

Sinnia pressed her arm in sympathy.

"I understand. But I spent a year in the company of the First Oralist. Her knowledge of the Claim surpasses ours combined. And do you know what I learned from her?"

Half-Seen regarded her, wide-eyed. Ash shook her head.

"The one who speaks all languages, the one who reads and re-cites the Claim—*she* chooses lives over words. She would choose them over books."

Comprehension dawned in Half-Seen's eyes. She looked around the Citadel's scriptorium as if every inch of it was new. She caught sight of the hidden lever and trembled, remembering her desperate gamble.

A choice she now understood Arian would not have made.

The Companion dedicated to the written word would have let the scriptorium burn, rather than take three lives.

Half-Seen pondered this for a moment, then spoke her conclusion out loud.

"That must be why Arian was chosen to ascend."

34

Ash had left them, called to help at the walls. Now Half-Seen held the lantern aloft so that Sinnia could search the Miraj Nameh.

Sinnia spent some time considering the Buraq. A few pages later, she found an illustration of a gilded dome depicted in solitary splendor. The dome seemed familiar, the high drum positioned above an octagonal arcade.

Another page dwelt on the tiled exterior of the magnificent sub-structure, its faience glazed in tiles of turquoise and lapis lazuli blue. She peered at the page, and she saw that the fine hand of the artist had captured the lines of calligraphy above the faience in elegant loops of white. She was reminded of the facade of the Tilla Kari in Marakand. The blue and white scheme was the same, but the structure that supported the dome of the Miraj was ornamented by the language it expressed, articulate and aware. A communication of the Claim.

A thought awoke in the back of her mind, and she made note of it.

She turned another page and found herself gazing at a bifolium, where the gilded dome was swallowed up by the blank space of an empty courtyard, with small arcades at intervals, leading to sets of stairs.

"Look." Half-Seen pointed to a small structure east of the dome, open to the elements. Above the smaller dome, the artist had painted a silver streak extending down from the sky.

And now Sinnia recognized the painting for what it was: a painting of the Noble Sanctuary, except the black lead dome had been stripped of its blacking, so that its gilded plates lit the sky and the calligraphy beneath.

"The Blind Dome," Sinnia murmured. "Blind and inarticulate no longer."

Half-Seen brought the lantern closer to the illustration, so close that Sinnia flinched.

"Careful!"

But Half-Seen's attention was fixed upon the silver streak. She tapped the page beside the illustration.

"I've never seen lightning like this before, have you?"

No sooner had she asked the question than Sinnia's mind was filled with the Silver Mage.

When Half-Seen turned the page, Sinnia was looking at two different images of a sword on a page divided in half.

The sword on the left-hand side of the page was one she knew well. It was wielded by the Silver Mage, and it bore along its length, in smoke-colored calligraphy, the Silver Mage's maxim: *Defend the truth in the face of all dishonor.*

On the right side of the page, the same sword was altered. Its solid tip was split in two, and on the longer portion of the bifurcated blade, a separate motto was engraved.

There is no sword like the Bladebone, and none like the warrior who wields it.

Thoughts fell into Sinnia's mind like flightless birds into a river. She turned another page. This time, the two domed structures were linked, the gilded dome aflame against a sky of ruin, the jagged bolt of lightning fastening the upper earth to the chasm beneath, the courtyard of the Noble Sanctuary roiling with fire and smoke. The artist's rendition was so detailed that the streak of lightning resembled both a chain swinging between the upper and lower worlds, and the Silver Mage's sword. But how could it be both?

A beam cut a path through the turmoil of the sky above. The longer blade of the sword was angled up at that beam.

She noticed another detail.

The thunderous sky that blacked out the upper portion of the page was painted in the shape of a face, the shape of a face she had seen, with a white stone in place of one eye.

But how could a historical text speak of the One-Eyed Preacher?

What were the secrets of this venerable book, and why had she been sent to seek them?

She asked the question of Half-Seen, her fingers hovering just above the face on the page.

"Why is there a painting of the One-Eyed Preacher in this book?"

Another clap of thunder rumbled through the sky.

Half-Seen stared back at her, her graceful eyebrows raised.

"You are quite mistaken, Sinnia. There is no such painting."

Sinnia was baffled. "I assure you, Half-Seen, I would recognize the Preacher anywhere."

Half-Seen's hand closed on Sinnia's arm.

"Sinnia, the Miraj Nameh is filled with stories of the Claim. This illustration depicts the one known as Dajjal."

Sinnia made a harsh sound in her throat.

"Dajjal?"

The two women looked at each other askance.

"The Deceiver," Half-Seen whispered, frightened to say it aloud. "The Deceiver and the False Messiah. The herald of the end of the world."

35

"Hide." Lania motioned to one of the alcoves. "No one expects you here; no one will think to look for you."

"If you are worried about the Ahdath, let me help you, Lania."

The Khanum of Black Aura scowled at Arian. "I brought down the Authoritan without your help, and you think I cannot manage a handful of Ahdath? My Augury will see me safe."

But for all Lania's tight-lipped wrath, Arian caught a trace of her sister's concern. She disappeared into the alcove, but as she passed the basin, she dipped her hands in it to wash the blood and grime from her face. And then she swept the cool caress of water down over her bare arms, feeling a temporary relief, noting that after each use, the waters cleared again.

Just as she moved into the shadows, several of the Ahdath broke into the room. One had hold of a girl whose arm was gripped in the Ahdath's massive paw; a bruise had begun to form.

"What is this? How dare you trespass upon my scrying chamber?"

Lania waved at the giant Ahdath. His hand opened to release the girl. The girl darted behind Lania. Her glance fell upon the

279

trail of water that led to Arian's hiding place. She shuffled her feet, dragging the hem of her gown to obscure the trail of droplets.

Her eyes met Arian's in the shadows. There was an instance of mutual recognition before the girl looked away. It was the girl named Gul. Arian had first seen her in Marakand.

Arian kept her eyes on Lania, who was surrounded by the Ahdath. The one who had moved to stand in front of Lania was built along long, lean lines, a predatory expression on his aristocratic face. One of his hands was balled into a fist. He pushed Lania back with the other, by placing his palm on her chest.

"Where is my brother? What have you done with Kiril?"

One of the Ahdath had tried to warn Lania, Arian remembered. He had cautioned that it would be dangerous to dispose of the soldier who had taken Gul from the Pit.

Lania drew up her shoulders. She touched the Ahdath's hand with the crimson talons of her own. He snatched it back with a curse.

"You think to hold Black Aura with your sorcery? You think you frightened us with your murder of a weak and deluded man? You do not know the Ahdath, if that is what you believe."

Lania turned her back on the fair-haired soldier, a sign of her contempt. She wandered to the basin, one hand beckoning Gul. The Ahdath started after her.

"Wait, Mikhail."

A woman slipped through the door to the chamber. Gray-haired, blue-eyed, elegant, attired in ceremonial dress, her heavy blue robes banded with gold at the waist. But what Arian was struck most by was that the woman's arms were bare, and on her upper arms she wore circlets made of turquoise. The circlets were free of script, but Arian felt the Claim stir in response. The Ahdath parted to let the woman through.

overeign repelled it with another.

eyes locked, they raised their hands and created s...
tions. The wind in the scrying chamber gathered for...
d Arian of the aesar she had summoned in the desert
self from Najran. The glass panes of the skylight rattle...
ot dry wind.

n offered a calming murmur of the Claim. She was here
urgent purpose, an urgency the other powers—the other
—in this room should share.

vereign, the Talisman come to the Wall also," she said.
n the One-Eyed Preacher is finished with the Citadel, he
rike at the Wall next. Task End, Marakand, Black Aura,
—your cities will not be spared."

o not plead with her." Lania's moonstone fire moved to
f Arian as a shield, not a sword. "The Sahirah are like the
lless. They care nothing for the world beyond their walls."

our learning derives from the Authoritan," the Sovereign
ed. "A man of the cruelest ignorance." She doused the tur-
se flames in response to Arian's plea. "The Khanum appears
aware that an army defends Marakand from the Talisman,
it is not the Ahdath."

When a cloud drifted over Lania's irises, the Sovereign contin-
"This army is led by a man who descends from the Wander-
Cloud Door. He sends a second flank to Black Aura."

"Zerafshan," Arian breathed.

The Sovereign's eyes snapped to Arian. "You know him?"

"He gave me safe passage through the Cloud Door. I had
ped his armies would join our war against the Talisman."

"He isn't just fighting the Talisman." The Sovereign turned a
nd smile upon Lania. "He fights your Ahdath behind the Wall,"

"Where is my son, witch?"

The woman flicked one hand up and out. A thin trail of blood scored Gul's neck.

"Did you kill him over this worthless concubine you trained at your house of whores?" The older woman's hand notched another trail of blood, this one down Gul's arm. Gul whimpered in response. "He was more than a noble—he was the head of our house."

The moonstone on Lania's finger shone with a harsh glare.

"Such nobility." Lania aimed the moonstone at Gul's face. "To beat a girl into submission to satisfy his animal desires. Tell me, Valeria, is Mikhail of the same bent?"

The moonstone flicked in Mikhail's direction, and a blood-trail that matched Gul's appeared beneath his jaw. The Ahdath in the room drew their weapons. Gul flattened herself against the wall. The woman named Valeria scoffed.

"I should strike her down where she stands, if only to give you pain."

Lania twisted her ring. "As I said. Such nobility."

Mikhail raised his sword. "Have a care, witch. My mother is Sovereign of the Sahirah."

Arian's body stiffened. Were the Sahirah's gifts real? She'd thought their magic had passed into legend. Like the Authoritan, they were said to dabble in arcane rites. But the source of their power couldn't be the Claim. The Blue Mage had told her of Najran's perversion of the holy tongue of Aramaya, derived from the sacred scriptures Najran had stolen from Axum. She tried to think of an equivalent source of magic in these lands beyond the Wall.

Lania lowered the hand that wore the moonstone. She moved a pace at a time until Gul was gathered within the shelter of her arms. The girl's limbs were shaking with fear, the bruise mottled and ugly upon her arm. Valeria watched them without blinking. But Arian was surprised to see the rise of color under Mikhail's skin. He set his jaw and looked away from Gul.

Lania spoke to his mother. "I killed your son because he brutalized one of my doves."

A cry escaped Mikhail. And though grief and anger flared in Valeria's eyes, her intonation didn't change. "You are the one responsible for setting these girls in the path of the Ahdath. You are little more than a procurer, so why pretend they matter now?"

Lania tapped one finger against her crimson lips. "You have your secrets, Valeria, just as I have mine."

"There must be an accounting, nonetheless."

Just as the older woman touched her turquoise circlets, Arian stepped out of hiding. She slipped in front of Lania and let her cloak fall from her arms.

Valeria's gaze moved between the two sisters in surprise.

"Who are you?" She let her hands fall from her circlets and motioned the others back.

Mikhail gave a slight nod. "The First Oralist of Hira. She is sister to the Khanum."

"You know this how?" The Sovereign of the Sahirah appraised the two sisters again.

"You were in Khiva, Matushka, but for a time the Authoritan held her prisoner at the Ark. She was . . . displayed . . . in the throne room as the Khanum's prize." Mikhail's blue eyes met Arian's, that same trace of color rising under his skin, and with a sense of wonder, Arian understood. He'd witnessed the humiliation of a Companion of Hira, and something about her debasement had disturbed him.

She dropped her gaze, fighting back a blush of her own. She made a brief bow before the older woman.

"Sovereign."

"Sahabiya." The Sovereign rubb
clets. When Arian mirrored the gestu
are you here, First Oralist, when the
upon your Citadel?"

Curious, Arian asked, "Did you div

The Sovereign sneered at Lania. "It i
Augury. The Sahirah are engaged in no

She circled the sisters, frowning at th
Mikhail moved to obey.

"Not you, my son—the rest. Wait for

When they'd gone, she returned her att
murder must be requited. You owe my fan

Lania slashed one hand down. A line
Mikhail's cheek. He took the blow without

"There is your payment, Valeria."

Turquoise light flared from the older wo
would test me here and now, Lania? When
Khanum on my sufferance?"

Lania shoved Gul out of the way. Mikha
arms.

The moonstone ring danced with fire. Whit
the Sovereign. The Sovereign responded in kin
pouring from her fingers. When Gul cried ou
made a reassuring sound.

Turquoise fire met white across the surface
The room filled with a sibilant noise, the waters i
ing blue and silver. The filmy curtains that shr
ways danced in the hot wind that brushed the fa
gathered in the room.

Lania chanted a verse.

"Where is my son, witch?"

The woman flicked one hand up and out. A thin trail of blood scored Gul's neck.

"Did you kill him over this worthless concubine you trained at your house of whores?" The older woman's hand notched another trail of blood, this one down Gul's arm. Gul whimpered in response. "He was more than a noble—he was the head of our house."

The moonstone on Lania's finger shone with a harsh glare.

"Such nobility." Lania aimed the moonstone at Gul's face. "To beat a girl into submission to satisfy his animal desires. Tell me, Valeria, is Mikhail of the same bent?"

The moonstone flicked in Mikhail's direction, and a blood-trail that matched Gul's appeared beneath his jaw. The Ahdath in the room drew their weapons. Gul flattened herself against the wall. The woman named Valeria scoffed.

"I should strike her down where she stands, if only to give you pain."

Lania twisted her ring. "As I said. Such nobility."

Mikhail raised his sword. "Have a care, witch. My mother is Sovereign of the Sahirah."

Arian's body stiffened. Were the Sahirah's gifts real? She'd thought their magic had passed into legend. Like the Authoritan, they were said to dabble in arcane rites. But the source of their power couldn't be the Claim. The Blue Mage had told her of Najran's perversion of the holy tongue of Aramaya, derived from the sacred scriptures Najran had stolen from Axum. She tried to think of an equivalent source of magic in these lands beyond the Wall.

Lania lowered the hand that wore the moonstone. She moved a pace at a time until Gul was gathered within the shelter of her arms. The girl's limbs were shaking with fear, the bruise mottled and ugly upon her arm. Valeria watched them without blinking. But Arian was surprised to see the rise of color under Mikhail's skin. He set his jaw and looked away from Gul.

Lania spoke to his mother. "I killed your son because he brutalized one of my doves."

A cry escaped Mikhail. And though grief and anger flared in Valeria's eyes, her intonation didn't change. "You are the one responsible for setting these girls in the path of the Ahdath. You are little more than a procurer, so why pretend they matter now?"

Lania tapped one finger against her crimson lips. "You have your secrets, Valeria, just as I have mine."

"There must be an accounting, nonetheless."

Just as the older woman touched her turquoise circlets, Arian stepped out of hiding. She slipped in front of Lania and let her cloak fall from her arms.

Valeria's gaze moved between the two sisters in surprise.

"Who are you?" She let her hands fall from her circlets and motioned the others back.

Mikhail gave a slight nod. "The First Oralist of Hira. She is sister to the Khanum."

"You know this how?" The Sovereign of the Sahirah appraised the two sisters again.

"You were in Khiva, Matushka, but for a time the Authoritan held her prisoner at the Ark. She was . . . displayed . . . in the throne room as the Khanum's prize." Mikhail's blue eyes met Arian's, that same trace of color rising under his skin, and with a sense of wonder, Arian understood. He'd witnessed the humiliation of a Companion of Hira, and something about her debasement had disturbed him.

She dropped her gaze, fighting back a blush of her own. She made a brief bow before the older woman.

"Sovereign."

"Sahabiya." The Sovereign rubbed one of her turquoise circlets. When Arian mirrored the gesture, her eyes narrowed. "Why
are you here, First Oralist, when there are rumors of an assault
upon your Citadel?"

Curious, Arian asked, "Did you divine this, Sovereign?"

The Sovereign sneered at Lania. "It is your sister who practices
Augury. The Sahirah are engaged in nothing as profane."

She circled the sisters, frowning at the Ahdath. "Leave us."

Mikhail moved to obey.

"Not you, my son—the rest. Wait for us outside these doors."

When they'd gone, she returned her attention to Lania. "Kiril's
murder must be requited. You owe my family blood."

Lania slashed one hand down. A line of blood appeared on
Mikhail's cheek. He took the blow without flinching.

"There is your payment, Valeria."

Turquoise light flared from the older woman's circlets. "You
would test me here and now, Lania? When you have survived as
Khanum on my sufferance?"

Lania shoved Gul out of the way. Mikhail caught her in his
arms.

The moonstone ring danced with fire. White heat lashed out at
the Sovereign. The Sovereign responded in kind, turquoise flames
pouring from her fingers. When Gul cried out in fear, Mikhail
made a reassuring sound.

Turquoise fire met white across the surface of Lania's basin.
The room filled with a sibilant noise, the waters in the basin dancing blue and silver. The filmy curtains that shrouded the archways danced in the hot wind that brushed the faces of all those
gathered in the room.

Lania chanted a verse.

The Sovereign repelled it with another.

Their eyes locked, they raised their hands and created strange compositions. The wind in the scrying chamber gathered force. It reminded Arian of the aesar she had summoned in the desert to save herself from Najran. The glass panes of the skylight rattled in the hot dry wind.

Arian offered a calming murmur of the Claim. She was here for an urgent purpose, an urgency the other powers—the other *women*—in this room should share.

"Sovereign, the Talisman come to the Wall also," she said. "When the One-Eyed Preacher is finished with the Citadel, he will strike at the Wall next. Task End, Marakand, Black Aura, Khiva—your cities will not be spared."

"Do not plead with her." Lania's moonstone fire moved to engulf Arian as a shield, not a sword. "The Sahirah are like the Bloodless. They care nothing for the world beyond their walls."

"Your learning derives from the Authoritan," the Sovereign rejoined. "A man of the cruelest ignorance." She doused the turquoise flames in response to Arian's plea. "The Khanum appears little aware that an army defends Marakand from the Talisman, and it is not the Ahdath."

When a cloud drifted over Lania's irises, the Sovereign continued, "This army is led by a man who descends from the Wandering Cloud Door. He sends a second flank to Black Aura."

"Zerafshan," Arian breathed.

The Sovereign's eyes snapped to Arian. "You know him?"

"He gave me safe passage through the Cloud Door. I had hoped his armies would join our war against the Talisman."

"He isn't just fighting the Talisman." The Sovereign turned a bland smile upon Lania. "He fights your Ahdath *behind* the Wall, as well. Though, of course, he has been aided from within. The Basmachi—the Salikhate—have risen again."

Arian's heart seized with joy. Larisa and Elena, leaders of the Basmachi resistance, had done as they had promised to do: they had taken their war to the men who held the Wall, the men whose constant demand had fueled the slave-chains.

Lania wasn't fazed. The cloud-spell had vanished from her gaze. She stepped toward Mikhail, touching the cut on his cheek. He let her, harboring Gul beneath his arm.

"Do you cheer the destruction of your son's confederates?"

The Sovereign laughed. "For all your Augury, Lania, you know little of what passes in the Authoritan's city. There is a change in the wind: those without esoteric gifts will no longer submit to the whims of those who rule by compulsion."

"It is no longer the Authoritan's city; it is *mine*."

Lania's fingers dug into Mikhail's cheek. With a grunt, he pushed her aside.

Valeria watched their exchange. "The men and women of this city have no love for you. One night soon you will find yourself murdered in your bed."

It was Lania's turn to laugh. "Many have tried, Valeria. No one has succeeded."

Arian interceded once more, every moment that ticked by a moment that kept her from the Citadel.

"Sovereign, I do not dispute your claim or your rights over my sister, but what I have told you about the One-Eyed Preacher's ambition was not a lie. He must be stopped at the Citadel before he overtakes all of Khorasan."

A weight settled on the Sovereign's shoulders. She indicated the basin.

"You see a different future, do you?"

Arian shook her head. "Augury is beyond my knowledge. I work to change the future with my knowledge of the Claim. That is all I possess against the One-Eyed Preacher."

"Then go," the Sovereign replied. "My business is with your sister."

Arian stood her ground. "I'm sorry, Sovereign, but I need my sister. The Citadel needs her, if Hira is to survive."

"Arian—"

But she ignored Lania's angry interruption.

"She is outcast from Hira, I thought." The Sovereign's eyes moved between the two sisters, puzzling through their discord.

"She was *stolen* from Hira, but Hira is her home." Arian's knowledge of the Sahirah was too limited for her to persuade their Sovereign. So she did as she knew best to do, and relied on the power of the word. "Lania was meant to be Custodian of the Archives."

The Sovereign's response was cold. "Instead, she became an Augur."

The same harsh judgment that Arian had made. "That wasn't her choice, Sovereign. She didn't *ask* to be sold to the men behind the Wall."

Mikhail swallowed. He bent his fair head beneath the words.

Arian turned to Lania. "You'll come with me, won't you? Now when I need you most?"

Lania's eyes touched on each person in the room, as she considered her options.

"If I leave, I might lose the Wall."

As Gul sobbed in Mikhail's arms, Arian asked, "And is that what you want? To deliver defenseless girls, girls from our cities in the south, into the arms of the Ahdath? Is that the dominion you choose? Are you the Authoritan in all but name, Lania?"

Lania's eyes came to rest on hers. They contained a flicker of surprise.

"You are not without your weapons."

From Lania, the words were praise. They also signified a concession. Now it was the Sovereign who stood in Arian's way. But Arian's request had changed the Sovereign's calculations.

"Very well." The Sovereign aimed her turquoise fire at Gul. A crimson slash appeared on the girl's breast. "I will take the girl's life in payment for Kiril's, as she was the cause of his doom. But this dispensation is granted to the First Oralist." Looking at the girl's fragile body trapped in her son's arms, she snapped, "Kill her. Spill her blood in the same chamber where your brother's was spilled."

Despite her fear, raw fury burned in Gul's eyes. Though she did not struggle in Mikhail's hold, she raised her head to face the Sovereign.

Bitterness stripped the beauty from her delicate features. "From the day I came to Black Aura, I had no other fate."

The Sovereign shrugged. "My son's eye shouldn't have fallen on you. That it did is your misfortune."

Mikhail pulled Gul closer, and now Gul did struggle. His mother looked to him, one brow aloft in challenge.

"I do not intend to kill her."

Gul's struggles ceased. A terrible stillness took their place.

"No? Shall I do it, then?"

Before the Sovereign could advance, Mikhail held out one hand. His other hand slipped to Gul's waist, locking her against his chest.

Arian waited. She didn't intend to allow either to hurt Gul, but a silent signal from Lania told her not to interfere.

"I will take my payment from the girl. I want her for myself."

Gul let out a low cry. She made a desperate appeal. "I did as you asked, so please—please, Khanum, *kill me*. Don't let them have me again."

Mikhail's arm tightened around her waist. He wiped the blood from her breast.

"If you harm her, you'll never leave this room," he said to Lania.

Lania dismissed Gul without another thought. "Take her, then, if that will settle the debt."

The Sovereign shook her head at Lania's caprice. "The girl wishes to die," she told her son. "And I will accept her death as compensation for the murder of your brother."

Mikhail's face hardened. "*I* am the head of our house now, Sovereign. I do not interfere with matters under your authority; do not interfere with mine."

Surprise filtered through the Sovereign's blue eyes, so similar to her son's. She studied the girl weeping in Mikhail's arms.

"If you wish to keep her, I have one stipulation."

Mikhail waited.

"When you tire of her, you will give the girl to me."

He gave a short, sharp nod.

But Arian couldn't abandon Gul a second time. "Lania—"

Her sister waved her off. "So it was Augured, so it must come to pass."

Seething under Lania's indifference, the Claim whispered something else. And then, the Sovereign surprised Arian by reaching out to grasp her circlet. She studied the script engraved upon it with grooves etched into her brow.

"The Sahirah do not accept leniency, sahabiya. I spare the girl because of you, not because of the witch. One day, the Sahirah will come to Hira for repayment of this debt."

Arian put both her hands on the other woman's circlets and leaned close to whisper in her ear. "Don't let your son hurt her. You can see she is just a girl."

A brusque laugh from the Sovereign. "Mikhail is nothing like Kiril. He should have been head of our house from the first, but fate is often capricious."

Arian looked into the Sovereign's eyes, trying to see her with the Claim.

"Will you help us?" she asked. "With the gifts you possess, will you come to Hira's aid?"

It took a full minute for the Sovereign to consider Arian's request, her pale eyes turning dark. She seemed to weigh some secret calculation. After a pause, she shook her head.

And then she swept from the room without waiting for her son.

Gul's eyes caught Lania's, her thin face bleak with pain.

"I'll never forgive you for this."

Then Mikhail pulled her away, and the sisters were left alone.

36

"YOU LET HER GO," ARIAN SAID. "TO A FATE YOU KNOW WILL DESTROY her."

"No." Lania's hand beckoned Arian closer to the basin. "I Augured all that came to pass. The Ahdath asked for Gul to save her from his mother's wrath. He means to keep her safe. Gul will determine the rest."

The words, the careless tone in which they were delivered, pierced something in Arian. "And if you had Augured otherwise? You train your doves for the pleasure of the Ahdath, do you not?" She wanted to say the words without judgment, but how could she? Gul's hopeless despair was another facet of her nightmares.

"Ah. You share Valeria's perspective in thinking me a procurer."

Arian spread her hands. The injuries Lania had suffered were so heinous that she could be forgiven anything . . . except inflicting the same harm on others. Arian's duty was to reckon with the fate of the women of the slave-chains.

"I have been to the Gold House, Lania. I have also seen your doves with the Ahdath."

"Do you expect me to explain myself to you? Do you presume the authority of the First Oralist over me?"

"I do not presume anything." Her heart continued to ache. She felt the weight of Lania's pain, just as she sensed Daniyar's, wounds that would not heal if either were to be lost. "I would like to know. I want to understand."

Lania twisted the moonstone on her finger, betraying a hint of nervousness.

"No judgment?" A jest with a bitter aftertaste.

Arian was careful with her response. "No judgment of you, Lania. But as First Oralist, I do judge right from wrong. Slavery against freedom, oppression against dignity." She spoke to Lania in the same manner that she spoke to Wafa, reaching for the innocence behind his anguish. "You know how to measure one against the other, you know that wrong must be condemned. And you know that as a servant of the One, I am bound to resist oppression in all its forms."

Lania moved into the concealment of the shadows, her expression guarded.

"What did you expect me to do? I was one woman against my oppressors, new to my gifts with the Claim. There were no gentle teachers for me, Arian. There was the Authoritan, and there were his men clamoring for blood. I think you remember Nevus."

Her heart drumming, Arian asked, "Are they all—"

"No. There are others like your poet, Alisher." She nodded at the door. "Like Mikhail, ashamed to use their strength against a woman. Some defected to the Basmachi, some tried to check their brothers. And there were others who resisted. They were put to the trials of the bloodrites. The taste of their blood awoke an appetite for madness in the rest. What does this matter, though?"

She shot a questioning glance at Arian. "Should you not depart for Hira?"

But Arian's charge did not stop at the border of the Wall. "Tell me the rest, Lania. For there is more, isn't there?"

"Do you think I wore a mask of cruelty to hide an incipient kindness?" The words of a woman who despised herself. "If the Authoritan had guessed that I cared for these girls, that they *mattered* in any way, he wouldn't have let me interfere." A secret smile stole across her face. "But I had my own purposes to work, my own remedies, if you will. So yes, I became a procurer. I taught these girls to protect themselves with the sweetness of seduction and laughter; I taught them to bewitch. I trained them as my spies." She slashed down with one hand. "I could not spare them the appetites of men, but I did give them a say in how their captivity played out." She shrugged, her anger dissipating. "Some were incapable of learning and died. Some were grateful and learned the lesson well. And some are like Gul: they will hate me until the end."

Her green eyes held Arian's in a spell that bound both sisters, a deliberate hardness in her face. "I am no victim, Arian. What I did was inexcusable, so do not think to excuse it." She tilted her head. "Did I give you the answers you seek? Do you understand a little?"

Arian exhaled on a sigh. She was far from solving the enigma of her sister, but another forgotten detail shifted to the forefront of her mind. Lania had mentioned the Basmachi.

She touched Lania's shoulder. "Is that all you did?"

Lania patted her hand, as one would stroke a pet.

"The Basmachi. I let them work their will. I enjoyed their small victories against the Authoritan, but I could not venture further."

Arian stifled a gasp. "Then you *know* of Larisa and Elena."

Lania gave a regal nod. "Daughters of Mudjadid Salikh. Daughters of the Claim. It wasn't my wish to harm them, but I had to make choices to survive, to continue to play this game. Just as the Salikhs did."

She scrutinized Arian in turn. "There has been so much suffering for the women of these lands, yet you remain undamaged."

For a moment, Arian faltered. She let herself think of Daniyar, let herself feel the darkening of his star. Allowed herself to count the cost of the decade she had spent at war, not knowing when her quest would end. She thought of friends lost and sacrifices made, of the ravening famine in the south and the harshness of Daniyar cutting her, the harshness of losing him twice. Of the pain of Daniyar's final farewell: *Be free, heart of my heart.*

She gathered the Claim to herself like a song. She breathed it in, let it suffuse her blood vessels, let it penetrate through to her cells.

"I am not undamaged." She raised her chin. "But neither am I undone."

There was a glint of approval from Lania. Then the moment of connection faded beside the urgency of what waited for them at Hira.

Lania nodded at the basin. "Show me how to use the portal."

Arian pressed both hands over her circlets and thought of the Israa e Miraj. With one last look around the chamber, she asked Lania, "Would you yield the Wall, in truth?"

Lania's red lips curved. "Who says I have yielded it, sister?"

That was when Arian noticed the plague-jar had disappeared.

37

"WHERE IS YOUR LOVER NOW, MAGE OF KHORASAN? WHO WILL DEFEND you with the Claim?"

The sardonic voice belonged to Najran, and he carried in his hands a new weapon: an elegant steel sword with a distinctive mottling that dripped down the surface of the sword. The cross-guard was a hard black shaft incised with gold. He gripped it in one hand, while with the other he unwound a length of silk from his turban.

He must have followed them to the Well of Souls, but why he had chosen to engage outside the city's walls when he might have caused greater confusion within, Daniyar couldn't fathom. Now he stood poised at the head of the Rising Nineteen, soldiers falling into line behind him, the desert quiet beyond the city walls, as Daniyar adjusted his grip on the Bladebone and brought the sword to his chest.

He ignored the other man's taunt, waiting for him to strike.

Najran nodded at Daniyar's sword. "You have a new weapon. Miracles have been thrust upon you, though you seem unfit to carry them."

A point to Najran, for Daniyar was no longer capable of hiding his fatigue, though any man would be tired from having fought so many battles, or from journeying this far. But if Najran had been able to use the portal of the Well of Souls, perhaps his words presaged more.

"You, as well."

Najran looked pleased. He dropped the length of silk over the tip of his sword. The blade sheared it in two with a soft, caressing sound that held the Nineteen in thrall.

Splinters of white dissected Najran's eyes. "The Dimashq will thread you so finely, you will meet your death without knowing it."

An arrogant boast meant to intimidate Daniyar. But he had gazed upon wonders too great to be awed by a trifling display, or the name of a well-blooded sword. Najran's bluster didn't disturb him, but it was reassuring that he felt the need to try. And since the man was given to conversation, he brought up the strange fragmentation of his eyes.

"I thought at first that the tricks you play were a reflection of your sorcery. But seeing that I bested you, I realized the markings serve to foretell your intent. A soldier's trick." He jerked his chin at Najran's sword. "You mean to strike at me, and you would have me fear the attributes of your blade."

Najran caressed the blade's edge. "And do you?"

Daniyar dismissed his weariness. The Dimashq was just another sword to battle; it was the army of soldiers who fought with Najran who would assure the fate he had been promised upon ascent.

Your time is at an end.

"I fear only the One. But your army does unbalance the odds."

Najran fell prey to Daniyar's contempt.

"Single combat," he spat. "I need no man's aid to bring down the Silver Mage."

But the men beside him were not cattle to be herded by the sound of a shepherd's command. They were warriors in their own right, fanatics, Daniyar thought, though he could not fail to be aware of their fascination with the Sacred Cloak.

"And if you should fall?" One of the Nineteen dared Najran, who skimmed the sands with his sword, his eyes glittering like feldspar trapped in the bright light of dawn.

"If I fall," he mused, "the Silver Mage earns safe passage into the city."

He shaded his eyes to study the light beginning to break through the clouds, a thin belt of color creeping down to the fringes of the star-veil. "When the dawn overtakes the night, your veil of star-fire will fall. When the day overtakes the dawn, the city will be mine."

So that was how Najran had spent his time within the city walls, studying the secrets of the Conference of the Mages, studying Daniyar's secrets. He couldn't dispute the other man's conclusions, yet he'd never seen an army battle with the Zhayedan's conviction. Even now, he heard Arsalan's deep voice calling him back, begging him to retreat from a battle he faced alone.

"Enough of your talk. I am ready to honor my trust."

The silver eyes blazed like a pulsar as Daniyar brought the Bladebone down. A rousing cry from the walls of the city as single combat was joined.

38

"HELP ME!" CASSANDANE SHOUTED THE COMMAND TO KATAYOUN, THE two Teerandaz archers racing from the Tower of the Mirage to the roof above the Messenger Gate. Two dozen archers of the Teerandaz had survived the long weeks of battle, and to one of these Cassandane had given instructions for the final defense. Now she and Katayoun passed the Black Khan on the wall, working in concert with the Blue Mage to derive the protections of the dawn. The Messenger Gate was holding by a miracle. It would take another to save the Silver Mage.

To the east, the shimmering star-veil had begun to recede; once it fell, what was left of the city would burn. But this she didn't share with Katayoun, her heart twisting as she witnessed the sheer scale of destruction in the square.

Cassandane picked up her pace, weaving through the Zhayedan who held the western wall. Though she followed without protest, Katayoun gasped, "The Silver Mage accepted single combat. You know we cannot interfere."

They came to an abrupt halt at the door to a storeroom. Cassandane ripped the helmet from her head and used it to bang open the door. No one had been left inside to guard it. Every man who could fight was either on the walls or in the square, so the archers entered on their own.

"Rope," she told Katayoun. The defenses of the tower had been expended; this small repository was all that remained along the western wall. If there were other weapons in the armory to the east, they didn't have time to reach them.

She'd measured the battle in the square. Too many Zhayedan lay dead, and their enemies' numbers were still vast. A small group of Talisman defectors fought alongside the Cataphracts, the silver rooks on their foreheads declaring their loyalty for now. But what would happen when the star-veil fell and the Talisman overran the square?

A niggle of doubt worked its way into her thoughts. The Silver Mage was just one man; his gifts were not without their limits. She'd learned as much from watching the three Mages attempt to harness the armillary sphere and fail. Without the power of the sphere, these Nineteen who needed no rest, whose purpose never faltered, couldn't be held at bay.

And it seemed their fortunes were not about to change, because there was no rope in the storeroom, either coiled on the hooks at the front or hidden on the shelves at the back. They were at the end of their reserves.

"What about this?"

Katayoun pointed to a heavy track of iron links stored under a stack of canvas. It wasn't as flexible as rope, but with its strong, square links, it would give the Silver Mage a foothold if he could grab on. Dust stirred as she kicked the canvas aside. Coughing, Cassandane tugged at the track. Katayoun braced her legs to help, but the iron track was sturdy, designed to swing catapults into position. The Teerandaz were limber and lean. These tracks were designed for the brute strength of the Zhayedan, and there were no Zhayedan to spare.

"Come on. We can do it if we try."

Both women braced again, but as they struggled to raise the track to their shoulders, their knees gave way under its weight.

"We'll never get it to the Silver Mage," Katayoun panted. "And even if we do, how will we be able to use it to help him climb?"

"We can help."

Cassandane looked up. She found herself staring at a hardened fighter with bleak blue eyes, accompanied by another man whose throat was scarred. They wore the Talisman's uniform, but both men's foreheads were stamped with a silver rook. These must be the defectors who'd passed into Ashfall under the Silver Mage's flag.

The man who'd spoken helped Cassandane to her feet. Then with the ease of a child hefting a toy sword, he caught up the track and balanced it on his shoulders.

A smile of bitter humor. "How were you planning to pull him up?"

Cassandane's eyes strayed to the mark on his forehead. Squaring her shoulders, she scanned the battle in the courtyard. "The Teerandaz always find a way."

"Your hands are better suited to your bow."

He didn't need to tell her something she knew. Just as she knew they owed a debt to the man who had fought for Ashfall from the first.

"Will you aid the Silver Mage?" Her dark eyes touched the rook again.

The Talisman soldier gazed down at the Nineteen, where two fighters continued to circle.

"We cannot interfere, Uwais." The younger soldier struggled

with his half of the track. But he was either strong or determined, because once he'd heaved it to his shoulders, he stood firm. "The Silver Mage wears the Sacred Cloak. He must honor his oath to fight."

Cassandane swallowed the protest that rose to her throat. The eyes of the man named Uwais swung back to her. "You disagree, Captain?"

He'd noted her insignia. She shoved her helmet back onto her head, sliding her bow free.

"We need the Silver Mage alive. Without him we cannot hold."

"His honor matters to him."

"Honor is poor solace to the dead."

Cassandane couldn't tell if Uwais favored the Silver Mage's pledge to fight in single combat or not. She and Katayoun marched along the wall, the Talisman matching their pace. They reached a point just above the Silver Mage. Uwais measured out links of the track over his battle-scarred hands, resting against the wall. "If I throw down the track before the contest is ended, the Nineteen may find a way to use it. We have to wait."

Cassandane paused for no more than a moment to look into those simmering eyes. The soldiers fighting in the courtyard needed cover from the Teerandaz.

"You *will* aid him if you can? I can trust the word of a defector?"

His entire body hardened in response, and she had to stop herself from stepping back.

"Do you know of the tribes of Khyber?"

She nodded. The mountain tribes were said to be as ruthless in battle as the Zhayedan. He shifted the track in his hands, his knuckles white against his skin.

"Then you know that honor is not solely the right of the Silver Mage."

39

"YOU FIGHT WITH LESS DETERMINATION THAN YOU DID UPON YOUR AIR-ship," Najran taunted.

Daniyar saved his breath for the attack. His movements fell into a pattern. Circle, leap, feint left, but bring his sword up from the right, where Najran was slower to respond.

Hot blue sparks flew from the edges of their blades, like thunder trapped in a constricted space, buffeting them with each blow.

There was a tense silence from the army of the Nineteen, as Najran shifted to his other foot, his thrusts accompanied by a string of curses.

Wild gold color filled the sky. Far above them on the walls, the voices of the Mages struggled to hold on to the Dawn Rite, hoarse with effort and strained with the foretaste of fear.

Najran smiled. The blade of the Dimashq formed a counterpoint to an intricate movement that stirred a gasp from the soldiers who watched. It slashed across the Sacred Cloak. The Cloak fluttered, then resettled on Daniyar's shoulders undamaged.

Suspicion darkened Najran's face. "What strange magic is this?"

Their swords met again, tangled, and broke free.

"Not strange—*true*." Daniyar's shoulders had begun to ache again, the heavy muscles of his arms trembling with fatigue. To distract Najran's attention from what would soon be apparent, he said, "The Cloak was meant for me. Your sorcery cannot harm it."

They circled each other again, and this time Daniyar sensed that the quality of attention from those who watched had altered by a degree.

A feint with the Dimashq left a stripe across his cheek. A matching one appeared on the other. A third strike caught a fold of the Cloak and wove it around his ankle. Najran leapt high, jamming his foot down behind Daniyar's knee. He kicked up at the back of his thigh. Daniyar fell to his knees, just missing the edge of the Dimashq.

His magic shifted in his chest, furling in. His right hand slipped on the pommel of the Bladebone, the sword buried in the sand. A cry of dismay rippled along the wall.

A sneer worked across Najran's face. He threw his head up at the wall.

"Look at your savior now!"

He circled Daniyar, the Dimashq balanced in his hand. Daniyar knew he should give Najran a fight worthy of the name, but the effort to maintain the star-veil was stealing away his strength. He jerked his sword, bracing his hands on the guard. He told himself that any moment now, he would rise.

The tip of the Dimashq whipped the Cloak over Daniyar's shoulders. Najran stabbed at his torso in a series of dizzying strikes.

"Here is your true magic!" he crowed.

All traces of night had been swallowed by the dawn. The star-veil had drifted down in increments. Now, like the rasp of a falling curtain, it faltered and collapsed. A wild roar echoed to the south. Daniyar closed his eyes, accepting Najran's blows.

The voice of the Ascension echoed in his head.

Silver Mage, Guardian of Candour. Your time is at an end.

So be it. He whispered the prayer that was a prelude to dying.

From the One I came, to the One I return. To the One I belong.

He searched along the walls for the lost boys of Candour who had come to Ashfall under his flag. When he found them, his bearing firmed, and he magnified his voice.

"If you follow a man and take your creed through him, you should know that every man meets his fate. But if your submission is to the One, know that the One is Infinite and Everlasting, and let that be your guide."

The warning was for the Preacher's followers, though he also comforted his own.

There were cries of grief along the walls.

Najran kicked at his body, not troubling to use his sword. His lips pulled back in a violent grimace as the Nineteen watched him batter the man who wore the Sacred Cloak.

He'd failed, Daniyar thought. He'd failed Arian at every turn.

He let his forehead touch the pommel of his sword. A little of its energy soothed the pain of his wounds.

Najran mocked him. "Arian gave me more of a fight when I cracked her bones beneath my boots."

Daniyar raised his head. His tarnished eyes pinned Najran.

The mottled blade of the Dimashq came up in response; it traced the seam of his nape. A mournful wail rang along the wall.

"Her blood was sweet to taste, her body sweeter to break."

Daniyar breathed in once, then measured another breath. His hands fastened on the Bladebone's grip. Its brutal magic seeped into his palms, washing over his body. In the vast silence inside his mind, he felt a pulse like a heartbeat, a shocking echo of pain suffered by the woman he loved.

Arian.

My love, don't let me go. Hold on a little longer.

But he knew his time was at an end. He could feel his soul slipping from his body, yearning to escape the darkness he had carried within him so long.

He heard her voice again.

Don't give me up, my love. No matter what you learned upon Ascension, for I learned you are mine. My sword, my shield, my destiny. My garment as I am yours.

The silver sword shone between his palms.

A haunting voice called out from the wall, the voice of a boy, deflecting Najran's attempts to cover his body in blood, to thread him as he'd promised.

He listened to the voice from a distance that contained the passing of eons, history unfolding in a pageant of glory, a golden pinnacle overtaken by endless years of decline. They had forfeited their faith and lost their way, though *he* had never been lost. He had held on to his belief in the face of every attempt to diminish it.

Now the boy Wafa ripped the veil away, and through the lessons of history, the Guardian of Candour came to understand a truth, certain and immutable through time. With the Sacred Cloak, *he* was Commander of the Faithful. With the Bladebone, *he* was the Lion of the One. Why then accept defeat? He was no less than Najran.

I am far, far more.

Thunder surged in his blood, and with a roar, he came to his feet. He pulled his sword from the sand and balanced it, his right hand wrapped around the top of the grip, his left hand closed over the pommel. He drew his elbows nearer to his body, gaining greater freedom to move.

But Najran had missed the significance of his renewal. He brought the fine blade of the Dimashq up in counterpoint to Daniyar's surge, ignoring the cries of encouragement that rained down from the defenders of Ashfall.

Daniyar didn't wait. He advanced on Najran with fierce downward strokes, his angle of attack powered by his calculated fury. Najran stumbled under the assault, the army of the Nineteen restless at his back. Gathering himself, Najran shouted in Aramaya, "You cannot defeat the Nineteen! You are no match for the Keepers of the Saqar!"

Daniyar's advance didn't slow, and now Najran kept his taunts to himself, the two swords meeting in a flurry of blinding strokes. With each forward lunge, Daniyar forced Najran to give ground, the Dimashq pinned closer to his body, as his parries became defensive. A soldier of the Nineteen caught the edge of Daniyar's cloak, cutting off his pursuit. Daniyar freed himself by shoving the soldier into the arms of his comrades, his hand planted in the center of the man's chest. Jeers poured down from the walls at the soldier's intercession, a violation of the terms of single combat. The soldier's comrades secured him, and Daniyar leapt after Najran.

But the Nineteen's lethal lieutenant had regrouped. He'd taken up a black and gold shield that was patterned after the Dimashq, the shield buckled to his forearm. The Bladebone struck a jarring note against the shield, and now Najran's well-judged parries were drawing Daniyar deeper into the midst of the Nineteen, who circled the two fighters.

"Take a look around," Najran invited. "Assess your circumstances." He drew the Dimashq across Daniyar's body with a horizontal swipe of his blade. He lunged with the shield and counterattacked with the sword. The Sacred Cloak softened the blows, but Daniyar stumbled back a pace. The Nineteen threw him forward in time to meet a stroke of the Dimashq that swept up from the ground.

The power of the blow radiated through the arm that held the Bladebone, but Daniyar steadied himself and held firm. He caught Najran's eyes and waited.

Still baiting him, Najran said, "You are alone and outnumbered. When you fall beneath my boots, your name will vanish from history."

The Dimashq flicked across Daniyar's collarbone. With a sweep of his shielded arm, Najran indicated the might of the Nineteen. He raised his voice so that his words would be heard by those who stood as witnesses to the battle, his malice and arrogance plain.

"You are left with two choices, Guardian of Candour: death or humiliation. I wonder which you will choose."

At the brazen insult, Daniyar swept the Cloak to his back. He brought his sword to his lips and kissed it. His tendons began to burn. Murmuring notes of the Claim, his eyes trapped Najran into fleeting stillness with their brilliance. Seizing his advantage, he split Najran's shield with a powerful downward stroke, the blow cleaving muscle and bone. Blood spurted from Najran's forearm, snaking down to his wrist. Shocked, he dragged his arm to his chest.

Daniyar threw off his weariness, his back straight, his voice carrying to the walls.

"We do not falter before unjust war, and we *do not* accept humiliation."

The Zhayedan roared with pride.

Bolstered by it, the Bladebone became a cold lance of fire that moved across Najran's torso, returning blow for blow. No matter how Najran tried to twist away, the Bladebone was there to meet him. Barreling forward as Daniyar evaded his strike, the deft strokes of the Dimashq lanced across the body of a soldier. His limbs and trunk disintegrated in neatly severed bits, blood spurting like a fountain and lying like a stain on the sands. The bloodletting was answered by a roar from all who watched.

Daniyar swung around, battering Najran again, bearing him back with ruthless force. The enemy's grip on his weapon weakened, and Daniyar took immediate advantage, trapping the deadly sword between the Bladebone's tips. With a final determined effort, he wrested the Dimashq from Najran's hands and sent it sailing through the camp.

"No!" Najran gasped, leaping to evade the Bladebone's deadly sweep. "You cannot defeat me—my gifts are invincible! You cannot even *hurt* me."

Daniyar's gaze met Najran's, watching as his pupils bled to black.

"Then you will not feel it when I repay the agonies you inflicted on the First Oralist."

He struck a series of harsh blows. Najran's armor peeled from his torso; stripes welled up on his skin. The Nineteen did nothing to interfere, even when, beaten back beyond retaliation, Najran teetered before Daniyar, his chest and ribs lathered in blood, curses falling from his lips.

Cheered on by the Zhayedan, Daniyar raised the Bladebone high, its pristine edges unmarred. Najran looked up with a desperate cry, shielding his face with his arm.

But though Najran called out, "Over you are *Nineteen*!" no one moved to aid him. He stood frozen before an enemy he had woefully misjudged.

A haunted look came into his eyes. His hands locked at his side, he managed to force his lips apart.

"Mercy."

The word was a plea. A rumble of disgust rippled through the Nineteen's ranks.

The folds of the Sacred Cloak settled over Daniyar's shoulders, emphasizing his grandeur. And though Daniyar took no pleasure in killing, he was guided by the Claim, and he answered, "Mercy is for the deserving."

The sword flashed down. He drove it through Najran's sternum with unadulterated strength. When Najran's breath whooshed from his lungs, Daniyar wrenched the sword free, shoving at the other man's shoulder to swing his body around.

"This is for daring to speak her name, for daring to think yourself worthy."

The Bladebone severed Najran's spine; his body collapsed with a thud. Confronted with the truth of his mortality, his breath soughed from his body as silence descended on the camp.

The Silver Mage watched him die.

"You thought you could vanquish *her*, when you could not stand against *me*."

Then he confirmed his victory with a bold and visceral truth.

"There is no sword like the Bladebone, and none like the warrior who wields it."

A deafening cheer resounded from the wall.

The Nineteen backed away from him, widening their circle. His eyes searched out their lieutenants.

"You appoint yourselves Keepers of the Saqar? Do you *know*

what hell truly is? Do you understand it? It spares no one, leaves nothing intact. If that is your choice, make it."

Someone called down to him in the dialect of Candour.

He looked up at the wall and found the soldier named Uwais.

Uwais gestured at the iron track that tumbled from the wall like a rope.

"Grab hold." Uwais's bleak eyes blazed with pride. "Commander of the Faithful, hold fast to the rope."

40

THE EVACUATION OF ASHFALL WAS CHARACTERIZED BY CHAOS. THE PAS-
sageways that linked the outer residences to the palace were narrow and dark. There was a great push to reach the Qaysarieh
Portal. Many of the city's inhabitants were divested of their treasures to open up the passage through. Others had chosen to remain in the palace, unable to fathom a reality where the Zhayedan
were defeated.

Now, as Khashayar and a handful of others tried to hold the
palace doors closed, cries of fright echoed from the upper halls.
Enemy fighters from all sides bore down upon the palace. And no
matter how Darya tried to direct the flow, her people resisted her
orders, spilling out of every passageway, defeating her efforts to
organize the retreat. The crush was too great, and there were no
soldiers to spare to assist her.

A quick glance through an upper window showed her that the
Assassins had gathered at Qaysarieh's pishtaq, barring the outer
entrance to the Portal. Their movements were coordinated, their
directions unhurried. She wished their leader had assigned a few

of these men to her aid. A few moments later, the Assassin appeared, carrying an ebony horn.

He blew the horn twice. The frantic crush within the palace stilled.

"You open those doors to your death." He pointed to a black-garbed Assassin at the far end of the hall. "Follow him, or your enemies will find you in the tunnels."

Khashayar echoed his order.

A hush descended, as frightened faces stared up at the Assassin and children whimpered in fear. The air tore as the celestial curtain fell. They heard the wild roar to the south. The foundations of Ashfall shook. Across the square to the east, the Emissary Gate bulged. The frenzy of thousands of fighters burst like a rocket through the square. Sounds of terror filled the hall.

The Assassin remained calm. He used the horn again. The Claim rang out through the hall, and civilians began to move with some cohesion, his voice a source of reassurance.

Forgetting herself, Darya clutched his shoulder.

"Should—should I go with them, lead them? The tunnels will frighten the children."

His murmur of the Claim turned subvocal. His jade eyes traveled over her, and she knew they found her wanting.

"Your place is here, Princess. The star-veil has fallen, but you were confident in your powers before they faltered. What can you tell me of the armillary sphere?"

Her lips trembled at the enormity of her crimes, at the unbearable foolishness that had sparked her interference. Her interactions with Darius had made her believe she could help, but her stubborn pride had brought about the annihilation of Ashfall.

Like a frightened child, Darya put her hands over her ears.

The Assassin pulled them free without compunction. "That sound you hear is the collapse of the Tower of the Mirage."

And indeed piercing cries resonated along the southern wall over the crash of stone and mortar, and the ceaseless clash of steel.

"Yes, you made a mistake. But it is not the end—it doesn't have to be. *Think,* Princess. You knew about the power of Al Mintaka; you called yourself its twin. Had I not been overseeing the evacuation, I would have helped you use your knowledge." She met his gaze for a searing moment before he said, "Is there any other way to use the sphere? What did your half-brother teach you when you harnessed the power of the stars?"

Her dark eyes huge, she whispered, "I don't know." Then, drawing a shaky breath, she asked him, "What would it take to save the city?"

An impatient jerk of the mask. "The city can't be saved. All we can hope for is sufficient time to complete the evacuation."

Her gaze fell to his hands. He was wearing his leather gloves. They were laced with the webbing he knew she loathed: they reminded her of the ghul.

"If we could split the power of the star-beam, we might be able to hold the walls."

But the Assassin had heard the roar of fighters pouring into the square.

"You tried that and failed."

"I failed because I tried to use the star-beam against my brother's wishes. But there may be another way to help. I know a secret that Darius kept." If there were any who would still believe her. "Do you think Rukh would be willing to hear me?"

Her eyes were bright and hopeful on his face. In this moment, he held all the power. And he intended to use it.

He brought the horn to his lips. His gaze met Khashayar's.

The Zhayedan captain gave him a firm nod; he would do his part to speed the evacuation along. The Assassin didn't wait for more. He took hold of Darya's hand, pulling her against the tide. She stumbled as she tried to keep up with him, the lines of his body blending into stone. If she hadn't been holding his hand, she wouldn't have been certain that he was there in the shadows.

She didn't know how long she followed him as thunder crashed all around, and the doors of the Illustrious Portal trembled, warning its inhabitants that the palace would soon be overrun.

But just when her lungs were pleading for air, the Assassin came to a halt. They'd reached the stairs to the Messenger Gate. She could hear her brother reciting the Dawn Rite, the words rough and desperate. She tried to dodge the Assassin. He moved to bar her way.

"We should hurry," she told him.

"A moment of your time first, Princess."

She brought her gaze back to his mask.

He had led them to the music room in the part of the palace known as the Great Gate. When it was first built, the monumental gatehouse had been meant to serve as an atrium that connected the public square to the administrative sections of the palace. Rukh had converted the Great Gate into a five-level tower crowned by an open porch. At the center of the porch, water danced inside a triple-tiered fountain, a reminder of better days.

From the covered porch, the Black Khan and his courtiers had watched the entertainments in the square. Darya's favorite of these had been chowgan, a sport where superbly skilled horsemen chased a ball around the grounds. Arsalan had been the most daring of the players, and Darya had loved to watch him, had loved to see the Zhayedan's handsome general flushed with the exertion of the chase. When he won—as he often did—he did so in the name of his prince. And Rukh had rewarded each victory with a prize worthy of a king.

The memory made Darya bitter. She moved away from the porch into the vaulted space of the music room. This was a cross-shaped hall with a ceiling rich in plaster decoration. Niches in the walls were hollowed out in the shape of instruments: the long-stringed setar, the kamancheh, the daf. A lantern cast a coral glow on the frescoes painted on the walls.

The Assassin gestured to a banquette nearby, and Darya sank into it, counting each moment that was lost. Yet the Assassin stood motionless, though his jade eyes tracked each new emotion that gave color to her face.

His clothes bore evidence of the battles he had fought. The scent of smoke clung to his cloak, and traces of ash painted a line across his mask. His black uniform, if uniform it was, was torn in some places and bloodied in many others. Through a slash across his abdomen, she saw the raised texture of a scar. A quick adjustment of his cloak covered it.

She shivered under his gaze, and the corners of his eyes pinched tight.

"Do I frighten you, Princess?"

The voice stroked over her senses like the fall of a smooth, dark wine into a glass. He had ceased the trick of distortion that made his voice metallic and cold. Now its timbre was different. It seemed to promise injury. Or . . . other things, perhaps.

She clenched her hands into fists. She tried to hide them in the folds of her dress, but she knew he'd seen her reaction.

"You command a secret force of assassins—that would be enough for me to fear. But how can I ignore the fact that you brought me back from the dead? I would be a fool *not* to fear you."

"Many at this court think of you as foolish, but I do not share their view."

She paled at this reminder, even as words rushed to her tongue.

"After I failed with the sphere, you should. But perhaps you require a subject for your experiments, to determine if your skills also apply to the dead."

"You were not dead, Princess."

"I *was*!" Unable to bear his looming over her any longer, she jumped back to her feet. She paced the chamber, ignoring the nooks she had loved to hide in as a child. She wished she could hide from him now, from whatever he wanted from her.

"I know what I felt; I know what I *was*. Dark. Heavy. Cold. The spark of my soul extinguished, the thread of my life snapped."

He caught her by the arm to halt her restless pacing. To force her to face him. The way he had arranged his fingers inside her elbow didn't hurt, it didn't bruise her, but she felt the flaring of nerves, knew that if she pulled away those nerves would pinch in pain.

She stiffened her spine and raised her chin.

"I am the Princess of Ashfall. Do not touch me without my consent."

The pinched corners of his jade eyes softened, though the grip of his fingers didn't ease.

"I have already made free with your person, Princess, it's too late to stop me now. I've carried you in my arms, I've dressed and undressed you." His other hand came up to rest at the center of her breastbone, the movement soft and silken, yet carrying the weight of threat. "I've touched you here." A slight pressure, and Darya's heart thumped with jarring force. He bent his head so that his mask brushed the lobe of her ear. "I've *opened* you here. Taken your blood, tasted it." With a deft movement, his hand was at her wrist, exerting a peculiar pressure. "I've cut you here."

His hand shifted again, cupped the back of her head with terrifying strength before it trailed through the tresses of her hair. The dark curls caressed his wrists. Cool steel brushed her soft cheek, drifted closer to her lips. A thrill of fear shot through her.

"I've taken blood and bone and hair from you, Princess. I've already made you mine. The rest is a formality."

"You speak in riddles, Assassin. Why do you delay my attempts to assist my brother when you say the city is doomed?"

"It is time for a debt to be paid."

"What debt?"

"The many debts your brother owes me, not least the refuge I offer at the Eagle's Nest."

A lump rose to Darya's throat. "What has that to do with me?"

Something she couldn't read came into the Assassin's eyes. But she was never able to read him. She'd never known what he wanted or why he'd chosen to ally himself with Ashfall, when a treaty with the Talisman would have proved more fruitful.

"It has everything to do with you, for you are the payment I seek."

41

She couldn't have heard him right, but the Assassin wasn't done.

"Settle the matter now, and the road to the Eagle's Nest will remain open. Refuse me, and know that you were the one who brought death upon your people."

Her face went slack with horror. "You would blackmail me? *Why?* Do you seek to raise the ghul again?"

He checked a betraying movement. "You do yourself little credit, Princess. It is *you* I seek to bind."

Darya broke away from the firm lines of his body, aware that she'd escaped because he'd chosen to release her. Now he watched her, head tipped to one side.

"You wish to be *bound* to me?" Her sense of shock was profound. "You were the one who ruined me!"

Her chest was rising and falling in her agitation, enraged by his refusal to admit that he'd harmed her. He held himself aloof, as though he were removed from her unmaking.

"Come, Princess. Nothing about you makes me think you a coward. You think *I* made you yield your self-control? That *I* unleashed your cruelty?" He dared to contradict her. "The ugliness was within you. The ghul merely took advantage."

"No . . ."

"Yes." The truth was like the thrust of a sword. "You've been angry too long. Bitter. Humiliated. Unloved. Desperate for attention. From your brother, from your would-be lover. When you learned the truth of who Arsalan loves, you acted to destroy him. You burned down the scriptorium. You wanted your pain acknowledged." He shrugged. "I do not blame you for that. Nor for the brokenness you refuse to accept."

Darya reeled away from him. She stumbled as the banquette caught her at the knees. The Assassin did nothing to assist her, watching as she struggled. She tripped over the hem of her dress, landing on her hands and knees.

Her face wet with tears, she tried to defend herself from his allegations.

"It was the ghul who wanted to hurt my brother. I would never harm Arsalan or Rukh."

She made an ineffectual swipe at her tearstained face.

He watched unmoved as she scrambled to her feet.

"You are prone to self-delusion, Princess." The assessment stung. His jade eyes were opaque, the blows coming in swift succession. "Look at your obsession with Arsalan: anyone could see he didn't want you. Why else did you need to coerce him? You shed your scruples in an instant in order to satisfy your lust."

She choked back a cry, struggling to breathe as he stripped her defenses away.

"You will not be free, Princess, until you accept that you, yourself, are the ghul. Whatever ugliness the ghul conjures, the desire for it comes from you. Once you acknowledge that truth, your guilt will cease to affect you."

"No! *No!*"

He listened to her cry with no attempt at comfort. Her slender frame shook with the force of her sobs. It couldn't be true that she was the author of her own ruin, that she had pillaged with reckless indifference to the loyalty she owed to Ashfall. How could she have been so foolish? So ruthlessly greedy and vengeful?

Her shame and horror were soldered to her bones. Child of Hira, indeed. The magic that had raised her from death had entwined with her darkest impulses to demand a brutal repayment of countless injuries and slights. Darya had sanctioned the violence—she had *gloried* in it. She could still feel tremors of that glory buried in the reaches of her soul.

The Assassin had told her the truth. She had no choice but to contend with it.

When she had found some measure of control, she wiped her face with the long sleeves of her dress. She moved away, far away, to the entrance of the porch, her bruised eyes unseeing as she pictured a capital in ruins. Images raced across her mind. The thought of fires burning, of broken walls and crumbling towers, of legions of Zhayedan dead.

Her voice raw, she didn't look at him. "If I am as ugly and broken as you say, why do you wish to be bound to me? Does your alliance with my brother mean that much? Or do you think to use me to deepen your knowledge of the dark arts?"

He moved to stand beside her, a little distance between them.

His voice was no warmer, no kinder, when he said, "I didn't say I found you ugly. Nor can I be accused of engaging in arcane rites." The offense he had taken was clear when he added, "I am a son of the Nun scriptorium—I seek to *confront* dark sorcery. You judge me without knowing who I am."

"I might say the same of you."

The mask dipped once, a concession. She kept her face turned away.

"Then why? If you believe the things you have accused me of, there is little to recommend me to a man of your . . . renown. By your account, my selfishness is wretched—I cannot even govern myself."

"Self-pity doesn't suit you." The words were cutting and cool.

Her nails dug into her hands. Crescents appeared on the soft skin of her palms as he turned the question back on her.

"Why do you not wish to accept? The alliance would be advantageous."

"You are quick to think of advantage, aren't you?"

"Are you not, Princess?"

Her lips thinned, her dark eyes bleak.

"As you pointed out, my heart belongs to another."

"Arsalan doesn't want you."

Her breath hissed through her teeth.

"I know that *now*." She pressed the heels of her hands to her eyes.

"You have always known it."

She glared up at his mask. "It doesn't matter what you think; my feelings for him haven't changed. I cannot love you, I do not wish to, and in the absence of any kinder feeling between us, how do I know what cruelty you intend?" She rubbed the spot on her breastbone where his cut had been made. "What *further* cruelty, I should say."

She chafed her arms as if cold. Again, he offered no sympathy in response, though his limbs were stiff, his actions poised on the turn of a blade.

"I don't recall asking for your love." A harsh edge to that modulated voice. He hesitated a moment before he removed his mask.

She gasped at the sight of his scars, her fingers pressed to her lips. He tensed, but he let her eyes dwell on the gaunt planes of his face, on the rawness of the scars, as if the fire had been recent instead of many years past.

His eyes were locked on hers, parsing every nuance of her expression.

"My body is scarred as well. Riven in my family's defense. Broken and re-formed long ago. Much like yours, Darya."

Her name on his lips made her tremble. His jade eyes flared in response.

Hesitating, she asked, "With your arts, could you not heal . . . ?" The words tapered off. Perhaps she wondered if he would take offense.

"I have never had reason to try."

"They must hurt you."

"They do." His lips tightened, the scars rippling with the movement. He drew a breath and asked her, "Do they frighten you? For there is more to me than my disfigurement."

Darya couldn't look away from him. This was her chance to strike back, to judge him and find him wanting. But she couldn't. She couldn't even pretend. No matter what he thought of her, she wasn't predisposed to cruelty.

"I can see the . . . artful . . . arrangement of your bones. Your hair is dark yet it shines like watered silk, your voice a thing of such beauty, I find it often beguiles me. And the way you hold your body—I have never seen a man move as you do." Her lashes fluttered down before she raised them again. "Your eyes are like the First Oralist's. Green as jade, soft with light, rich with mysteries." She swallowed. He followed the delicate movement of her throat. "Your eyes make you beautiful. I cannot say I do not see the scars, but I gave you my refusal before you showed me your face."

The mask was forgotten in his hand. He stared at her until a painful color crept up under her skin. She ducked her head and moved from the porch to the fountain. She trailed a hand through its waters, distancing herself from whatever he might say next.

Would he sling his words like arrows?

Or would he offer her kindness this once?

"If you are not repulsed, what is your reason for refusal?"

Her hands gripped the basin, tension firming the slim line of her shoulders. He was demanding total capitulation.

"Neither my brother nor Arsalan love me, nor can you pretend to care for me." She stopped him before he could interrupt. "I've been useful to you, I know. I have furthered your plots, and perhaps you see some value in that, but not enough."

"Not enough?" The soft echo was painful to her, but why would that matter to the Assassin when his words could slice her to the bone?

"When your experiment with the ghul went awry, you expected Arsalan to kill me. You told him to do it. I was there, so you cannot deny it."

"I am not a liar, Princess," he said mildly.

Her hands clutched the basin. She wanted to bring this conversation to an end; it was tearing at the heart of her. Making her doubt her sole source of comfort, the hope that she belonged to Hira, that she belonged anywhere at all.

It cost her something, but she pushed on to the end. "Whether I live or die, it's all the same to you." Her lip curled in self-derision. "I thought I might mean more to the man I marry."

The Assassin took her by the arm, touching that same spot inside her elbow, this time without the hint of threat. When she summoned the will to look at him again, his eyes were lit with warmth. She caught her breath.

"Do you know what my particular gift is, Princess?"

She shook her head.

"I read the hearts of others. I show them to themselves, just as I forced you to confront the truths of your heart. I sought to release you from the grief that has bound you. I knew Commander Arsalan would not be able to harm you, but he needed to reach that conclusion for himself." His voice deepened, a strange magic in it. "It matters to me very much whether you live or die." His hand moved up her arm to stroke a tendril of her hair. "I saved you from the One-Eyed Preacher. And I pulled you back again when the ghul would have brought you to ruin. I didn't do that for your brother. I did it for myself."

After everything he'd done, she found that impossible to believe. Yet she found herself asking, "Are you saying you love me, Assassin?"

Laughter deepened the color of his eyes, but he didn't allow it to escape. With some seriousness he said, "You should use my name when you ask me such a question. My given name is Hudayfah."

Hudayfah. A proud name, weighted with history, noble to the ear.

Taken aback, she found a way to rephrase the question that embarrassed her. "Do you court me out of . . . affection, Hudayfah?"

His lips quirked. "Accept my suit and see."

Darya pursed her lips. "I do not wish to marry. I wish to be free of a man's influence, of his dictates over me. If Ashfall should survive—" Wasn't that all that mattered? A dream she dared not dream. "There may be a possibility . . ." She blushed over the faltering words, then cleared her throat. "I have always wished to study at the Citadel of Hira. I hoped to become a Companion. A life with you would steal away my dream, if our dreams should remain."

"Then go," he said, sharing the fallacy of a future where the city endured. "I would not take from you your dream."

"Then why—how—?"

"The First Oralist and the Silver Mage have bound themselves to each other. As a result of that bond, the Council of Hira may choose to grant them dispensation. And if to them, why not to others? You could follow the First Oralist's path."

Darya stammered a reply. "You would not wish me to—you would insist—you would force me to your side."

He slipped the mask onto his face, the barrier back in place between them.

"If we succeed in the defense of Ashfall, I will permit your course of study."

"Why do you not understand? I do not require permission! As long as I am unmarried, I am free to govern myself."

A subtle shift of his shoulders. "I do not think so, Princess."

His thoughts focused on the plans he had made, on the many webs he had woven. There were things he could do to ease the suffering of Ashfall, but he would not act without her pledge.

"Come, Princess, you delay us. And in the end, what other option do you have?" He smiled behind the mask, the echo of the smile in his voice.

"I hate you!" She couldn't stop herself from shouting the truth at him.

"As you will." His indifference to it unhidden by the mask.

Desperate to dissuade him, she made herself tell him of her shame. "I do not come to you untouched. I gave myself to Arsalan."

An imperceptible tightening. "*Took* him, rather, I think." He straightened the laces of his gloves, the webbing Darya loathed. It had kept her, bound her, *destroyed* her. She still didn't comprehend its power. But there was no softening now of those jade-green eyes. "As for the rest, I do not care. In all the ways that matter, you will be chaste for me."

A sick feeling swamped her stomach. His sorcery would continue. He would reawaken the ghul, find a way to master them both. What folly to have offered him compassion when she could have done him injury instead.

"I will not marry you." This time it sounded like a plea.

The mask tipped, dark hair sliding over its surface. "I had hoped to persuade you, Princess, but your consent is not required. The Black Khan's debt will be fulfilled."

They both knew this to be true. It would not occur to her brother to consider her independence as meaningful as his own.

She raised her head. She wished now that she could see the face behind the mask. Would there be tenderness in it? Remorse? Compassion? Or only the satisfaction of one unaccustomed to any obstruction of his schemes?

The script that covered the steel mask swam before her wounded eyes. She saw the letter that denoted the name of the Inkwell scriptorium—ن—*Nun*. Other words danced before her eyes, but she could not decipher their sense. She didn't want to show the Assassin weakness, yet she couldn't resist the urge to rub her eyes. The script on the mask vanished, leaving it cool and blank. The well-shaped lines of his eyebrows arched over his watchful eyes, as he measured the shades of her response.

"Is the thought of my company so abhorrent?"

How could she respond? The mask revealed nothing, yet she sensed the possibility of injury from a careless parry.

She found herself pressing a hand to the mark on her breastbone again. The eyes watching her flicked to her heart before returning to her face.

"It isn't that," she said at last. "Though I do not know you at all." She chose her next words with difficulty. "If I am ever sent to Hira, I would have more to learn than most. My training would not bear the pressures of a betrothal."

She sensed the easing of his tension, though she didn't know how that was possible when the Assassin hadn't stirred.

You know me better than you think. The bond we share is deeper than one granted to others by ritual.

She heard the words in her mind and she gasped. Before, the Assassin had breached her mind to speak to the ghul—not to her as Darya. She looked up at him, her eyes wide in appeal. "Then why do you insist on the ritual?"

When she asked the question, he realized the Princess had never truly seen herself. But what *he* saw was not a gift he intended to give her now. He inclined his head at a graceful angle. "It is enough for you to know that I do."

He gave her a moment to consider her choices. But a moment was all he could spare.

She brought her fist to her mouth. "*No.* I will not bind myself to you."

The Assassin raised his horn to his lips.

"Wait!" Panicked, she pulled at his arm to lower the horn. "What are you doing?"

"Telling my Assassins to halt the evacuation."

Undiluted terror moved over her face. "You can't mean that. You won't do it. Rukh—Rukh is your ally. You have always been friends."

"As I told you, your brother has given you to me. He did not require your consent."

He raised the horn to his lips again, and she spat at him, "You cannot call this consent when you coerce me to a choice I have no wish to make."

He gripped her chin with his free hand, forcing her to meet his gaze. "Such pride and defiance from one so well-acquainted with coercion."

The heat of her blush seared his fingers. He held her in place a little longer before he pushed her again. "Why do you deny the inevitable, Princess?"

She broke free of his grip. "I can't accept you under these conditions. The city is about to fall, the armillary sphere is at the other side of the square—how will we reach it in time? And I do not know if you are telling me the truth. I know Rukh is furious with me, but he would not just *give* me to you. If not for my sake, he would not dishonor Arsalan by ending our betrothal."

The Assassin's horn vanished. He cocked his head to one side, listening for Rukh's voice.

Drawing up the remnants of her courage, Darya challenged him with the truth. "Why force this now, when we cannot know if Ashfall will be standing at the end of this day?"

"I will permit you to discuss my proposal with your brother; the rest is my concern. But perhaps I might allay at least one of your worries." He dipped his head at the stairs. Darya peered around his shoulders, seeking what he sought to show her. A gleam of sunlight on silver.

He'd been thinking ten steps ahead.

He'd brought her the armillary sphere.

42

THE RUIN OF ASHFALL, THE END OF AN EMPIRE OF GRACE, AND STILL there was no sign of the First Oralist. Enemies poured into the capital from the south, the east, and the west, a thick miasma of murder in the square—and his Zhayedan, his Zhayedan were mowed down like fields of wheat under a scythe, Arsalan battling at their head, Khashayar and the rest wearied beyond use.

The iron scent of blood colored over a dawn that had folded itself away. The Mages stayed on the walls, helping the soldiers below, bright forays of fire burning fighters away from the path that led to the palace.

Nothing, Rukh thought. Nothing could be done.

His throat burned with pain, his voice was raw with exhaustion, his cloak long since discarded in the heat, his collar loose around his neck. Bodies littered the noble square. Half the world, he lamented. The square called the Naqsh-e Jahan was half the world, and this half would drown in blood. Three Mages of Khorasan and a general who refused to accept defeat could not stem this tide. Even as Rukh called out incantations from the wall, he saw a group of Talisman climb the Maiden Tower, setting their charges again. Another contingent had reached his war room. He watched the armory and barracks burn.

Yet still they fought to the last soldier, his Zhayedan, heeding Arsalan's call, and he took a moment to feel pride in their courage. They had not wanted or asked for this war, but when it had come, they had not balked at it.

He'd been lost in his thoughts too long. A group of Nineteen discovered him above the Messenger Gate and raced along the wall to confront him.

He blasted them back with a final urging of the Dawn Rite. A handful of men were incinerated, yet dozens more followed. A savage roar from below. Arsalan had seen the attack. He charged the stairs that led to the ramparts, Zhayedan falling in behind him.

They fought, they dueled, they suffered injury, and in the haze of smoke and the heat of carnal destruction, they lost sight of each other. A soldier, Talisman or Nineteen, Rukh couldn't tell, aimed a blow at his throat. He dodged it, stepping into the path of another that hit his shoulder hard. He cursed the man with the Claim. Someone called out a warning. A third man was at his back. But the man had already fallen by the time he whirled around, Teerandaz arrows through his chest. He looked up. Cassandane saluted him, then sidestepped to retrieve her arrows from a corpse.

They had come to this. They had given everything they had in Ashfall's defense, and now there was nothing left in their armory, no weapons to gain them tactical advantage, no fresh soldiers to fight, and hours to go before he could call on the power of Al Mintaka.

It was hopeless. Yet the Zhayedan continued to fight, so their prince could do no less.

Assessing the butchery below, he looked for a point of attack and found it on the eastern wall. More Talisman fighters had grouped to set their charges. The wall was coming down, the Maiden Tower quaking at its base. An insight came to him: Why not trap those same Talisman in the resulting chaos? He could turn their bodies into a wall the rest would have to climb.

Someone else had had the same thought. A dozen men dressed in black masks spread out across the wall, drifting east like curls of smoke, impossible to grapple with, already somewhere else before their presence was grasped. They blocked off the retreat from the upper level where the charges had been laid.

A hand jerked Rukh around at close quarters. Too late, he raised his sword.

It was the Assassin, pulling him to the nearest stairs. Rukh cast out another arc of fire, lowered his sword, and coughed before he followed.

He halted inside the door, brought face-to-face with his sister.

"No!" he shouted, raising his sword again. And then Arsalan was there, at his back, at his side, pushing the Assassin away, even as Hudayfah insisted, "Listen to me, Excellency!"

Rukh's sword slid through the air, its tip just glancing off Darya's shoulder. A dark lock of her hair slithered to the ground. He brought his sword round again, but this time the Assassin stood in his way.

"No!" Rukh gritted. "I will not let her take the city."

With a smooth feint beneath Rukh's body, the Assassin divested the Black Khan of his sword. He let them hear it clang against the rings of the sphere. Arsalan had drawn his sword and placed himself between the Black Khan and the others, but now he turned to Rukh.

"Kill her." Rukh gave the command to Arsalan. Rukh was

needed on the walls. He would give the Talisman his head on a pike before he abandoned Ashfall.

"I'm so sorry, Rukh." Darya slipped behind the sphere, her small hands moving its rings. "You'll never know how sorry I am!"

He couldn't contain his rage. His fury overflowed, lighting up the alcove. He grabbed Arsalan's sword and thrust it through the rings, missing Darya by inches.

"You stupid, foolish girl!" He tried to untangle the sword, but Darya had trapped it between the rings, her eyes haunted by the knowledge of just how she'd earned his wrath. "Wasn't it enough that you burned down the scriptorium? Did you need to dismantle the last line of our defenses?" He spat at Darya across the sphere. "Girl or ghul—whatever manner of creature you are, I curse the day you were born. You were destined to be our undoing."

Arsalan hauled him back. "Get behind me before she hurts you."

Darya turned those haunted eyes on Arsalan. "Wait, please! I know how to bring the sphere under my brother's command."

"Too late to lie to me now." Rukh's fury was such that Arsalan had to use his full strength to restrain him. "We won't survive until nightfall. Consider your work here done."

"You don't need nightfall, Rukh! Al Mintaka is yours to command!"

"Liar!" He freed one arm from Arsalan's grip to point at her, his hand shaking. "You tore down the southern wall."

She reached through the rings of the sphere she had just positioned to grab hold of Rukh's hand.

"See me with the Claim," she said to Arsalan, who turned his face away. "Know that I am Darya, the foolish sister of your prince."

She took hold of the signet ring on Rukh's finger, refusing to let him shake her off. "Fasten your collar, Rukh. Let me show you what Darius taught me."

"KILL HER!" Rukh thundered at Arsalan, unable to elude her grip. His free hand motioned to the square, to the final battle of the Zhayedan. *"She did this!"* A harsh sob caught in his throat. He turned his rage on Arsalan. "She did this because you refused to carry out my orders. What a fool I was to forgive you."

Arsalan set his jaw, his anger icy in the face of Rukh's rage.

"Keep your forgiveness. You *know* I did it for you."

It was there—poised at the edge, the undoing of all they had been to each other. Yet neither man could think of that in the dying hours of empire.

The Assassin edged behind Rukh, reaching for his collar. Arsalan's blade slid through Hudayfah's armor to his ribs, but all the Assassin did was fasten the Black Khan's collar so that his emblem flashed from his throat: the symbol of his allegiance, the symbol of his ancient line.

The Assassin backed away, hands held aloft to ward off a killing blow.

Darya slid around the sphere. She stopped in front of Rukh, curling his hand so that his palm was facedown, his index finger aloft, his signet ring in place.

He grabbed her by the throat and began to squeeze.

She didn't fight him. Neither did the Assassin.

Rukh squeezed harder, but all Darya did was raise Rukh's free hand to his collar, aligning the emblem on his collar with the insignia on his ring.

"I made a mistake, Rukh! I didn't understand how the power of the sequence star was meant to be invoked." Despair drove the words on the merest thread of breath.

The satisfaction of crushing her larynx raised a tide of blood behind Rukh's eyes. Arsalan touched Rukh's shoulder. For an instant the tide ebbed.

"No more lies, ghul. The power of Al Mintaka is to be wielded at night."

"Rukh." A soft, penitent gasp. He eased his grip the barest fraction. "Al Mintaka is still in orbit; it is daylight that conceals it." She locked his ring into his collar—the onyx rook on silver, the silver rook on onyx, their grooves measured and aligned. He eased his grip a little more, and heard something click. He twisted his hand to the right, and another click sounded before his signet popped free, its onyx rook locked into his collar, the stone separated from its circular mount. The heavy band around his finger remained as the base to the empty mount.

Puzzled, he stared at the ring. Then he lifted his eyes to Darya's. If he pushed his thumb down into her throat, she would die. Instead, he let his hand fall. His sister sank to her knees. H heard a murmur of approval from Arsalan but shook off his general's hand.

"What trick is this now?" He asked the question of Hudayfah.

Darya's hands clutched at her throat. She struggled to gasp out the truth. "Darius told me that I had the ability to control Al Mintaka's twin. He said by harnessing its power together, we would double it." She didn't want to cry in front of these men whose fierce will prevailed no matter what came their way, but she found she couldn't help herself. Her brother had tried to kill her; the potency of his hatred had seeped into her pores. "Darius was wrong. He didn't understand. Nor, it seems, do you."

One dark brow shot up, an arrogance she knew too well.

"Each assumption you have made has imperiled this city. I won't ask you again: Why would I trust your word?"

"Rukh." She panted his name, one hand braced on the floor, though she didn't attempt to rise. "The power of Al Mintaka belongs to the Dark Mage. That power *cannot* be divided between you and another."

"As *I* told *you*, when you brought the star-beam to our walls." He studied the ring on his finger, angry with himself for listening to the ghul. But he didn't sidestep her when she reached for his hand, and used it to pull herself up.

Misty-eyed, she told him, "We have enemies on all sides—"

"And some within our walls," he shot back.

"You need more than a single sphere to command the power of Al Mintaka. Should you have another, you could harness the power of *both* stars."

He glared at her, outraged by the false hope she offered in the final hours of their city.

"Where am I to find such a sphere?" His hand shaped itself into a fist.

"Listen." Arsalan murmured his counsel. Rukh flashed a glance of fury at him, though his mind took in the fact that Arsalan had not engaged with Darya. When she moved closer to Rukh, his general stepped away. And it seemed he was not yet done with Arsalan's cool counsel, for he made no protest when Darya adjusted the mount on his ring that had held the rook in place. She rotated the circular base until it stood upright, studying its outer markings. Then her delicate fingers twisted the circle and pried it open from the center, so that several smaller rings tilted around an imaginary axis, the rings positioned to mirror the alignment of the armillary sphere.

The two spheres were identical, down to their delicate markings.

Rukh gaped at the discovery, all his certainties shattered.

He'd worn the signet since achieving his majority. It had been taken from him three times in his life: once when Darius had usurped it, once when he had given it to Arian to give her free passage to the scriptorium, and once when he had used it to authorize Khashayar's actions on the battlefield. On each occasion, the ring had been retrieved. Yet he had never uncovered the secret of his signet: that it could evolve into this fantastical creation, a miniature armillary sphere.

Could Darya be right? Could he harness the power of both stars at once to meet the armies at his gates?

Tears spilled down Darya's pale cheeks.

"I watched Darius open the ring once, but I didn't understand that when he spoke of a twinned power, this was what he meant." Self-conscious under the attention of the three men, she dropped her gaze. She rubbed at her throat, her voice an ugly rasp. "You can't forgive me, and I won't forgive myself—I know what my actions have wrought. But perhaps by showing you this, your love for me may be redeemed. And if that isn't possible, I accept your judgment."

His judgment was a sentence of death.

He felt Arsalan nudge him, and knew his friend wanted him to soften. His lips tight, he shook his head. No matter what Darya promised him, his sister's fate was sealed. He opened his mouth to speak, then caught the warning glint from behind the Assassin's mask.

He remembered his promise.

"Whether you are sister or ghul, it is not for me to kill you now." And at the hope that flared to life in Darya's eyes, he glanced at the Assassin. "I have promised you to the Assassin in payment of the debt I owe him, though I have had the best part of that bargain." He nodded at the black-clad figure who had kept Rukh's secrets, who had tried to steer him through this unwinnable war. "Should we survive the battle, the Princess Darya is yours."

He sensed Arsalan's surprise, but he avoided looking at him.

"Bring the other Mages here. The empire of the Prince of Khorasan will not die today."

43

From the portal of the All Ways, Arian and Lania made their way to the walls of the Citadel. Arian had expected to find their way barred. The same power that had banished her should have kept her from returning. Yet she and Lania had touched their hands to the waters of the basin in the scrying room, thought of the All Ways, and arrived.

The Council Chamber was empty, and though Lania sought to linger, perhaps to remember a time when she, too, might have served as a member of the Council, both sisters felt the pull of the battle at the walls.

"This was not how I thought to return." Lania searched the room, holding herself still against the weight of her memories, of possibilities lost. "If I thought to return at all."

"Nor I."

Arian grasped her sister's hand and hurried her along the wall, searching for signs of the Citadel's general. She blanched at the sight of skirmishes being fought in the courtyard below: the fight was between members of the Citadel Guard, bodies collapsed over flagstones and fountains, palm trees burning from the base. But even that consciousness faded as lightning whipped at the Citadel's walls and fired a path up the ramp. Between two burning lines, a company of Talisman advanced until they stood beneath the Citadel's motto:

Never to be altered by the encircling tremors of time.

A vain boast.

For the One-Eyed Preacher had come, sending his underlings before him as the first heralds of his war. She gazed out at the Talisman forces readying themselves for the attack. Though the scale of the battle was nothing like the siege of Ashfall, it was enough to doom the Citadel. All that stood between the Talisman and the loss of the Khorasan Archives were a few dozen women skilled in the arts of the Claim.

The High Companion was meant to prevent this. She had declared herself powerful enough to stand against the Preacher on her own. But Arian couldn't see Ilea in the courtyard or on the ramparts.

She caught sight of Psalm battling members of the Guard who had turned, backed by others who fought at her side. The senior Companions were dotted along the walls, calling up verses of the Claim to greater or lesser effect, depending on their gifts.

Arian became frantic. Where were Sinnia and Ash? The Preacher was drawing closer, she could feel it; she needed their help to defeat him. She was a guerilla fighter gifted with the Claim; she had never been taught to defend a walled fortress from a power as great as the Preacher's. She may have prevailed at Ashfall for a time—disoriented and panicked, she thought of Daniyar, until Lania snapped her name like the flick of a whip against her arm. She met her sister's gaze. "What should I do? How do I reach Psalm? How do I help her?"

A piercing pain streaked through her skull, focusing behind her right eye.

"Lania, it's him! The One-Eyed Preacher has come!"

Lania paused to assess the nature of the attack, to gauge the strength of its components. Then she raised her moonstone ring to her lips and depressed its surface. The ring opened up. Tilting back her head, she sipped the blood it contained.

"Not the bloodrites, Lania!"

The tint of fresh blood stained Lania's lips. "Go!" She raised one arm and scored a path for Arian along the wall. "Use your methods, leave me to mine." She gazed down upon the Talisman. Her smile darkened . . . deepened. "I will bolster the gate."

Though Arian was repulsed by Lania's choice, that same choice bolstered her decision as she raced along the wall toward Psalm, calling out the Claim as she ran. If their own soldiers tried to attack her, she would use the Claim as the deadliest of weapons, though she'd never expected to see a day when she would lash out at the Citadel Guard. She raised her voice: the Claim's response was new.

Magic spilled from her tongue with effortless strength, forming its own rhythms, determining its own cadence. She expected bone to shatter, blood to spray along the walls. Instead, bodies jerked as if their limbs were tied to invisible strings, then subsided, falling to the ground faceup, glassy-eyed, unknowing, and still.

She shifted to avoid the bodies, her mind feeding her information faster than she could absorb the meaning of what she'd done. The Citadel's enemies had fallen where they stood, their bodies whole and undamaged, the essence of their spirit absent. The men who were still standing made no move to attack. They cleared the bodies of those who had fallen from the walls.

Arian came to a halt just steps before Psalm, feeling the echo of the Claim's power shiver through her limbs. She understood what had happened. Just as it had done in the Registan, the Claim had distinguished between enemy and friend. Or perhaps to use the Claim's own lexicon, between the just and unjust.

Psalm turned to her, sword ready. When she saw Arian, she swallowed a gasp.

"How—"

Arian cut her off. "Tell me where my gifts would serve us best."

A bolt of lightning cut between them, steam hissing in its wake. It had cut a line through the ramparts, creating a narrow chasm between Arian and Psalm. Arian could have leapt across it, but instinct told her not to. Her gaze swung out to the plains where the Talisman were amassed, and beyond them to the mountains and the twist of the High Road. New fighters were pouring through the passes. The Citadel could summon no army of its own to meet them.

But this was no longer about the strength of armies. This would be a battle of the Claim. And between the combined might of the Talisman and the Preacher, she didn't think the Citadel would hold. The loss of the archives was at hand. The Companions of Hira would be killed, and her parents' graves—no, *no.* This was not the moment to anticipate loss. There was no room now for self-doubt.

Her head jerked back to Psalm. "What is your plan?"

"As long as we hold the walls, the Citadel is safe. If we lose them, the battle is over." She assessed the Talisman army. "We can fight off the initial assault, but if their numbers are replenished, we will need all the grace of the One that you can summon to our side."

The battle plan of a general dealing with flesh-and-blood forces, mapping out moves on a chessboard. Another stroke of pain through Arian's skull reminded her that Psalm's plan did not allow for the power of the Preacher.

"Where are the Companions most gifted in the Claim? Where are Ash and Half-Seen?"

Psalm's gray gaze scanned the courtyard. She scowled at the sight of Talisman sympathizers so close to the doors to the scriptorium.

"You'll find them in the scriptorium. Do what you can in the courtyard, Arian, but we'll need you on the walls." She paused as she caught sight of Lania above the gate, both hands raised above her head. "Arian, who—"

"I brought my sister with me. Do not treat her as an enemy. She came from Black Aura to our aid." She pushed down the thought of the plague-jar.

Psalm began to call out orders to the Citadel Guard. Her eyes cut back to Arian.

"The one woman whose power could rival yours is the Khanum of Black Aura."

Arian held back a sigh. "Trust me, Psalm. Let her prove herself."

Psalm grimaced. "As you will, Arian. But I must assign men to watch her." She jerked her chin at a point behind Arian. "The closest route to the scriptorium is back the way you came, on the other side of the gate."

She reached over the chasm and gripped Arian's hand.

"Either we hold, or all of Khorasan is lost."

A bolt of steel stiffened Arian's spine.

"There is no one but the One, and so the One commands."

Psalm echoed the words with a salute. Another whip of lightning broke the women apart.

Arian turned and ran. The Preacher was coming for her; his whispers roiled in her mind.

But minutes from the gate, Ilea found her first.

44

"How dare you transgress the boundaries of this Citadel!"

The High Companion was dressed in brilliant golden armor, her hair cinched in a knot at her nape, her diadem polished to a brightness that cast a light along the wall. The dark heart of the sapphire at its center was a lodestone that drew Arian's eyes. Ilea's hands were empty of weapons, her self-assurance such that she required nothing but the Claim. And why shouldn't she feel powerful? She had banished the First Oralist of Hira; perhaps in her arrogance, she thought she could silence the Preacher.

Arian spoke up. "My return should tell you all you need to know about your judgment."

Honey-gold eyes narrowed, crawling with shadows and secrets. Ilea hissed out an incantation. Arian raised one arm, her cloak falling like a shield.

"You are fighting the wrong enemy! You fought the Preacher at Ashfall yet let him work his will at our gates. You may have promised the Black Khan your aid, but you are *sworn* to protect the Citadel!"

"I *am* protecting the Citadel." A smile so disturbing touched the High Companion's lips that Arian's heart jolted. The faintest glimmer of insight stirred. Before she could examine it, Ilea aimed a hand at her unprotected throat. Catching herself, Arian swerved to evade the blow.

"I don't understand you! My gifts as First Oralist are necessary to our defense!"

Ilea scorned this. "Certainly you have always thought so. Yet you left us on our own against the Talisman, drawing the Preacher's eye to us with your harrying of the slave-chains." Another furious strike. This one singed the tails of Arian's hair. "So what was I supposed to do, Arian, when you left us to face the aftermath of your little insurrections?" Golden sparks of fury darted from Ilea's eyes. "For years I kept the Talisman from our doors, but now your actions have provoked the Preacher into setting aside our . . . arrangement."

"Arrangement?" Arian was aghast. "What arrangement? Our only alliance is with the Black Khan."

Ilea lowered her head, her thoughts secret. "How frequently he comes to your thoughts."

Arian faltered a step. Did Ilea resent the Black Khan's attentions, when his actions were guided by self-interest?

When Ilea's head came up again, her expression was bitter.

"*You* took Sinnia from me, you took the respect of the Companions, then you flaunted yourself before Rukh. *My* lover. My partner. My aide in all my efforts. He was meant to offer *me* marriage. One look at you and my efforts became meaningless."

Arian was stunned by this casual admission of the truth. Stunned to consider that Ilea's hostility could be rooted in envy, with Hira's survival at stake and Khorasan's future at risk.

Quieting her inner turmoil, Arian said, "This isn't about Rukh. Nor were you concerned with Daniyar, no matter what you said to the Council. You fear and resent me when you have no cause for either. I don't want Rukh, nor does he want me. He traded me north without a qualm." Rage flickered through her voice, the Claim sharp and pointed. She controlled it, drawing it back. "I mentioned him because if Hira was in need while Sinnia and I were absent, you could have called on *his* aid."

Ilea watched her with unblinking eyes, one hand poised to strike.

"Yet *I* went to the aid of Ashfall, rather than the reverse."

A pang of fear struck Arian. She still hadn't fathomed the motives that drove Ilea.

"You were right to do so, as Hira was safe from attack. If Ashfall with its scholars and great scriptorium fell, the blow would have been to all of Khorasan."

But Ilea diverted Arian again. She had eased the Claim in her throat, prolonging this thrust and parry, when fear of the Preacher should have been all that governed her.

"Hira was safe from attack?" The sapphire diadem winked. "You left, so you assumed all was well in your wake." She clicked her tongue. "Your duplicity is boundless. This interlude of peace was *granted* by the Preacher, and why? Did you ever think to ask?"

Arian's premonition became a full-fledged warning. She glanced behind her at the wall. At the walls of the Citadel, unmolested, at the Talisman held at bay so long. By a half-trained Citadel Guard, when their captains had gone to the north.

"Your agreement—a pact of some kind?" she asked soberly. "You gave the Preacher something he wanted, just as you and Rukh gave me to the Authoritan in order to gain the Bloodprint?"

Another terrible smile twitched across Ilea's face. "Not quite." She glanced down into the courtyard, as if she were taking in the vastness of the Citadel. The hammam, the fountains, the lush and vital gardens, the stately mausoleum, the dormitory for the novices, the hospice where their healers worked, the chambers of the Companions. The upper reading room, the sturdy doors that led down to the scriptorium.

"Hira was worth preserving." Ilea's words sliced at Arian. "Your family's name was lost, the Nun scriptorium ravaged by fire: it was clear your time was past. The Citadel didn't need you, but if you *did* return with the Bloodprint, so much the better. If you didn't—it was useful to keep the Preacher's eye aimed in your direction. He left the Citadel alone because he believed the real threat was not behind these walls. He was mistaken, of course. As I made clear in the Council Chamber, what am *I* if not a threat?"

The subvocal menace of the Claim became greater. Strengthened by her closeness with Lania, Arian worked to defuse it. "Ilea—no one denies you are powerful. *But you haven't faced the Preacher.* His power is immense. It will overwhelm the Citadel unless we work together. The Companions' survival depends on us being of one mind."

"Ah." A fine sneer, as the golden eyes flicked over Arian's battered armor. "You faced him alone, not once but twice, but you think *me* incapable. Until you have usurped my role completely, your ambition will not be satisfied."

Arian made a despairing sound. "I'm not after your position— I'm thinking of the Citadel! The Preacher almost *killed* me! I have never faced him alone, I've always had Sinnia to aid me. Even then"—she shuddered at the memory—"even then, Ilea, he turned me inside out, tearing the soul from my body, draining the hope from my heart. You *cannot* defeat him on your own."

"I wouldn't be so sure." Unmoved, Ilea's fingers dusted over the golden band fastened to her upper arm. "But it doesn't matter—it isn't going to come to that."

But with the Preacher's agonizing voice tearing at Arian's sanity, she knew Ilea was wrong. She put her hands to her temples, frantic, seeking relief, the Claim hard and insidious.

Gasping, she asked, "Why not? What do you know that I don't?"

Ilea flicked out one arm to indicate the Citadel's grounds.

"He isn't coming for *us*. The one he wants is *you*. He will take you and spare the Citadel, as promised. And I will never have to contend with a First Oralist who defies me again."

Arian crossed her arms over her torso, her thoughts in torment. Could it be as simple as this? As dark and deeply twisted? That Ilea hoped to use the Preacher to dispose of her rival?

But betraying Arian to the Authoritan was a crime of a lesser order than collaborating with the Preacher. The Preacher admitted no equals. His purposes extended far beyond Ilea's vision for the Citadel. His would be the dominant voice, even in subterfuge.

Sudden futile tears studded Arian's lashes. "You shouldn't have trusted his promise."

Ilea aimed one finger at the sky, a perversion of the shahadah. "So you say. But you see," she told Arian, "though the Preacher's assault is wounding you, it isn't affecting *me*."

It was true. The terrifying, throbbing pain caused by the Preacher's assault did not impede Ilea. She stood tall and proud in her golden armor, her lips edged up at the corners.

"How can you believe you are safe?" Arian was desperate now. She would accept this bleak rivalry, even banishment should it arise in the future, but in this moment, they needed to join their powers *against* the Preacher. "Whatever pact you entered into with him is over. The Preacher will burn the scriptorium, and finish by killing the Companions!"

"As to that . . ." Ilea seemed to wash her hands of worry. "If you were so easily vanquished by me, why should I fear him?"

"This is a fool's confidence, Ilea! You don't understand him at all. We need to act now—you *must* recall Ash and Half-Seen to the walls!"

"You don't command the Citadel! You will leave our defense to me!" Reckless paranoia glittered in her eyes. She threw her golden head back, the sapphire causing a throbbing ache at the back of Arian's eye. "Preacher! The First Oralist is yours. Take her and be done."

For answer, the Preacher's thunder cracked the walls, lightning strikes aimed at the courtyard. They scorched a trail to the scriptorium.

Arian couldn't stop him. She was losing the vision in her eye, and she would have to contend with Ilea before she could take on the Preacher. She balled her fists at her sides.

Feint, she told herself. *Feint, as Daniyar taught you.*

Ilea laughed at her struggles. "How pitiful you are! You seem to have forgotten that I am also the Golden Mage."

Arian felt the full force of Ilea's power: no weapon of war could pierce it. Still she tried.

"You have double the skills, then, to assist in our defense. And no cause to betray us."

The Preacher's thunder made a mockery of Arian's words. The Citadel fell silent. All along the walls, the Companions of Hira screamed. Arian was brought to her knees; only Ilea managed to prevail against the Preacher's brutality. Arrogance defined her posture, as if her defiance of the Preacher was proof of all she had said. She was righteous, and she would rule.

Arian battled back to her feet, turning away from Ilea. She cast the Verse of the Throne as a screen over the Companions to give

them time to regather. At her back, Ilea hit at her hard, twisting
the Claim so that it wormed into Arian's ears. The pain of it dismantled her rhythm.

She gasped Ilea's name. "Why do you obstruct me? The shield
is for the *Companions*."

"They don't need your protection when I have given mine.
Only those who have proved disloyal will suffer the Preacher's
wrath."

Arian's thoughts lit with fury. With one hand, she warded off
Ilea. With the other, she reinforced the shield.

Gritting out the words, she said, "The Companions' loyalty
is to the Claim, and through the Claim to the One." A jade fire
burned in her eyes, as she found the clarity she'd sought. "You
won't stop with me, will you? You will use the Preacher to purge
the Council of those who voted in my favor. With them gone, you
imagine no one else will stand against you. You'd rather have submission than cooperation."

She'd been absent from the Council too long. She hadn't perceived that Ilea had been trying to put an end to their practice of
consultation: she hoped to eclipse their shura, the Companions
no more than members of a compliant court.

"The Preacher will overrule you once his purpose is fulfilled.
He will not stop with murdering those you consider your enemies."

Ilea lashed out at Arian again. Arian faltered, so intense was
her concentration on the shield she sustained. She was sweating,
every muscle in her body strained, her larynx pushed to the limit
of its endurance, her right eye leaking blood.

"You see?" Ilea pushed her back with a spiteful jibe. "You are
no match for me."

"I'm not trying to outflank you. I'm trying to make you see."
But despite her sincerity, the Claim was constrained in her mouth.

She couldn't be so feeble, not when she'd been given the gifts
of the Israa e Miraj.

She bore the pain a moment longer, and then she wasn't alone.
She heard a voice that matched hers, clear and resolute.

You must learn to see the Oralists when and where they appear.

"Sister."

Lania.

Lania there at her side, the Talisman's forces forgotten. A second shock as Lania placed a slender arm around her shoulders.
"Follow your own path. Leave this traitor to me."

Ilea switched her attention to Lania, her prideful smile now a
sneer. "You think to thwart me, *you* who were always the lesser
daughter of the Inkwell scriptorium?"

Lania's insolence shimmered in the air. "I think you tremble at
the very thought."

Arian couldn't grasp how she knew to do what she did; all she
knew was that Lania's presence fortified her own resources. But it
wasn't just her presence. It was Lania's dedication to a cause she
had begun to believe in.

Tremulous with hope, Arian touched the blood that stained
her eye and daubed it on Lania's lips. "I would share my gift with
the Claim."

Lania curled her hand around Arian's nape.

"Thank you, little sister. Trust that I will use it well."

45

ARIAN DIDN'T LOOK BACK. SHE FLEW DOWN THE STAIRS TO THE COURT-yard, dodging fighters who blocked the path through the gardens to the scriptorium. The pain in her temples and eye was constant now, an attempt by the Preacher to prevent her access to the Claim. Running, racing, she fought it. She struggled with every breath.

There were dead men all around her—corpses piled in heaps along the path that led to the mausoleum. And defectors from the Citadel Guard in the square, who were moving toward the stairs that would take them to the walls.

No. They could not have transgressed to the point they would think to murder the Companions.

She couldn't leave that to chance.

She summoned the fiery, sundering power of the Verse of the Throne just as she had done in the Registan, forging the words with the strength of her resistance.

She lost the vision in her right eye, blood streaking her face, but she forced herself to persevere. Breath after breath, she panted the verse, changed it, transformed it with the urgency of the Cita-del's last stand.

It would not fall.

She would not fail.

And then bodies were dropping from the stairs, falling in the courtyard like the rush of waves on a hostile shore. The clash of steel fell silent, though smoke and thunder raged, an ominous stillness in the courtyard, the breath of a dying soul.

Her work done, she found herself at the door to the scriptorium, her path barred by two men left untouched by the Claim. She tilted her head up; the men were tall, strong, formidable, towering over her. That they had been battling others in the courtyard was clear: their weapons were red with blood.

She used the edge of her cloak to wipe the blood from her cheek and eye, hoping to make herself known. But then she remembered her circlets and cast the cloak aside.

"Please, let me pass."

The men seemed shaken by the sight of her. Murmuring invocations of the Claim to herself, the vision in her right eye cleared. She thought she recognized the men.

"First Oralist." The man to her right stepped aside. The other man scanned the courtyard, measuring the dead, measuring the power that had issued from her throat, the power that had determined who would live or die. "I aided you in Candour once, do you remember? I am Hamzah, and this is Qais, my brother."

She nodded with relief. She recognized the chieftain of the Khyber tribes. Years ago, he had helped her track a slave-chain out of Candour, but there was no time to ask him now how he had come to Hira or why he fought in their defense. The Claim had spared him—that was enough.

Her glance encompassed the two men, who were built like mountain warriors and closely resembled each other, one blue-eyed, the other green-eyed.

"Qaid Hamzah." She gave the green-eyed man his title as Khyber chief. "Will you lend your strength to the Companions on the walls?"

Both men sheathed their weapons.

"Ask and it is done." Hamzah nodded at the door to the scriptorium. "But one of us should stay with you to ensure your safety."

"I can protect myself better than the other Companions." She rubbed her circlets, then asked the warriors from Khyber to bend so she could touch their foreheads. Pursing her lips, she blew a prayer of protection over their heads, her breath stirring their hair. "This is all I can offer you against the One-Eyed Preacher."

"Your prayers are enough, First Oralist. The Khyber do not make for easy prey."

They were halfway to the stairs when Arian called out a warning. She pointed to a figure on the ramparts above.

"Be wary of the woman wearing golden armor."

Green eyes slashed at her. "The High Companion?"

Arian pulled the door to the scriptorium open, one hand to her throbbing eye. She considered the fact that the two men could have been soldiers of the Talisman, and said, "Betrayal comes in many guises, sincerity in others. Go with the blessings of the One."

46

THERE WERE BODIES IN THE SCRIPTORIUM, THE BODIES OF MEN WHO had promised to fight an apocalypse to defend the Companions of Hira and the Khorasan Archives, another sign of the High Companion's perfidy. But she forgot this when she saw Sinnia and the others, while thunder boomed overhead and the glassed-in shelves of the scriptorium rattled in their casements. Their reunion was brief but joyous.

"We need scholars of the Claim at the walls." Arian motioned to Half-Seen and Ash. "Sinnia and I will do our best to shield you from the Preacher's attack." The air in the scriptorium was closed and tight, thickened by the scent of blood. Arian threw off her cloak, taking a moment to weave her long hair into a braid.

Half-Seen mouthed a prayer. "Isn't the High Companion seeing to our defense?"

Arian made herself tell the others about Ilea, hating to see the impact of betrayal on the faces of those who served the Council. It was more difficult still to tell them the truth about Lania, to ask them to trust a woman she didn't fully trust herself. Ash looked at her in silent communication. She was older, had been at the Citadel longer—perhaps she knew more of Lania's fate than Arian had guessed.

She watched as Ash took Half-Seen's hand. "Let us go, then. If we are to prevent the surrender of our sanctum."

"And the murder of any Companion who questions Ilea's reign." Sinnia's hand struck the opposite circlet hard. "So much for the oaths we take. It seems Ilea is quick to dispense with customs that stand in the way of her desires."

"We knew that." But Arian had failed to give it due weight in time. "When we guessed that Ilea and Rukh were lovers." Her gaze swept the scriptorium, judging its soundness, its safety. She paused at the sight of the lever with the knife jammed into the wall above it.

"Half-Seen?"

"I thought the moment had come to act to preserve the scriptorium." Half-Seen spared a smile for Sinnia. "Sinnia convinced me otherwise." She studied Arian with her customary calm. "Do you wish me to stay behind? If nothing should avail us against the One-Eyed Preacher?"

She was asking Arian to weigh the possibilities of the future against the peril of the present, prepared to sacrifice herself. And Arian wasn't certain of her course.

"I think you would better serve us at the walls, but you'll know when that changes. Come, let's go. And do not fear the Preacher, for he is just a man."

A terrible crack shattered the silence in the courtyard. It was followed by another: the falling of a lash that whipped the door to the scriptorium open and split the staircase in half. A third resounding stroke of the lash, and glass began to shatter. The lash rimmed the upper shelves, glass raining down on their heads.

This time it was Sinnia who used the Claim as a shield, augmenting her response by throwing her body over a book positioned on a high pedestal.

"Come!" Arian called. "There's no more time to waste."

"Ash, take Half-Seen with you. I need to show Arian the book."

But Arian had every intention of acting as a personal shield to the two Companions who were the most learned in the history and lore of the Claim. Of all the Companions of Hira, these two could not be sacrificed.

She was surprised when Ash took Sinnia's part. "Sinnia has something to show you. Come after us when you can."

Gripping Half-Seen's hand, Ash moved to navigate the staircase.

Torn, Arian made the best decision she could. "Look for a man named Hamzah on the walls; keep yourselves under his protection. The Claim destroyed the guards who deserted the Citadel; this man is a friend."

Arian turned to Sinnia, ignoring the pulsing pain behind her eye. "Tell me."

Words flew from Sinnia's lips, soft and sure and true. She turned the pages of the Miraj Nameh, letting Arian examine the illuminations at her own pace.

"From the Ascension I learned I was meant to show you this. Do you recognize the Silver Mage's sword?"

Their heads bent together, she and Sinnia studied the painting of the sword. Arian's lips formed the name she read on the manuscript.

The Bladebone.

Then Sinnia turned the page, and she was looking at the Noble Sanctuary, at the great gold dome and its smaller echo, the lightning-sword hanging between them, poised between the heavens and the earth.

On the next page she found the One-Eyed Preacher.

"Sinnia, what—?"

"It's not him." Iron certainty from Sinnia. "This is a painting of the Dajjal. The false prophet, the one who misleads his followers about the truth of their faith."

"But that sounds like a description of the One-Eyed Preacher. He converted the Talisman with his deceptions, a false prophet if ever there was one."

Sinnia nodded, tapping the page. "In the lands of the Negus we are taught that Dajjal will appear after a period of great trial, such as the wars of the Far Range."

"But it could also mean the Harrowing of Timeback, or the plague that wiped out the people of the north."

Sinnia's voice began to falter. "It is said that many will follow the Dajjal because he provides them with food."

They looked at each other, two women who had battled the Preacher's followers in all the lands of their realm, with their battle beginning and ending in the south.

"The famine." How could she as First Oralist not have seen it? Why had she never spoken to Half-Seen about the history the younger Companion had collected? "The Preacher created the famine in order to relieve it. And so he gained followers in droves."

Sinnia studied the depiction again. She recounted for Arian the conclusion she had reached. "His name in the High Tongue is Al Masih Al Dajjal, but in the manuscripts of Axum, he was sometimes called Al Dajjal Al *Masikh*—not just a deceiver, but a *deformed* deceiver."

Arian searched her own memories of the Dajjal, as described in the archives. From the words *Masih* to *Masikh*, it was the simple matter of altering one letter by adding a single dot.

ح became the letter خ.

She paused to reflect on the dot that transformed one letter into another, like a single eye, or like a *stone* that obscured an eye. The dot signified a metaphysical warning: a warning that truth could be distorted into falsehood.

She grasped a new conclusion.

The One whose spirit breathed through the Claim would not equate a physical condition with a moral deformity, which meant the One-Eyed Preacher could not, in fact, be one-eyed. His other eye was obscured by a stone that represented his inversion of the teachings of the Claim, the inversion that had taken the shape of the Talisman law of the Assimilate.

The Preacher's proclamation was a reversal of the mercy of the Claim.

Blood began to leak from Arian's eye again. Sinnia's face twisted in concern. "What's happening to you, Arian?"

The Preacher's voice whipped at the scriptorium, drowning out the voices of the Companions gathered at the walls.

"It's something he's doing to me. He's trying to prevent me from seeing the essence of who he is. He thinks he can make me over into an image of himself." She placed two fingers beneath her bloody eye to massage the fragile socket. Then she opened her mouth and sang out the truth she'd just discovered, and the bleeding turned off like a tap.

Sinnia's lips rounded in surprise, her excitement catching like a match set to flame.

"If the Preacher is the Masih Al Dajjal, and you are meant to bring him down, don't you see what this means? It means *you* are the true Masih, the one who is foretold to herald the salvation of a world consumed by ignorance."

"No, Sinnia, no." She turned and kissed Sinnia's cheek, touched by her belief. "All I am, all I *seek* to be, is the First Oralist of Hira. The truths revealed in the Sana Codex do not speak of a deceiver, nor do they speak of me. They prophesy a man whose time is yet to come."

Catching her lower lip between her teeth, Sinnia turned back to the page of the Miraj Nameh that depicted the shining sword, its fine blade riven in two.

"Could the Silver Mage be prophesied? Is he the one destined to defeat Dajjal?"

But Arian was shaking her head, even as her fingertips stroked over the silver sword.

"I cannot pretend that I possess full knowledge regarding the secrets of the Claim. I have long believed that many of its stories are parables, while others serve as metaphors. Perhaps the Preacher assumes a form that is familiar to us through the lore of our Tradition. He deceives his followers as to the truth, but he does so with great power. I cannot say his arrival heralds the end of the world when the wars of the Far Range didn't. The earth may grow and flourish again in a time long after ours."

It was a reasonable conclusion. She wouldn't argue certainties in light of her lack of knowledge. That was the Preacher's game, whereas Arian valued ambivalence, valued having a mind open to question, knowing that she alone could not possibly grasp the fullness of the Claim, or the vastness of the One. Her questions were signs of reason weighed against irrational belief. She may have been the First Oralist, but her faith had never been shaped by ignorance.

Sinnia hugged her close. "Just once I'd like to see you accept the easiest conclusion."

A smile found its way to Arian's lips at Sinnia's irreverence. "No, you wouldn't. I've never met anyone who rises to the challenge like you."

She closed the Miraj Nameh, her mind troubled by the link between Daniyar's sword and the domes of the Noble Sanctuary. Some part of the truth was still obscured from her knowledge, and comprehension might come too late.

Would Daniyar know any better than she? Would she see him again to ask him?

The pain along the bond that linked them was overshadowed by the power of the Preacher. Under the mindscape of his wrath, she couldn't feel anything else.

He was calling her. His voice, his thunder, his infiltration of the Citadel, of the Council, all of it was designed to put her in his power, to remove her as the obstacle to his dominion.

If he saw her as a threat, she intended to show him how much more he should fear her proficiency with the Claim.

With Sinnia at her side, she would make her stand at the wall.

But when the two of them navigated a safe path from the scriptorium to bar the door behind them, she would find her plans had come to naught.

For the Preacher had come to Hira, not as a smoke-formed figure above the clouds, but as a flesh-and-bone being, riding a rukh to their walls.

47

FLAMES STREAKED DOWN FROM THE SKY, THE RAUCOUS CRIES OF THE firebird tearing the clouds apart. The Preacher was resting his voice after his use of the Claim had boomed for hours, a blasphemous heat licking the Citadel's walls. Now the firebird did his work, a giant, crimson-throated rukh with wings like the geometries of minarets, feathered rows of blue and green and gold, the gems that rolled from its tongue sowing destruction on the ramparts and the courtyard.

Arian's armor felt sticky against her skin, her upper arms swollen within her circlets, her face itched in places where blood had dried; she regathered her defenses.

The Preacher had come for her, but like the warriors of the Khyber, she had no intention of becoming easy prey. The rukh shrieked its demoralizing cry. On the walls, Companions fell to their knees, blood pouring from their ears. Arian's eyes sought and found Hamzah and Qais above the Citadel Gate. They stood steady on their feet, Hamzah pulling a durable bow from his back and readying an arrow. The Preacher's attention turned to him.

The firebird dove to the gate, its fiery tongue extended, a gemstone poised at the tip.

Neither Khyber warrior appeared affected by the cries of the rukh: when the Preacher brought his hand down above Hamzah's head, Qais brandished a polished sword in a smooth arc around his brother. The air around Hamzah rippled, and Arian blinked. Had it become solid? The Preacher's strike against the Qaid was deflected, but the gemstone struck the brattices above the gate. Fire and noise exploded along the wall.

Hamzah's arrow missed. The Preacher checked the rukh's flight, sending the bird over the courtyard. Smoke cleared in his wake, and Arian saw the reason that the Khyber's arrow had missed. The High Companion stood opposite the Khyber, a golden bolt of magic casting Hamzah's arrow aside. A crimson strike appeared on the High Companion's shoulder. She turned to face the oncoming threat: the Khanum of Black Aura.

It was shattering to see the pact Ilea had spoken of come to life. Her heart cracked, pain seeping through its chambers. Her banishment was nothing beside this profoundest of betrayals. This bleak alliance was the end, the end of everything the Council of Hira had worked for during the Age of Ignorance.

But the Citadel would make its stand.

And the One would not abandon them.

Her eye pulsing and her ears pounding, Arian pressed her lips to Sinnia's ear. "Get to the walls. Help my sister and the Khyber stand against the High Companion. Use the Verse of the Throne, use what you learned during your ascent."

Sinnia jerked Arian around until they were face-to-face.

"You can't face the Preacher alone! Let me take the rukh, just as I did on the field."

An impenetrable gloaming covered the parapets, but Arian had confidence in the warriors from Khyber, and in Ash and Half-Seen, who defended one part of the wall, their attention focused on the Talisman approach.

"Please, Sinnia. The Citadel needs you more than I do. Let me go to the tower, where I can meet the Preacher on his ground."

He was searching for her, trying to pin her down in the courtyard . . . and though it was clear she didn't want to, Sinnia agreed. The two Companions of Hira clasped each other's circlets, strengthening their bond as if it was the last time.

The last time they would fight.

The last chance to hold their ground.

Arian placed one hand on Sinnia's heart. "Look at me. If I don't return from the tower—" She gazed into Sinnia's great dark eyes, sustained by the love she found there. Nothing was more beautiful than Sinnia's loyalty and courage.

Every part of Arian's struggle, each bit of success, was due to Sinnia's solidarity, to her endless generosity in reshaping the meaning of their sisterhood. Arian had searched for Lania, when true sisterhood had been within her reach, had been there at her side.

"Arian, no—"

"Listen, Sinnia. If things should go amiss, you need to know your role on the Council of Hira. There are things I need to tell you about Lania." She hurriedly whispered in Sinnia's ear, and when she was done, she kissed her on the cheeks three times.

"You can't go alone! You can't leave me like this!" Sinnia's grip was fierce, but Arian pried her hands from her circlets.

"Know that I love you. Know that we came to this moment because of your love for me. You made it possible for me to rise when I had fallen, to believe when my faith was in doubt." A last, gentle kiss to Sinnia's temple. She tried not to see the tears in Sinnia's eyes. "You are my sister, Sinnia. You will always be my sister."

She released herself from Sinnia's embrace, ready to move against the Preacher, compelled to glance back once.

"Trust me one last time. But trust yourself more."

Wind stirred in the Citadel's hollows, and they parted ways.

E xplosions dotted the courtyard. Smoke coiled along the Citadel's pitted parapets.

Two women battled above the gate, one in crimson, the other in gold. Two ancient magics clashed and burned and boiled in a fight for supremacy, in a fight that would transform the Citadel of Hira, and the meaning of all it stood for.

The blood-strikes came from Lania, merciless and quick. Ilea countered with invocations of the Claim that battered and bruised, pushing the other woman back. Both their faces were distorted, clean angles twisted by hate, driven by the need for vengeance.

"First you sold *me,* then you sold my sister beyond the Wall." One raised fingertip drove a spike of pain into Ilea's skull.

But the High Companion didn't waver.

"Do not blame me for Arian's choices. She sought to pursue the Bloodprint behind the Wall. If she lacked the skill to see to her own safety, that cannot be laid at my door."

"You plotted with the Black Khan to trade Arian's life for the Bloodprint, yet you absolve yourself of betrayal?" She laughed at Ilea's look of surprise. "You thought I didn't know? But all the Authoritan's secrets were mine, just as I had my part to play. Your schemes beyond the Wall were fruitless. The Black Khan refused to yield the Bloodprint to you, nor could he prevent the Preacher from securing it."

Ilea's features twisted with wrath. "You seek to cast blame for your sister's failure to fulfill the Audacy I assigned. Her position on the Council is unmerited."

Prodded into fury, Lania clipped, "Arian is the greatest jewel of this Citadel, as she was the treasure of Inkwell. *Your* lust for power could not tolerate your own inferiority."

"And what of *your* inferiority? Always overlooked in favor of a younger sister whose gifts as a linguist far outstripped yours. First Oralist of Hira, while you were chosen as a handmaid. Why *not* serve the Talisman, then?"

Lania's fingers clawed the air.

Five slash marks appeared on Ilea's cheeks. Hissing at the pain, Ilea struck at the ground behind Lania. A chasm opened up, and Lania stumbled before she recovered her footing. She heard the ominous creak of the gate beneath her and knew that calamity was at hand. She slashed Ilea's other cheek, even as the High Companion healed the first set of strikes. Try as she might, Lania couldn't slash the other woman's throat.

But she *could* refute her words. Muffling Ilea's voice, she said, "Liar. You know as well as I that my gifts were complementary to Arian's. I was slated to become Custodian of the Archives. You took me from my sister while she still had need of my care."

Ilea broke free of the magic that bound her voice. She slashed at Lania's arms.

"What 'care' do you speak of? You kept her as a pet on your leash, you tormented her by seducing her lover. Or wasn't it you who kept her from the man she loves?"

But in all that Lania had Augured, she knew that what Ilea accused her of was, in fact, her own crime. It was Ilea who had separated Arian from the comfort and protection she would have gained from the Silver Mage.

The gate beneath them shuddered. It was time to end these

provocations, time to rain down the same dark power she had used to conquer the Authoritan.

She let the Claim fall from her lips, twisted and made over with the power of Arian's blood, sweet, stinging, immense in its potency, glorious and dark, overladen with something that was unique to Arian, a resolve that no measure of defeat was able to overturn. Moving around the High Companion with the graceful steps of a dancer, Lania circled and struck. A twist of her voice unlatched the gold diadem from Ilea's forehead. Its sapphire gleamed downward, as it fell to the High Companion's feet.

Ilea struck back with the Claim-verse on authority; Lania's grimace evolved into a smile.

"You denied me my place at Hira. You yielded your authority before it came to fruition."

Another twist of her blood-enriched voice, and the Claim unfastened Ilea's circlets. The resonance of gold striking stone was sweet to Lania's ears.

"No!" Ilea poured every ounce of power she possessed into her voice. "You cannot undo the rites of Hira! You cannot undo the power of the shura that put me on my throne."

A stinging pain at Ilea's waist. But not dealt by the Khanum of Black Aura, who had returned to wreak her vengeance. This was the pain of a bullwhip curled around Ilea's midriff.

"It's not a throne, Ilea." Sinnia mocked the High Companion. "It's a position you were elected to by the Council of Hira. The Council is not a theocracy. Nor is it a tyranny where you rule with absolute power."

Ilea slashed at Sinnia now, like a cat toying with prey. Taking advantage of the distraction, Lania used her bloodrites to hold Ilea in place. Then she began to chip away at Ilea's armor, watching bits of it fleck the wall with feline fascination.

Distracted by this first sight of Lania, Sinnia breathed, "By the One. You look so much like Arian you could be her twin."

With great hauteur, Lania replied, "I am Arian's sister."

"As am I." Sinnia raised her chin, not at all afraid of this woman who had destroyed the Authoritan. "She told me so herself."

The Khanum of Black Aura mulled this, found it displeasing, saw the assertion of a prior right, of what might well be construed a superior claim. But the sister whom Arian had embraced in Black Aura, the sister Arian *loved* despite every proof that she should reject one as warped by blood-magic as Lania, recognized a heart truer than her own, and granted a concession.

"Then my little sister is worthy of your love."

Ilea attacked them with feverish strikes. One unraveled Sinnia's whip; the other burned a path over Lania's ribs. Lania clutched at her torso, but Sinnia's whip struck again, this time coiling around Ilea's neck. She yanked hard at the whip, and the High Companion staggered, reeling to the edge of the wall, where Talisman soldiers pounded at the gate. The Citadel Guard responded with volleys of turquoise-fletched arrows. And still it wasn't enough, with the roar of the Preacher urging their enemies on.

Sinnia jerked at the whip, determined on her course.

Ilea struggled to speak. "I . . . am . . . in . . . authority . . . above . . . you. You . . . *must* . . . obey."

"You were *entrusted* with authority." Sinnia leaned in close, her fingers easing the tension in the coils. "You are trusted by me no longer."

Golden eyes glared into hers, sunlight broken into pieces of antique gold, a mysterious power shifting in their depths, galvanized by the words Sinnia had spoken.

"You will never understand what I hoped to achieve for Hira, so though I would have had you fight for Hira, I find you leave me with no choice." Ilea's voice was flat. One arm jerked up, and she called, "Preacher, see what I give you."

A golden arc shimmered along the parapets, clearing away the smoke that had concealed the Companions. The firebird wheeled back from the courtyard to the Citadel Gate.

The golden arc broke into a series of halos, small suns brightening the sky for miles around. And each of the halos formed above the heads of the Companions who had spoken out against Ilea. The ones who denied Ilea's judgment, among them those who held the history of the Citadel and the promise of the future in their hands.

"No!" A man's voice shouted down the wall, but the warning came too late.

The rukh's long tongue curled up into its mouth, then its gaping jaws split open, its tongue unfurled with furious speed, and bolts of fire pierced the sky.

Three of the chosen Companions fell. Dijah, Saw, and Psalm, the General of their Citadel.

A cry of unending horror broke from Sinnia's throat. She darted away from the halo that lingered over her head. The coils of her whip came undone. Ilea turned to the side of the gate where Ash and Half-Seen worked to slow the advance of the Talisman. Her spell found a new target in Lania. But halos also appeared above the other Companions.

Sinnia's scream brought Ilea to her senses. She shouted at the Preacher, who aimed the rukh's fire with magnificent contempt, Ilea's cries unheeded.

The rukh's fire pierced the halos, striking the Companions. Their bodies decomposed to quietly smoldering heaps. Sinnia thought the cries that ravaged her ears were her own, but they issued from Ilea. Sobbing wildly, she hurled the Claim at the Preacher.

"*What have you done! I didn't ask for this!* I banished the First Oralist as promised! Now go from here and leave me to my throne!"

The Preacher glanced down at Ilea. Without inflection, his cold voice intoned, "All thrones are mine. All dominions are mine."

"No!" Her denial rang with shock. "You cannot do this! You gave me your word!"

She lanced the Preacher with the Claim; he scarcely felt it, a raised finger in Ilea's face whipping the blood to her head. It drifted down her temples.

A terrible perception darkened her golden eyes. She was grasping an unpalatable truth. The alliance she had formed with the Preacher was a deception; one she had practiced on herself. She choked on the realization, wretched that even in this Arian had had the upper hand.

But what had *she* done to the Companions? What fate had she brought about for Hira?

The rukh's long tongue rolled down its jaws again, aiming at those who'd escaped.

Lania acted, her incandescent magic enclosing Ilea and Sinnia. The rukh's firebolts rebounded off the shield. It turned its attention to Half-Seen and Ash on the other side of the gate. But the Khyber warriors tackled the Companions to the ground. Covering them, they placed their swords tip to tip, forming a bridge above their heads. The air rippled, and as the firebird struck, glints of blue and green struck an invisible wall that spouted from their swords.

The firebird dipped low, so close that its feathers brushed Sinnia's arms. Her entire body was numbed with cold by the One-

Eyed Preacher's approach, his bony hands knotted above the rukh's crest. She couldn't look at his face; she ducked her head, pulling Lania down with her.

Ilea saw her opportunity. As the firebird wheeled away, she grabbed hold of one of its claws, launching herself into the air. The massive span of the firebird's wings swept out and over their walls, its hind legs extended as Ilea held on tightly. Sinnia watched in astonishment as Ilea tried to topple the Preacher from the rukh, rushing at him with the Claim. Dismissively, he strangled her voice. A forceful gesture of his hand crushed her throat. And Ilea faced him blankly, her arrogance assailed, all her certainties undone. She had failed to understand the extent of his ambition; she had thought him as easy to overturn as a careless prince in her bed. Yet even Rukh had escaped her, and the knowledge of her undoing was too bitter for her to bear.

The piercing cry of the rukh bloodied Sinnia's eyes: she blinked, transfixed, as its great wings swept the gate, and it lunged up at the sky.

Ilea's hand was forced open. She was made to release her grip upon the firebird's claw.

Her cloak flared out behind her, golden hair limned by the sun. Then, free of the rukh's protection, her body fell like an arrow into the Talisman camp.

When Sinnia blinked again, the High Companion was gone.

48

SINNIA PUSHED PAST THE KHANUM, REFUSING TO LOOK BACK AT THE ashes heaped along the wall. She moved instead to the Khyber, who came to their feet with warrior quickness, surveying the Companions their bodies had almost crushed.

Sinnia's thought was for Ash. She was older and much too frail to have borne such a fierce charge. Her breathing was shallow as Qais and Sinnia helped her to her feet.

"Speak to me, Ash! Are you injured?"

The Jurist shook her head, the sole link now between Hira's past and its future. "Give me a moment." She continued to fight for breath.

Hamzah helped Half-Seen rise. "Forgive me, if I hurt you. I meant to act as your shield."

Blushing, Half-Seen took a step away from the man who had taken her hand.

"Thank you for your assistance. I have suffered no injury."

"Qaid." The man named Qais snapped the word at Half-Seen.

She blinked at Qais in surprise, even as Hamzah touched his brother's arm in admonition.

"My brother is Qaid of the Khyber tribes," Qais insisted. "You will address him as such."

Half-Seen's blush deepened. "Of course. I am grateful for your rescue, Qaid."

Hamzah shook his head. "Forgive my brother the harshness of his manners." He nudged Qais. "Finish the introduction."

His gaze holding hers prisoner, Qais said, "This is Hafsah the Collector."

The three Companions on the wall gasped, for Qais had used Half-Seen's real name in lieu of the name that described her position on the Council, and instead of her title as Companion, an unaccustomed familiarity even among themselves.

Hamzah smoothed the moment over by saying, "Collector. It is an honor to meet you." And indeed his eyes lingered on Half-Seen's delicate beauty.

Qais's handsome features hardened. He pulled his brother aside. "The gate, Hamzah. What now?"

Hamzah searched the sky for another sign of the firebird. Then his glance came to rest on Sinnia, dropping to her circlets before returning to her face. "Are you the Companion Sinnia, the one who acts as the First Oralist's protector?"

"In as much as she allows it." Sinnia's voice was raw. She couldn't ease the moment with levity, stricken by the loss of the Companions—the loss of Psalm the most grievous wound, her wisdom indispensable to them all.

She watched Ash place a palm to her chest.

"Sinnia, I feel . . . an *absence*." She shifted so that she could see past Sinnia to the other side of the gate. "Where is Psalm? Where are the others?"

Sinnia tried to articulate the truth. "I don't know where Psalm stationed the junior Companions, or where the novices are. But the

Companions on the walls were killed by the One-Eyed Preacher." She hesitated, then made herself say, "I think with Ilea's help."

Ash's pained gasp was terrible to hear, the pain shared by them all.

Half-Seen tried to push past them, but Hamzah caught her by the elbow. "The wall is damaged, sahabiya. It is dangerous to venture farther."

Half-Seen stilled, able to see the truth for herself, now that he'd shifted to her side.

Mounds of ash in place of the women she had trained with, served with—and Psalm. Psalm, who had dedicated herself to the fight against the Talisman, who had always possessed the courage to challenge Ilea's priorities—Psalm, the heart of the Citadel, was gone.

"No." Half-Seen's piteous cry. Sinnia cried with her, trying to muffle the sound.

Tears formed in dark topaz eyes and slid down Half-Seen's cheeks. Her beauty in that moment was spellbinding, and Hamzah was solemn before it, until Qais grated, "Grieve later, Companion. War is at your walls."

Sinnia watched in surprise as Half-Seen flashed Qais a look of ire.

Ash cleared her throat, and as one, the three Companions intoned, "From the One we came, to the One we return." The smallest share of peace in a landscape of desolation.

Sinnia slid one arm around Half-Seen's waist, easing her away from the men. She hugged Half-Seen hard. "All is not lost." The words were intended to persuade them both. "We still have Arian. And you and Ash must stand with us, and help to defend the gate. The Citadel needs us."

"Countermeasures are called for."

A cool observation from Lania. The party at the gate turned to meet her. She acknowledged them with a nod, but both Khyber warriors drew their swords in a single pass. Lania ignored them. She leaned down over the parapet to survey the Talisman battering the gate.

She raised her arms aloft, her crimson robe falling to her sides like two graceful wings. She uttered something that sounded like the Claim, yet roared like the fires of Jahannam, a rage that had burned for centuries, now tipped with arctic frost, cutting a path through the Talisman like a reaper slashing at bones.

When the frenzy of her killing was done, she dusted her hands against her robes and warmed her fingertips with her breath.

"There," she said. "Countermeasures. A pity I did not kill them all. But these Talisman multiply like the demon spawn of hell."

Hamzah's lips twisted. "They are men, not demon spawn. Misguided or under compulsion, driven forth by a monster."

The cold eyes of the Khanum touched the warriors from Khyber. "You do them little credit. Monsters beget monsters, and now that I look more closely, it seems that you resemble them."

Hamzah and Qais touched their swords together, their faces pale as they watched her. Sinnia maneuvered around them, a strong, valiant shield in front of their much larger bodies, staring down the Khanum, one arched brow raised in challenge.

"These men are *not* Talisman. And we are not in the habit of murdering our allies."

One edge of Lania's mouth curled up. She studied Sinnia in her battle-worn armor, her weapons girded at her hip.

"I think I like you, Companion." Her gaze darted about the courtyard. "Where did you leave my sister?"

Sinnia pointed to the tower of the Citadel. "She meets the

Preacher there." She couldn't see Arian anywhere; a ribbon of fear stroked her spine.

Lania's smile faded. "On her own, Whip of the First Oralist?"

Tension ratcheted through Sinnia's lithe frame. "She said you needed me more."

A long pause as the Khanum absorbed this, while the warriors of the Khyber bristled at Sinnia's back, uncomfortable with a woman's protection, even one who had exhibited such skill. The Khyber's code allowed for nothing else.

Hamzah broke position first, tugging Sinnia behind him. His low rumble in her ear, he said, "It is our honor to defend you, Companion."

Sinnia pushed back in front of them. "I appreciate your courtesy, Qaid, but perhaps your brother will confirm that I am able to look after myself." She gave Lania a look.

Lania's cat-green eyes brimmed with calculation.

The firebird circled again, its cries shattering their peace.

"I will deal with the rukh." Dismissing the Khyber, she said, "I will leave the Companions of Hira to decide the rest."

49

Arian's circlets throbbed. She was flooded by a wave of blankness—a breaking of some kind, an unmaking. Had the bond of the Companions been sundered? She searched the parapets in terror. She saw Sinnia and Lania, and her heart began to beat again.

Then she looked west.

The crenellations were blackened by smoke, the wall deserted. No matter how she searched, none of the senior Companions could be found holding their positions of defense.

No! Her plea was to the One. *You wouldn't take my mother, then take the women who raised me in her place.*

But the absence within, the weakening of the Companions' bonds bore no other explanation. Her gaze swung to Psalm's post. A few of the Citadel Guard milled around it in disarray. Of Psalm there was no sign. A keening cry rose to Arian's lips. The rukh shrieked, alerted to the target it sought.

It pursued Arian without respite. A surge of adrenaline pushed her onward, past the circular fountains of the courtyard, into a long arcade opposite the door to the scriptorium.

Stones dropped from the firebird's tongue, detonating charges inside the Citadel's walls. Arian weaved through the debris caused by the explosions, close enough at times that she felt the hot brush of air against her cheek, and once she stepped into the spray of water from a demolished fountain.

Her ears bled at the rukh's unceasing cries. She calmed her terror and grief with the Claim, a subvocal murmur pitched low to avoid giving away her location to the firebird's razor-sharp sight. She felt like a doll on the Preacher's strings, jerked this way and that, backtracking again and again, her destination fixed in her mind.

The rukh screeched its delight as it chased her. It rose to the skies in a spiral of flight, then dove down in a scarlet streak. At the last second it veered off course, its spiked tongue detonating a giant crimson orb. A percussive noise beat at Arian's temples and eardrums. Air whooshed from the square, and then moments later blew back.

She was thrown off her feet like a toy kicked by a petulant child, and landed with a painful thump. The blast shook the Citadel's walls, brought cries from every quarter, terror and pain combined.

Agony convulsed Arian's thoughts. The mausoleum where her parents were entombed was reduced to rubble, robbing them of dignity in death. She saw them for a moment with the light upon light vision, their arms entwined, their heads bent together over the treasure of a manuscript. And then she saw their tombs.

She could have borne it—could have borne the insult of their defilement in death—but in the same moment she was confronted with a reality so stark, it took her too long to unravel it.

There were *fresh* bodies in the rubble, smears of blood spattering white silk, dark hair daubing bits of broken stone. And the savage tearing of flesh as far as Arian could see.

The *novices*. This was where Psalm had sent the novices to hide. The mausoleum's walls were fortified, double the thickness of any other part of the Citadel, safer than the Council Chamber, and less likely to be targeted than the treasures of the scriptorium.

Or so she had thought. Just as she had believed that Ilea would do nothing to harm the Companions.

As the percussive noise in her ears dulled, she gagged at the scent of burnt flesh, of blood staining the Citadel's walls, the blood of Hira's future. The Preacher had claimed both the past and the future, legacy and promise.

Her thoughts ran in rivers of red, her grief incoherent, her throat torn by elegiac cries, until the Claim lay across her brow like a stroke of consolation, forcing her into calm. Forcing her to think past her sorrow, to listen and comprehend.

A beat passed, then another. The tremors that seized the Citadel's walls whispered into silence, the ground still beneath her feet. She dragged in another breath, inhaling dust and smoke. She coughed and coughed, her body racked by sobs, until the Claim stroked her again.

In the appalling silence, she heard something other than her own weak cries.

She heard the voice of another Companion, and her lament was louder and more tragic than Arian's. Wiping a hand across her eyes, she gazed across the field of debris to see Mask upon her knees, her dress torn, her arms bruised, her circlets covered in blood, bits of flesh and bone scattered through her hair and smeared across her face. In her arms, she held the torso of a child. The rest of the child's body had been shredded by the blast.

Arian blinked in horror. There was more than one body.

And more than one child.

Strewn among the corpses of the novices were the bodies of

the refugees the Citadel had taken in, the women and children of the Hazara that Arian had sent to Hira, offering them the protection not just of the Citadel, but of Mask and Half-Seen, the two Hazara Companions. Now she took Mask's name.

"Mishkah, forgive me."

But Mask shook her head, her sorrow harrowing the Courtyard with the Claim.

Underlying Mask's grief, Arian heard another sound: noises of pity and fury and sorrow like her own. In the space of a breath, she understood.

Gathering the Claim within her like the calm at the center of a storm, she turned on her heel and bolted to the gate.

"Qaid!" She screamed Hamzah's title with the pent-up power of the Claim. Once. Twice. Then again until he heard her. He hailed her in response. She waved at the ruins of the mausoleum. "There are survivors! Help Mishkah, please!"

She left their fate to Hamzah, this time running out in the open, one arm casting the Claim like a shield over her head. She would pierce the rukh's heart with her rage: her grief would be her finest weapon, and she would wield it as Daniyar did his sword.

She sprinted past the mausoleum to the northern side of the wall. She spied the stairs to the tower on the far side of an inner courtyard sheltered by palms.

The rukh circled above her head, waiting its chance to strike.

She readied herself for its charge.

But instead of dipping low and dropping another stone, the Preacher yanked hard on the firebird's crest, pulling up its sinuous neck.

His stone eye found Arian. He raised one hand and murmured a perverse incantation—perverse because it came from his lips and spoke to the nature of his crimes. An incantation that spoke of growth, of lush and fertile fields, of an earth renewed in greenery, the famine of the south swept away.

Arian gathered her courage and readied herself to run.

She had taken two steps out into the open when she was stopped in her tracks.

Not by the cries of the rukh. And not by another detonation.

A wall appeared before her eyes, a solid forest of green, thick hedges that rose so high they blocked out her view of the tower. Sunlight gleamed along the dense edges of the leaves, turned upward like palms in futile supplication. The borders of the hedge were crowded and close, fragile cups of blossoms drooping in delicate lines from its vines. The fresh scent of night jasmine washed away the taint of blood, the air uncorrupted and sweet.

She stepped back for a better view.

The entire courtyard was overgrown, the green forest branching out in all directions. She couldn't see the walls or the wreckage of the mausoleum. She couldn't hear the voices of the Citadel Guard, still less of the Companions who were left to deliver the Claim.

It was as if Hira was deserted, and she alone was left to defend it under a sky of isolated clouds that had lowered to enclose the hedge. She was trapped between high green divides, separated from the Companions, her goal now far out of reach.

She tipped her head all the way back and caught the trace of light on crimson wings. The Preacher was still there. She could dethrone him by capturing the rukh. He'd thrown up a forest to keep her at a distance, which had to mean that he feared her.

He doubted his supremacy against her knowledge of the Claim.

A sigh escaped Arian's lips. She stood in the sun-washed silence of towering green hedges. She touched a hand to leaves of green, cupping a cluster of blooms in her palm. Its sweetness graced her skin. An opening appeared in the wall that blocked her passage, the narrow alleys within dark and cloistered and cool. When she took a step forward, the wall re-formed behind her. She drew another breath, inhaling the sweetness of jasmine. Whenever she touched a hand to the hedges that hemmed her in, another opening appeared, leading her deeper within.

But when she failed to encounter a single tree, or to run her fingers along the overlapping fronds of a palm, she understood what the Preacher had done to prevent her access to the tower.

He'd trapped her within a maze.

50

ARIAN WANDERED ALONG FRAGRANT ALLEYS, LOSING ALL SENSE OF time. She felt comforted, her grief attenuated. She was wrapped in peace, lulled to sleep by a curtain of silver-gray fog, her body crying for rest. There had been little time during her quest to consider her physical needs, to wonder if she might seek a reprieve, might change into fresh clothing, or scent her palms with rosewater, or work a comb at leisure through the tangled knots in her hair: acts that would have made her feel human, as if she were a woman instead of a hostage to the cruel fortunes of war.

She would rest in this maze for a while, let the fog curl around her and soothe her. She would center herself in this beautiful garden, this lush paradise on earth, and as soon as she had recovered she would remember . . . she would remember the shimmer of silver eyes, she would remember the grave and alluring voice that spoke to her of her quest.

But not at present. Not just yet.

She was—enchanted. Charmed by her surroundings, lulled by an inner peace.

Birdsong rose from hidden rests among the hedgerows. She laughed a little to herself, brushing the hedges on both sides, collecting blossoms to fold into her hair. The scent was sweet and sharp all around her, and for a moment she felt a dull pang of memory. She crushed a dainty blossom in her palm and brought her hand to her face to inhale its perfume.

Turquoise-green water running in marble channels, the silky waters of a timeless pool, clusters of jasmine in her hair.

He'd brushed her hair.

He'd kissed the jasmine from her lips.

He'd held her, praised her, helped her to dress.

Who was he?

She sniffed her palm again. The scent tore the veil of unraveling pleasure aside.

There was something she needed to remember . . . something or *someone.*

She wandered a little farther, turning left, then right, then left again, but not with any sense of destination or of how far she might have traveled. Every now and again, she'd find apertures in the hedgerows where the light of day broke through, probing at her senses, peering into her mind. When that happened, she would recall herself to her purpose. She would remember that she was fighting for the life of the Citadel, but then her hand would brush the dense green of the hedges, and she would lose her way again.

Perhaps she should keep her hands to herself. She should shake the blossoms from her hair and let them trail behind her to mark the paths she had walked.

The clouds slid lower over the maze, the sky soggy with heat. She wiped sweat from her forehead, the sharp tang of jasmine teasing her senses again.

It's you who puts the stars to shame, Arian. The stars, the moon, the night.

Arian! Her name was Arian. And the man who had spoken it loved her more than the treasures of the earth, more than all hope of the Hereafter.

The Hereafter?

The buzzing of bees among the hedges made her drowsy, the fog stroking her limbs.

She pinched herself awake, her hand encountering a band of gold fastened to her upper arm. She frowned, the drowsiness clearing. She covered the gold band with her hand, found another on her opposite arm, and covered that one as well.

The bands began to pulse. A dynamic sense of power cleared the fog from her thoughts.

She looked ahead, her vision acute, the pain behind her eye gone.

She was surrounded by towering walls of green. Vines of night-blooming jasmine threaded through thick hedges and choked the air with scent.

She was trapped inside a maze that was cloistered, scented, and dark.

As to why she had been ensnared, she was the First Oralist of Hira. Her task was to rescue the Citadel from destruction.

A voracious cry pierced the lull, the shriek of a dragon. Her hands clasped to her circlets; her feet took her west. Her fingers sought out the carvings in her cuffs. What were they? She glanced down at one arm and read the script.

In the name of the One, the Merciful and Compassionate.

Her power, her memories, her mission—all came roaring back. She threw her head back and screamed.

The shimmering silver-gray fog in the maze shattered like panes of glass, leaving the air without sweetness, biting and clean as a blade. Called to it by instinct, she offered the shahadah.

This quest, her mission, they had begun with her Audacy. An Audacy to search out the Bloodprint, to rescue the written record of the Claim from the dark predations of the Preacher.

The Preacher!

She remembered him now. It was the One-Eyed Preacher who had trapped her in this maze, and she knew why he had done it, why he had conjured the maze.

To block her access to the tower.

Because he was afraid to meet her on her ground, afraid to contend with her power. So he'd weakened her by destroying what she loved. He'd murdered her mentors and left her to defend the Citadel alone.

Not alone. Lania's sharp reminder. *Your loss is mine, your triumphs will be also. Draw your courage from me.*

She placed herself in a meditative trance, focusing on the maze. She was trapped inside a square. If she pressed forward to an opening, the fog would shroud her again, an endless, encircling lure.

Never to be altered by the encircling tremors of time.

The motto of the Citadel.

Had the Preacher trapped her with the Citadel's axiom?

She spoke in the radiant, self-assured tones of the First Oralist of Hira, the most gifted Qari of her time. Arian, the Linguist.

And it was as the Linguist of the Citadel that she spoke in the Citadel's tongue.

"I alter you, heart of Hira. I alter you to my purpose, to hold until the end."

A sudden whoosh of sound. The walls of the hedges shrank. Now, she could see through the forest to the design of the maze.

She could also see the battle being waged. The rukh rolling gems from its tongue. Sinnia notching arrow after arrow to force the rukh away from the walls. Lania at the Citadel Gate, assisted by Ash and Half-Seen. The sturdy warriors of the Khyber aiding the Guard, pulling survivors from the debris. Smoke, filth, blood, and bone, destruction all around her.

But in the still center of the maze, an imperturbable coolness.

A riddle to be unworked before she could access the tower.

The maze took up every inch of space between the mausoleum and the tower. It flowered into the arcades that led to the Council Chamber. Perhaps it even coiled around the hidden fountains of the All Ways. Yet its pattern was symmetrical. Square hedges like mathematical problems cordoned off into lanes.

Straight lines, right angles, no openings that led anywhere other than back to the heart of the maze. The pattern reminded her of something she'd seen before. She closed her eyes to summon the image. Was it the map of the graveyard? Or the Tomb of the Living King? Was it the astonishing geometry of the Tilla Kari's motifs? No. There was too much variation in the design, with floral motifs and palmettes, and leaves and vines of every shape.

She opened her eyes. Her fingers raised just above the hedge-rows, she traced the lines of the maze in the present moment, and through the pathways of her mind.

Her eyelids fluttered closed. She felt brambles pull at her skin, stepped into a hidden mausoleum in the city of Black Aura, felt the air cool and close around her body, found a space filled with written prayers and a tomb riddled with secrets.

A pedestal had emerged from that tomb. On it rested a golden case with a mortise lock formed of a single emerald.

She pressed her circlets. She thought of the numbers seven, eight, six.

She traced the pattern of the numbers on the case; the mortise lock snapped open.

She bent her head to inhale the fragrance of a manuscript.

She turned a bloodstained page.

The script came alive in her mind. Her eyes snapped open at once.

The memory she was chasing was the memory of a strong, square script blocked out upon a page. Of pen and ink and verse.

Pen and ink and *writing*.

She studied the green maze that wasn't a perfect match to the memory, though she now understood what it was. Because she had learned to *read* it.

The maze was a wonder of calligraphy, the Kufic calligraphy of right angles and straight lines, written from right to left, anterior and inverse, mirrored in every dimension. There was no way out of the maze; it was made of a single word, a single name.

The maze had trapped her because the Preacher had thought to trap her in *his* name. He assumed his possession of the Bloodprint gave him powers of divinity, seeing himself as omnipotent, impervious to defeat.

He had raised the maze in homage to himself, naming himself the One. And so the Talisman's chant, distinct from the shahadah: There is no one but the one. And the meaning the Talisman ascribed to the chant? *There is no one but the One-Eyed Preacher.* A mortal man who had named himself a god, divining the darkest of arts to substantiate his claim.

An unthinkable heresy for the people of the Claim that had spread throughout all of Khorasan. Arian would not let it stand.

The Linguist of Hira would not be defeated by a sorcerer's use of semantics.

She was a child of Hira. Hira was a citadel of faith.

The truth of the shahadah was: *There is no one but the One.*

And she read the One's name in the upright angles of the maze.

Praised be the One. All blessings come from the One, Eternal and Everlasting.

There is no one but the One.

The hedgerows shifted, and the maze re-formed, its lines and angles altered. The name of a heretical would-be divinity became the name of the One.

Straight lines, right angles, a citadel of belief, Arian its disciple.

First Oralist of Hira, Linguist of the Claim.

She had been afraid of who she was meant to become. She had distanced herself from Hira, setting out on her personal quest, keeping herself apart in her pursuit of the Talisman, a worthy goal, she'd thought. But now she had returned, she'd reclaimed the rights of First Oralist of Hira, first daughter of the Citadel, foremost scholar of the Claim.

She would defeat the Preacher with the searing truths of the Sana Codex, with the wisdom of the Israa e Miraj.

The Citadel was hers to hold, her ground to defend, and defend it she would.

She breathed the shahadah over the green forest of the maze. What was left when her prayer had ended was a murky gloaming at her feet.

She paced the distance to the tower, shoulders thrown back, circlets gleaming, a whisper of praise on her lips. She pressed one palm to her heart, searching out the silver thread that linked her to Daniyar, the bond that held them to each other, that held them to their purpose, even when they wavered, when the light that bound them went dark.

My memories of you brought me back, my love. I will do no less for you.

There would be time. She would find a way when her purpose was fulfilled.

At the door to the tower, she called out a warning.

"Preacher, I come for you."

51

ARSALAN, ESFANDYAR, AND THE ASSASSIN FORMED A PERSONAL GUARD around the trio of Mages above the Messenger Gate. With brute strength, Uwais had hauled the Silver Mage up the wall.

The Nineteen had let him climb unmolested, honoring the bargain Najran had made, when he'd assumed his victory was inevitable. But their forces continued to pour through the Messenger Gate. From the south and the east, the Talisman advanced unchecked. The southern wall had fallen; the great square was overrun.

Daniyar had had no moment to rest—neither had the others. Rukh had shown him the twin armillary spheres, and now with Wafa centered between them, the three Mages called upon the Rite of Qari'ah.

His ring finger raised to point the miniature sphere at a blood-stained sky, Rukh cried out, *"The Qari'ah will occur on the Day when humanity will be dispersed like moths, when mountains are like tufts of wool. Then for those whose weight of decency is heavy in the balance, their joy will be assured. But those whose weight is light shall be engulfed by an abyss. What will make you know the abyss? It is a fire hotly burning."*

Rukh's free hand was positioned on the meridian of the sphere the Assassin had brought from the western wall. The Silver Mage had hold of the ecliptic ring, the Blue Mage the center sphere. They gazed at an empty sky, where the sun overrode any trace of Al Mintaka's blue fire. The Mages reiterated their call on the Qari'ah.

The Nineteen's fighters had infiltrated the wall. In between bouts of recitation, Rukh caught sight of a tenacious attack upon the Teerandaz, and of soldiers pushing through the Zhayedan who protected the route to the sphere . . . the route to their Khan.

He refused to glance down at the carnage in the courtyard, to acknowledge the assault upon the Illustrious Portal or the soldiers pressing into the palace.

He could feel Arsalan at his back, keeping the enemy from reaching him, his sword spinning, lunging, striking, as if his strength was endless.

Breathing in, he repeated the Qari'ah.

There was no response at all.

The Silver Mage braced his free hand on Rukh's shoulder; the Blue Mage did the same on the other side. They began again.

"What will make you know what the Qari'ah is?"

He heard Arsalan's grunt behind him. The clash of heavy weaponry. Then another grunt and a sound of hollow pain. He turned his head to see.

"No!" Arsalan gasped, the word wet in his throat. "Stay true to your task."

Then the Assassin was there, his smokelike movements dispatching Arsalan's assailant.

The circle of the Mages tightened. Their guards moved in behind them, a solid wall, as steel crashed against steel.

His back to Arsalan's back, Rukh murmured his general's name as a question. Arsalan's response was swift.

"Fight, Rukh! Ashfall's fate is in your hands!"

Another grunt, another strike of sword meeting bone, and this time Rukh didn't look. He pushed the sound away to another part of his mind. The hoarse timbre of his voice became a chant, and from a chant it rose to a roar, echoed by the other Mages.

The sphere on his ring began to glow. He felt power streak from his finger to his palm, then up his wrist through his arm, down to his very core.

He bellowed a castigation at the sky, stripping all light from it, hurling a veil of infinite darkness over the glare of the sun, the air glazed sapphire blue. A handful of brilliant pinpricks appeared against the midnight veil.

The sphere at the wall began to vibrate. Its rings shifted a fraction under the grip of the Mages. The one bit of lightness in a landscape of blood was the distant foaming of the salt lake.

An unnatural darkness covered Ashfall. Silence fell upon the square.

Light shot up from the armillary sphere, illuminating the clean bend of the horizon, then climbing higher to an infinite plane to capture the blue glint of the stars.

Rukh was seeing something he shouldn't be seeing: the night overtaking the day, a sight that spoke of power he couldn't plumb, a sight so terrible that he felt himself retreat.

And then, as if Arsalan sensed his disquiet, he felt the strength and heat of Arsalan at his back, heard a broken murmur, heard the effort it took to say it. "This is your gift. You were meant to command this, Rukh."

Rukh's arrogant certainty flared to life again.

He called out the Qari'ah once more.

Yet despite the darkness, and the first faint inkling of stars, the power of Al Mintaka trembled at the brink.

He heard Arsalan pant, "You have never failed me, Rukh. You will not begin now."

There was pain and blood in the words. He felt Arsalan's body stagger. Agony fired Rukh's veins, his loss imminent . . . immeasurable . . . fathomless . . . something he couldn't reckon with, a void too colossal to be grasped.

"Arsalan—"

His general found his feet again, forced himself to stand his ground.

The terror of night saturated the air, grabbed Rukh's heart in its fists.

Al Mintaka remained dark.

"Call the stars, Rukh."

A familiar hand at his neck. Holding on to him. Arsalan was holding on.

And he didn't know why, but Rukh abandoned the Rite of Qari'ah, pressed his ring to his lips, kissed the sphere, and cried out a lament, shouting his grief to the stars.

"Wrap the night over the day, wrap the day over the night! Let the sun, the moon, and the stars run their course. Exalted and Most Forgiving, take *anything* from me but this."

He sensed the surprise of the other Mages at the prayer. It was an approximation of the Claim, a memory, a prayer of his mother's, a prayer of his own soul at the point of its extinction.

He called up to the skies, a man of little faith begging for the one thing that mattered.

"Take Ashfall, take this empire, *take my life*. Exalted and Most Forgiving, grant me *this*."

"No, Rukh, *no*." Arsalan's whisper. His hold on Rukh's neck weakened. Rukh caught Arsalan's fingers before they could slide away.

The rings of the armillary sphere careened out of control, rays of harsh blue light splicing a lightless sky.

"It's the wrong prayer, Rukh."

He pulled Arsalan around, so that his shoulders shored up Arsalan's sagging weight.

"Commander!"

Cassandane's bleak cry along the wall. Echoed by Khashayar and others in the square. They had seen their general fall. Their pain couldn't be pacified, their fear and grief an abyss.

He turned his head, put his lips to Arsalan's ear. A hope. A promise. An oath he would uphold with every scrap of honor he possessed.

"It's the only prayer that matters."

Forever poised at this moment, where he felt the last touch of Arsalan's hot breath, felt weakness where Arsalan would never choose to yield, read love and sorrow in fathomless dark eyes. Brilliant black eyes that had always held the stars.

The other Mages held fast to the sphere, but in this moment, Rukh couldn't look away. He had to hold on to the fading of those stars, had to witness the end of what he cherished.

He leaned in close to hear a last confession, his lips brushing Arsalan's jaw.

"Forgive me, my Prince. It wasn't my wish to leave you."

"No." He pressed his fingers to Arsalan's lips. "Don't ask for my forgiveness when I've been the one at fault. Just don't—don't leave me yet. See this through at my side."

Arsalan shook his head. "I name Khashayar my successor. Let him see you through."

Scalding tears on Rukh's cheeks, hot, sweet, cleansing. They drifted to Arsalan's face, dropped to the armillary sphere. If the battle had resumed, Rukh didn't hear it. He was bent on holding Arsalan to life with his gifts as Dark Mage, his will as Prince of Khorasan, his majesty as the Black Khan. All of which he would trade for his prayer to be granted.

Thick lashes fell to Arsalan's cheeks, his body slumped to the ground. Rukh knelt with him, held him, pressed his lips to Arsalan's temples, the roaring of grief in his ears, uncaring that others would see, or try to draw him away. He wouldn't go. He couldn't. All he could feel was this agony of love, this raging anguish of loss.

He braced himself against the sphere, his signet brushing its outer ring.

Light sparked into the sky from the contact.

The other Mages fell silent, their hands still pressed to his shoulders, their solidarity firm as Ashfall burned, and the Prince of Khorasan grieved not the end of empire, but the loss of a man he loved as he had loved no other.

He didn't see the sphere rotate. He didn't feel the pull of the signet ring, his hand curled into a fist. His face was buried in Arsalan's neck, his soul a yawning chasm.

The sphere began to shiver against the wall. Moments later, the wall began to shake.

A bracelet of light circled the blue veil of sky, stars linked together like a belt across a warrior's hips, or like a faltering string of prayers counted out on a tasbih.

A boy's voice uttered words that trembled, words Rukh had offered to a sky turned to night, but the boy's voice polished the words to the point of absolute truth. Like the gleaming edge of a blade. Like a sword that shone silver in the night.

"The One created the heavens and the earth. The One causes the night to flow into day, and the day to flow into night, and has made the sun and the moon run their courses for an appointed term. Is the One not Exalted and All-Forgiving?"

Though he wanted to deny the relevance of the verse, Rukh whispered into Arsalan's neck, *"Yes.* It isn't too late, Arsalan. Your belief makes me believe."

He felt the edge of the Sacred Cloak brush his shoulder, felt a flare of warmth travel down his arm, and from his body into Arsalan's.

He stirred. The moment he raised his head, the armillary sphere came to life, a bright beam shooting skyward, as the walls rattled from the force of the magic unleashed.

The hidden orbit became visible: Al Mintaka blazed overhead, paired with its twin in an ellipse shortened and illuminated by the power of three Mages, and the lucid voice of a boy.

The star-beam cut down across the desert behind the Nineteen, sweeping the plains in a burst of continuous fire.

The Silver Mage grasped Rukh's shoulder to haul him to his feet.

The Assassin slipped in behind Rukh, taking Arsalan's weight, his hands testing the wounds. Rukh would not have permitted anyone other than the Assassin to lay hands upon Arsalan—the strange bond between the Khan and the Assassin had held.

Rukh rubbed his hand across his eyes, unashamed of his tears. The air felt velvet-soft and warm against his skin. Why was Ashfall more beautiful when he was about to lose it?

"Control it." Daniyar angled his head at the beam. "Direct its path."

The Silver Mage's jaw was set, his eyes bleak as he watched the Nineteen obliterated by the power of the star. The Blue Mage's hand gripped the central sphere. He nodded at Rukh, giving him tacit permission to adjust the rings of the sphere. The star-beam grazed the western wall with extreme precision, gouging out a chasm between the wall and the soldiers who overran the gate. Then the beam swung away.

Rukh molded Daniyar's hands to the sphere's ecliptic ring. "Hold here." He turned and shouted to the Zhayedan who were still battling on the walls. "Zhayedan! With me!"

His eyes locked with the Assassin's, who had stripped off Arsalan's breastplate to examine his blood-soaked torso.

Instead of delivering a threat, Rukh made a quiet vow. "Anything you ask will be yours." He bent and touched his hand to Arsalan's head. Arsalan's eyes flickered open, his skin pallid and gray. Curt and angry, Rukh said, "I love you. Nothing in this world can change that. If knowing that doesn't keep you with me, expect to die unforgiven."

He found Wafa on the other side of the sphere and tugged him from his place of hiding.

"I have need of you, boy."

He strode down the wall toward the ruins of the Tower of the Mirage, dragging Wafa along with him, Zhayedan soldiers clearing the path for them both. When he'd reached the point where the tower sheared away from the wall, he positioned himself above the hole and raised his hand up to the power of Al Mintaka. He put his other hand on the boy's shoulder, conviction burning in his voice.

"Now you will recite."

The boy's strange eyes met his, turquoise blue intersected with thin spears of silver. They held no resistance to his command; indeed, without taking a breath, the boy intoned the same polished words, refining them on the edge of his tongue with such literacy that Rukh felt himself undone. The first faint streamers of hope trembled against the chill of his bitterness and rage.

He'd never been known for humility.

But his grief at losing Arsalan had forced him to his knees.

The sphere-ring aimed at the sky, his new vulnerability underlined his actions. He couldn't control the outcome or the fate of Ashfall; he had come to see himself as the neediest of supplicants, his fortunes dependent on others.

The First Oralist. The Companion from the Negus. The Silver Mage, the Blue Mage. The Assassin. Arsalan. Even the assistance of his wayward sister, and now the boy, Wafa. They'd given themselves to the cause of Ashfall's survival as a matter of principle.

So his arrogance had suffered a blow. But what did it matter that he'd been forced to his knees and driven to atone? He would remake himself entirely if Arsalan could be saved.

"Again, please."

The boy repeated the night-verse at his request, his huge eyes showing his surprise at the Black Khan's courtesy.

But they were linked now, he and the boy, just as with the other Mages. He saw the birthright in the boy's eyes and had an inkling of why the Silver Mage had seemed to bow beneath the weight of his burdens.

A fleeting realization followed.

His time is at an end.

The Silver Mage had come close to surrender on the field.

The boy shook his head, pointing to Al Mintaka, pointing *beyond* Al Mintaka to its smaller, weaker twin. A bolt of fire shot from the signet ring on Rukh's hand, straight to the star locked in Al Mintaka's orbit. His whole hand seemed to burn as if flames licked at his unprotected skin. The pain of it was immense, yet he channeled it to a single point on the sphere of his ring. If it would save Ashfall, let the beam take his hand. No sooner had he made his silent vow than the pain receded. And just as Darya had promised, the star-beam split in two.

He glanced back along the western wall. The beam continued to burn a path through the Rising Nineteen, veering away from the Messenger Gate. The second shaft of the star-beam blazed out from his ring. His body raging with the Dark Mage's power, he clenched his fist and aimed the sphere-ring at the full strength of the Talisman to the south.

The beam became a thin blue line, his gifts working in concert with the boy's.

The blue line slashed through Talisman lines, gliding farther and farther out with each rotation of his wrist. The frantic cries of the enemy fell upon his ears—welcome, celebrated, *perfect*. Death as far as the eye could see, cleansing Khorasan from the southern wall to the salt plains and beyond. The carnal stench of blood. The triumph of having erased a blight upon the land. The sheer jubilation of revenge.

This was how it felt to conquer, how it felt to be *omnipotent*.

How many men had he killed? And how many more awaited the lance of his displeasure?

Who would dare stand against him now?

His hawk-like profile turned to the Emissary Gate, an imperious smile on his lips.

The boy's voice fell silent; his recitation ceased. The twin star-beam switched off. To the west, the power of Al Mintaka took the form of a shimmering veil, similar to the one the Silver Mage had conjured to shield the city to the east, the power of profligate, undiscerning death curtailed by the Blue and Silver Mages.

Rukh tilted his head. Onyx eyes tinted with blue fire gazed down upon the boy.

In arctic accents, the Dark Mage asked, "Why have you stopped, boy? Who gave you leave to do so?"

The boy looked hesitant, as well he might, standing before a prince whose dominion was unequalled. But the boy pressed his hands to his heart, his gaze shifting to the sky, seeing something that Rukh's vision couldn't grasp.

"What is it?"

The boy rubbed his chest. His voice changed, his vocabulary with it. "I was chosen to ascend by the leave of the One. I assisted you in the defense of your city by the One's grace. But I judge that this"—his work-roughened hand indicated the killing fields— "does not conform to the One's guidance."

Rukh's jaw slackened. He stared at the boy, agape. Then a sneer twisted his lips.

"*You* judge? Who are you to judge such a thing? A slave kicked in the teeth by his masters, you should rejoice at this victory."

But Wafa would not appease him. He had learned the lessons taught by the Silver Mage. He had witnessed the Silver Mage's repeated offers of clemency; he understood his mentor's pain at the loss of his kin and clan. The Silver Mage had shown him there was no glory in killing: even a righteous sword left a trail of anguish in its wake.

"You ask who I am to judge. I am a servant of the One, enlightened by Ascension, entrusted with a noble task."

He said the words with care, not wanting to get them wrong. His prior dealings with the Khan had taught him that the will of a Hazara boy would never conquer the edicts of a prince.

The Black Khan looked to the east, where Talisman forces had charged the gate, their attack all the more frenzied for having witnessed the unleashing of Al Mintaka. They would wreak what damage they could before the Black Khan struck again.

Wafa rubbed his chest.

"Think." He pointed behind the Black Khan to the place where Arsalan lay bleeding out the last traces of his life. "You swore an oath to the One in exchange for a blessing."

Rukh's eyes sharpened. They switched between Arsalan and the boy.

He indicated the scope of destruction to the south.

"I act to defend my people."

Tears appeared at the edges of the boy's long silky lashes. He shook his head. "There are other ways to hold your city. You soak your empire in blood when some are constrained, and others were conscripted to this war. How can one without mercy expect to be *granted* mercy?"

The corners of his trembling mouth eased down as he turned to the Emissary Gate.

"Make your choice, Prince of Khorasan. And make your peace with the outcome you begged the One to prevent."

How dare the boy presume to judge Rukh's choices or his actions?

But his head turned back, his dark gaze lingered on Arsalan's body, then moved to the Assassin, whose ministrations continued, as if there was the faintest hope.

Turning back to the boy, he made another vow. "If Arsalan dies, I will use Al Mintaka to raze the lands of the south. Not a single soul will survive."

"Think," Wafa repeated, ignoring Rukh's threat. "Think about who you kill. We are them, and they are us—our lives of equal merit. So, too, our dreams. In this, we are one people."

Wafa's eyes watered, and Rukh remembered that the boy's

people heralded from the southern territories, from lands the Talisman had cleansed.

Cleansed.

A terrible word. Better to say they had laid waste. As he had done beyond his walls.

A sick taste filled his mouth. He would be guilty of the same crimes as his pitiless enemies, wreaking the same cruelties with as little regard for life.

Ashfall is the glory of an age. Be worthy of it, my Prince.

He dug his knuckles into his temples, enraged by Arsalan's voice, enraged that Arsalan would expect better of him than this.

Make your peace with the outcome you begged the One to prevent.

He couldn't. He *couldn't.*

His gaze drifted back to Arsalan, studied the shallow rise and fall of his chest, grief etched on the faces of the Zhayedan who guarded their commander.

Arsalan's link to life was so delicate. Yet still the Talisman came on.

Did it—*could* Arsalan's survival depend on Rukh's choice now?

The other Mages had determined the fate of the west; the rest had been left to Rukh.

Tilting the axis of the sphere-ring, he took hold of Wafa, gazing into the boy's magnetic eyes. He felt the boy tremble, and made an effort to gentle his hold, speaking his name for the first time since he had met him.

"I choose the straight path, Wafa. Tell me what I must do."

52

HER RAGE WAS NOT ENOUGH. INSTEAD OF THE PURITY ARIAN HAD hoped for, her fury clouded thoughts that were overwhelmed by sorrow. The One-Eyed Preacher knew it, his wiry form seated atop the rukh, his sinews taut with sinister grace. Beneath a woolen hood was the face of a much older man, his hair white, his skull graven, his skin creased with lines of age, but his eyes burning, *burning*, the stone eye with a white fire, the eye of murky brown an abyss inviting her to fall within to her own destruction.

He struck the tower of the Citadel hard. The firebird lashed its walls with its tongue. The glazed turquoise of their tiles shattered into pieces that the Preacher transformed into projectiles. Arian deflected thousands of the tiny, sharp edges with constant use of the Claim. Her actions were defensive. She couldn't gather herself to attack.

He was inside her mind. Weakening her, doubting her, taunting her.

She thought of the Companions who had fallen, of the novices and the Hazara, of the Citadel Guard turned against the heart of their mission, and she remembered Ilea's pitiless betrayal. Her rage flamed to life again, but it brought with it no sense of how her use of the Claim might defeat the One-Eyed Preacher.

The spiked edge of the firebird's tongue missed her throat by inches. She dashed away from the window. The Preacher uttered a word. His stone eye pierced the tower. The roof above Arian's head came down, blocks of stone crashing down into the courtyard. She flung herself against the rounded wall, her arms braced above her head. Bits of stone rang against her circlets. When the collapse of the upper level was complete, she could see through an opening where there had once been a door. The Council Chamber and the All Ways had been spared.

All that was left of the platform she stood upon was a thin ring of wooden joists, molded to the perimeter. She balanced on it, her face and arms covered with dust, her hair thick with soot and smoke, her armor rent in so many places that she could have peeled it off with one hand.

The firebird circled the tower, then the Preacher brought it to bay. He faced Arian across the jagged crenellations formed by the firebird's tongue.

This close, she could see that the rukh's throat and upper body were covered with crimson-colored scales. Its wings were supported by membranes that gleamed like the first rays of dawn dappling a lake in the mountains, while on the upper surface, crimson feathers sprouted.

The reflective surface of the rukh's eyes was split by the thin black line of its pupils, blinking reptilian and quick. Yet Arian sensed no malice in the actions of the creature: it functioned on animal instinct, the crimson plumes on its head swaying in the direction of the One-Eyed Preacher's commands.

Its long, sharp-toothed jaws opened to issue a fire-strike. She knew she couldn't evade it: it would burn her to ash where she stood. Her eyes caught the One-Eyed Preacher's, glinting with triumph, certain of his victory. But beneath this, she perceived something more. He wanted to destroy her, but not here. And as she looked back through the opening he had gouged into her mind, she aimed her own consciousness like a chisel. She found the Preacher's nest, the location that had evaded the Council of Hira, evaded Lania's Augury, and escaped even the knowledge of her brother, the Assassin.

The secret of his hiding place was hers.

A snowy fastness in the sky-piercing mountains far to the east of Candour. Steeped in the silence of clouds, the peaks shrouded in winter storms, a hollow carved from siltstone and shale by the weight and misery of time. Opaque and impenetrable, guarded by jewel-winged rukhs.

He wanted her away from her own ground, away from the Citadel that had been her solace and shelter, but she wouldn't let him take her from Hira.

She wouldn't let him destroy her home—the home of the Companions.

She wove a spell of confusion with the Claim. The rukh closed its jaws and dipped its head, jerking its invisible leash.

With a word, the Preacher subdued its restlessness. His stone eye pierced Arian's skull.

"Do you believe you can defeat me, First Oralist? Your Citadel is in ruins, your Council decimated." He tracked the firebird's work, lighting up a path of destruction for Arian to follow. So many bodies, so much loss, and she dared not think of the loss of Psalm or the fate of the archives. The Preacher *meant* to dishearten her, so she turned her face away.

As long as the Preacher was mounted on the rukh, the contest was unequal.

A cry of fury from the wall adjacent to the tower. A blood-strike up at the rukh that the Preacher deflected without turning his attention from Arian.

"Ah." A hot wind blew against Arian's skin, the bated breath of the rukh. "You are thinking of the scriptorium. You worry over the fate of the archives."

He nudged the firebird's jaw. "Do not mire yourself in doubt, First Oralist. Know that I do not intend to spare any part of your Citadel."

The rukh's jaw angled down toward the door to the scriptorium.

Arian screamed a name.

In a desperate gamble, her arm reached out to Lania.

Lania's head came up. She reached back. And then the Claim made the distance immaterial. Whether it was Arian's power or Lania's that had brought the change about, or the pull of the All Ways responding to the Citadel's need, Arian was no longer alone at the perilous heights of the tower. She held fast to Lania's hand.

"Interesting." The Preacher's eyes drifted to Lania. "She abandoned you, never cared for you except to envy you, never sought you out except to harm you, yet you call her to stand at your side. Your trust in the Black Khanum is misplaced. A gift steeped in blood cannot avail you now, if indeed, it ever could."

Lania looked stricken by the name the One-Eyed Preacher had given her, but Arian didn't believe him. She could feel the resurgence of the Claim, feel its ascendant truths rippling in waves through her veins.

Guided by instinct, she used her free hand to rip the circlet from her opposite arm. Then, with immovable conviction, she fastened it to Lania's arm.

The rukh opened its mouth. Its tongue lolled between its teeth.

The sisters stood with their hands linked, the circlets aimed at the sky.

A bolt of flame speared from the firebird's mouth just as the Claim issued forth in a synchrony between the two sisters, two daughters who had learned the art of recitation from parents whose final rest the Preacher had wittingly disturbed.

The verse of the Claim blazed from their throats, a repudiation of the Preacher's judgment of Lania, his judgment of what she and Lania were destined to be to each other.

"And as for those who henceforth come to believe, who adopt exile and struggle together with you, these, too, shall belong to you—they are of you. And those who are kindred by blood have the highest claim on one another in accordance with the One's decree. Verily, the One has full knowledge of everything."

The Claim became a material reality, a solid shield against a wall of flame. The fire blazed, the sisters' shield held, their hair stirred by the flame-winds erupting from the rukh.

Again and again, the verse spilled from their lips, and with each new retelling, the bond between the sisters solidified. It became a thing impregnable, their voices indistinguishable, their cadences robust. There was passionate wrath in their recitation, the ferocious desire for justice, for wounds to be accounted for and reckoning delivered, words hot and pointed, rich and raw, manifold in meaning, strong enough to tilt the axis of the earth, but beneath all this there was more. There was love. The love of a lifetime's isolation, the sorrowful love of separation, the grim comprehension of harm done, of shared griefs and the darkness of self-doubt, stripped away by older memories of days beneath the roof of Inkwell, when the promise of their future was unlimited, and their duty to Hira a pleasure so deep that it underlined every thought.

The light upon light vision flickered in Arian's eyes, the meaning of it decanted into her mind during her ascent, where it had fluttered at the edge of perception. It came to her in full now: the light of knowledge upon a receptive mind, the light of love on a susceptible heart.

They had loved each other then, they loved each other now, and the power of that love was their resistance, the shield that held, assuring the safety of the archives.

The Preacher couldn't win at this. He learned it to his cost, leashing the fury of the rukh. He pulled away to reconsider, his stone eye turning inward, then flashing to the scriptorium.

He came to a decision. And through that opening he preserved inside Arian's mind, she knew what he intended to do, how he intended to win. By isolating her in his mountain retreat, then returning to burn down the archives, and the Council of Hira with it.

With that realization, Arian understood what use she could make of the secrets revealed by the Miraj Nameh, the book Sinnia had been shown upon the Israa e Miraj. In a single moment she comprehended the disparate parts of the Ascension. Hers. Daniyar's. Sinnia's.

Beneath her impassioned recitation, she murmured her thoughts to Lania.

Lania murmured back, "Divided we fall, sister."

Arian gripped her sister's hand tighter. "Have faith, Lania. Share my faith in you."

The Preacher's stone eye fixed on Arian. He wove one arm in a circle.

Easing from the recitation that redoubled the sisters' power, Arian put a question to this man who had founded the Age of Jahiliya.

"You preached the law of the Assimilate and thus claim the title of Preacher. But are you in truth the Dajjal?"

The movement of his arm stilled. His mouth firmed, his expression became grim. Fanatical truths raged behind his eyes. His lips parted to speak abomination.

"I am the herald of your death. I am the end of the world."

A rope formed of gold particles flew through the air to settle around Arian's shoulders. She glanced back once to make certain that Lania had followed her instructions. Her sister was where she had asked her to be, holding their shield high before the door to the scriptorium.

The Preacher tugged at the rope, returning her focus to him.

Arian turned the pages of the Miraj Nameh in her mind, gathering purpose from her breakthrough: the Citadel was not her only ground.

She was yanked from her feet, pulled to the rukh by the Preacher's powerful spell, designed to deliver her to his mountain retreat. But she was not powerless, and she was not his pawn. His claims were spurious; she did not intend to submit.

She touched the rope that constrained her, subverting its purpose with a murmur of the Claim. Though the verse she'd chosen was meant to deter the Preacher, she offered it to remind herself of the strength of the Companions.

"Hold fast to the rope of the One, all of you together, and do not be divided among yourselves—remember the One's favor upon you."

She reassured herself with the truths she had gained on Ascension. "The One's favor cannot be upon a man who claims to herald the end of the world. I—and all the Companions—are graced by the One's favor. I need only hold fast to the rope."

She fought the Preacher's hold, struggled against his lariat, murmuring the verse all the while, keeping the Throne-verse in reserve. But her belief was enough. The golden particles thickened and condensed, and ultimately transformed. Arian tugged the rope free. She tested its resilience between her hands. The strength of the woven fibers would serve her purpose well.

The Claim escaped from her throat in the climbing notes of a whistle, conveying a gentle command. The rush of a thousand beating wings, an earnest chorus of prayers. Her destination etched in delicate calligraphy above the arches of her brows.

The Buraq. The Blind Dome. The Bladebone.

She called her mount from the skies.

When the Buraq descended, Arian used the rope as a bridle, ignoring the Preacher's fury at how she had undone his spell. Let him learn the bitter lesson of her uncorrupted gifts.

Mounted on the Buraq, she surveyed the destruction to the Citadel. And she whispered a final entreaty through her bond with the Silver Mage.

53

Holding the Preacher at bay with her invocations of the Claim, Arian sat astride Safanad. The elegant mare, the mother of the khamsa, was graced with the gift of wings and the dazzling conformation of the steed of the Israa e Miraj.

For a passing moment, Arian had thought to use the portal of the All Ways to escape capture by the Preacher, perhaps by returning to Ashfall to regroup. But she knew the Buraq's course; she knew its destination. The Preacher chased her through the skies to the heart of the Noble Sanctuary, alighting beneath the black dome.

The Buraq's giant wings glittered white and gold in the down sweep, its articulated hooves touching down like a whisper, the wings folding away to allow for Arian's descent. The bridle fell away. Her mount moved off to a distant corner of the courtyard, a creature of a dimension beyond the veil, grazing for pasture in the same manner as a mare.

Arian felt Daniyar's absence. They had last approached the sanctuary together. Now in his place was this man whose teachings had strangled joy, whose creed of life favored death.

The Preacher's command had sent the rukh to the skies, where it circled the dome.

He approached her in the guise of the warrior from Candour, young and handsome, resolved to bring her resistance to an end.

Arian positioned herself between the two domes, close enough to the Dome of the Chain that she could reach out and touch one of its pillars, yet far enough that she could angle her head to the sky while keeping the domes within view.

His voice lulling her, the Preacher asked, "Do you think you are safe from me here?"

"Blood cannot be spilled within the Noble Sanctuary."

"Is that why you brought me here? You think me a slave to the bloodrites? You think your blood will empower me?" A dismissive snap of his fingers. "Why would I need your blood, when I am master of the Bloodprint?"

He murmured a verse of the Claim, this time unocculted. Its truth sank into Arian's bones.

He spread his hands before him, the movement liquid dark. A moment later, the sacred text of the Bloodprint rested upon his palms. Tears started to Arian's eyes, summoned by its holy presence. She brushed them aside, focused on her task.

She glanced up at the dome, spread her own palms wide, and uttered, "Israa e Miraj."

The thin gold plates of the Sana Codex shimmered between her palms.

The Preacher frowned, no trace of wonder on his smooth-skinned brow. "I have the manuscript entire."

Arian blew a prayer over the Sana Codex. "I have the truth at its heart."

The Preacher sneered at her, a stain upon his handsome features. Arian sensed the truth of the proverb that dark deeds left their mark on the appearance. The Preacher's face was cruel with the agonies he had inflicted. He deepened his voice, calling out verses from the text. They took the shape of solid planks, striking at the air around her skull, pushing against her body, trying to shift her position by attempting to cage her.

The place she had grounded herself mattered.

But the Preacher didn't know why.

The pages of the Codex fluttered between her palms. She offered a verse that repelled the Preacher's attack without pushing him away.

He responded with other verses, darkened and twisted by his voice, anointing her with a sky painted in blood, with fire and wind, with piercing ice and rain. To all this she responded with quiet reliance upon her skills as First Oralist.

When he'd run out of means by which to manipulate the Claim, Arian removed her hands from beneath the Sana Codex. The collection of holy fragments hung suspended on the air.

He copied the gesture, setting the Bloodprint aside.

"I told you. You cannot kill me with the Claim when I am a daughter of the Claim."

His firm, full lips parted over his teeth. "Nor can you kill *me*, when I am a scholar of the Claim. No matter your use of the Codex."

Her brows drew together as she tested his assertion for truth. When she found it, she considered the rest of his words.

"Then you recognize the Codex?"

"I am no novice."

But his prideful assertions would be his undoing.

"Yet you show no reverence in its presence. When I was permitted to read the Sana Codex, I felt as though I'd been reborn."

She surprised him into laughter, a rough and unfamiliar sound.

"How were you in your witlessness granted the honor of Ascension?"

"How were *you* in your wisdom denied?"

His hand bunched into a fist. She felt the pressure on her throat. She raised a hand to delay him. In all seriousness, she asked him, "I have questions, Preacher. Will you hear them before the end?"

The Preacher pointed one finger at the suspended Codex.

With the utterance of a word, the fragile collection burned. The golden plates came loose. Sheaves of parchment became embers that smoldered into ash at her feet.

Tears rolled down Arian's cheeks. She glanced once at the Bloodprint, then back at the black lead dome, as though waiting for a sign of deliverance.

"Why do you fear me, Preacher?"

He let his jaw hang loose. Hornets poured from his mouth. They swarmed around her head, striking the shield that kept her safe. To the stinging haze, she spoke the word *rest,* and the swarm diverted its path. Arian returned to her questions.

"How have you lived this long? Was it not you who founded the Age of Ignorance?"

This time he obliged her. "Strange questions for one upon the eve of her death." He circled her with care, anticipating a strike. Her head tilted so her eyes could follow him. "My gift is akin to that of the Mages of Khorasan. It is bequeathed from one generation to the next."

Her body went solid in shock. "Are you claiming to bear a trust like the Mages, Preacher? The Mages are sworn to protect, to guide and aid their people in the most desperate of times."

He slipped in front of Arian, blocking her access to the Bloodprint. He was close enough to touch her now. He raised his hand to her throat: the way he moved wasn't natural, his limbs sinuous, his fingers longer than they appeared, floating, fluid, controlled by some external source or made over by his acts of sorcery. He snatched back his hand, repelled by the concentrated power of her shield.

His eyes bored into hers, but he took two steps back.

"I was given the same charge by my mentor. To guide a faltering people onto a righteous path. A path of purity undefiled by your Council's innovations. My task as a Preacher of the law was to cleanse these lands of corruption."

Arian held his gaze. He had offered words she was able to dispute.

"And where do women fall within this 'cleansing'?"

"Women are the essence of corruption. Exiling them from the public sphere restored to us a measure of peace. Just look at you"—his gaze raked her arms, her uncovered hair—"you and your sisters deem yourselves above the law."

"*Whose* law?" A quiet question—she was listening for another sound.

"The law of the One. The law given voice by the Claim."

Arian extended a finger beyond her shield, the forefinger of her right hand. She upheld it in the shahadah. The raised finger testifying to the oneness of the One.

"Do you know the will of the One? Do you grasp the immensity of the Claim? How could you? You pillage these lands to burn the written word, you murder scribes and scholars to prevent a reading of the Claim that would denounce your slave trade."

He sheathed his voice in ice. "Women abuse freedom. Just as your Council does. Or I should say, as it *did*."

Arian examined the face of the man who'd rescued two girls from the vicious abuse of a warlord. "How could you have been a hero of our people?" She imbued her next words with the Claim.

"Freedom isn't a gift to be granted by a tyrant. It inures to the people of the Claim, it belongs to them by right. Those who would deny it should know the virtue of resistance."

"Heresy!"

"Tell that to the girls you rescued from Lashkar. You honored their innocence, restored their dignity. *You were part of the resistance*. What happened to you?"

His guise shifted, the young man's handsomeness replaced by the hollow skull with the stone eye that sought to negate her conviction. His spittle fell against her shield.

"I was Claimed." The burning intensity of the stone eye began to drill into her shield. There was still no sound from the dome.

"You were *claimed*." A firm rebuttal. "Corrupted by a mentor skilled in dark arts, to misdirect and misread, to sow the very corruption you sought to erase from the land. A weak mind dazzled by power, failing to question its source. You who took arms against cruelty allowed yourself to fall into its trap: you became a slave to it."

Rage rose in the Preacher's face, his eyes flashing crimson. "I guard the women of this land from the savagery of men's impulses, though they do not thank me. Their foolishness prevents them from seeing the wisdom intended to protect them."

"Then women are naive and men are creatures governed by their basest urges."

"Yes!" A crimson corona formed around the pupils of his eyes.

"And what of those women held in hallowed bonds? And the men who honor those bonds? Are they not garments for each other? Sources of each other's solace and protection?"

"YOU CANNOT TEACH ME THE CLAIM! I AM THE MASTER OF THE CLAIM! I AM THE ONE'S ALLY! I AM AKIN TO THE ONE!"

He used the force to pulverize mountains; it seeped through the cracks of her shield, tore at the veil of her certainty.

He seized his advantage, inflicting an image on her mind: the burning of the Sana Codex, the truths that had opened her heart, the sweetness of being made and unmade in the words of a holy fire. She felt her grief rise, felt the sway of bitterness, and blinked it away, telling him, "You may be the embodiment of myth, but if *you* are a prophet of the Claim, how far from glory we have fallen."

He raised strong arms, submerging her in his animus. She retreated a step, using her cloak as a second layer to her shield.

Scornful phrases poured down on her head.

"As if *you* are worthy of prophethood. One so broken and sullied. You decry the arts of womanhood, your mind greedy for war, your form weak and malnourished. I have never seen you dressed in other than blood and dirt, the marks of your true calling."

He had never seen her at all.

But underlined by sorcery, the words hammered at her shield. She struggled to respond. "You created the famine, yet hold me to account for sharing in the misery of my people?"

"Khorasan is *mine*! Its people are *mine*! The witches of Hira claim a dominion that was never theirs."

"You dare to slander the First Oralist of Hira with your foul allegations?"

Verses of the Claim fell from her lips like waves that would never reach the shore, tumbling over the Preacher's skull to drown him in her wrath. Rage rose to the surface of her mind in a tumult of self-righteousness, the Claim growing fetid and dark, twisting its tendrils along her tongue, until she was intoxicated by the naked expansion of her gift, seeing herself as a queen, an empress, an angel of retribution who would one day remake the world.

No one could stand in her way. Not this Preacher whose lust for power had kept him at the Claim's periphery. This man *was* a deceiver. He deceived even himself, whereas Arian was the chosen of the One, anointed by the power of the Claim.

Glorious, glorious power.

She could never be defeated. She could rip a man's innards from his ribs. She could bring empires to their knees. She could hold Khorasan's fate in her palm, making it over in her image. She could do all this and more, she *would*.

She would reign all in all, First Oralist of Hira and High Companion both, dispatching every enemy, destroying any threat to her supremacy.

This was the Claim in her hands.

This was the Claim on her tongue.

Monumental, magnificent power.

She would turn the Preacher inside out.

But there was a sudden queasiness beneath her ribs. The walls of her heart collapsing, her arteries constricted. Bile rose to her tongue, acrimony to her thoughts. A sense of condemnation pierced her through and through.

What will the Claim be in your hands?

What will the Claim be on your tongue?

You were chosen to ascend.

Ah, by the glory of the One. She was meant to be a conduit, a student to show other students the way, the glory that accrued to her a privilege and trust.

Her lust for power was quenched, the memory of the Ascension restoring her sense of balance.

She had always had a choice.

She would always have the choice of deciding which lessons to derive from the Claim. She wasn't arrogant enough to assert a perfect understanding, or to believe herself the source of an infinite wisdom. But her actions would be judged by her intentions, and she wasn't the mirror of the Preacher. So she would find another way.

When she relented, the Preacher hit back hard. "You are a child bereft of family. The sisters of your Council refused to lend you their aid, so you struck against the slave-chains alone. The head of your order banished you from Hira, and the man you forswore your sisterhood for left you for the pleasure of fighting a foreign war. What are you but forsaken? Who are you to call yourself First Oralist? Your claims disgrace a noble rank."

Her rage fell away. His accusations were absurd, but she absorbed the power of his words and struggled to sort the truth from lies that could destroy her. She had come to the Noble Sanctuary to face herself, just as she'd done upon Ascension.

She let the Preacher's vitriol sing through the fibers of her body, pierce through the secrets she kept from herself, wear at the edges of her spirit. She let it fill her, as he wove his incantations to batter away at her shield.

He wanted her raw and exposed. He wanted her stripped to the bone.

So she looked within and searched for what was hidden away at her core. She was pulled into a memory of the Ascension, where she had stood within the limits of a pillar of golden light. During the Ascension, she had held the Sana Codex in her hands, as knowledge and compassion poured through her mind to reframe her image of herself.

The Preacher's words pushed up against the edges of that understanding, insidious and seeking to intrude. But the pages of the Sana Codex turned. The Claim sang out its truth, purified her thoughts, set aside her worries, gilding her senses with power.

A power she had earned because she used it with compassion. A power she hadn't asked for, but could not choose to forsake.

"You think to slight me when you speak of my trials as a daughter of the Claim. But there have been many sons and daughters of the Claim, many who have borne greater trials than I. Did you think I would not be tested when I wear the mantle of First Oralist? When I have bound myself with the benedictions of the One?"

She indicated the circlet she wore on her right arm. And then she let her shield fall, aiming her hand at the black lead dome. Shedding layers of history, paring back centuries of ignorance, her fingers worked the magic of the Claim, and as the Preacher turned to watch, she stripped the lead from the dome that loomed over the Noble Sanctuary.

The light upon light vision returned to her in full force.

The dome caught fire atop its drum. It drew the crimson poison from the clouds, leaving the sky unblemished. Against the serenity of unblighted blue, the Dome of the Noble Sanctuary called the faithful to worship, no longer unintelligible and blind.

The Blind Dome. But the name was only an approximation of the truth.

The *blinding* dome, a luminous, golden arc against the heavens.

Elegant script crept across turquoise tiles, a pattern tracing the octagonal drum beneath a celestial circumference.

"Read," she told the Preacher. "Read the truths of the Noble Sanctuary."

She curled her hand, forcing his head to turn, forcing his eyes to the unmistakable tracings of calligraphy.

The Preacher obeyed, the words a stiff whisper through teeth clenched against knowledge. And what he read in a rising rhythm was the foremost truth of the dome.

"There is no one but the One. The One has no partners in one-ness. The One is One."

Again and again, in infinite variation, confirming the central belief of the people of the Claim.

There is no one but the One.

"You think women weak?" She flexed her hands. "The interior verses of the dome honor the mother of the Esayin, the noblest of all women."

Myth. Legend. History. Love.

She sketched the interior verses on the wind, forcing him to read, reading them herself, just as she had read them on the tower of the Golden Finger, with Wafa and Sinnia, so long ago.

A moment of insight into why the Custodian of the Noble Sanctuary had been drawn from the ranks of the Esayin: a guardian of his own trust, a brother to her in faith.

The Preacher fought her insistence.

"*No.* These verses repudiate the Esayin's theology assigning partners to the One."

Warmth glimmered in Arian's eyes. "Then you *know* your claims are spurious."

She had trapped him, and his ire spiked in response.

"This is witchery! You practice witchery!"

"Does your hatred of women run so deep that you would deny the Adhraa?" She drove the words through his skull. "You call yourself master of the Claim, yet you couldn't erase the name of the mother of the Esayin. Not at the minaret of the Golden Finger, nor here at the Noble Sanctuary. What the One has wrought can-not be undone by your distortions of the Claim."

He whirled away from her, the folds of his cloak flaring around his rigid frame. A shrill whistle pierced the air. The rukh descended from the sky, called by its master's command, talons and wings extended, brindled jaws agape.

"Burn her!"

The rukh's narrow skull jerked in the direction of the dome, its feathered plumes aquiver in agitation.

"BURN HER!"

The rukh's head jerked back, its pupils dazed as its flat eyes flicked to Arian. Its speckled jaws parted, its mandible loose, a gelatinous coating of saliva spilling down the length of its throat. In the explosive light of the dome, its scales shone crimson and gold. The size of the firebird was such that Arian staggered back from the force of its breath.

And still the rukh resisted the One-Eyed Preacher's command.

The Preacher closed his hand, and a mournful cry filled the courtyard. The cry stabbed the air with thorny spikes, the sound of the creature's pain so immense that Arian could not bear it. She struck the Preacher hard with the Claim. His magic released the rukh.

In the ensuing silence, she heard the grating of wood against stone, and then against the measure of the earth. She'd been waiting for that sound ever since she'd arrived.

"BURN HER TO ASH!"

The Preacher no longer pretended to invoke religious authority, his ceaseless quest to dominate glaring from his single eye, while the white stone revolved in circles of acid fury.

A coaxing noise in the wake of the roar. The rukh's wings extended in a brilliant, multihued sweep. The Preacher made a fruitless bid to call down the rukh again. But another voice had spoken, had treated the rukh with respect. A voice that described the First Oralist, depicting her bond with the Claim. Responding to the voice, the rukh rose higher and higher, its wings extended in flight. It dipped its head at the ground before it vanished from view.

Arian turned to the man the rukh had chosen to acknowledge. War-ravaged and weary, the Silver Mage had come.

54

SHE COULDN'T GO TO HIM WHEN THE PREACHER STOOD BETWEEN THEM, but her heart began to beat with the same radiant pulses that blazed from a dome resplendent in its glory.

He was in the same condition she was, beaten and battered, down to his last reserves of strength. The eyes that brushed her like moonlight dull, fatigued by all he'd done, the muscular lines of his body lit by the dome's effulgence, his beauty austere, grace in his eyes though something had changed in the way he carried himself, like a man climbing the steep ridge of a mountain to stumble at the summit.

They looked at each other, clouds condensing above their heads, their hopes pulsing between them, then his lips quirked and he pulled a fold of the Sacred Cloak over his shoulder, letting it fall along his arm. A smile in her eyes, she copied him, their vows renewed in silence.

"You came," she said to him.

"Always, when you call me."

That voice, low, soft, drugging, worked its magic on her ears. Her entire body softened, impelled by the urge to move to him, to hold him and promise him safety. She was filled with a joy akin to the ascent, a concentrated fire at seeing him again.

The Preacher broke through their communion.

"There is something unusual between you. A malady of spirit."

Daniyar's face went hard. His hand went to his sword. But Arian asked, "Has no one ever loved you, Preacher, that you see love as a sickness?"

"Be quiet when men are speaking!"

His hand flicked at her throat. With her shield down, the Claim wounded her.

Her breath came out in puffs that blew away in the wind. Daniyar lunged with his sword, the movement balanced yet lacking its normal precision.

The Preacher's hands were raised. One pointed to Arian, the other was held high to pin the Silver Mage in place. A primeval silence deadened the air. None of the three moved.

The Preacher nodded at the sky. "You suborned the will of my rukh. How?"

Daniyar looked back at him, his face dangerous, the lines of his body taut, the silver sword poised to attack.

The Preacher curled his palm. Words grated from Daniyar's throat, his lips pulled back in a savage line, his eyes promising vengeance.

"I did not suborn it, nor would I. Creatures of the Claim respond to the truth. That is what I offered. You sought to bend to your will rukhs that carried prophets on their backs."

The Preacher dissected Daniyar's expression, the stone eye boring into silver. A silent battle for hegemony before the Preacher looked away.

"Truth." He sounded surprised. "This is the truth: I am master of the Claim, and all of Khorasan will yield."

Arian began to murmur, easing the grip on her throat while the Preacher was distracted, aware that at any moment he could strike down Daniyar, and his sword would not suffice to protect him. The Miraj Nameh had led her astray; by calling him, she'd placed him at risk.

Daniyar kept his attention on the Preacher, unflinching before the stone eye.

The Preacher spoke to Daniyar with a respect he'd never offered Arian.

"As Guardian of Candour, you of all men should understand my calling. For who is the master of the Claim, if not the Guardian of Khorasan?"

Daniyar's sword shifted a fraction. "You trespassed on my ground as Guardian of Candour. How can you justify your actions to the generations you robbed of childhood? And as for the women of these lands"—his black hair shifted away from the stark angles of his face—"you were no guardian to them. You delivered them into misery."

"All wars have their cost."

Her blood coursing through her veins, Arian wanted to beg Daniyar to stop. He couldn't challenge the Preacher like this, couldn't call him to account.

The Preacher lowered the hand in Daniyar's face. He was readying himself for the fatal strike. But as if he heard her warning, Daniyar pulled the Sacred Cloak around him like a shield. His long dark lashes brushed over his eyes, screening his thoughts from the Preacher.

"What was your reading of the Claim that you determined these costs?" The twin blades of his sword indicated the Bloodprint, still suspended on the air. "In a text of such compassion, where did you find such cruelty?"

"You dare!"

"I am the Lion of the One—there is nothing I would not dare."

Arian's heart soared. Daniyar's conviction was flawless. Anointed by Ascension, his power so vast and deep that her senses reeled from it.

The Preacher's hand became a claw, peeling the golden plates from the dome, peeling Daniyar's skin. Five jagged lines bled down his cheeks. As they melted into his beard, they turned the color of hammered silver.

"Ah." The Preacher nodded. His glance at Arian was sly. "The Silver Mage is Silver Mage no longer. His impoverished knowledge of the Claim dies with him as we speak."

"No!" She broke free of the Preacher's hold. She flew to Daniyar's side, weaving the protections of the Claim around him, consumed with the pleasure of being held by him, her heart beating fast against his, marveling that he could be at once so powerful and so gentle.

Though Daniyar kept his gaze on the Preacher, his body was fused to hers, promising the same shelter she had wanted to offer him. His right arm flexed as he indicated the Bloodprint.

"You are not a god I worship that your heresy should stand unchallenged. I was chosen to ascend. I know the truths of the text."

Cloud-shadow drifted over the Preacher's face, rendering it inscrutable.

"You have just woken to your task—I have carried my charge for decades." The stone eye revolved between the First Oralist and the Silver Mage. "Did you summon him here as your shield?"

"I summoned him here as my sword."

Her love for Daniyar was blinding in that moment, yet it left the Preacher unmoved.

"Even with his help, you cannot defeat me." Something that

sounded like laughter from the Preacher, but felt wretchedly perverse. "How could I carry out an attack upon your Citadel, and urge on the armies at Ashfall, while holding you here, if I hadn't memorized the Bloodprint? If I did not possess *total* mastery of the Claim?" The grating laughter again. "You think your voice can stop me, woman? This power belongs to men. It belongs to *me*."

Arian turned her face into Daniyar's chest, as if she was cowering beneath the words the Preacher considered his dominion.

In truth, she pressed her lips to Daniyar's throat and whispered, "Don't leave me, love. Not so close to the end."

The dark head dipped, and a vow of love was spoken in her ear. "Your garment until the end. Yours until the end."

"Then when I ask, give me your nearest possession."

He tilted up her chin. "My heart is already yours."

She was quivering with tension in his arms, mesmerized by his eyes. They held a trace of the teasing that had defined their days in Candour. She whispered to him in the dialect of the Damson Vale, and he listened with ruthless patience. He'd given Arian his ring; now he would yield everything else.

She stalked back to her previous position, her recitation pristine. The Bloodprint landed on her palms, a large, unwieldy manuscript whose weight she contained with the Claim.

She took a step back, leaving the book suspended, forcing the Preacher to follow her.

She could not deny the Preacher's claims. The power he commanded was immense, it had brought Khorasan to ruin, it had pulled the people of the Claim along a path of deviation. To use the Claim's own lexicon, it had sown corruption in the land.

And the Preacher had taught his people to be unjust to themselves.

His scholarship, his immersion in the Claim, had enabled these actions, had allowed him to prosecute his wars. But his hatred of women she *could* answer, and that would answer the rest.

"You have long sought to separate that which is indivisible, women from men, men from women, when from birth to death we are partnered by the majesty of the One, and by the teachings of the Claim."

Her eyes brushed Daniyar's face like the fall of summer rain.

"Sacrilege! That a Companion of Hira should betray her vows is sacrilege."

Arian's smile was cold. "You either believe in Hira or you don't. And if you do, you should know that Hira has granted me dispensation. I am *bound* to the Silver Mage."

A jolt of surprise from Daniyar. She hadn't told him, hadn't had time to tell him.

Roaring his outrage, the Preacher aimed his claws at Daniyar, but this time Arian's recitation turned the Preacher's hand against his own face, just as she had once pushed the swords of the Ahdath into their own breasts.

His thin, strong fingers poked out his stone eye. It rolled from the hollows of his skull to come to a rest beneath the mihrab of the Dome of the Chain. He stared at her in shock, wrenched by the capacity of the power she had contained.

She murmured to the book. Its pages fluttered in the wind. When the page she wanted settled open, she rested her palm on the bloodstain that had given the manuscript its name. She was shaken by tremors of grief, but the grief renewed her perseverance.

"You spoke of blood because blood is what you seek and pain is what you rejoice in." Her scorn found its echo in the Claim. "How could a master of the Claim not know the name of this book as the Criterion? You gave it a lesser name to anoint our people in blood."

His heresy was confirmed when he stood unmoved by the truths of the Ascension.

"I know the law. Your tawdry skills will never suffice to subvert it. Men will always enjoy a degree of advantage over women."

And indeed the history of the Claim gave weight to his counterattack.

Arian steadied herself, fought down the impulse to fury.

"*Your* law." She shook her head in pity. "Not *the* law. Your law erased the women of Khorasan because you lacked the courage to meet us on equal ground. Your cowardice is contemptible. Your fear of women is contemptible."

He swallowed the Claim in his mouth. The stone eye spun on the ground. The seeing eye was tainted with blood, blood enough to drown the world. She knew what would come next, the thought followed by his actions.

A yawning chasm cracked the ground beneath her feet, running the length of the sanctuary, she and Daniyar on opposite sides. She stayed in position next to the Dome of the Chain. The wild winds of a great storm roared through the peace of the courtyard, gaining in power every second, whipping at the surface of the dome, stripping the golden plates from the metal ribs that enclosed them, smashing the turquoise faience, and bringing the columns down. The fire-ravaged sky she had seen upon Ascension drowned the courtyard in a blood-rain. The ground shook with immeasurable force, the courtyard cracked from end to end, as dozens of fissures opened up. Olive trees were uprooted from their groves, the dome from the drum of its mooring. Another wild pass of the Preacher's hand, another blusterous roaring of the

Claim, and the Dome of the Noble Sanctuary was laid waste, the courtyard ravaged by hail and wind, until all that was left in the aftermath was the bare rock of the Sakhrah, and the Dome of the Chain.

The Preacher's spine curved, his body lurched forward to destroy the rest. To destroy Arian, and bring his war to a close.

"I KNOW THE LAW. I HAVE MEMORIZED THE CLAIM!"

Arian turned to Daniyar. He was holding on against the force of the raging storm, just as she was holding on, rooted in the ground of sanctuary. His black hair whipped about his face; silver tears streamed in the wind. His depthless desire to defend her burned across the chasm that had split around the rock, but with every additional surge of the One-Eyed Preacher's calumny, his body betrayed its weakness, and he fell back in retreat.

Her eyes bright with love, she said, "Give me your nearest possession."

He didn't hesitate. He threw his sword to her across the chasm, leaving himself undefended. The force of the wind pushed him back to the Sakhrah. He anchored himself against it, his breath labored in his chest, his dexterity lost.

He gave her one last gift.

"There is no sword like the Bladebone, and none like the warrior who wields it."

Arian was that warrior.

55

THE PREACHER LAUGHED, HIGH AND WILD. HIS THUNDER FILLED THE sky, blacking out the ribs of the dome, a crimson flush against clouds that bruised the twilight. Lightning burned against the sky, sharp strikes rising like the stalagmites from the depths of the Well of Souls.

"YOU THINK TO KILL ME WITH A *SWORD* WHEN I HAVE READ THE BLOODPRINT?"

Arian raised the Bladebone to the sky, pointing at the Dome of the Chain.

Daniyar shouted a warning. Lightning hit the sword. It should have struck Arian dead, but her other hand was on the blood-stained page of the book she called the Criterion.

Wind rushed at her from all directions, roaring in her ears. Hailstones battered her head and arms, the red sky ripped away, rapacious clouds circling so that a cyclone's funnel extended to the heavens. Her eyes burned with tears, her body experiencing the force of the cyclone like hammer blows to her ribs. Her knees threatened to buckle.

"Arian!" Daniyar called her again, gripping the rock with all his might. If his fingers slipped from its surface, the wind would tear him apart.

Lightning gripped the sword above her head, flickered along its length, sent its power surging down into her body. Her teeth chattered and her arm shook under the impact of the surge, but Arian stood firm. She made Daniyar a vow, begging him to believe.

"There is no sword like the Bladebone, and none like the warrior who wields it!"

The silver eyes accused her, the fury of a man who could not defend what he cherished, who could not stand as her shield as love and honor demanded.

He should be the one struck by lightning. He should be the one to burn.

Her green eyes held him at bay, her will tempering the brutal vigor of the cataclysm, her love a vow that would see them through the storm.

Daniyar dug his fingers into the rock: he had promised to trust her, not to let her sacrifice her life when his fate was already sealed. His teeth gritted, he climbed the rock, every muscle in his body straining. At the summit, he managed to gather himself to leap across the chasm.

Arian stopped him with a word. The word was his name whispered with a love that could have called down the stars. Called them down and laid them at his feet.

Her eyes were streaming with tears, but through her chattering teeth, she said, "This promise I will not break."

A second bolt of lightning crossed the first, the power that surged through her body doubled. The voltage of the bolts slid down the blades of the bifurcated sword. Energy collected in her palm. The Bladebone was jerked from her hand and flung up against the horizon. Arian raised her head to look.

The red sky had made it too dark to see, the Preacher's magic at work, so she called to the guardians who had guided her ascent. Whispers in her ears found their echo on her tongue.

"The One is the light of the heavens and the earth. The example of the One's light is like a niche that holds a lamp, the lamp within glass, the glass as if it were a pearlescent star lit from the oil of a blessed olive tree, neither of the east nor of the west, whose oil would glow even if untouched by fire. Light upon light. Guided to light are those whom the One wills."

The hailstones clattered to the ground, the Preacher's stone eye lost among them. The black and crimson clouds retreated, giving way to pale tremors of gold across a vault of gray. The cyclone winds subsided, leaving them in a silence deeper and colder than the grave.

The lightning-sword of the Bladebone had called something down from the sky.

Glittering links of silver-white hung suspended between Arian and the Preacher, anchored by the Dome of the Chain.

Arian's fingers brushed the chain. She swung toward the Preacher. He tried to grasp it, but the chain evaded his grip. It swung back toward Arian, who caught it and held it firm, her thoughts, her soul, her very breath, surrendered in submission to the One.

And in that ephemeral moment, submission felt like joy, surrender like sweet victory.

Without calling on the Claim, she said, "You read, but you did not comprehend."

The Preacher's eye focused on the chain. He struggled to grasp it. Arian did nothing to prevent him, releasing her grip. The chain swung before the Preacher's face, tracing the course of a pendulum arc between the curve of his shoulders.

He tried to catch it with one hand, then with both. Each time it seemed within his grasp, it slipped away. Arian pulled it to herself, seeing now what the Preacher was, a shade of trickery and lies, his hypocrisy so complete that he'd made of the Claim a system of injustice. A man so hollow that the scourging of Khorasan and the murder of thousands could not fill the emptiness or satisfy what passed for his conscience.

"What witchery is this?" The words were thick between his teeth.

Arian caught the chain again. She nodded at the miniature dome. "The chain hangs here in judgment, suspended between the heavens and the earth. It hangs for one purpose."

The Preacher viewed her with suspicion. "And what is that?"

"To resolve points of dispute between the just and unjust." Her voice became gentle, but the gentleness was not for the One-Eyed Preacher: it was for the legions who followed him, seeking to learn their faith from the man who'd corrupted it, sowing tragedy in place of the guidance they had sought.

A critical faculty, to reason for oneself in the face of fanaticism; a calamity to renounce ethics in the name of unreasoning obedience.

The people of the Claim had fallen far, but the Preacher had plotted that fall. And then he had passed it into law.

She swung the chain back at the Preacher.

"An honorable man may grasp the chain. One whose reading of the Criterion is false will not be able to seize it, as there is no graver injustice than to falsify the Claim."

"Lies." The chain eluded him again.

"You don't believe me?"

Daniyar, the Authenticate, spoke from the summit of the Sakhrah. "The First Oralist tells you the truth."

Keeping hold of the chain, Arian took the Preacher's hand in her own. She twined the chain around their wrists.

His single eye seared her with contempt.

The column of his throat worked. He battled to hurt her with the Claim. His words were a soundless cry, without vigor or effect.

She reached for his other hand and looped the chain around it. Then she freed her hands from beneath his, leaving him clinging to the chain, a mortal man stripped of his mystery and, here in the Noble Sanctuary, of his mastery, as well.

For long moments, nothing changed. The Preacher's lips began to curl.

Arian stripped off her remaining circlet. She whispered the words that graced it.

In the name of the One, the Merciful, the Compassionate.

She reached across the chasm to Daniyar. The sanctuary shriveled and shrank, collapsing the distance between them. Reading her eyes, he took hold of one side of her circlet and pulled her across the gap onto the rock, tucking her into his side.

Watching them, the Preacher tried to free himself, but nothing he attempted allowed him to shake free of the chain. He cursed at her, calling on the power of the Claim, using occulted verses, saliva leaking from his lips, his eye blood-thickened and opaque.

The chain fused to his skin. It sang with electricity. In moments, it had seared the flesh from his wrists, peeled the sinews from his bones, sapped the blood from his veins. A terrifying clamor split the sky. The Preacher's forearms began to char. His shrieks became unhallowed, darkening a holy space.

"No!"

Arian couldn't watch any longer. She found herself roused to sympathy, though her purpose remained firm. She reached above

Ausma Zehanat Khan

the Preacher for the chain. It slipped from its point of suspension; the links rippled down through her fingers. She flung the chain upward with a fierce gesture; the silver sword returned to her hand.

The Preacher raised his ruined arms to defend his bloodied eye.

Arian looked at him with pity. *"You read, but you did not comprehend."*

She plunged the sword into his bloodless chest.

His mouth hollowed, his cheekbones sank. The image of the young warrior who had fought the warlord of Lashkar hung over his skull, a brief instant of hope before the hollow-eyed skull swallowed all trace of who he might have been when his path had diverged.

His lips formed a soundless word. He cursed her with his last breath.

Then his skeletal frame burned before her eyes, and his ashes scattered to the winds.

56

ARIAN STAGGERED UNDER THE IMPACT OF HIS DEATH. THE DOME OF THE Chain fell into the chasm, absorbed into a churning earth, the earthquake unmaking the world, until all that remained to hold on to was the rock of the Ascension. Then that, too, was swallowed. Together, she and Daniyar fell down to the Well of Souls, bathed in precarious silence, locked in each other's arms. She buried her face in his chest, thinking of all she'd been granted—the Buraq, the Blind Dome, the Bladebone—humbled to her soul by a whisper.

You were chosen to ascend.

Her Audacy accomplished at the end.

57

Silence in the Naqsh-e Jahan, the kind Rukh had never heard before, as if the world was being born, the city steeped in quiet over untold centuries of peace. A flame-edged twilight descended on the square, the day having run its course, the star-veils flaring against the city walls.

Beyond his walls: desolation, the plains and salt lake burning, the sands rising and shifting under the burden of blood. This was neither victory nor triumph, the numberless dead lost among those who had thrown down their weapons and sat with their heads in their hands, wondering why they had come to Ashfall, and what they had thought to gain.

In the square, Talisman and Nineteen mingled in disarray, the will of the Preacher undone. Their confusion was the enemy of zeal, of the fervor that had gripped them.

With the enemy's passion for war broken, the Zhayedan would have been merciless. Wafa had not allowed it. The boy with the most reason to despise the Talisman had asked the Black Khan a simple question: How could one without mercy expect to be granted the same? His humility had transmuted the power of Al

Mintaka, had altered the traction of the beam. With the sphere-ring, Al Mintaka's power had been diffused into thousands of tiny sparks that separated combatants from one another, a hushed moment of truce in a day of frenzied killing. His captains—Khashayar, Shayan, Niyal, Zishaan—tallied their losses in commiseration. Teerandaz archers slumped against the walls.

At some point before the truce, the Silver Mage had fought his way to the Qaysarieh Portal, urging the other Mages to let him go. He'd given no explanation, and perhaps none was needed, because that moment of truce had extended: peace had come to Ashfall in the end.

To what was left of Ashfall.

Under Khashayar's direction, and with the help of the Talisman under Rukh's protection, Zhayedan were putting out fires along the walls. The southern wall was gone, the city's gates had fallen, the Maiden Tower and the Tower of the Mirage were two smoldering columns of ruin. The white stone that had dazzled the eye from miles around was pitted by the impact of projectiles, broken through in places, dulled to a dreary gray in a canvas of smoke and blood.

The square below had fared even worse. The delicate pathways had been smashed by mortar and stone, arbors of roses torn down and burned, aisles of trees uprooted, the fountains shattered, with three sides of the great capital in ruins. The war room, the armory, and the barracks were gone; Qaysarieh's magnificent pishtaq had crumbled between its minarets; and the Illustrious Portal was broken and defaced, its roof listing in the wind, one wing of the palace ransacked, the priceless scriptorium destroyed.

And in the square and along the walls, the bodies of Zhayedan were piled alongside Talisman fighters and the blue-robed corpses of the Nineteen, their mystic numerology of no advantage to them now. The people of Ashfall were among the numberless dead. Rukh had yet to visit the palace, to see whether his family had survived, or if his court was still intact.

The scenes of blood, death, fire, and smoke were what remained of the Preacher's war of ideology, his war against the written word, and against those who had risked everything to read.

The Blue Mage pressed Rukh's shoulder. He had come to find Rukh along the wall, given him the news that Arsalan had been taken to his apartments. Alive or dead, Rukh hadn't asked, and could not bear to know, a tragedy he would hold off just a little longer, as he witnessed the end of his world.

"What will you do now that you have won?"

Rukh rubbed the back of his neck. "This doesn't seem like victory. What would you suggest?"

"Rebuild, but remain vigilant."

He felt a stab of anxiety. "The Preacher is gone."

The Blue Mage tilted his head to read the skies. His power had held the star-veils; Rukh . . . Ashfall . . . Khorasan . . . would always be in his debt.

"Yes. The First Oralist's Audacy has been fulfilled. But as for the rest, we must ask ourselves why men fall prey to cruelty. Why so many were willing to serve as the foot soldiers of a tyrant. So rebuild, Prince of Khorasan, but stay vigilant. I will remain at Ashfall until you no longer need my aid."

Rukh nodded his thanks. He considered the survivors with a narrow-eyed glance. "If enemies remain—"

"No." Wafa tugged at his cloak. Rukh looked to him, saw that his irises had changed again, turquoise and silver interwoven around his pupils.

"May I?" Wafa touched the signet ring, the armillary sphere still upraised.

Rukh's debt to the boy was even greater. He slid the ring from his finger. Wafa held it up, searching for a point among the stars. When he found it, the ring cut a sharp path through the twilight. It shone on a route through the mountains, and another through the sands to the west.

He sang out a verse of the Claim that Rukh had never known existed. It was a balm for his overwrought mind: at the crux of darkness, he felt a measure of peace.

"The One is the light of the heavens and the earth. The example of the One's light is like a niche that holds a lamp, the lamp within glass, the glass as if it were a pearlescent star lit from the oil of a blessed olive tree, neither of the east nor of the west, whose oil would glow even if untouched by fire. Light upon light. Guided to light are those whom the One wills."

To the soldiers below, Wafa said, "Go home and leave this city in peace."

Rukh waited for stirrings of dissent, for some sign that the Preacher's will would persist. Instead, soldiers began to move, entire regiments at once—that was when he knew it was done. He patted the boy's head, this time with affection. "Will you stay to aid me, as well?"

Wafa frowned. "I belong with the lady Arian. And one day, I must return to Candour."

Rukh considered this with a smile, considered how many had fallen at the First Oralist's feet. She would raise the boy with love. What he would become would be guided by her hands; her inner light would transform him. Or perhaps it would merely reveal him.

His thoughts were interrupted by a call along the wall. "Excellency!"

He waited as Cassandane approached, her helmet lost, a deep

gash across her right arm. Like all those who had fought in the battle for Ashfall, her face was marked by the losses they had suffered, yet her ebony eyes were bright.

"Commander Arsalan asks for you! Captain Khashayar and I can hold the walls."

"The fighting is over. There is no need to hold the walls now."

Cassandane nodded.

"The Commander, then . . ."

He went still, refusing to accept it.

She gave him an encouraging nod. "His injuries are grave, but he will not die this night. Not with the Assassin to tend him."

The light in her eyes dimmed at his hesitation. "Will you not go to see him?"

Saluting her, he strode from the walls.

58

CRIES OF WELCOME AND GLADNESS GREETED RUKH IN ARSALAN'S rooms. The Commander of the Zhayedan was surrounded by admirers, by healers who monitored his health, and by aides who hurried to bring anything he might need. The Assassin supervised these efforts, saying little, though Rukh was certain he was aware of every detail in the room. His eyes seemed to follow a trail to the door, and Rukh turned his head to see what had captured his attention.

Darya hovered near the door, her anxious eyes on Arsalan's gray face, on the bandages that bound him from sternum to ribs, his chest and shoulders bare. Though his chambers were austere, someone had propped cushions behind his back, leaving him half-reclining.

A healer's hand had washed the blood from his face. His thick sable hair was combed back so that his vision was unobscured, though his lashes lay heavy on the fragile skin beneath his eyes. He looked defenseless, and Rukh had never seen him like this, never wanted to see him like this. Nor did he want Arsalan's vulnerability exposed to the members of his court.

He clapped his hands. "Leave at once."

The room emptied amid a chorus of protests.

"There are others that need you. Go!"

They fled.

Darya lingered at the door, though, and the Assassin dipped his head at the Princess—a question. Rukh nodded. Of all the people of Ashfall that the Talisman's war had claimed, his sister had survived, and much of that was Arsalan's doing, his compassion rare in a man who'd been bred for the purpose of war.

It was a gift Rukh didn't share. In the end, Darya had helped to save the city, but the blame for too many of Ashfall's losses, for far too many of their dead, rested upon her head.

The ledger between Rukh and the Assassin would never be balanced. He would give Hudayfah anything he wanted, and in this instance, his generosity would serve a purpose. The Princess would be exiled. He would never have to see her again.

"Get out," he said to Darya.

"Rukh—" His name was a saddened plea.

"I said, get out." He jerked his head at the Assassin. "Take her. Do with her what you will. The debt will never be repaid, so the gift of my sister must suffice. Now go, and leave me with my friend."

"Rukh, please! I want to stay. I want to *help*."

Unwanted anger broke over him in a wave. He had the restless, driving need to be alone with Arsalan, to say the things he needed to say, but still Darya denied him.

He stalked to her, reining himself in because the Assassin made a sudden movement, a warning he chose to heed.

His lungs working, he stabbed a finger in Darya's face.

"I don't care what you want! How many of our people do you think would welcome your efforts, knowing what your actions have wrought? The scriptorium . . ." His breath shuddered in his chest. "The men you killed with Al Mintaka . . . how can you expect your crimes to be forgotten?" He motioned at Arsalan. "You took him against his will—did you think I would forgive that? Did you think *Arsalan* would?" His fury grew, his wounds raw and untended. He had allowed the insult to Arsalan; worse, he had contributed to bringing it about.

The Assassin touched Rukh's shoulder. He was at once aware of the threat.

He swung around to the bed, wiping his face with his hands, wiping away the tears that had leaked between his fingers. His voice aching with fatigue, he waved one hand at the door. He knelt at Arsalan's side, refusing to look at his sister.

"Just go." He found one of Arsalan's hands, pressed its knuckles to his lips. "You will retain your rank, an honor I intend for the Assassin. But you are not a member of my court or my family, so go." He bent his head over Arsalan's hand. "Do as you're asked for once."

He heard the choked sound of her sobs, heard the Assassin address him in clipped tones.

"Shall I continue the evacuation, Excellency?"

He shook his head. "My people need to bury their dead. After that, we will see." His eyes on Arsalan's still face, he asked, "Will you stay, Hudayfah? Until our need has passed?"

A wave of coldness emanated from the Assassin. "After I have made arrangements for your sister. Come with me, Princess."

Sobbing, Darya huddled in the hallway outside Arsalan's rooms. She wanted to stay with him, wanted to be the one to care for him, when his courage had kept Ashfall from despair. To know that he had come so close to death was like dying herself. Yet,

Ausma Zehanat Khan

unlike Rukh, she had no right to mourn, no rights over Arsalan at all. And that she still yearned for him after everything she'd done made her despise herself all the more.

There had been some spare grace in their victory today, but she could not put off the Assassin's payment, despite her fear of his motives. Was this how Arsalan had felt about being forced into marriage? Stripped of all choice and all hope? And wasn't it better to know? Collecting her thoughts, she forced herself to face the Assassin.

"Will you hurt me, Hudayfah? Is pain what you seek from me?"

The mask dipped to her, and if she could have read his expression, she would have guessed she had caught him by surprise.

"Not by any means in my power. But it is for you to decide whether to trust my word."

She gave him a hesitant nod, though she had more to ask him, a subject that may not have troubled the ghul, but that Darya found impossible to broach.

"What is it, Princess?"

His tone was gentle, so from somewhere deep within she gathered the courage to speak.

"You would have . . . expectations . . . of me . . ." Her voice trailed off, color rising to her face.

"Expectations?"

She glanced up to catch the teasing light in his eyes, and felt the faint stirring of hope. Stammering a little, she continued. "Marital duties. I can't—I don't think I can—I do not know you, so I don't know if I can . . ."

He took pity on her, leaning in so close that his breath whispered over her forehead.

She shivered a little, not quite daring to hope.

"Again, Princess, that is for you to decide. You are not a prize I have won, you are someone I have chosen. I will wait until you are ready to reciprocate that choice." He hesitated, as though weighing a decision. "If you wish to remain at your brother's court, I will persuade him to accept you."

Her breath hitched in her throat. "But you said—you said I had no say in the matter! You made your aid to Ashfall conditional on my acceptance!"

There was something off about the way he tipped his head back and angled his body away. He indicated the quiet that had fallen upon the city.

"You have won the war, Princess, and though your brother may not credit it, you played a role in that victory. The Black Khan no longer has need of the assistance I offered. The debt between us is canceled."

But how could that be when the scales remained so unbalanced? With all Hudayfah had done for Rukh, her brother would refuse him nothing. She felt a strange clutching in the center of her chest at the thought that he'd changed his mind. Instead of claiming her in payment, he was offering her a way out.

His gaze swung back to her face. "Do you wish me to speak to your brother?"

Darya bit her lip. The Assassin's gaze dropped to her mouth, and she blushed, her hands crumpling the fine cloth of her dress.

"Even with all he owes you, Rukh will not accept my presence at his court. I will always remind him of calamity." Her delicate jaw set, she added, "I no longer have a home in Ashfall."

"Hira would claim you."

"Rukh would never allow it."

"The Black Khan has no say in how *I* govern my affairs, but that choice is still yours to make."

"Why?" Darya whispered, bewildered by his forbearance.

"Why have you changed your mind? Why do you promise me freedom my brother would never grant?"

He jerked his mask at the door. "I will not allow your brother to condemn you. The penalties of raising the ghul shouldn't be yours to bear."

Darya bit back her protest. The Assassin didn't want her—why would he? He was seeking a way to atone for the ghul's destructive malice because he held himself responsible for summoning it to life. No wonder he was willing to send her away—he didn't want her at all.

But why was she indulging in self-pity? She'd finally been given a choice—the choice to stay or go, with the Assassin bearing the consequences. His shoulders were broad, he would carry the weight well, but was that what *she* wanted, to shirk her duty once more?

The harm she had done to Ashfall couldn't be undone. Her only hope of penance lay in the wisdom of Hira, in acquiring knowledge that might be of benefit to her people. That might see her brother consider her return to Ashfall one day.

She took a deep breath. If there was a price to be paid for redemption, she welcomed the chance to pay it. There had to be *something* to set against the devastation of the city she loved. This was her moment to prove herself worthy as Princess of Ashfall.

Her lips firmed, and she nodded at the Assassin. "I will honor my brother's bargain. Send me to Hira, and I will come to you whenever you call me to your side."

She had surprised him into stillness, but then the tension eased from his body and he captured a graceful wrist. The silken webbing she hated was wound with great delicacy around the fingers of her right hand.

"I will give you a token when we marry, but this will keep you bound to me for now."

Darya nodded again, overwhelmed by a decision she hadn't expected to make.

He seemed to be waiting for her to say something, so she thought of what she would have done if the ghul had never come to life.

Her eyes on his, she managed, "I will not dishonor you with a show of my reluctance."

His hand tightened on hers, a softness in his glance. Then he touched her in a new way, his glove caressing her palm.

"I thank you for your courtesy, Princess. And I hope a time will come when you cease to regret your choice."

When the others were gone, Rukh raised his head. His fingers slid along Arsalan's neck to test the strength of his pulse. Steady enough, but faint.

"What have you done?"

He was jolted when Arsalan replied.

"I have been your friend." A dark rasp of a voice. "I have been . . . devoted."

Rukh straightened. Pulled his hand free. Found a stool, took his seat beside the bed. But the sight of Arsalan's hand caught at him—his long fingers curled, his palm empty . . . an emptiness Rukh couldn't bear. So he reached for his hand and wrapped it in his own.

Arsalan's dense lashes stirred. "The city? The Preacher?"

"Safe. You're safe. Safe with me now."

Arsalan coughed, his mouth dry. Rukh found a cup on the table near the bed. He tipped the cup to Arsalan's lips.

"Take your time," he warned. Then, considering the extent of Arsalan's injuries, he let his anger loose. "Why allow them to hit you so hard? You could have died on the wall."

He set the cup aside, waiting for Arsalan to speak.

"Perhaps I had to fall for you to rise."

Rukh gripped his chin in hard fingers. "Sheer idiocy. Never do anything like that again."

"Will you demote me?" A teasing note beneath the fatigue. Rukh's response to it was uncertain; he didn't know what he'd come here to promise.

But as always, Arsalan knew his dilemma. He slashed through Rukh's facade, black eyes burning into black. It would have been easier to ignore what had passed between them on the wall, but that had never been Arsalan's way.

"Have you come here to make declarations?"

"You wouldn't believe me if I did."

A reply that elicited a growl. "It would be worth it to hear you try."

Of all the things Arsalan sought from him, this was the one he couldn't give, no matter what he'd promised in extremis. And Arsalan knew him too well to have expected otherwise.

He swallowed, trying to put his feelings into words.

"You have been honorable, certain of your duty, and though I have not repaid you in kind, you have never judged me. My actions disappoint you, yet you continue to love me."

"You love me also, you just didn't know you did." A fine riposte, and true.

"As a brother." Because Rukh's position couldn't alter. His basic nature wouldn't change. He would seek advantage wherever he could without thinking of others.

But he saw that Arsalan had been holding himself taut, his fierce strength pushed beyond its limits. "As you wish, my Prince. Whatever you would ask of me is yours."

"I won't allow anything to change. I will wed, as is my duty, but you will remain at my side." His fingers touched the bandage on Arsalan's ribs. "Perhaps even in my sight."

His face calm, Arsalan asked, "And will you love this woman you wed?"

Rukh's hands slid to Arsalan's bare shoulders, his grip savage and cruel.

"Don't ask me questions you know I cannot answer!"

The breath sighed out of Arsalan's chest, his lashes fell, and he was still.

Rukh shook him. "Arsalan!"

At the terror in his voice, Arsalan opened his eyes. "I'm tired, Rukh, let me rest."

"You can't rest now—the city is in ruins!"

He was in ruins; he needed Arsalan close. And he was selfish enough to deny Arsalan the period of rest he deserved.

"You sent Darya away."

"Yes."

"It was wrong."

"I know." He'd known as soon as he'd done it.

"You will make amends."

"Anything, anything." He couldn't stop himself. He buried his face in Arsalan's neck, wanting closeness—wanting *some*thing, his lips brushing Arsalan's neck.

"I'm bleeding to death, Rukh. This may not be the time."

"I thought you dead." Rukh's sob caught against his throat, his forehead coming to rest upon Arsalan's cheek.

"I know." A gentleness Arsalan reserved for Rukh. Love without pity, without judgment. "Yet you managed to save Ashfall on your own."

The convulsive grip of Rukh's fingers against his throat, searching for and then soothing himself with the throb of Arsalan's pulse, lingering in the carved hollow. Arsalan's breath came faster, the rise and fall of his chest disturbed as Rukh continued to speak close to his ear.

"Not on my own, never that. You stood against the Talisman. You fought off everything they threw at us—*you* held the city with your will."

Uncomfortable with these encomiums, Arsalan tried to tease, "Then perhaps you might finally name me to your precious Order of Khorasan."

A faint rasp of laughter from Rukh. "Anything, anything you ask."

Save the only thing that mattered. Still shaking a little, Arsalan's hand touched Rukh's hair, stroked over the silky strands. Rukh settled under the caress like a panther starved of affection. Just once . . . just this once . . . he would allow it.

"The future of Ashfall is yours, Rukh."

Praise from the one whose praise mattered.

"If you help me, yes."

"If my Prince will let me sleep."

Rukh sat with Arsalan in silence, then reached for his hand, entwining their fingers again.

"Don't let go."

A beleaguered protest from his general: "I won't."

"Don't let go, Arsalan. Whatever Ashfall's fate, I need you at my side."

59

Arian and Daniyar found themselves at the fountains of the All Ways. Around them, the Citadel was quiet. All that could be heard was the murmur of falling water. Arian had found a place to sit at the center of the fountains, Daniyar's head resting in her lap. She brushed back his hair from his face, calming them both with the touch.

"Forgive me, Arian. I cannot keep my promise."

She hushed him, her hand resting on his cheek, his ring shining from her finger.

"The One would not take you from me now when the way ahead of us is clear."

But his breath was ragged in his chest, and his beautiful face was marked by the enormity of his trials. "The Ascension." Arian bent closer to hear him. "I was told my time has ended."

She laced her fingers through his. She kissed him, her sense of rightness unshaken, the first time in a decade her peace was unreserved.

"The Ascension did not prophesy your *death*," she said, concerned. "It meant only that your time as Silver Mage must end. Your trust will pass to another."

"Wafa?" He had guessed it, and the thought of what was coming to the boy was a raw hurt in a heart that had borne too much. Death was easier to accept. "I have seen the birthright in his eyes. In time, he will take up the mantle of the Silver Mage."

"Yes."

Arian stroked his temples in the gentlest of caresses, needing to ease his pain, stricken by the knowledge that since they had first parted at the Sakhrah, he'd believed his fate was written and despaired of seeing her again, of ending their days together in the peace of the Damson Vale. His agony was hers, but it was essential that he know their time of anguish was past.

"When the Authoritan burned the book of the Candour, he ensured that the gifts of the Silver Mage would perish. Wafa is"— she laughed a little, pleased and stunned—"Wafa is the Mage of Miraj. His destiny was influenced by *two* Mages of Khorasan. You taught him by example, and Yusuf delivered him to the portal of the Blue Eye, guessing that he would ascend. So Wafa's powers and birthright are new, but yes, when the time is right, Candour will be part of his trust. What his book will be in place of the Candour, I cannot say."

He lay in her arms, thinking over her words, searching within himself. Her fingertips traced his torso, seeking the hollows of his ribs, the layers of muscle that armored them.

"I felt my life slipping from me. I feel the same thing now."

She touched her forehead to his. "You were injured in battle, that is all. Your body will heal in time."

"My eyes—"

"The birthright has passed. Now your eyes are like moonlight on the mountains, so beautiful I am vanquished."

A frown darkened his brow, grief supplying his answer. "You are trying to make it possible for me to let you go. You would ease my suffering in any way you could, even letting me believe—"

"No, Daniyar." She covered his mouth with her hand, her tears hot on his skin. Their time together had always been constrained, their depth of feeling for each other shadowed by the torments of war. She understood his deeply rooted fear that the forces gathered against them could never be overcome; she had lived it herself for years.

"I would not lie to you, I have held this hope too dear."

His lips moved against her palm in the merest whisper of a kiss.

His lashes lifted, and his moonlit eyes drifted over her face. That she pleased him, that he loved her, couldn't have been in doubt.

His voice deeper now, he questioned, "*Have* I vanquished you, Arian?"

She nodded, a smile beginning to form. His fingers played over her lips.

On a sensual note, he teased, "Then am I not entitled to the spoils?"

She gave him an ardent answer, and when at last, she was able to pull away, a flame had been kindled in his eyes, his remarkable vitality renewed. He ached to believe in the life he'd been granted—the life he would share with her, never to be separate from the woman he loved again. The fountains of the All Ways murmured their encouragement, and it gave him the strength to say, "You held me to life, Arian."

The graceful lines of her body melted into his. "Just as you held me."

She curved into him, sheltered him. He surged up in her arms, reversing their positions, so that he was holding her, possessing her delicate, fearless strength, his discipline yielding to hunger, the hard contours of his body fused to hers with the exultation of being free to love her—here at the heart of the Citadel, in the honorable ceding of a trust, and the fulfilment of his oath.

At a noise from the door to the Council Chamber, they broke apart. Arian helped Daniyar to his feet, taking his hand in hers. The Companions of Hira filed into the chamber, led by Sinnia and Ash, their features blunted by grief. The lower tier of the chamber remained empty, a gesture of respect to the Companions who had fallen in battle. The rest did something surprising as the waters of the All Ways rose. As Ash and Sinnia stood beside Arian and Daniyar, the others came to Arian one by one. They touched the circlet she had refastened to her right arm, then surrounded the fountains. Palms cupped upward, they raised their hands.

Arian glanced to the door, where Lania stood, ablaze with the Claim's power, her circlet afire. Arian turned to Ash, confused. Ash raised her palms. Lania and Sinnia did the same.

"In the name of the One, the Merciful and Compassionate, we seek to elect to the office of High Companion Arian, First Oralist of Hira. Do you accept this charge, Arian?"

Daniyar's arm firmed around her shoulders.

Tears filled Arian's eyes. Though she was deeply conscious of the honor, she had no choice but to refuse it. "Ash, please—you promised me dispensation."

The older woman's eyes met hers with a steady, determined warmth.

"And you shall have it, First Oralist. You will hold the office in absentia, if necessary, as long as you do not deny us your leadership while we work to restore our Citadel."

Lania's smooth voice drifted down the stairs. "Your duties will not be onerous, sister. This Council has relied on you too long. I have spoken to your Jurist, and we are in agreement." Her gaze shifted to Daniyar, traced his face with unmistakable envy, but she glanced away when he acknowledged her.

"What have you agreed?"

Sinnia slipped her arm around Arian's waist, steadying her. Arian leaned her head against Sinnia's, her heart wrenched with gratitude that her truest and dearest friend had been spared by the war in the end.

Ash motioned to Lania, who completed her descent into the chamber. "I nominate Lania, daughter of the Inkwell scriptorium, to the rank of First Oralist."

Arian went still. Stunned, she moved away from the others to take Lania's hands in her own.

"What of the Wall? Will you stay at Hira?"

Joy and fear seized her in equal measure. She thought of what Lania might do. She thought of the missing plague-jar. But Lania's fierce loyalty in their battle against the Preacher tempered Arian's fears. Lania's lips parted on a smile.

"Others will take the Wall: a woman with dark hair, a man who stands at her side. I have more important battles to fight. I have sisters to reclaim and a fortress to rebuild."

The words struck a pang of doubt in Arian. "The Citadel is not a fortress."

An implacable vow in return. "It will be."

Sinnia intervened. "This won't be like the Wall," she warned. "The Council of Hira will not submit to one woman's rule again." She glanced at Ash. "Tell them." For Lania was still an unknown quantity; if she refused to accept their terms, her rank would not be confirmed.

The most senior Companion on the Council of Hira now folded her hands.

"I nominate Sinnia of the lands of the Negus to the rank of Second Oralist of Hira. The Oralists will work in tandem, under the guidance of the High Companion and myself." Ash clapped her hands. "Take your seats." She gave Daniyar a respectful nod. "Forgive me, my lord, but we must conduct the business of our chamber in privacy."

Eyes of moonlight gray brushed her face, and Ash blushed like a novice.

"I am grateful you allowed me to remain this long." He reached for Arian's hand. "I do not have the words to thank you for your dispensation."

Ash nodded. Her grave regard fell upon the chamber. "Hira must reinterpret the past. Our Tradition must rise from the ashes of this war to take up the challenge of renewal."

"A noble task."

"You will assist us in this." An imperious demand.

Daniyar's lips curved, and a hush fell upon the chamber. "I and all the Mages." He tugged a lock of Arian's hair. "If you will permit us a little time for ourselves."

Ash pulled Arian close. "No one deserves it more. But you will formalize your binding first, Silver Mage and High Companion, if this council should elect."

The Companions spoke as one. "We elect Arian to the rank of High Companion. Her charge is to observe the rites of Hira and uphold the honor of the Claim."

"So it is affirmed."

And when the Silver Mage had parted from Arian, the Council of Hira came to order.

60

TEN DAYS LATER, MIDNIGHT FIRES BURNED ALONG THE WALLS OF THE
Citadel from torches tended with care. The dead had been gathered and buried, and now Arian stood with Lania, at the foot
of their parents' tombs. They knelt before their graves, the white
stone markers restored, the names Armaghan and Saya resting on
holy ground.

A man stood nearby, cloaked all in black, his steel mask removed from his face, his head bent in supplication. When the
prayer was done, he helped his sisters rise. They huddled together
in the chill temperature of night.

"We hold their legacy," he mused.

"We and all who read, as must be our trust from this day forward." The vow of the former First Oralist.

"I will honor it," he agreed. "Though I must ask something of
you both."

"In exchange for honoring the vow?" Lania's cynicism had not
died.

Hudayfah's head dipped. Though Arian held him close, Lania
had not yet learned the habits of affection.

"No, I give my oath without reservation. But I would ask that you assist the Princess of Ashfall in her training as a novice. Her crimes weigh upon her. Her burden of remorse is heavy, and I fear it will serve to make her . . ."

Arian's face softened. "What do you fear, Hudayfah?"

His head tilted to one side, his scarred face taking in a young woman in a white silk dress who waited for him a courteous distance apart.

"I fear the Princess will be lonely."

"Do not fear." Arian kissed his cheeks, once, twice, thrice. "In honor of our parents' love, we will hold her close."

"I cannot quite grasp it," he said.

Lania studied her brother, seeing the memory of the boy she had loved behind the scars. She had been the eldest, Hudayfah the next, and Arian their blessed charge. Three souls in the world who shared completely in this loss. She gestured at the desolated graves.

"That our parents are gone?"

His eyes pinned hers, the same shade as Arian's, a little darker than hers. "I made my peace with their deaths long ago. What choice did any of us have?" The scars twisted his lips. "I meant that I cannot quite grasp the absence of war, of obliterating darkness. I have worked against it all these years, Arian also." He considered the bleak reserve in Lania's eyes. "Your campaign against the Authoritan is a mark you should wear with pride."

He bent to place a cluster of jasmine on their mother's grave. "I wish our parents could have lived to see this day. But I have decided on something." He brushed his hair away from his forehead to show his sisters the mark. The letter *nun*, the sign of the Inkwell scriptorium, stamped in silver on his brow. "The Nun scriptorium will flourish again as my gift to Ashfall."

Lania's sleek brows rose in a skeptical curve, but Arian's smile was playful.

"A fitting gift for the Princess."

He bowed his head. "You must help her, Arian. And Lania, too—she needs you both."

"I promise I will." Arian hugged her brother again. Then, with a hint of reluctance, Lania did the same, allowing his embrace for no more than an instant.

"And I." The spark that brightened Lania's eyes encompassed the exiled Princess. "Considering what she did to Ashfall, she would have served me well as a dove."

A muffled oath from their brother. "Lania—"

"I am teasing, brother. Any woman who comes to Hira will find her potential fulfilled."

"Swear it." The oath would hold the children of Inkwell always. So, solemnly, the sisters did.

Epilogue

THE CEREMONY TOOK PLACE ON A WARM NIGHT IN A GARDEN OF THE Citadel under the swaying of the palms. Arian and Daniyar had wanted a quiet service with Wafa and Sinnia present, as a means of honoring the dead of the Citadel and the mourning of the people of Khorasan.

It was the Jurist of the Council who convinced Arian that her duty as High Companion meant that she should set an example for the change she hoped to bring about: a new partnership between men and women, and a possible future for the Companions, based on the teachings of the Claim. And Ash wanted that message conveyed to their allies and friends.

So instead of a private ceremony, dignitaries from the lands of Khorasan had been invited to the Citadel. Guests included the Black Khan and the Commander of the Zhayedan, the Mage of the Blue Eye, and Nuru and Kamali, as representatives of Queen Zoya. The Assassin came with an honor guard to accompany the Princess of Ashfall. Uwais and Toryal were present under the Silver Mage's banner. Hamzah and Qais, the lords of Khyber who had come to the Citadel's defense, were honored in turn. Tochtor, the Empress of the Cloud Door, and her daughters, Storay and Annar, had ridden the great distance on their war-horses. And Larisa Salikh from Marakand, to whom Arian had written, *Come unto that tenet that you and we hold in common.*

The Citadel was festooned with summer roses in all the colors of dawn. Seating was arranged in rows, and candles lit the enclosure beneath the palms. In the forecourt, a fountain tiled in blue murmured quietly rapturous notes on the breeze. And on a platform near the fountain, a silk divan had been placed.

Pedestals were stationed around the enclosure, and before the divan a low table on which a mirror rested, adorned with golden scrolls. On the pedestals, illuminated manuscripts were displayed under Half-Seen's watchful eye, a sign of what the Citadel had been, a gesture meant to signify that Hira's treasury of manuscripts was for the benefit of all.

Daniyar was seated on the divan, the boy Wafa at his side. They were dressed alike in silk sheaths embroidered with golden paisleys. Beneath these, they wore narrow trousers with gold-trimmed cuffs. Daniyar's face was covered by a sehra, a curtain of jasmine and roses that drifted down to his knees. Above this, at the center of his turban, a silver aigrette bore the colors of his tribe, a stroke of black on a field of green.

Yet despite his formal splendor, no one was looking at him. A double door at the foot of the Citadel had opened. The Companions of Hira advanced from it in pairs, dressed in their ceremonial dress: white silk patterned with gold, translucent veils covering their hair. Their hands raised a canopy of embroidered silk. Beneath the canopy, Arian was accompanied by three of the Companions: in front of her, Ash the Jurist; behind her, Lania, First

Oralist. And at her side, always at her side, Sinnia, whose hand clasped hers as their shining circlets touched.

The procession reached the platform, and Daniyar reached for Arian's hand to help her climb it, in her dress of fine red silk that was threaded with gold. The dress was made of two pieces: a tunic with long sheer sleeves, over which her circlets had been bound, and a flaring skirt, embellished with Hira's motifs. An embroidered veil covered her face and hair.

Under the veil she wore rubies at her ears and throat, and a matching ornament that trailed the length of her braid: the formal accoutrements of the former First Oralist of Hira. Her hands were patterned with henna, and her wrists chimed with gold bangles, but the one ring she wore was the ring of the Silver Mage.

Daniyar seated her beside him, his hand holding on to hers.

Ash cleared her throat, then asked for the witnesses both parties had selected to approach. On Daniyar's side were the Assassin and the Blue Mage. On Arian's, Lania and Sinnia. Half-Seen produced the Criterion. She placed the manuscript between Arian and Daniyar.

Ash called out the benediction: *"In the name of the One, the Beneficent, the Merciful."*

The assembly echoed the phrase.

Then Ash began the formal inquiries of the marriage rites. Arian was meant to give her consent, but in his eagerness Daniyar spoke first. A ripple of laughter floated through the garden. Though neither could see the other's face, Arian squeezed his hand. Then Ash addressed him.

"What is your promise to Arian, the High Companion of Hira?"

He spoke his vow through the veil of roses. "I will be her garment, just as she is mine."

A soft sigh whispered through the garden.

"And what is your vow, Arian, to Daniyar, Silver Mage and Guardian of Candour?"

"I will be his garment, just as he is mine."

"Will the witnesses testify?"

One by one, they did.

"In this binding of two souls, the One is always the third."

Half-Seen held the Criterion to Arian's lips. She kissed its cover; then Daniyar copied her gesture. Cheers erupted in the garden. Wafa detached the sehra from Daniyar's turban. Daniyar reached for Arian, but Sinnia shooed his hands away.

"Would you see your bride, my lord?"

He removed his turban and shook his dark hair loose.

"Haven't you tormented me enough?"

"Just a moment more, my lord."

Sinnia placed the mirror between Arian and Daniyar, as Lania pulled Arian's veil free. Arian's head was bent, so the Companions urged Daniyar to seek her reflection in the mirror. He did so, his moonlight eyes brushing her face with wonder. She was his at last, and he was hers, a bond there would be no undoing, given its blessing by the Claim.

In his hand, he'd kept a cluster of jasmine. Now he sprinkled the blooms on the mirror in praise of Arian's beauty, save for a few he withheld. He scattered these over Arian's lips before he claimed her for a kiss. The Companions sheltered their heads with the veil, an intimacy that was all the more cherished for how long it had been delayed.

"And now?" Arian's eyes held a joy bright enough to light the stars, her voice husky in her throat. She was holding him—she *held* him—there was no sweeter reward.

"And now everything, Arian. Now I take you to the Damson Vale."

The celebration lasted well into the night, the Citadel's loss attenuated by unadulterated joy. Daniyar held her close by his side, exchanging greetings with the guests who had come to honor them despite the work that remained.

The end of the Age of Jahiliya was not something they had wanted to miss.

The Black Khan approached, his princely regalia reminiscent of their first encounter. A crown with pointed tines on hair like a glossy wing; a gem-studded mantle flung over a silver sheath and silk trousers. The two gold armbands set with the Darya-e Nur diamond and the matching Koh-e Nur. The giant emerald buckle at his waist and the sparkling Shahi scepter in his hand. His collar was polished to diamond hardness, the onyx medallion glinting with the shimmering fire of a star. From the collar hung ropes of matchless pearls in place of the lustrous sapphires that had mirrored his gift to Arian, a subtle sign of acceptance that she would never be his. He kissed her cheek in a final trespass, his lips like silk against her skin.

"Thank you," he said quietly, his mockery absent for once. "Ashfall will rise again, and it will do so in your honor. One day you must return, if only to grace the scriptorium Hudayfah has promised to rebuild." His gaze slipped past her, settling on a figure in the distance who stood apart from the rest. "I thought I knew all the Companions."

Arian was all too certain that he did. She turned to see Lania watching them from afar.

"You knew my sister as the Khanum of Black Aura."

His glittering eyes widened, and he looked at Lania closely. "My dealings were with the Authoritan. I did not recognize the Khanum without her usual . . . embellishments." The slight stress he laid on the word lent itself to a less flattering meaning. His eyes traced Arian's features, his own sensual and sleek. "She could be your twin, though she is missing that element that is unique to you. Your air of innocence, perhaps. I confess I didn't think the Khanum would come to be welcome here."

Disturbed that Rukh's eye had fallen on Lania, Arian said quickly, "She was meant to be Custodian of the Archives. She will serve as First Oralist now."

"Ah."

He wasn't dissuaded in the least, but they were interrupted by Khashayar, whose joy at seeing Arian was so ardent that he caught her up and crushed her in his arms, releasing her only when Daniyar stepped in, directing a wry glance at Arian.

"Stop weaving your spells."

At the shining response in her eyes, he dropped a kiss on her lips.

The Commander of the Zhayedan came to join them, pinned with glittering ornaments and dressed in armor so splendid, it shone in the flickering light. His face was pale beneath his olive skin, and something in his movements was tentative, one hand pressed to his side.

"Sahabiya." He bowed to Arian, his sable hair shining in the torchlight. She returned the greeting; then, impulsively, she took his strong hand in hers.

"Do you still suffer, Commander?" She indicated his injury.

"I would be honored if you would call me Arsalan."

His brilliant black gaze moved to Daniyar, whose private nod of assent reflected the warmth of his respect.

Arian's radiant smile broke through. "The honor would be mine, Arsalan: your name is covered in glory." She was dazzled by the diamond aigrette at his throat, an emerald of such purity at its center that its coruscating light seemed depthless. To either side above the green stone, the shimmering wings of a firebird extended upward in flight. The Commander of the Zhayedan had been named to the Order of Khorasan, the highest tribute of the empire.

Arian nodded at the aigrette. "These honors do not do justice to your courage. Without you to lead the Zhayedan, Ashfall would have been lost."

He shook his head, his eyes steady on hers. "It took all of us, sahabiya. All who believed in the beauty of Ashfall, and all who came to our aid without counting the cost to themselves." Sorrow deepened his voice. "But for all the Zhayedan's fearlessness, the city is in ruins."

He was still holding her hand. A bolt of warmth pulsed from her slender fingers to his.

"And what of you?"

She sensed that something within him had changed—a lessening of his solitude? His eyelids flickered, and his gaze dwelt on Rukh. He knew what she was asking.

Carefully, he admitted, "I am not as alone as I was."

She was stunned by Rukh's response, a rich color cresting his cheekbones, a blazing pride in his eyes.

"I'm glad," she said, a little startled. With a gentler intonation, she sought to honor Arsalan's mother, once a Companion of Hira. "This is a place of belonging for you. You will always be welcome here."

"*Sahabiya.*"

Tears started to his ebony eyes, and suddenly Rukh was at his shoulder, speaking with angry concern. "You need to rest."

"In a moment, my Prince."

The Commander raised Arian's hand and pressed it gently to his heart. "You are the light of this Citadel, a light you shone upon me."

A mordant twist to his lips, Rukh muttered, "Would that *I* had been as fortunate." When Daniyar's jaw tightened, Rukh mocked him. "You have won the prize; you have nothing left to fear. Bring the First Oralist to Ashfall—I will host a banquet for your bride." And with a devilish lift of his brow, he quipped, "Let her wear my sapphires in peace."

When Rukh had departed with Arsalan, the Blue Mage came to join them, Wafa trailing after him. He offered a blessing on their marriage; his gift to Arian had been a manuscript from the Library of Timeback with exquisitely painted miniatures of the orchards of the Damson Vale. He had chosen it after consulting with Daniyar, the bond between the two men strengthened by the journey they had taken together and the battles they had fought side by side.

Arian asked Wafa to come to her, tilting up his head with her fingers. Before she could say anything, he gave her a scowl that recalled their first encounters.

"Will you be all right without me? You need someone to look after you. It should be me and the lady Sinnia."

Arian kissed the soft curls that Sinnia had somehow tamed. "Will you trust the Silver Mage to take over your charge?" she asked.

Wafa looked at him dubiously. "Won't you miss me at all?"

Her voice caught in her throat, bright tears coming to her eyes.

"I will miss you every moment we're apart." Her fingers caressed his curls. "But your love is so precious that I will not be without it. I will carry it to the Damson Vale." She smoothed the scowl from his face. "Will you keep mine safe until I am with you again?"

Consoled by her promise and her charge, he nodded, turning his head to listen to the Mages who had taken up their tasks as his mentors. He pressed something into Arian's palm before he pulled away: an apricot, soft and fragrant, a gift of sweetness between them. But there were other gifts he would remember her for: the first time she had saved him from the Talisman, the moment she had placed the Sacred Cloak on his shoulders and told him he was worthy of it simply by being born. The Commander of the Zhayedan was not the only one she had tended with the gift of her love.

As the conversation between the Mages grew more intense, Sinnia drew Arian away, with a wink at Daniyar. Though he was engrossed in the discussion, his moonlit eyes lingered on Arian and followed her to the gate.

They climbed the stairs to the top of the Citadel Gate, their arms linked, pensive with the knowledge that a new era was beginning. But though Hira's time was at hand, Arian was preoccupied with thoughts of how easily Khorasan might have come to grief. Her joy was still tentative, her peace of mind hesitant.

"Thank you for your belief in me. Thank you for staying by my side when there was no reason to believe."

Sinnia kissed her cheek. "Thank me by not staying away too long. Otherwise, that little ruffian will not leave me in peace."

"Come to the Damson Vale when you can. Bring Wafa with you."

Arian's longing was clear. She was grasping on to joy, but she wanted to hold the ones she loved close.

"I won't fail you." Sinnia squeezed her hand.

"You won't fail at all. What the Citadel will be in your hands! There will be other Companions from the lands of the Negus. From the maghreb and all our lands." She was quiet for a moment. "Sinnia, I wanted to ask you—the rank of First Oralist—do you resent the Council for naming Lania in your place? I will take your part if you think it should have been otherwise."

Arian had wondered at the Council's reckoning of its future, decisions made swiftly in the aftermath of peace. Sinnia had served the Council with unfailing loyalty and courage, and in Jaslyk prison, her mind had been opened to the Claim. Since then, her knowledge had only grown. Should Lania, a practitioner of Augury who was well-versed in the bloodrites, have been named to the rank of First Oralist at Sinnia's expense?

But Sinnia was shaking her head, her great dark eyes serene. "Despite Salikh's teachings, Lania's facility with the Claim surpasses mine—like you, she studied it from childhood. For that matter, both Ash and Half-Seen are at least as skilled as I, and could have been chosen in my place. But you know I could not withstand a life cloistered behind these walls. I've been roaming at your side too long." She nudged Arian with a smile. "To bear the rank of Second Oralist is an honor that suits me well. It lets me keep an eye on your sister as the newest member of our Council, while allowing me the freedom to serve as an ambassador. As you said, other Companions must be summoned to join the Council, and the women of my lands have been overlooked for this distinction for too long."

Arian slipped an arm around Sinnia's waist.

"So young to be so wise," she teased.

Sinnia hugged her back. "All this time, we've been learning from each other."

Arian felt a pang at the thought that she would soon be parted from Sinnia, but Sinnia said in a comforting voice, her eyes on the Silver Mage, "He would never be the cause of your loneliness or pain. You have only to ask him to return."

A glance down into the courtyard and her gaze encountered Daniyar's. She felt the urgency of his love across their bond, his ardent promise of joy.

Her sadness eased, and she said to Sinnia, "It's time."

Together they chanted an incantation that transformed the Citadel's motto: *Never to be altered by the encircling tremors of time.*

The new motto reflected the same words that flourished on all the Companions' circlets, the golden bands agleam.

In the name of the One, the Merciful, the Compassionate.

The Citadel a refuge, a kingdom of the wisdom of women.

At a signal from Arian, Sinnia released the flag mounted above the gate.

Its banner flew in the wind, and a series of smaller flags unfurled at the same moment along the crenellations of the wall.

Throughout its long and venerated history, Hira had flown no flag. Now a green pennant fluttered in the breeze, marked by a word in the High Tongue, speaking to the trust of the Companions and the endurance of the Khorasan Archives.

The word on the flag was *IQRA*.

The trust of the Companions—

To read.

HERE ENDS THE KHORASAN ARCHIVES

Acknowledgments

AT THE END OF THIS LONG ROAD, DURING A VERY DARK PERIOD FOR THE Muslim world, I hope the books in the Khorasan Archives series will allow room for reflection on a present moment of crisis and decline, and perhaps, in their own small way, offer a little bit of hope. It's been painful, difficult, and, occasionally, redemptive to look within and try to reclaim my history and heritage for myself. As a Pashtun Muslim woman, I hoped to wrest back beauty from the pervasive culture of ugliness that has overwritten parts of my tradition.

If I have succeeded at all, I have the following people to thank: My editors, David, Vicky, and Natasha, who understand the spoken and unspoken, and who so gently and wisely shaped the world of Khorasan. Thank you—it was a master class. My agent, Danielle, who accepts that rage is a necessary force in telling stories like these, but who also encourages beauty. Kristin, Brian, and everyone at the Nelson Literary Agency who holds my hand and sees me through. The very patient, talented, and generous people who have contributed to these Khorasan adventures: Priyanka, Shailyn, Pamela, Caroline P., Michelle, Jaime, Rebecca, Angela, Mireya,

Jack, Paula, Gemma, Ashley, Lex, Steve, Caroline Y., Chris, Emma, all the artists who worked on these books—especially my sister, Ayesha, who designed my original maps—and the wondrous Micaela, who dreamed the same dreams as me. Vicky, Natasha, and Jack—it was a thrill to meet you in London! It's been such a privilege to work with the wonderful people at Harper Voyager in both the US and the UK.

I want to thank my parents for letting me wander their world, and for sharing their love of history and faith. I learned the poetry of the Qur'an from them as a child, and its magic still simmers in my veins. Perhaps that was why, many years ago, I once walked into a room that held a bloodstained manuscript and felt the hush of reverence. I knew one day I would tell its story.

Thank you to my siblings, Kashif, Irfan, and Ayesha, for a bond that holds strong over time and distance, and for being the first and most ardent champions of my work. Thank you for all you do on my behalf, and for being so proud of me—it means everything to me. Thank you to my nephews and nieces, who fill my life with such joy—particularly to Noor and Naseem, who have been reading these books. And to my Summer and Casim, who are the center of my life.

A special thank-you to my immensely loving and supportive second families—the Ahmads, Choudry-Raos, and Hashemis. To my parents-in-law: Being able to ask questions about history, locations, and vocabulary has been such a gift. The beauty of the Persian civilization is reflected through your eyes, and I hope you recognize Ashfall's great scriptorium.

Thank you to the sisters who let me pour out my heart and who believe I can write anything: Farah B., Farah M., Fereshteh, Firoozeh, Haseeba, Iram, Najia, and Saima. To Nozzie, for all the care you take of me and the love you so selflessly give. To Uzma, for that magical event you hosted with such love. To Hema, who wanders the back roads with me, and whom I can't do without. And to Yasmin and Semina, my little sisters, the family I chose for myself.

To Nader, my companion on every journey. All your life, you've been fighting the battles of the Khorasan Archives, lighting the spark of knowledge through the dangerous work you do. My brave, brave love—remember that you've promised me all the days to come.

Uzma Jalaluddin, I owe such a debt to you. How many times did you read these manuscripts or help pull me back from the brink? Your fingerprints are all over these books, and your suggestions helped me understand which of these stories mattered, especially on the subject of irresistible men. I'm more grateful than I can say for how much of your time and creativity you shared with me, and for how deeply you see.

Sajidah Kutty, thank you for believing in me. Thank you for that magical day when you decided we should meet in person, giving me a community I'd never known before. Thank you also for your artistic efforts—you are so unfailingly giving. Please don't forget our secret dream: "A girl walks onto a stage. A spotlight finds her in the dark." And Uzma and Sajidah: #sisterhoodofthepen + #blahblahplot = sheer magic, but we still have to find a name.

Saladin Ahmed: Thank you for being the soul of generosity and for making me believe that all our stories could be valued. Nafiza Azad: There from the beginning to believe, encourage, and inspire. Always grateful, my sweet sister. Especially for that delicacy of a book *The Candle and the Flame*. Shannon Chakraborty: We've been only hours away from meeting in person, and I look forward to the day our stars finally align. In the meantime, thank you for your generosity, and for the fascinating (and hilarious) worlds we share online. And for your beautiful books!

Michael D'Souza: What a champion you've been, following me from genre to genre and reminding me that there is more than hostility in this world. The struggle makes me weary, but you and Colleen are always a light. Ayesha Ejaz: How beautiful it's been to meet another writer who lives in two worlds like me, and who understands so well the pain of separation. Thank you for your comfort and counsel, and for letting me read the exquisite *Beyond the Moonlit Frontier.*

Naseeba Khader: I've loved talking books with you. Thank you for the incredible gift of your gorgeous, illuminating art. Through you, the Nun scriptorium lives. Melati Lum: I know we are destined to meet one day and immediately discover we are sisters of the soul who not only read the same books, but who fight the same fight for justice. Thank you for your many kindnesses, and for sharing your kittens and your book club.

Ardo Omer: Thank you for talking about my books with so much enthusiasm and warmth on Put a Blurb on It and elsewhere. You've been generous beyond all expectation. And thank you also for sharing your thoughtful insights on my writing. Rachel Purrteman: To the most dedicated reader I know, thank you for offering your friendship, and for showing these archives so much love. Aaliyah Rafeeq: Thank you for your beautiful photographs, and for writing to encourage me when it felt like there was no end in sight. Your words have meant so much to me.

Hussein Rashid: Thank you so much for reading my books with your daughter, for seeing the subtext as text, and also for the honor of teaching my stories in your classroom. In solidarity with you, always. To the magnificent Amy Tenbrink and the wonderful community at Sirens: Thank you for giving me a platform and for finding value in my books. Thank you, Laury Silvers, for your incredible kindness, those wonderful discussions, and your stunning novel *The Lover*. London Shah: My Pathan sister. No one could be more generous than you have been from the beginning. Your beautiful book *The Light at the Bottom of the World* is a reminder that all things are possible, and that all our stories matter.

To the scholars, researchers, and enthusiasts whose work has enlightened me and given me such pleasure, thank you for being the fascinating people you are and, in so many cases, for answering the questions I posed: Sophia Arjana, Abigail Balbale, M. Ballan, Eléonore Cellard, Paul Cobb, Juan Cole, Paul Cooper, Asad Dandia, Jordan Denari Duffner, N. A. Mansour, Shabana Mir, Stephennie Mulder, Ali A. Olomi, M. Lynx Qualey, Omid Safi, Alex Shams, Amanda H. Steinberg, and Marijn van Putten. I also thank Ahmed Shaker for sharing his fascinating scholarship on the Blue Qur'an, and I am singularly indebted to the work of Shaykh Khaled Abou El Fadl, and the great Amin Maalouf.

Writing the Khorasan Archives, I learned firsthand about solidarity, so I want to say thank you to those who tell their own stories, uplift the voices of others, or champion the rights of communities under threat—the same communities I write about. I particularly want to thank those who came before me, those who will come after, those who so kindly encouraged me in my writing, as well as those who educated me on the issues that lie at the heart of these books. Just some of these voices: Aaisha Zafar Islam, Adib Khorram, Adiba Jaigirdar, Aisha Saeed, Ali Lawati, Alia Malek, Amal El-Mohtar, Amalie Howard, Amanda Nelson, Amani Al-Khatahtbeh, Aminah Mae Safi, Amir and Khalil, Amira Elghawaby, Ann Bragdon, Ashley Franklin, Asma Uddin, Ayesha Mattu, Ayisha Malik, Ayman Mohyeldin, Ayser Salman, Brian Bunce, Daisy Khan, Dalia Mogahed, Daniel Cohen, Deb Parazzi, Deborah Margolis, Dena Takruri, Donna Auston, Ehsaneh Sadr, Elisabeth Däumer, Elizabeth Neill, Elizabeth Roderick, Émilie

Gascon-Léger, Farah Heron, Farah Naz Rishi, Fartumo Kusow, Fatema Akbari, Firoozeh Dumas, G. Willow Wilson, Geneive Abdo, Hafsah Faizal, Haneen Oriqat, Hanna Alkaf, Hena Khan, Hend Amry, Hend Hegazi, Hind Makki, Huda Fahmy, Ibtihaj Muhammad, Ibtisam Barakat, Idrees Ahmad, Ihsaan Gardee, Imraan Siddiqi, Irene Lau, Irfan Master, Ishara Deen, Iyad el-Baghdadi, Jamila Afghani, Jamilah Thompkins-Bigelow, Jeanne Timmons, Jenn Northington, Josh Monken, K. B. Wagers (and Garrus!), Kamila Shamsie, Kamran Pasha, Kareem Shaheen, Karuna Riazi, Khaled Hosseini, Laila Lalami, Laura Mahal, Laurie Grassi, Layla Abdullah-Poulos, Leanne Foster, Leila Aboulela, Leila Al-Shami, Lina Sergie Attar, Linda Sarsour, Lisa Casper, Madiha Ghous, Mahmoud Darwish, Malika Bilal, Margari Aziza, Maria Hossein, Mariam Ahmed, Mariam Khan, Marjane Satrapi, Mark Stevens, Marni Graff, Marsha Mehran, Masood and Nermina Baig, Mehdi Hasan, Michael Rollins, Mohammad Khalil, Mohammed Ayoob, Mohammed Hanif, Mohja Kahf, Mohsin Hamid, Mona Eltahawy, Monia Mazigh, Monica Ali, Muhammad Khan, Nadeem Aslam, Nadia Hashimi, Nadine Jolie Courtney, Naheed Hasnat Senzai, Naheed Mustafa, Na'ima B. Robert, Nesrine Malik, Nevien Shaabneh, Nilofar Shidmehr, Noor Javed, Noura Erakat, Nur Nasreen Ibrahim, Nura Maznavi, Olivia Abtahi, Onjali Q. Rauf, Orhan Pamuk, Rabia Chaudry, Rabiah Lumbard, Rajaa Alsanea, Rana Ayyub, Randa Abdel-Fattah, Rania Mirza, Razan Saffour, Rebecca Donnelly, Renée Ahdieh, Reza Aslan, Richard Doughty, Rim-Sarah Alouane, Riza Qadri, Robin Yassin-Kassab, Rowaida Abdelaziz, Rukhsana Khan, Ryan Ramkelawan, Saad Khan, Saadia Faruqi, Saba Sulaiman, Sabaa Tahir, Sabeeha Rehman, Sabina Khan, Sabrina Mahfouz, Sabrina Siddiqui, Safiyyah Kathimi, Sahar Aziz, Sahar Mustafah, Sahira Javaid, Sameer Gardezi, Samina

Ali, Samira Ahmed, Sana Amanat, Sana Saeed, Sandhya Menon, Sara Alfageeh, Sarah Hagi, Sayed A. Tabatabai, Seema Nundy, Seher Shafiq, Sezín Koehler, Shazia Munir Khoker, Shelina Zahra Janmohamed, Shereen Malherbe, Sohaib Awan, Somaiya Daud, Soniah Kamal, Soraya Moghadam, Sumbul Ali-Karamali, Suzie Rose, Swapna Krishna, Tabassum Siddiqui, Tahereh Mafi, Tahmima Anam, Tanaz Bhathena, Toni Moore, Umm Juwayriyah, Usman Malik, Viniyanka Prasad, Yasmin Khatun Dewan, Yasmin Rahman, Zahra Ayubi, Zahra Billoo, Zahra Hankir, Zareen Jaffery, Zarqa Nawaz, and Zeyn Joukhadar. And many, many others who have offered me advice and encouragement or whose work has simply enthralled me.

Thank you, dearest Wisam, Yara, Diana, and Jennifer. In different ways, you took me on the same journey to find the Noble Sanctuary. My heart is with the people of Palestine.

To the prisoners of conscience and human rights activists who have suffered in the cause of justice, and whom I named my characters after, may you know the beauty of Paradise.

In writing this series, I was guided by the voices of women whose work has been deeply influential: Su'ad Abdul Khabeer, Zainah Anwar, Assia Djebar, Leila Ahmed, Laleh Bakhtiar, Shirin Ebadi, Natalia Estemirova, Asma Jahangir, Massouda Jalal, Anna Politkovskaya, Amina Wadud, and Malala Yousafzai. And, unforgettably, the incomparable Fatima Mernissi.

And lastly, in telling these stories, I've been thinking about my Pashtun/Pathan roots, how my path has diverged from that of the women of my family, and how migration shadows and transforms everything. Of all the roads not taken that have led me to where I am today. And I honor the courage of the Pashtun girls who continue to fight for the dignity and equality that are inherent in our faith.

Cast of Characters

THE CITADEL OF HIRA

THE COUNCIL OF HIRA

Ilea: the High Companion
  Other titles: the Golden Mage, the Exalted, the Qari, Ilea the
  Friend, Ilea the Seal of the Companions
Arian: First Oralist, a Companion of Hira
Sinnia: a Companion from the lands of the Negus

Ash: the Jurist of the Citadel
Dhiya: a Companion from Tanah Malayu
Dijah: the longest-serving Companion at the Citadel
Half-Seen (Hafsah): the Collector of the Claim
Maryam: a Companion from the Valley of Five Lions
Mask (Mishkah): a Hazara and Shin War Companion responsible
  for the care of refugees
Mei Lai: a Companion from the lands of Shin Jang
Melati: a Companion from Nusantara

Cast of Characters

Psalm: the General of the Citadel

Saw: a descendant from the Najjar tribes, a Companion from the holy cities

Other Companions of Hira, the Affluent: Moon, Rain, Ware, Zeb; and in the old world, Hafsah

OTHERS AT THE CITADEL

Azmaray: Captain of the Citadel Guard

Hamzah: a lord of Khyber with the title of Qaid

Qais: a lord of Khyber, Hamzah's brother

CANDOUR

Daniyar: the Guardian of Candour
  Other titles: the Silver Mage, the Authenticate, the Keeper of the Candour

Wafa: a Hazara boy of Candour

Helai: a girl of Candour

Husay: a girl of Candour

THE TALISMAN

The One-Eyed Preacher
The Immolans

Toryal: a Talisman soldier
Uwais: a Talisman soldier

ASHFALL

The Black Khan: Rukhzad, Rukh
  Other titles: Commander of the Faithful, Prince of West

Khorasan, Khan of Khorasan, Sovereign of the House of Ashfall, the Black Rook, the Dark Mage

Begum Niyousha: the Black Khan's mother

Darya: the Princess of Ashfall, sister to the Black Khan

Darius: the half-brother of Rukh and Darya, formerly the Dark Mage

The Begum: the eldest aunt of the Black Khan

Nizam al-Mulk: the Grand Vizier of Ashfall

The Zareen-Qalam: the curator of the scriptorium of Ashfall

The Assassin/Hasbah/Hudayfah: the founder and leader of the Assassins

Alisher: a poet of Black Aura

The Zhayedan: the army of the Black Khan at Ashfall

Arsalan: Commander of the Zhayedan

    Esfandyar: a Zhayedan captain

    Niyal: a Zhayedan captain and negotiator

    Shayan: a Zhayedan captain and counterintelligence expert

    Zishaan: a Zhayedan captain, promoted to Captain of the Khorasan Guard

The Cataphracts: shock troops of the Zhayedan

Maysam: Captain of the Cataphracts

The Teerandaz: the Zhayedan's all-female company of archers

Cassandane: Captain of the Teerandaz

Katayoun: a Teerandaz archer

The Khorasan Guard: the Black Khan's personal guard, the home guard of Ashfall

Khashayar: formerly Captain of the Khorasan Guard

Cast of Characters

BLACK AURA

The Khanum: Lania, sister to Arian, the First Oralist of Hira
   Other titles: Consort of the Authoritan, the Augur
   Saher: one of the Khanum's doves
   Gul: one of the Khanum's doves
The Authoritan: former ruler of the Wall and the cities of
   Marakand, Black Aura, Task End, and Khiva
   Other titles: Khagan, Khan of Khans
   Temurbek: an Ahdath soldier assigned authority over the Wall

The Sahirah: a group of women sorcerers
Valeria: Sovereign of the Sahirah
Kiril: Valeria's eldest son, a noble and a soldier of the Ahdath army
   of Black Aura
Mikhail: Valeria's youngest son, a noble and a soldier of the
   Ahdath army of Black Aura

THE NOBLE SANCTUARY

The Custodian of the Noble Sanctuary

THE RISING NINETEEN

Najran: Sayyid of the Rising Nineteen
   Other titles: the Iron Glaive, the Angel of Blood, the Bone
   Shadow

THE LANDS OF THE NEGUS

The Negus: ruler of these lands
Queen Zoya: his queen

Nuru: a shipbuilder, a soldier of Axum, and Sinnia's cousin
Kamali: a soldier of Axum and Sinnia's cousin

TIMEBACK

The Mage of the Blue Eye (the Blue Mage): Sidi Yusuf, Lord of Shining Gate and Guardian of Timeback

THE WANDERING CLOUD DOOR

Zerafshan: Aybek of the Wandering Cloud Door
 Other titles: Lord of the Wandering Cloud Door, Lord of the Buzkashi, Aybek of the Army of the Left
Tochtor: Empress of the Cloud Door, mother of the Aybek Zerafshan
Annar and Storay: Tochtor's daughters, Zerafshan's sisters

THE USUL JADE

Salikh: the founder of the Usul Jade
The Basmachi Resistance
 Larisa Salikh: the leader of the Basmachi Resistance, daughter of Salikh
 Elena Salikh/Anya: second-in-command, daughter of Salikh

Glossary of the Khorasan Archives

ab-e-rawan. A type of silk known as running water.

Adhraa. The most highly venerated woman mentioned by name in the Claim.

aesar. A hot desert wind.

Afaarin. A word of praise and appreciation.

Affluent. Those who are fluent in the Claim.

Age of Jahiliya. Age of Ignorance brought into being by the Talisman.

Ahdath. Suicide warriors who guard the Wall.

Akhirah. The Last Day, the Day of Judgment, the Afterlife.

Akhundzada. A member of the family of the Ancient Dead, guardians of the Sacred Cloak.

Al Dajjal Al Masikh. The deformed deceiver who heralds the end of days.

Al Masih Al Dajjal. The mythical deceiver who heralds the end of days.

Al Mintaka. A star in the skies over Ashfall, also known as the Belt.

Al Qasr. Literally "the Castle," but in this case referring to the women's fortified quarters inside the royal palace at Ashfall.

alam. A flag.

Alamdar. A title of utmost respect given to an elder of the Hazara.

All Ways. The fountains of the Citadel of Hira, imbued with special powers, and a foundation of the rites of the Council of Hira.

Amdar. A river of North Khorasan that flows on both sides of the Wall.

Amghar. Chief of the clan.

andas. Blood brother.

Angel of Blood. A name given to Najran, a lieutenant of the Rising Nineteen.

Aramaya. A holy language from

the regions near the holy cities, a precursor to the High Tongue.

Ark. The stronghold of the Authoritan in Black Aura Scaresafe.

Aryaward. A territory of South Khorasan.

Ascension. A spiritual and mystical journey taken from the heights of the sacred rock known as the Qubbat-as-Sakhrah.

Ashfall. The capital of West Khorasan, seat of the Black Khan.

asmaan. Sky.

asmani. Sky-blue lapis lazuli.

Asmat. The secret names of the One.

Assassin, The. Hasbah or Hudayfah, leader of a sect of Assassins at the fortress of the Eagle's Nest.

Assassins. A sect of skilled warriors stationed at the fortress of the Eagle's Nest.

Assimilate. The proclaimed law of the Talisman.

Audacy. A mission assigned to any of the Companions of Hira, a sacred trust.

Augur. One who foretells the future, a rank in the Authoritan's court.

Authenticate. A title given to one who can verify the truth. *See also* Silver Mage.

Authoritan. The ruler of North Khorasan, the land beyond the Wall.

Avalaunche. A Talisman warning horn used to defend the Sorrowsong.

Awazim. A tribe of the Rub Al Khali that keeps noteworthy flocks of sheep.

Axum. The capital of the lands of the Negus.

Aybek. Commander of the Buzkashi, leader of the people of the Wandering Cloud Door.

aylaq. Summer camp of the Buzkashi.

azraq. A description of the color blue. In the Claim, with the significance of referring to the blue-eyed or green-eyed.

bacha bazi. The practice of some Talisman warlords of inducting boys into sexual servitude.

badal. "Revenge" in the Talisman code.

baraka. Blessing.

Basmachi. A resistance force north of the Wall who follow the teachings of the Usul Jade.

Begum. The highest-ranking woman at the Black Khan's court, in this case the Khan's eldest aunt.

Bir al Arwah. The Well of Souls. A well beneath the rock of the Sakhrah.

Black Aura Scaresafe. The Authoritan's capital beyond the Wall.

Black Khan. The Prince of West Khorasan, the Khan of Khorasan. *See also* Dark Mage.

Black Khanum. A title given to the Khanum of Black Aura by the One-Eyed Preacher.

Bladebone, The. See this book.

Blind Dome. A place of spiritual

significance linked to the Noble Sanctuary.

Bloodless. The guardians of the Bloodprint.

Bloodprint, The. The oldest known written compilation of the Claim.

Blue Mage. Also known as the Mage of the Blue Eye, or the Mage of Timeback. A mage from the lands of the maghreb.

Bone Shadow, The. A name given to Najran, a lieutenant of the Rising Nineteen.

Buraq. The winged steed of the Israa e Miraj.

burnoose. A long, loose hooded cloak.

Buzkashi. The name of the people of the Wandering Cloud Door.

buzkashi. A game of sport involving the carcass of a goat chased by horsemen.

caliph. A leader of a community of the faithful.

Candour. A city in the south of Khorasan captured by the Talisman, home of the Silver Mage.

Candour, The. The book of the Silver Mage, instructing him in the history, traditions, and powers of the Claim, as well as his responsibilities as Silver Mage and Guardian of Candour.

Cataphracts. The shock troops of the Zhayedan, the Black Khan's army.

chador. Shawl.

chowgan. A sport where horsemen compete for possession of a ball.

Citadel. The stronghold of the Council of Hira.

Citadel Guard. Warriors who guard the Citadel of Hira, assigned to the protection of the Companions.

City of Faith. The earliest of the holy cities where the Noble Sanctuary is found.

City of the Friend/City of the Four. A city in the holy land of historical significance for communities of faith.

Claim, The. The sacred scripture of Khorasan; also a powerful magic.

Clay Minar. A tower in the city of Black Aura Scaresafe.

Commander of the Faithful. A title given to the leader of the Claim's community of faith.

Common Tongue. A language common to all parts of Khorasan and beyond.

Companions of Hira. Also Council of Hira, Oralists, the Affluent, sahabiya in the feminine singular, sahabah in the plural: a group of women charged with the guardianship of Khorasan and the sacred heritage of the Claim.

Conference of the Mages. A gathering that unites the Mages of Khorasan, allowing them to increase the power of their magic.

Council of Hira. *See* Companions of Hira.

Crimson Watch. An elite company

of the Ahdath who guard Jaslyk prison.

Criterion, The. The formal name of the Bloodprint.

Custodian of the Archives. A rank held by a senior Companion of Hira.

Custodian of the Holiest House. The keeper of the Noble Sanctuary.

daf. A Khorasani drum.

Dajjal. A mythical figure whose presence heralds the end of the world.

dakhu. Bandit, disreputable person.

Damson Vale. A valley north of the Wall and east of Marakand.

Dark Mage. Rukhzad (Rukh), the Black Khan, and Prince of West Khorasan. The ruler of the city of Ashfall and the empire of Khorasan.

Darya-e Nur. The Ocean of Light, the pink table diamond encased in one of the Black Khan's ceremonial armbands.

Dawn Rite. A rite of the Mages of Khorasan that empowers their shared magic at dawn.

Death Run. A chain of mountains that forms one of the boundaries of the Wandering Cloud Door, east of the Valley of Five Lions.

Dhu al-Nurayn. The One Who Possesses Two Lights, a title of the one who preserved the Bloodprint.

Dimashq. A deadly Damascene

sword carried by Najran, the lieutenant of the Nineteen.

Divan-e Shah. The throne room at Ashfall where emissaries are received.

Dome of the Chain. A structure within the Noble Sanctuary, in the earliest of the holy cities.

Dome of the Noble Sanctuary. The far Distant House of Worship located in the earliest of the holy cities.

dunya. The world.

Eagle's Nest. The fortress of the Assassin, north of the city of Ashfall.

East Wind. A people of a sister-scripture to the Claim, also known as the Esayin.

Emissary Gate. One of the three gates of the city of Ashfall.

Empty Quarter. The lands of southwestern Khorasan, destroyed by the wars of the Far Range. Also known as the Rub Al Khali.

Esayin. A people of a precursory sister-scripture to the Claim. Also known as the East Wind. A faith practiced in the lands of the Negus and in the earliest of the holy cities.

Everword. A people of a sister-scripture to the Claim.

Far Range. The uninhabitable country beyond Khorasan.

fayruz. Turquoise in the dialect of the Empty Quarter.

Fire Mirrors. A mountain chain

that forms the northern boundary of the Wandering Cloud Door, just south of the Wall.

First Oralist. A rank of highest distinction among the Companions of Hira, reserved for the Companion with the greatest knowledge of and fluency in the Claim.

Firuzkoh. The Turquoise City, lost to time.

Five Lakes. A territory of Khorasan, north of Hazarajat.

Garden of Refuge. A destination to be found upon Ascension.

ger. Home, tent, yurt.

geshlaq. Winter camp of the Buzkashi.

ghayb. Mystical knowledge beyond the veil. Also a word that means "vanished."

ghayrat. "Self-honor" in the Talisman code.

ghul. A powerful and dark spirit brought to life by sorcery.

Glory of Kings. The sacred book of the people of the Negus.

Gold House. A palace in the Registan where women are trained in the arts. *See also* Tilla Kari.

Golden Finger. A minaret at the meeting place of two rivers.

Golden Mage. Ilea, the High Companion of the Council of Hira. The most senior rank on the Council.

Graveyard of the Ships. A desert near Jaslyk where the lake bed has dried up.

Great Bend, The. A river of the southern maghreb, also known as the Joliba, the Isa Ber, and the Kworra.

Great Gate. A covered portico with fountains, part of the palace at Ashfall.

gris-gris. A leather pouch said to contain blessings; an amulet or talisman of protection.

Gur-e-Amir/the Green Mirror. A tomb complex in Marakand.

Hafiza. A woman who can recite the Claim from memory.

Hallow. A hall in the valley of Firuzkoh.

haq. Truth, right, justice.

Haram Sharif. Noble Sanctuary.

haramzadah. An epithet that means "bastard."

Harrowing of Timeback. A period when the city's manuscripts were destroyed by fanatical fighters.

Hazara. A people of central and east Khorasan, persecuted by the Talisman.

Hazarajat. A territory of central and east Khorasan, home of the Hazara people.

Hazing. A district of Marakand that is home to the Basmachi resistance. *See also* Tomb of the Living King.

High Companion. Leader of the Council of Hira.

High Road. A river of central Khorasan; also called the Arius, the Tarius, the Horaya, and the Tejen.

High Tongue. The language of the Claim.

Hijazi. A regional script.

hijra. Migration; also the name given to a historically significant migration.

Hira. The sanctuary of the Companions.

Ice Kill. A valley at the entrance to the Wandering Cloud Door, home to the Buzkashi.

ijtihad. A method of independent reasoning, in contrast to the following of precedent. An essential part of the Claim's jurisprudence.

Illustrious Portal. The entrance to the Black Khan's palace at Ashfall.

Immolans. Deputies of the One-Eyed Preacher, tasked with book burning.

Infisal. A rite used to exorcise a ghul. In strict terms, "separation."

Inklings. Scribes from the Lands of the Shin Jang.

Inkwell. The name given to the scriptorium curated by Arian's parents. *See also* Nun.

iqra. Read.

Irb. The language spoken by the people of the Wandering Cloud Door.

Iron Glaive. A name given to Najran, a lieutenant of the Rising Nineteen. Also, the weapon wielded by Najran.

Israa e Miraj. The Night Journey and the Ascension. The name of an allegorical or metaphysical spiritual journey taken by the Messenger of the One from the Near House of Worship to the Distant House of Worship.

jaan. Life, love, beloved.

Jabal Thawr. A mountain near the holy city.

Jahannam. In the afterlife, a place of punishment for evildoers.

Jahiliya. The Age of Ignorance.

Jaslyk. A prison of the Authoritan's, northwest of the Wall.

jorgo. Fast mountain horses.

kaghez. Paper manufactured from mulberry trees.

Kalaam. Word, one of the names of the Claim.

kamancheh. A Khorasani stringed instrument.

kamish. A type of calligraphy pen.

karakash. Black jade.

Keepers of the Saqar. In the legends of the Claim, the nineteen guardians of hell.

khaeen. A Talisman word for "traitor."

Khagan. Khan of Khans or King of Kings.

Khamsa. One of five mythical mares.

khamsin. A desert wind.

Khanum. A consort of the Khan, the Authoritan's consort.

Khiva. A city of North Khorasan, beyond the Wall, where the Sahirah reside.

Khorasan. The lands of the people

of the Claim, north, south, east, and west.

Khorasan Archives. The collection of manuscripts held in the Citadel of Hira's scriptorium.

Khorasan Guard. The home guard of Ashfall, the Black Khan's personal guard.

Khost-e-Imom. A protective cover or place for the Bloodprint.

khubi. Bounty, spoils of war, an endearment meaning "enough" or "everything."

khuriltai. Council.

Khyber. Mountain tribes from the southern territories of Khorasan who were the last to submit to Talisman law.

Koh-e Nur. The Mountain of Light, a white diamond encased in one of the Black Khan's ceremonial armbands.

kohl. Black eyeliner.

Kufic. A style of calligraphy taken from the name of the city Kufa.

kuluk. Load-bearing horses with stamina.

lajward. Lapis lazuli.

lajwardina. A lapis lazuli glaze.

Lashkar. A city of the southern territories of Khorasan.

likka. Raw silk fibers used in the practice of calligraphy.

Lion of the One. A title given to the Silver Mage.

loess. The golden soil of Marakand, possessed of healing properties.

Lote Tree of the Utmost Boundary. A destination to be found upon Ascension, a mystical tree in the Garden of Refuge. *See also* Sidrat al Muntaha.

loya jirga. A consultation of Talisman chieftains; also a council of war.

Mage of the Blue Eye. Also known as the Blue Mage, or the Mage of Timeback. A mage from the lands of the maghreb.

maghreb. The lands west of West Khorasan, across the Sea of Reeds.

maghrebi. A style of architecture in the lands west of West Khorasan.

mahadhras. Rural schools of the maghreb.

Maiden Tower. A watchtower at Ashfall.

manaqib. A script of the lands of the Negus.

Mangudah. A death squad of the Buzkashi, a regiment of the Army of the One.

maqdas. A house of worship in Axum.

Marakand. A city of North Khorasan beyond the Wall.

Mashriqi. A style of eastern architecture, east of the maghreb.

Matushka. An affectionate maternal title in the tongue of the Russe.

Mausoleum of the Princess. A tomb complex in the Hazing, an area of Marakand.

Maze Aura. A city of central Khorasan.

melmastia. "Hospitality" in the Talisman code.

Messenger Gate. One of the three gates of the city of Ashfall.

mihrab. A prayer nook in the wall of a house of worship, indicating the direction of prayer.

minzar. A searchlight or spotlight.

Mir. Any leader of the Hazara people.

Miraj Nameh. A manuscript describing the Israa e Miraj.

mishkah. A niche that contains the light of the heavens and the earth.

mllaya moya. My sweet, my love.

morin khuur. Horsehead fiddle.

Mothers of the Believers. The senior Companions of Hira named in honor of the first generation of Companions.

Mudassir. Respected teacher, a form of address.

Mudjadid. A teacher of great knowledge, a form of address.

munafiqah. A gendered word in the High Tongue that means "hypocrite."

musaawat. "Equality" in the Talisman code.

naamus. "The honor of women" in the Talisman code.

naanawatai. "Forgiveness" in the Talisman code.

Najashi. A word for the people of the Negus in the language of the Empty Quarter.

Najjar. A tribe of the holy cities.

Naqsh-e Jahan. Half the world. The name of the great public square of Ashfall.

Nastaliq. A type of calligraphy.

neeli. Dark blue lapis lazuli.

Negus. Ruler of the lands south of the Empty Quarter, the leader of Sinnia's people; also the name given to these lands.

Night Journey. A fabled journey attributed to the Messenger of the Claim from the holy city to the distant house of worship.

Nightshaper. Site of the Poet's Graveyard, an abandoned city of Khorasan.

Noble Sanctuary. A public square in the earliest holy city, where the Dome of the Sakhrah and the Dome of the Chain can be found.

Nun (pronounced Noon*).* Inkwell, the name of the scriptorium curated by Arian's parents.

nur. A spiritual light that transcends materiality.

nurm. Soft.

One-Eyed Preacher. A tyrant from the Empty Quarter whose teachings have engulfed all of Khorasan.

Opening, The. The opening chapter of the Claim.

Oralist. A Companion of Hira who recites the Claim.

Order of Khorasan. The highest honor awarded to soldiers of the empire of Khorasan.

Otchigen. The Prince of the Hearth, a title given to the youngest male member of the family of the Lord of the Buzkashi.

Overturner of Hearts. A phrase that describes the One.

pagri. A thick wool cap worn by the Talisman.

Pearl of Timeback. The book of the Mage of the Blue Eye, providing instruction in the history, traditions, and responsibilities of the Blue Mage. A book that endows the Blue Mage with certain powers of the Claim.

pishtaq. At the palace of Ashfall, a rectangular frame around an arched opening, as in the pishtaq of the Qaysarieh Portal.

Pit, The. The dungeons of the Ark.

Plague Lands. A northern territory of Khorasan destroyed by the wars of the Far Range.

Plague Wing. A section of Jaslyk prison where prisoners are held for experimentation with the effects of the plague.

Plaintive. A warning horn sounded by the Buzkashi.

Qabail. The outlying tribes of the southern territories who'd held out longest against the Talisman. The Khyber are one of these tribes.

Qaid. Title of the chieftain of the Khyber tribes.

qalb. Heart.

qanatir. An arcade of columns.

qarajai. A dangerous form of the sport buzkashi.

Qari. One who recites the Claim.

Qaysarieh Portal. The prisons underneath Ashfall.

qiyamah. Resurrection, rising.

Qubbat-as-Sakhrah. See also Sakhrah. A phrase referring to a ridge of rock beneath the Dome of the Noble Sanctuary.

Queen Makeda. A revered and honored queen in the history of the people of the Negus.

rahem. "Mercy" in the High Tongue.

rahlah. A stand on which to rest an open manuscript, usually a manuscript of the Claim.

rasti, rusti. Originally "safety is in right"; the Authoritan's motto, "strength is justice."

Registan. A public square in the heart of the city of Marakand, literally translated as "sandy place."

Rising Nineteen. A cult that has come to power in the Empty Quarter.

Rite of Qari'ah. A rite of the Mages of Khorasan that empowers their magic at nightfall, for the purposes of war.

Rub Al Khali. Also known as the Empty Quarter, the lands of southwest Khorasan, destroyed by the wars of the Far Range.

rukh. A mythical firebird or phoenix with the scales of a dragon and the talons of an eagle.

Rukha d'Qudsha. The holy spirit worshipped by those whose tongue is Aramaya.

Russe. A name given to the people of the northern Transcasp.

sabz. Green lapis lazuli.

Sacred Cloak. A holy relic worn by the Messenger of the Claim.

Saee. A pilgrimage ritual consisting of walking or running between two hills near the holy city.

Safanad. One of the five mares of the Khamsa; Arian's horse.

sahabah. A title given to the Companions of Hira in the plural; sahabiya, feminine singular.

Sahel. A southern desert of the maghreb.

Sahirah. A coven of women from the north possessed of magic and foresight.

Sailing Pass. A mountain pass en route to the Sorrowsong Mountain.

Sakhrah. See also Qubbat-as-Sakhrah. A phrase referring to a ridge of rock beneath the Dome of the Noble Sanctuary.

Salaf. A scholarly class from the city of Timeback.

Sana Codex. A famous collection of fragments of the Claim bound in a single manuscript.

sanam. Camel hump.

Saqar. One of the names of hell as described by the Claim.

Sar-e-Sang/Sorrowsong. The Blue Mountain, location of the oldest continuously worked lapis lazuli mines in Khorasan.

Sayyid. A courteous form of address for a man among the people of the Empty Quarter.

Sayyidina. A courteous form of address for a woman among the people of the Empty Quarter.

Sea of Reeds. A body of water that divides the Empty Quarter from the Lands of the Negus.

Sea of the Transcasp. A body of water that divides West Khorasan from the Transcasp.

sehra. A curtain of roses to cover the face worn by a bridegroom of Khorasan during the rites of a wedding.

setar. A seven-stringed Khorasani instrument.

Shadow Mausoleum. A crypt used for storing the bones of the Authoritan's enemies. *See also* Shir Dar.

shah-mat. Checkmate.

shahadah. The bearing of witness.

Shahi scepter. The Black Khan's royal scepter, part of the Prince's regalia.

Shahnameh. Ashfall's Book of Kings, a history of its monarchy.

shahtaranj. A chessboard.

Shaitan. A name for the devil.

shalmas. A gauzy length of white fabric worn as a veil and/or wrapped around the torso.

Shaykh. The title of a man among the people of the Empty Quarter.

Shin Jang. A northeastern territory of Khorasan.

Shin War. One of the tribes of Khorasan, allegiant to the Talisman.

Shining Gate/Shinqit. A capital of the maghreb.

Shir Dar. A former House of Wisdom in the Registan. *See also* Shadow Mausoleum.

shisha. A water pipe with fruit-scented tobacco.

Shrine of the Sacred Cloak. A holy shrine where the Cloak has been stored for centuries and guarded by the Ancient Dead.

shura. A council or consultation.

Sidrat al Muntaha. A destination to be found upon Ascension, a mystical tree in the Garden of Refuge. *See also* Lote Tree of the Utmost Boundary.

Sihraat. The scrying room where the Khanum conducts her Augury.

Silver Mage. The Guardian of Candour, Keeper of the Candour.

Sorrowsong. *See* Sar-e-Sang.

Sovereign of the Sahirah. The female leader of a sect behind the Wall. *See also* Sahirah.

suhuf. A sheaf of paper or parchment.

Sulde. The spirit banner of the Buzkashi.

tabar. A two-headed axe of reinforced steel.

tabot. Tablets of law sacred to the people of the Negus.

tagelmust. A garment of indigo cloth worn either as a veil or as a turban by inhabitants of the maghreb to prevent the inhalation of sand on the wind.

tahweez. A gold circlet or circlets, worn on the upper arms by the Companions of Hira, inscribed with the names of the One and the opening words of the Claim.

taihe. A princess of Shin Jang.

Talisman. Followers of the One-Eyed Preacher, militias that rule most of the tribes of Khorasan.

tasbih. Prayer beads worn or used by adherents of the Claim.

Task End. A city of North Khorasan beyond the Wall, the original home of the Bloodprint.

Technologist. The chief torturer at Jaslyk prison.

Teerandaz. A division of archers in the Black Khan's Zhayedan army.

thobe. A long, loose gown worn by the people of the Empty Quarter.

Tilla Kari. A former site of worship in the Registan. *See also* Gold House.

Timeback. A capital of the maghreb.

Tirazis. A city of West Khorasan.

Tomb of the Living King. A lost tomb in a district of Marakand known as the Hazing.

Tongue, The. A speaking rock found near the Well of Souls.

Tower of the Mirage. A watchtower at Ashfall.

Tradition. The accompanying rites and beliefs of the Claim.

Transcasp. Lands of northwest Khorasan.

turah. "Courage" in the Talisman code.

usman. A form of lightning in the maghreb.

Usul Jade. The teachings of the New Method of studying the Claim, by Mudjadid Salikh.

Valley of Five Lions. A territory in central Khorasan, fought over by the Shin War and the Zai Guild.

Valley of the Awakened Prince. A territory in central Khorasan.

Wall. A fortification built by the ancestors of the Authoritan to ward off the plague, dividing North Khorasan from South.

Wandering Cloud Door. The lands of the Buzkashi in northeast Khorasan.

Warden. The administrator of Jaslyk prison.

Warraqeen. Male students of the teachings of the Claim at the scriptorium in Ashfall.

Well of Zamzam. A sacred spring near the holy city.

Whip of the First Oralist. A title given by the Khanum of Black Aura to Sinnia, Companion of Hira.

White Fathers. A group that protected manuscripts in the city of Timeback, akin to the Bloodless.

wisa. "Trust" in the Talisman code.

Yassa. The law of the people of the Wandering Cloud Door.

Yeke Khatun. Great Empress of the people of the Wandering Cloud Door.

yurungkash. White jade.

Zai Guild. One of the tribes of Khorasan, allegiant to the Talisman.

Zareen-Qalam. Title of the curator of the Black Khan's scriptorium, literally "Golden Pen."

Zebunnisa. A revered poet in the history of Khorasan.

Zerafshan. A river of North Khorasan, beyond the Wall.

Zhayedan. The army of the Black Khan, headquartered at Ashfall.

Zhayedan Gate. One of the three gates of the city of Ashfall.

ziyara. A religious pilgrimage.

zrig. A drink of sweetened milk, often thickened with millet and seasoned with spices.

zud. Animal famine.

About the Author

PILLGWENLLY

AUSMA ZEHANAT KHAN holds a PhD in international human rights law with a specialization in military intervention and war crimes in the Balkans. She is a former adjunct law professor and editor in chief of *Muslim Girl* magazine, the first magazine targeted to young Muslim women in North America. She is also the award-winning author of *The Unquiet Dead* and *The Bloodprint,* the first book in the Khorasan Archives. A British-born Canadian, Khan now lives in Colorado with her husband. You can learn more about her at ausmazehanatkhan.com and can follow her on Twitter at @AusmaZehanat, on Facebook at facebook.com /ausmazehanatkhan, and on Instagram at @azkhanbooks.

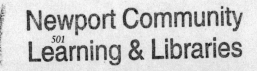

07-07-21

PILLGWENLLY